"Jam packed with page turning, heart-tugging adventure, *The Ryn* is a delightful tale not to be missed." -Jenny B. Jones, award-winning author of *There You'll Find Me*

"A perfect alchemy of fantasy and fairy tale, you'll willingly lose yourself in the story of a witty, pretty, totally relatable young woman who grows up, falls in love, and grasps her girl-powered destiny. This book will be a cherished read for all who understand that happily-ever-after dreams can still be made to come true." -Sandra Byrd, best-selling author of the Ladies in Waiting series, the French Twist Trilogy, and the London Confidential YA series.

"With *The Ryn*, a re-imagining of *Snow White and Rose Red*, debut author Serena Chase creates a story world that features a captivating cast of characters, fascinating locales, and a satisfying romance. I look forward to the second book in the Eyes of E'veria series." -Tamara Leigh, author of Carol Award-Winner *Splitting Harriet* and *Dreamspell*

"*The Ryn* is a beautifully rendered allegorical fantasy that captured my imagination from the beginning, my heart halfway through, and my soul by the final pages. . . . the perfect combination of whimsy and earthiness . . . Clever dialogue and delightful prose suggest Serena Chase has significant talent, the creative and evocative plot proves it. With action, chivalry, and sacrifice aplenty, this story will appeal to all ages. With shades of *The Princess Bride*, Lisa T. Bergren's River of Time series, and David Eddings *Belgariad*, this story is a keeper. Simply put, I adored *The Ryn* and can't wait to dive into *The Remedy*." -Rel Mollet, www.relzreviewz.com

Novels by Serena Chase

The Eyes of E'veria Series

THE RYN

THE REMEDY

Coming in 2014
Eyes of E'veria, Book Three

The Ryn

Eyes of E'veria

Book One

Serena Chase

THE RYN

Serena Chase

Eyes of E'veria, Book One

A young woman living in obscurity learns she is the long-lost heir to the throne and the key to defeating her Kingdom's most ancient enemy.

ISBN-13: 9781493551057
ISBN-10: 1493551051
Library of Congress Control Number: 2013920166
CreateSpace Independent Publishing Platform
North Charleston, South Carolina

Original cover photography (character) copyright 2012 Lincoln Noah Baxter / (background scenery) copyright 2013 Jodie Gerling

Cover design and Candent Gate logo design by JG Designs www.jodiegerlingdesigns.com, Manhattan, KS

Interior cover image of The Remedy:
(character photo) copyright 2012 Lincoln Noah Baxter/edited iris copyright 2013 Jodie Gerling/ Abstract flames image 63166120 Copyright Fenton, 2013 Used under license from Shutterstock.com/cover design by JG Designs, Manhattan, KS.

For

Delaney Olivia & Ellerie Victoria
...because some fairytales are more than true

Dave
...my knight in shining bib overalls

& Heather
... because you are appreciated
more than you will ever know

$\mathscr{P}$ ROLOGUE

$\mathcal{H}$iding in plain sight, the old man crept through the halls of the palace, his ancient heart keeping pace with the shifting of his black eyes. Festive gossip filled the air, but it held little information to aid his course. Instead, each phrase emptied the space of air and made him feel as if he could suffocate at any moment. Still, his keen ears captured each syllable, seeking some nuance that would serve as inspiration to help him bring an end to their joy.

The late evening hour found the idle gathered in the main kitchen. He passed among them, largely unnoticed but for a young serving girl who offered him a cup of ale. To her, as to the rest of them, he appeared to be a harmless old man, just one more member of the gathering staff and servants awaiting news of the birth. But while he *was* old—older than any of them could imagine—he was far from harmless.

"Should I brew her evening tea, I wonder?" A serving maid's question caught his attention. "Perhaps add a bit of honey?"

"Honey? Oh yes!" Another gushed. "It's not her usual preference, but honey is well known for easing a babe's passage."

The old man's beard twitched upward. The curse his kind had waited centuries to deliver to this family . . . served in a cup of tea? *Perfect.* Reaching for the wineskin strapped just beneath his tunic, the old man removed the cork and took a swig so quickly only the keenest eye could have marked the movement.

A fresh kettle was put to boil and a gilded tray was set with a cup and saucer, each delicate piece emblazoned with the flowery emblem of the mother-to-be. He inched closer. *Yes,* he thought, *this will do.*

The kettle whistled and the serving maid poured its contents over a small bowl of leaves. After a few minutes, the liquid was strained and transferred to the delicate cup.

The serving maid paused and turned to her friend. "You're sure about the honey?"

"Oh yes, dear," the older woman answered, nodding sagely. "It helped bring all four of my boys into the world."

Without earning so much as a glance, the old man, if that was what he could be called, whispered a word in his native tongue and plucked a hair from his beard. As soon as the maid finished her task he stepped out of the shadows.

"I beg your pardon, miss." He spoke humbly, carefully shaping each word to ensure his accent was hidden. "But might I have a drop of honey in my ale?"

The young maid paused. "The winter's got your throat a mite scratchy, does it?" She smiled. "Bring your cup here, then."

The cursed hair pulsed between his thumb and forefinger. As his hand passed over the hot, sweet liquid meant for the laboring mother's lips, he released it.

A fat glob of honey dropped into his cup of ale. He nodded his thanks and backed away. A moment later a fresh hothouse rose was set on the tray and it was carried from the kitchen.

Keeping to the shadows, he followed the serving maid until he was assured of the tray's destination. Satisfied that his curse would be delivered as intended, he made his way back down the stairs and into the courtyard. He meant to be well away before suspicion landed upon him.

He paused. Why hurry? No one would recognize a little old man as the famous enemy of their legends. To these common people, he and his kind were little more than a rumor, a tale to frighten children around the fire at night.

Yes, he would wait a bit. These short-lived simpletons couldn't possibly recognize him for what he truly was. They were far too removed from their history to recognize him as a Cobeld. Quickly but carefully, he moved out of the shadow, rounded the corner and—

"HOLD! What is your business?"

The Cobeld reached for his flask and took a quick swig.

The knight drew his sword. "Cobeld in the courtyard!" he shouted. "Sound the alarm!"

Shocked at being recognized, the Cobeld hesitated just long enough to find the sword's tip pushing his beard against his windpipe.

"Cobeld," the knight growled, "what is your business here?"

The Cobeld eyed the knight's gloveless hand. All it would take was one touch, but first . . .

"Death," he spoke the curse in the knight's own tongue, allowing a smile to part his beard. "My business here is death. Death for you, for the woman, and most especially for the child of the prophecy."

"Your blood will stain these stones before I let that happen." The knight pressed the Cobeld back until his spine met a solid surface. "Are there more of you here? Answer me!"

"Why need there be more?" The Cobeld smiled around the words. "One Cobeld, one hair of his beard, and one . . . little . . . whisper." He laughed again, reveling in the way the hairs on the knight's wrist stood up at the sound. "The curse has already been delivered. You are too late to stop it." Enough time had passed since the tray left the kitchen. It was as good as done. "The mother and her child will die. And so shall you!"

He lunged then, beard first, toward the exposed skin of the knight's hand.

But the knight was young and nimble. He swung his hand away and the Cobeld stumbled, falling face first on to the white stones of the courtyard. A second later the toe of a boot flipped the Cobeld on to his back and the sword was poised to strike above his neck.

"Killing me will not stop what has already begun," the creature said. "For two centuries the Cobelds have hidden in the mountains, waiting and watching for the prophesied child. My curse,"—*oh, he loved that it was his!*—"will stop the child's heart before she takes her first breath. My curse," he claimed it again, "will usher in our opportunity to finally take the Kingdom that should have been ours from the beginning!"

The knight's knuckles, wrapped about the hilt of his sword, whitened. "Tell me where I can find the cursed hair and how to destroy it." His voice was quiet now, but lethally so. "If either the child or mother is harmed we will wage a war the likes of which your kind hasn't imagined since the days of Lady Anya," he said. "But this time we *will* finish you."

"You will not succeed." The Cobeld's eyes shone with pride, for surely the curse was, even now, speeding through the woman's blood and finding its way to the child. He could almost taste his triumph. "Not without the child of the prophecy."

He felt it then, a freezing tingle of cold light expelling from the recently emptied follicle on his chin: the curse, delivered.

The knight's jaw went slack. "No . . ."

"Yes!" The Cobeld's laugh crackled with victory as three guards rounded the corner, "You are too—"

With an unearthly, grating sound of metal against metal, the knight's sword sliced through the Cobeld's beard, silencing his final whisper before it left his throat.

S ir Drinius de Wyte stared at the nearly motionless form of his Queen. He'd come as quickly as he could, but he was too late. The curse had been received.

Every moment she grew paler. Each breath was spaced too far from the last, and yet her tears, mingling with the King's, seemed to have no space between them at all.

She was slipping away. And there was nothing he could do to stop it.

Drinius spared a glance toward Sir Gladiel. Agony twisted just beneath the stony surface of the other knight's expression, a painful contradiction to the gaiety with which they'd slapped each other's backs, and the King's, hours ago when the Queen's pains had begun.

Gladiel met his eyes and one silent question groaned between them.

How had this happened?

They had posted additional guards. They had patrolled the surrounding areas for weeks to assure Daithia that her unborn child would be safe. How had the creature permeated their defenses? How had it gained access to the very cup meant for Daithia's lips?

Supported by the King's strong hand, the babe rested in the crook of her mother's arm, pink, healthy, and—most importantly—alive. Yes, the Cobeld's curse had been delivered. But not as planned. And not in time to reach the babe.

The Ryn.

With bright blue eyes and the same flame-born hair as the mother she would never know, this baby must indeed be the child of the prophecy. But it would be years before she would be able to embrace all that entailed, years before she would even be allowed to know who she was or what she was destined to become.

For now, they would call her Rose.

But that was not her name.

The baby startled. Daithia gasped. And then . . . her tears ceased.

The soft lament that issued from King Jarryn was so low and full of sorrow that it nearly hollowed Drinius's soul. Gladiel stepped forward and placed a hand on his sovereign's shoulder. Drinius moved to Jarryn's other side and did the same.

The King wept. And it was all Drinius could do not to fall apart beside him.

Queen Daithia was gone.

When the baby began to fuss, King Jarryn slipped the child from her mother's arms and into his own. He stood.

"Drinius," he said, his voice rough with grief. "You and Alaine were to be godparents. Are you yet willing to accept that charge, knowing how much more it now entails?"

Undertaking the hastily devised plan to ensure the child's safety would increase his responsibility a hundredfold, but Drinius would pledge nothing less than the Knight's Oath to see it done. "With all that I am and for all of my life, Your Majesty, I accept the care of your daughter."

"Thank you." The King's voice was a whisper, but Drinius had never heard words of gratitude so steeped in gravity.

The King cleared his throat. "And Gladiel," he said, turning, "if for any reason Drinius should be unable to serve in this capacity, will you take my daughter's well-being upon yourself?"

"With all that I am and for all of my life," Gladiel's deep voice rumbled with equal conviction, "I pledge my honor to that course."

The King looked down at the infant in his arms. Her blue eyes, still swollen from the rigors of being born, blinked up at him. He kissed her brow and traced the line of her jaw with his forefinger. When he spoke, his voice was barely loud enough to hear.

"It is the right thing to do," he said. "But I'm not sure I can bear to let her go."

Drinius exchanged a look with Gladiel. They were both fathers. The prospect of secreting his own child away, of disassociating himself even to the point of keeping the child's name from her, seemed a terrible burden to bear.

"But for her safety," King Jarryn said finally, "I must."

And then, placing his hand on her forehead, the King closed his eyes. "Sleep, child," he whispered, "until the sea is beneath you and you are well on your way."

The infant's eyes drifted closed. She did not even stir when her father's tears dripped on her cheek.

As Drinius took the hope of E'veria into his arms, he prayed that, somewhere within the baby girl's heart, she would treasure the "I love you" the King whispered just before he trusted his heir to a knight's keeping.

PART I: ROSE

ONE

16 years later

Rose took a deep breath, enjoying the crispness of the air and the free and joyful scent of snow, so recently delivered to the world. A sudden whirl of breeze lifted the glimmering dust of winter off a curved drift beside her mount. She held her breath as the tiny flakes danced circles with the wind before dipping into the shadow of the hill. Smiling, she lifted her face to the sky. Atop Lord Whittier's steed, on a hill overlooking Mirthan Hall, the air seemed newer somehow than it did in the wide valley below. Perhaps it was.

Or perhaps it just seems that way because I'm so seldom allowed this view. Her grin's mischievous path was arrested by a tiny pang of guilt. *Not that I've been allowed it, exactly, today.*

A cold, northerly breeze grabbed a lock of Rose's hair, momentarily tainting the clean, airy scent of the snow. She frowned. Borrowing a horse and riding beyond what Lord Whittier had deemed "a safe distance" from Mirthan Hall seemed a mild infraction compared to the constant scent of deception that was, even now, tickling her nose.

The blackened curl teased her senses with competing scents of the same lie. Every day she applied a sweet herbal tonic to her hair in the hope it would mask the darker, earthier scent of the ebonswarth root dye that lingered within each strand. Oh, how she detested that smell. It had been weeks since she had last applied the dye, but at times like this, when her nose was under a direct assault from it, proximity served as a pungent reminder of her promise to deceive those she loved.

Rose had given her word at the age of eight, too young to realize what such a vow would entail. And as soon as Uncle Drinius had obtained her promise, he had made an announcement that, however briefly, had broken her heart.

"You'll have more freedom in Veetri," Uncle Drinius had said after informing Rose that he would deliver her into the care of Lord Whittier de Barden, Duke of Glenhume. *"It will be an adventure,"* he'd said.

Oh, how excited she'd been to learn of their destination! *Veetri!* The land of the Storytellers! It sounded wonderful . . . until she realized that "delivering" meant Uncle Drinius would *leave* her there and it would likely be years until she saw him, or Aunt Alaine and Lily, again.

She had cried. Yelled. *Begged.* But there was nothing for it. Her father had ordered it. Her nameless, absent father. And not even Sir Drinius de Wyte would gainsay *him*. Not even if it broke a little girl's heart.

Rose scowled and buried her face in the roan stallion's mane. She inhaled deeply, hoping to drown the smell of that which blackened her hair in the much more pleasant scent of horse.

"Ah, Falcon," she sighed. "You're a beauty, you are. I'd dye my every garment with the rancid stuff if it meant I could ride you every day."

Falcon nickered as if he thought that a fine idea. And when Rose exhaled . . . her darker emotions drifted away on the wind.

It *had* been an adventure, coming here, Rose admitted, giving in to a slightly begrudging smile. Away from the over-protective eye of Uncle Drinius and the restraining, albeit loving, hand of Aunt Alaine, Rose's spirit had found its wings in Veetri. And although she grieved at being parted from Lily, who was more sister than cousin, in Veetri Rose had discovered a new family to call her own.

She had come to Mirthan Hall with nothing to recommend her but Uncle Drinius's word, but Lord and Lady Whittier had considered Rose a daughter from the beginning. Although she came with no official patronymic of her own, she had been effortlessly grafted into the family with an affection that never wavered.

Rose patted Falcon's neck. Indeed, it was a happy trade in the end, leaving the loving suffocation of Uncle Drinius's home for the adventurous camaraderie of three much-less-refined older brothers.

Kinley, Lewys, and Rowlen. Ah, but she missed them now that they were off in the world pursuing the adventures of men.

Falcon made an impatient noise and stomped his foot.

"Patience, now," she stroked the horse's neck. "I won't tarry much longer. After all, we wouldn't want to be found out, would we?"

Rose gazed down into the valley and at Mirthan Hall, firmly ensconced at its center. The view of her home never failed to fetch a smile. A large manor built from a yellowish native stone, Mirthan Hall exuded the same sort of cheerfulness as the merry occupants who called it home.

Well, most of its occupants, Rose corrected herself when the lone figure of Mrs. Scyles appeared. No one had ever accused the Head of Housekeeping of being cheerful.

Rose watched as the housekeeper looked all around, but not up toward the hill. Instead, Mrs. Scyles clutched something tightly to her chest and crossed the yard with hurried steps.

Rose held her breath and bit her lip. If Mrs. Scyles happened to look up and see Rose, her least favorite of all Lord Whittier's children, in an act of outright disobedience, she would be sure and report to the duke posthaste.

Lord Whittier's affection was constant, but his discipline was generally swift. No doubt his ire would be sparked a bit if he learned Rose was not only beyond the boundary he'd set for her, but atop his horse as well.

"Don't move, Falcon," Rose whispered, pressing her cheek to the horse's mane. "If we're still enough, maybe she won't notice us."

Mrs. Scyles would take too much delight in reporting Rose's infraction. She would consider it her duty. Mrs. Scyles took her job very seriously. The staff respected her—though Rose wondered if it was more from fear than genuine regard— and Lord and Lady Whittier often commented that it was Mrs. Scyles's efficiency that freed the family to so enjoy life. Whenever Rose or the boys complained of the housekeeper's sourness they received a reminder—sometimes a lecture— about respecting cultural differences, for Mrs. Scyles had been born into the desert clans of the Dwons province. And, if Lord and Lady Whittier were to be believed—and there was no reason they shouldn't be—the desert clans of Dwons were as different from the jovial Veetrish as an aged rooster was from a kitten.

Rose squinted at the swiftly moving figure. Mrs. Scyles had authority over all the staff at Mirthan Hall; therefore, the secretive way she moved across the yard was out of character. The woman seemed to be hiding something. And she was taking it to . . .

"The laundry shed?" Rose tilted her head. "I wonder what she's—?"

A distant sound turned Rose's head in the opposite direction. *Horses?* Rose sat very still as she tried to decide whether to wait and greet the approaching riders or flee. She didn't think they *looked* threatening, but as the old Veetrish saying claimed, *"The discovery of beauty is a feast to the eyes, but they that drink of that nectar could kiss death in disguise."*

She was just about to spur her horse toward home when something about one of the riders caught her eye. "No, it can't be." She peered harder. "Is it . . . ? *Kinley!*"

With a gentle tug of the reins and a quick tap of her heels into Falcon's sides, she took off toward them.

"Kinley!" she cried. She reined Falcon in, but slid out of her saddle before he came to a complete stop. "Kinley!"

"Whoa . . . whoa!" Lord Whittier's eldest son held up his fist and the other men reined in their horses alongside him.

"Kinley!" Rose ran toward them. "I didn't know you were coming! Did you write? Did your parents know you were on your way? Or," she paused, but not long enough for a breath, "is it a surprise?"

Her questions came rapidly, leaving no time for Kinley to answer, but since she'd been saving them up for three long years since his last visit home, she couldn't bear to leave one unspoken.

"How long shall you stay? Oh! You've been knighted, haven't you?" She laughed with a broad grin and sent a conspiratorial wink his direction. "It's the beard that gives it away, you know."

When she finally took a breath, Kinley rubbed his index finger and thumb over the short, triangular beard that circled his lips and came to a point just below his chin. "Yes," he said slowly, "I am a knight."

He dismounted and bowed. "Sir Kinley de Whittier, at your service. You have my deepest apologies, my lady, but I regret I cannot call you by name. I'm afraid you have me at a—" He froze. "Rose?" He blinked. "*Rose?*" His cheeks bounced into a grin. "It *is* you! Why, you were little more than a mischievous little imp the last time I was home! What has happened to you?"

"Did you think time would stand still at Mirthan Hall while awaiting your return, Sir Kinley?" Rose laughed. "If you did, I must disabuse you of the notion. I'll mark the end of my sixteenth year in two weeks' time."

Squired to a knight in the Sengarra province the same year Rose had arrived in Veetri, Kinley had been absent most of the years she had lived with his family.

"Sixteen? It hardly seems possible." Kinley's toffee-colored eyes blinked a few times more before he addressed the companions Rose had nearly forgotten in her excitement.

"Sirs Elden de Mars, Kile de Poggen, and Worth de Genner, may I present Rose de . . ." Kinley's brow furrowed. "Er, this is my sis—" He cleared his throat. "This is Rose," he finished rather lamely. "She's my father's ward."

Rose dipped her head as was expected, glad the action and the briskness of the northern wind would disguise the color that had flushed her cheeks at Kinley's inability to produce a patronymic to identify her father.

But how could he be expected to produce the name of a man for whom no one—least of all Rose herself—knew the identity?

"My lady," the knights greeted her in turn.

"Welcome to Glenhume." Rose made a point of addressing each man with a smile. Whether she suffered embarrassment or not, Lady Whittier would expect Rose to extend the warm hospitality for which the Veetrish were known. She dipped a curtsy. "May merry comfort keep you while you break your journey here at Mirthan Hall."

As her greeting made the circle of knights, curiosity overcame her shame. Since being delivered into Lord Whittier's care eight years ago, Rose had rarely met anyone from outside the Dukedom of Glenhume, and even fewer from beyond the province of Veetri. To meet three newcomers at once—two of whom were passing handsome, she could not help but note—was an unusual treat.

"We were given leave to visit our families," Kinley said when she finished, "before taking our commissions at Castle Rynwyk in Salderyn."

"In Salderyn?" Her eyes widened. "You've been assigned to serve the King?"

All four men beamed and nodded.

"Congratulations! That's—"

"Rose." Kinley's eyes narrowed on the horse behind her. "Surely that is not *your* horse, is it?"

Rose bit her lip for only a second before answering. "Lord Whittier was quite engaged in his study this afternoon," she said. "And Falcon, as you can surely tell by his form, requires more exercise than sweet old Bonnet. Therefore, I took it upon myself to exercise the poor beast on your father's behalf."

"I think what you mean to say," Kinley began, but his cheek dimpled twice before he gave in and let a laugh escape, "is that you snuck into the stable, saddled my father's horse, and rode—unaccompanied, I might add—well beyond the boundaries he established for you."

"It's been years since you were last here, Kinley." Rose lifted her chin. "Don't you think that perhaps he might have extended the boundaries since then?"

"Has he?"

"No." Rose admitted with a frown that quickly transformed to a grin. "But even you must admit that Lord Whittier would have no quarrel with me riding beyond the boundaries while I am accompanied by four such fine knights. The King's men, no less!"

Kinley smiled and shook his head. "Lewys was right."

Rose perked up at the mention of Lord Whittier's middle son, who was currently serving as squire to the same knight who had trained Kinley. "Lewys was right about what?"

"He said that I would have to keep my wits on the highest alert to be able to have even the simplest of conversations with you."

"Lewys is a flatterer."

"I'm not sure he meant it as a compliment."

"That will not stop me from accepting it as such." Rose gave the slightest whistle between her teeth and Falcon moved to her side. In one swift motion she put her foot in the stirrup and swung up into the saddle, skirts and all. "Shall we on then, knights? Having four extra at table will surely give the Asp a fresh reason to hiss if we don't give her enough notice."

"The asp?" Sir Worth asked. "Surely you don't refer to Sir Kinley's mother!"

"Hardly." Kinley laughed. "It's the nickname I gave to our housekeeper years ago. Her name is Aspera Scyles. *Mrs. Scyles*, I should say, as that is what she prefers to be called. She's originally from the Dwons province. And rather sour, even for one from Dwons."

"Ahhh," the other knights chorused.

Cultural differences, indeed, Rose thought. The knights acted as if Mrs. Scyles's province of origin explained everything.

"I can't imagine why she's stayed in Veetri so long," Kinley continued. "Our merrymaking causes her no end of misery. Which, of course, is why my brothers and I—and apparently Rose now, as well—have made it our mission to be as sickeningly jovial around her as we can manage. You'll see." He winked. "It's great fun."

Rose just smiled as the knights chuckled, but some of the merriness within her fizzled. When others were present Mrs. Scyles was the picture of reserve, giving respect to all members of the family, but when the duke and duchess were away, as they often were given Lord Whittier's popularity as a Storyteller, Mrs. Scyles's disdain for Rose was veiled with a sickening sweetness that was, at best, disconcerting. Although the woman had never said or done anything outwardly objectionable to Rose, she always felt an undercurrent of contempt when in the woman's presence. And after all these years, Rose was still at a loss to explain what she'd done to earn the woman's scorn.

"What say you, knights? Shall we *escort*," Kinley winked at Rose, "my sister back to the safety of Mirthan Hall?"

"If you wish to accompany me," Rose said, gently pulling the reins until Falcon faced the right direction, "you'll have to catch me first!" Simultaneously leaning forward in the saddle and tapping her heels into the horse's side, she cried, "Home, Falcon!" and Falcon leapt forward.

"Rose!" Kinley shouted after her. "Rose! Slow down!"

Looking over her shoulder, she laughed as Kinley and the other three knights raced to mount their horses and catch up. She was still laughing when she passed through the gate and angled Falcon toward the stables. Her laughter abruptly stilled, however, when Lord Whittier burst from the house and shouted for the guard.

"Whoa, boy," Rose pulled back on the reins. "Whoa."

She slid down from the horse and handed the reins to a stable boy whose face was as white as the snow beneath his feet.

"You're being p-pursued, Mistress Rose!" the boy stammered. "B-By four men on horseb-back!"

"Rose!" Lord Whittier's shout turned her head. "Rose, get to the house at once! Men, to arms!"

Lord Whittier blew across his palm. As the breath touched his skin a shimmering trail passed through his fingers and on to the ground.

Rose blinked. "What is he—?"

"And there suddenly appeared an army of knights, bound by honor to guard all those who dwelled within the manor," Lord Whittier shouted as he ran toward Rose, pausing only to send another puff of air across his palm, increasing the stream.

"Oh, no," Rose breathed.

Where each glittering breath landed, a translucent knight in full armor appeared, rising from the ground in the space of a heartbeat and keeping pace with the duke's long stride. With swords drawn, they screamed a battle cry.

"Well," Rose quirked a wobbly smile at the stable boy, even as her own heartbeat quickened, "you don't see that outside of Mirthan Hall every day."

She looked back toward the gate. Kinley and the other knights had just passed through. "You'd better take Falcon inside before he's spooked." Rose gave the stable boy a gentle push in the right direction.

"Yes, mistress." The stable boy clicked his tongue at the stallion, "C'mon now, Falcon. That's a g-good lad," his voice shook more than a little.

"Lord Whittier!" Rose picked up her skirts and ran directly toward the oncoming, ever-expanding army and the thin, pale-haired Storyteller leading the charge. Even knowing the knights were only Story People, it took every ounce of courage within her not to run the opposite direction. "Lord Whittier! All is well! It's only Kinley, come home from Sengarra!"

"Rose, get in the house! Bar the doors! Let no one—"

"It's *Kinley*!" Rose was almost to him, but she still had to shout to be heard above the racket of the Story Knights. She pointed toward the approaching riders and annunciated carefully, yelling as loudly as she could, "It's *Kinley*! *Your son*!"

The duke halted abruptly. "Kinley, you say?"

"Yes." Rose flinched, but the Story Knight who was about to barrel through her dissolved, as did his fellows. She let out a breath. "I'm sorry. I—"

"You're *sorry*? Rose, have you stopped to think what could have happened if it *hadn't* been Kinley you met in the hills?" He ran a hand over his pale blond hair. "You shouldn't have ridden outside the boundary I set for you. Especially not without an escort! How many times do I have to—urrgh!" He fisted both hands on his head as if to pull out his hair. "And to take Falcon? Without permission? Indeed!"

Rose bit her lip and looked down at the ground. The knights—the real ones—were nearing, now. Would they all bear witness to her reprimand and the doling out of punishment that would surely follow?

When Lord Whittier remained silent, she dared a glance at his face. When she met his eyes, his stern expression softened.

"You have your own horse. A safe horse. A gentle horse. You shouldn't have taken Falcon." His lip twitched. "I must say, though, that you handled him well. I should probably throttle you, Rose. But instead, I find myself wondering if I need to seek a new mount for you. A horse better suited to your skill." A bright sparkle lit his eyes, even as he shook his head. "That was an impressive bit of riding."

The glow of praise warmed her cheeks, but Rose had to press her lips together to keep from laughing. "And I must say, Lord Whittier," a tiny giggle escaped her mouth, "that was an impressive bit of Storytelling."

"You liked that, did you?" The duke's grin overtook his face, but he shrugged. "It just came to me as I was running. I'm no warrior, but I am not completely without the ability to defend those I love." He winked. "Even if that defense is little more than an illusion."

"It was truly inspired."

"It must have been, for I find no other explanation for it." The duke crossed his arms. "But neither my inspired Storytelling nor your skillful riding erases the fact of your disobedience. We will talk, Rose. Of that you can be sure. And there will be consequences."

TWO

Rose supposed it was unlikely that even Kinley's arrival would cause Lord Whittier to forget her need for discipline. Still, she was disappointed when the knock that normally summoned her to table did not come at the appointed time. And, when it did finally come, it was not a summons. It was Mrs. Scyles, bearing a rather sparse dinner and instructions that Rose was not to join the family at table or elsewhere until morning.

After setting the tray on the small table by the fire, Mrs. Scyles paused.

Unusual. A wave of dread passed over Rose. The rest of the household was at table, two floors below. Special attention from Mrs. Scyles could not be a good thing.

"Might I have a word, Mistress Rose?"

The Asp rarely spoke to her directly, but if she did it was most likely when they were alone, her words carefully crafted so that, even if repeated, Rose would not likely be able to prove they held a threat. But when Aspera Scyles made a special effort to address Rose, even the most innocuous comment seemed to be just that.

Rose nodded and took a step back as she waited for Mrs. Scyles to speak. Although quite tall, Rose always felt tiny next to Mrs. Scyles. Having little in the way of extra flesh clinging to her sturdy frame, the woman's largeness came from an impressive bone structure which made her small, pinched features even more surprising on such a solidly built woman. Her hair, which had given itself over to the dulled silver of time, was pulled tightly away from her face. Rose had often wondered if the slight downward tilt of the woman's eyes would be less so with a looser or higher bun, but she certainly wasn't going to be the one to suggest it.

Digging her fingernails into her palms, Rose finally spoke when it seemed the silence might stretch too long. "You wanted a word, Mrs. Scyles?"

Mrs. Scyles moved to shut the bedchamber door. "Yes," the whispered hiss set the hairs on Rose's neck at right angles to her skin. "Yes, I'd like a word, Mistress Rose." When she turned around, malice had replaced her usual bland expression, but sugary venom still infected her tone. "It's about your witchcraft."

Rose almost laughed, but caught herself just in time. "Pardon? I must have misunderstood. You did say . . . witchcraft?"

The Asp nodded. "You must desist with your evil practices on this family."

Rose blinked. "What are you talking about?"

"I found powdered ebonswarth hidden in your trunk."

The color drained from Rose's face in a rush of cold that left a sheen of damp behind.

"Ebonswarth is native to Dwons and does not grow in any of the other eight provinces of E'veria." She spoke as if giving

14

correction to a toddler. "I am of Dwons. Did you think that by hiding it in a wineskin I would not recognize it? Or by it, you, as a witch?"

"Witches are a Storyteller's invention, Mrs. Scyles. They aren't real."

"Liar!" Mrs. Scyles's hiss momentarily replaced the sickening sweetness in her voice. She straightened, took a long breath in through her nose, and when she spoke again her tone had normalized. "In Dwons, witches are very real, but they are not the hags the Storytellers make them out to be. They have no inherent magic, nor any inborn abilities like the Veetrish Storytellers or even the Andoven of Tirandov Isle. They have only knowledge and beauty at their disposal, but they use both for evil gain."

"Knowledge and beauty?" Rose asked. "But those are not bad things."

"They are in the hands of a witch!" Mrs. Scyles lifted her chin. "A witch of Dwons has knowledge of how to use the fruits of the earth in evil ways. And with beauty she can ease her way into the lives of those she wishes to use or destroy."

"I've never even been to Dwons. How could you think me one of them?"

"You have the powder." Mrs. Scyles said. "No one in the Kingdom of E'veria would dare possess it unless they intended to use it. I've never met a witch with eyes of your color, but since you have the powder, your beauty marks you." She lifted her chin. "I will not let you harm this family."

"I've no wish to harm anyone!"

The Asp disregarded Rose's protest as if no words had touched the air. "I've hidden the powder and I will destroy it as soon as I can. And I found it just in time, too, lest you use it to bewitch Sir Kinley or one of the other knights."

"Why would I want to hurt Kinley? He's like a brother to me!"

"Perhaps you envision yourself the next Duchess of Glenhume?"

"*What?!*"

"Indeed." The sweet tone disappeared, replaced by a low, dangerous quiet. "You are just like the black-haired harlot who stole my place within the clan! My husband was next in line to be Chieftain, he was. But he was tricked by a witch. She told him lies and he cast me out of our home. He exiled me from my clan and took her as his wife." Mrs. Scyles wrinkled her nose. Her nostrils flared. "He should have known she was a witch. Ebonswarth witches almost always have black hair. And black hearts to match. Like *you.*"

Rose's hand unconsciously reached up to touch her hair. Was that why Mrs. Scyles had never liked her? Because Rose's black hair reminded her of the woman who had stolen her husband?

But my hair isn't really black, Rose reminded herself. Not that she could let Mrs. Scyles know it.

Mrs. Scyles sniffed. "Of course, Sir Kinley, being the heir, would be an attractive proposition now that you're nearly of age." Her gaze was fixed nearer to the ceiling than Rose's face. She almost seemed to be talking to herself.

Rose shook her head. "Mrs. Scyles, I would never do anything to hurt my family."

"Your family? Pah! Lord Whittier is a duke! You are no one! No one," she spat, "but the cursed daughter of a witch and the knight she ensnared with ebonswarth!"

The knight? Rose's chin dropped. "Do you know who my father is?"

16

"It's rather obvious, I should think, to anyone with eyes." The Asp snorted. "Your black hair, your sudden departure from his home . . ." She shrugged.

Rose gasped. *Black hair. His home.* "You think *Uncle Drinius* is my father?"

Mrs. Scyles sneered. "Did it never occur to you?"

"Of course not!" Rose exclaimed. "That's absurd."

"Is it? Why else would a man go to such lengths to see a child cared for in such grand style, but yet keep her from claiming a father's name?"

The Asp's insinuations spun questions to life that, before now, seemed content to be ignored in the back of Rose's heart. Why *did* her father never allow her to claim his name? Was he . . . ashamed of her?

Uncle Drinius had told Rose that her mother died in childbirth and that her father was a knight.

Everyone knew a knight was expected to uphold the highest moral standard.

Uncle Drinius was a knight.

By hiding Rose away in Veetri, was he protecting himself from scandal?

Mrs. Scyles was exceedingly loyal to Lord Whittier's family, yet she had never, *never* transferred that loyalty to Rose. Did the Head of Housekeeping know something the duke and duchess—even Rose herself—did not?

Mrs. Scyles clasped her hands behind her back and leaned slightly forward. Rose shrank back.

"Perhaps the reason Sir Drinius brought you here," the housekeeper said, "was not to protect *you*, but to protect his *wife*. Perhaps Lady Drinius could no longer stand the sight of you, his child by another woman, in her home."

"No." Rose shook her head. Uncle Drinius couldn't be her father. He couldn't. "You're speaking nonsense. Aunt Alaine loved me. She cried when I left!"

"With joy, most likely." The Asp straightened. "I always knew there was something base, something dangerous about you, girl. And the ebonswarth powder proves it. You were born a witch."

"I am not a witch! And you should know better than to speak lies about a knight. Sir Drinius is an honorable man!"

"At one time I would have called my husband an 'honorable man,' as well. Alas, many honorable men have been ensnared by the craft of an ebonswarth witch." Mrs. Scyles clicked her tongue. "Think about it, girl. Sir Drinius has only visited you twice since he dumped you on the duke's hospitality."

Rose flinched. That much was true.

"Is that the act of one who is proud of his offspring? No. I'd wager the knight is glad to be rid of you." Mrs. Scyles sneered. "Good riddance to tainted blood, he's thinking."

"You go too far, Mrs. Scyles." Rose lifted her chin, but a tremor still remained in her voice. "As you said, I am considered a daughter of this house. When Lord Whittier hears of the disrespect with which you've addressed me, he'll—"

"Tell them of me and I'll tell them your secret." The revolting sweetness returned to her voice. "It would be a shame if I had to tell them about the ebonswarth." She smiled, her thin lips nearly disappearing. "Or that perhaps you used it to bewitch Masters Lewys and Rowlen?"

"I've bewitched no one! If you think I've hurt Rowlen, then perhaps you should ask *him*. He knows I have the powder and he knows why! He was there when the mineral springs washed the black away, leaving only red behind. He's the one who snuck into my room, got the powder, and helped me—"

18

With a shaking hand, Rose touched her lips. She had said too much. She had broken her promise to Uncle Drinius. But it was too late. She couldn't take it back. She could only speak faster and hope the Asp would not recall her slip.

"Rowlen will vouch for my innocence in this nonsense you've concocted," Rose declared.

"How inconvenient for you," the Asp mocked, "that he is not here."

Rose's heart raced as if trying to get ahead of her mind. Did Uncle Drinius know the powder was used in witchcraft? Is that why he cautioned her to keep it well hidden?

A swift series of taps on the door reminded her to breathe. "Come in."

The knob turned and Koria poked her head through the door. "Rose?" the tutor asked. "When you are finished with your dinner, please join me in the upper library. There were some errors with your sums from this morning that I would like you to try and fix."

"My sums?" Rose's morning lessons had not included any arithmetic that she recalled. She could only assume Koria had overheard part of her conversation with Mrs. Scyles. "Oh. Of course. I'll be there shortly."

"Will that be all, Mistress Rose?" The Asp's tone regained its normal tone.

"Yes." Rose nodded. But she knew differently. This was far from over.

THREE

Rose ate nothing of her dinner. Instead, she paced until she was sure Mrs. Scyles was gone and then raced down the hall to the upper library and pulled the doors closed behind her.

"She thinks I'm a witch!" Her voice was breathless and her skin tingled with fear. At Mirthan Hall, only Koria, the tutor Uncle Drinius had hired before they left for Veetri, knew about Rose's true coloring. It was she who assisted Rose with the dye each new moon.

"Mrs. Scyles found the ebonswarth powder, Koria! And now she thinks I'm a witch!"

"I know." The tutor's eyes slid shut.

"You heard?"

"Yes. I . . . heard."

"We have to do something." Rose wrung her hands and paced to the window and back. "She thinks I want to bewitch Kinley!"

"Where is the powder now?"

"I don't know!" Rose wailed. "She took it and hid it some-where while I was—" Rose's words halted as she remembered seeing Mrs. Scyles outside just before Kinley and his friends arrived. "It's in the laundry shed. It must be."

"The laundry shed?" Koria wrinkled her nose. "How can you be sure?"

"I saw her." Rose related the strange behavior Mrs. Scyles had displayed earlier.

"So a blessing has resulted even from your disobedience. Thank Rynloeft for guiding your eyes even though you did not allow your behavior to be so led." Koria closed her eyes, her mouth moving with silent words and her head tilted to-ward the ceiling. When she reopened her eyes a few moments later her look was stern. "Had you been in your room study-ing for tomorrow's geography exam as you led me to believe you would be, the powder would still be safely stowed in your trunk."

"I *did* study," Rose defended. "Give me the exam now if you don't believe me. I can draw all nine provinces of E'veria with my eyes closed. I can tell you their exports, and even how the Kingdom's people are distributed among them." She ignored Koria's crossed arms and stern expression. "From largest population to smallest, they are Stoen, Sengarra, Dynwatre, Veetri, Nyrland, Dwons, Tirandov, Mynissbyr, and Shireya. And, in case you doubt me, I can also list the nations, kingdoms, and empires E'veria considers her allies, as well as those we do not. I can name banner colors, capital cities, and recite lists of their most valuable—"

"No matter how quickly you speak," Koria interrupted, "you will not make me forget why you are up here rather than enjoying dinner with your family."

"I know," Rose sighed. "I should have told someone where I was going. I shouldn't have taken Falcon without asking. I shouldn't have gone further than I was supposed to." Her shoulders slumped. "I'm sorry. It won't happen again." At Koria's arched brow, she added, "Well, it might happen again. But not *exactly* like that."

"You must learn restraint, Rose. Patience. These are things I cannot teach you." Koria sighed and shook her head. "But we have a larger issue at hand than your developing character."

"I know," Rose groaned. "What if the red begins to show through?"

"We have at least a few more days before we need to worry about that." Koria pressed a calming hand on Rose's shoulder. "I hate to suggest a further act of disobedience, but if you think you know where the powder is, perhaps you should try to retrieve it after everyone else is abed." Koria rubbed her arms as if a chill had passed through the room. "I feel I'm betraying Lord Whittier by even suggesting you do this, but I'm afraid Aspera will destroy the powder if you don't find it first."

"You're not betraying Lord Whittier," Rose said. "I'm not *confined* above stairs. I'm just not allowed to join the family until morning. Lord Whittier never expressly forbade me from going outside."

"It was implied."

"Well, yes. I suppose. But as long as I slip in and out with no one seeing me—"

"Something I'm sure you've never done before." Koria rarely resorted to sarcasm, and when she did, Rose knew she tread on sensitive ground.

"Er . . . well." Rose forced a smile. "Perhaps my disobedience in the past has given me a skill that will serve as a blessing tonight?"

"You're using my words against me." Koria shook her head. "Be careful. To the laundry shed and back. No distractions."

Rose nodded. "I'd better get back to my room." At the door she paused. "Koria?"

"Yes?"

"About what Mrs. Scyles said . . . is it true? About the powder?"

Koria was silent for a moment. Finally, she sighed. "I'm afraid so. When ingested, the powder can incite normally benign people to murder, lie, steal, and commit any number of heinous acts based on lies told to them while they were under the influence of its poison."

"It's poisonous?" A sudden burst of anger made Rose cross her arms at her chest. "Is it poisoning me?"

"It must be ingested to affect the mind of its victim. Applied topically it has no known risks."

"No *known* risks?"

"That is why we go to the hot spring. Sulfur water is the only known antidote for ebonswarth poisoning. Be at ease." Koria smiled. "Using sulfur water utterly cancels the risk for you."

"Be at ease?" Rose arched an eyebrow and recrossed her arms. "Be at ease? When Mrs. Scyles knows about it?"

Koria's smile fell. "That does present a problem. Several, in fact, should she decide to tell of you having it." A pair of lines appeared between Koria's brows. "Especially considering that possessing ebonswarth in any form is illegal."

"Ach! So I'm a criminal as well as a witch?"

"You're neither," Koria shook her head. "I'm sure Sir Drinius would not have given you the powder without having taken pains to ensure it would not cause you ill through its use or possession."

It took a bit more persuasion on her tutor's part before Rose was convinced that the powder was benign. Finally, mind whirling, Rose headed back to her room where she attempted to wear a path in the floor over Koria's troubling words. Eventually she sat by the window and stared out into the night, her thoughts as dark as the sky.

The house had been still for a long while when Rose finally donned her sheepskin cloak and crept out of her bedroom. Many late night adventures with Lewys and Rowlen had taught her where each creak in the floor resided and which doors squeaked on their hinges or dragged across the floor. She avoided them accordingly, making her passage through the house entirely silent but for the sound of her breathing.

The lamps had long been extinguished on the first floor of the house. Although Rose had rarely snuck out in the night since Rowlen, the most mischievous of her adopted brothers, had left for his apprenticeship, she knew her way through the house well enough not to require illumination.

Outside, a waning sliver of light was all that was left of the month's moon, but it was enough to reflect upon the snow and ease her passage the short distance to the laundry shed.

In truth, she had rarely visited the small building. Treated as a daughter of the house, Rose never tended her own laundry. The only times she had come here were to join Rowlen or Lewys in a prank played on one of the good-natured members of the staff. Rose smiled, remembering the time she'd climbed inside the rag barrel and—

The rag barrel. That would be a perfect hiding place.

Rose winced at the loud groan the door made as it scraped across the shed's stone floor and only opened it wide enough that she could just slide through. Once inside, she put one hand against the wall and stretched the other out before her. Taking one tentative step after another, she moved around the left side of the shed's interior until her toe nicked against something solid. She lowered her hands and smiled. She'd found it.

Rose pried the top off the barrel and delved her hand within. The barrel was full of the discarded remains of the household's worn-out clothes. Using both hands, she dug down into the barrel until it had practically swallowed her, but finally her cold-numbed fingers grazed something that felt different than the cloth around it. Grasping its edge, she pulled.

It was a wineskin, but was it the *right* wineskin? With one quick glance toward the spare slice of moonlight coming through the cracked-open door, she pulled the cork out of the top of the skin. With a slight grimace she brought it to her nose, only to gag and quickly shove the cork back in to block the familiar reek.

Rose unfastened her cloak, tucked the powder-filled skin into the waist of her skirt, and pulled her cloak back in place. She slipped out the door, closing it entirely too loudly behind her.

Several snow-crunching footfalls later she had reached the stone steps. Her hand was on the door when a shadow moved and rent a squeal like that of a baby mouse, though thankfully no louder, from her lips.

Rose spun around. Her hand flew to the pocket of her cloak where she usually kept her dagger, but found it empty. "Who's there?"

Kinley stepped out of the shadow. "Have no fear, Rose. It's only me. What are you about, sneaking into the laundry shed at this hour?"

"Stop!" she whispered, lifting a hand to cover her eyes. "I'm not allowed to see anyone until morning."

"But you are allowed to wander about in the dark laundry shed?"

Rose frantically searched her mind for a plausible explanation to prevent Kinley from learning about the ebonswarth powder. In the split second before the silence between them grew awkward she decided that the truth, even if he did not receive all of it, was her best option.

"I needed to retrieve something from the rag barrel." She groaned inwardly as heat flooded her neck. Of all the possible explanations she could have concocted on the spot, she had chosen this one? "It was a rather urgent need, you see," she said, "and I didn't want to bother one of the maids at this late hour. I'm sorry. I know it's rather indelicate of me to mention, seeing as you're not used to being around women, but—"

"You'd best be on your way, then." Kinley quickly reached to open the door, but he avoided making eye contact.

Rose rushed in, mortified not only for what she had said, but what she had done. She had lied. To *Kinley*. A knight! Not outright, of course. Every word she'd said was true, but the implication was far from it. And that she had used the inconvenience of her gender to accomplish her means, embarrassing her foster brother in the process, sickened her.

Even in her haste, as had so often been the state of her return from various exploits with Lewys and Rowlen, Rose navigated around the creaks and groans of the house back to her room without a sound but the guilty beat of her heart.

$\mathcal{F}$OUR

$\mathcal{A}$ penitent Rose arrived at the duke and duchess's bedchamber door just before the appointed time for breakfast. After apologizing for her behavior the previous day, she followed them downstairs. Already seated at the long table, the knights rose as the trio entered.

"Good morning, knights. And might I have the pleasure of presenting—" Lord Whittier paused. "Well, *officially* presenting, as it were, since it would seem introductions of a sort were made yesterday afternoon, my ward, Rose. Rose, I believe Kinley introduced you to Sirs Elden, Kile, and Worth?"

"Good morning," Rose curtsied. "Please accept my apologies for being unable to attend dinner last night. I hope you all slept well?"

"Very well." Sir Worth smiled. "And might I say it's lovely to see you this morning?"

"Indeed," added Sir Kile. "A pleasure, Mistress Rose."

When Sir Elden nodded, his cheeks turned nearly as pink as the side of bacon that had just been delivered to the table.

"An honor, Mistress Rose. You're lovely. Er—" He cleared his throat. "What I mean to say, is that it's lovely to see you."

"The honor is mine." Rose ducked her head.

Lord Whittier moved to hold a chair for his wife and Rose stepped toward her usual spot.

"Allow me," Sirs Worth and Kile said in unison, but Sir Elden was nearest her chair and held it out for her.

At the foot of the table, Lady Whittier lifted a hand to her mouth. Rose was sure it was to hide the evidence of the girlish giggle that had just escaped her lips.

Not since her first breakfast at Mirthan Hall had Rose been such an object of interest at the table. No matter what subject Lord Whittier brought up, at least one of the knights sought Rose's opinion on the matter. It was, for a girl used to being somewhat secluded from the outside world, a bit overwhelming.

"You look tired this morning, Kinley," Lord Whittier addressed his son, and then his wife. "Don't you think so, Capricia?"

Lady Whittier eyed her son. "Did you not sleep well, Kinley, dear?"

"I confess that I am a bit tired this morning." After a quick side glance at Rose, Kinley smiled at his mother. "I suppose my mind was too occupied with the odd little details of home to settle at a sensible hour.."

"Ah, it's to be expected after so long away." His mother patted his hand. "But you will have plenty of time to rest while you are home."

"At least a day or two," Lord Whittier said with a laugh. "Isn't that right, Capricia?"

Lady Whittier's eyes sparkled as brightly as her laugh. "It is at that!" With long straight hair the shade of nutmeg and eyes to match, Lady Whittier was a beautiful woman, but it was her youthful charm that made her so easy to love. "I am afraid I may need to infringe upon you and your friends just a bit." She winked at Kinley. "All in the service of merriment, of course."

Rose's gaze traveled to the knight she considered a brother. But for his size, Kinley really did look a lot like his mother. His narrow nose and topaz eyes had clearly come from Lord Whittier, but his brown hair and high cheekbones were so like Lady Whittier's. He was broader and more muscular than Lord Whittier—the difference of a knight's life to that of a Storyteller's, she assumed—but he was such a perfect mix of both his parents that she couldn't help but feel at home in his presence, regardless of the length of time he was away.

That is, until he met her gaze and she remembered what she had implied the night before.

Rose hastily reached for her bread and set her concentration on applying honey to it while Lady Whittier addressed her husband across the expanse of the table.

"Infringe upon us, Mother?" Kinley asked. "And how?"

"Would you like to tell them, Whittier, or shall I?"

Lord Whittier chuckled. "I would not deny you the pleasure, my dear."

"Wonderful!" Lady Whittier reclaimed Rose's attention with her enthusiasm. "As you knights undoubtedly know, Sir Kiggon's company will arrive at Mirthan Hall in two days' time and—"

"Sir Kiggon's company? Will Lewys be with them?" Rose's words tripped over the duchess's. "Pardon me, my lady."

"No, no. It's fine. And yes, my dear. Lewys will be with them." It was all Rose could do to contain a squeal of delight. "And, although we had originally intended for it to be a surprise, I find that I can no longer hold it in!" Lady Whittier continued, "We're hosting a little gathering while they are here. It's not every day your son is knighted, after all!"

"But Kinley's knighthood is not the only thing we'll celebrate," Lord Whittier interjected. "Do tell, Capricia. You're nearly bursting with it."

"Rose's birthday!" Lady Whittier clasped her hands. "We will celebrate Kinley's knighthood and Rose's sixteenth birthday together!"

"My birthday hardly ranks with Kinley being knighted!" Rose laughed. "But I will not object the inclusion. Will there be dancing?"

"This is Veetri, my dear," Lord Whittier laughed. "Of course there will be dancing!"

$\mathcal{F}$ I V E

$\mathcal{U}$naccustomed to the doting attention of men not of her family, Rose was mentally exhausted by the time the household turned in for the night. Kinley's friends were kind, but she sensed a friendly competition of sorts among the three knights. She couldn't help but be flattered by their efforts to win her favor, but to attend the knights equally while all three vied to impress her was tiresome. She was just about to ready for bed when a knock sounded at her door and she remembered Koria's plan for the evening.

Rose groaned, retrieved the ebonswarth powder from its new hiding place, and slipped on her sheepskin cloak.

"I thought tonight we could view the Shepherd's Staff constellation," Koria said as they started down the path into the woods.

"I'm exhausted." Rose dragged her feet. "For once can't we just do what we need to do without a lesson?"

Koria smiled. "I know you're tired, Rose, but it is rather difficult to view constellations in the daylight hours. It's a beautiful night, the sky is clear, and since Rynloeft created us with an endless supply of curiosity with which to find reason to fill our minds, it would be a shame to miss an opportunity to learn."

"My supply of curiosity must be dwindling, for I find that the only thing I want to learn tonight is how my pillow will feel beneath my head." Rose rubbed her arms. "Besides, it's cold."

"And you have a very warm sheepskin cloak."

Rose grumbled all the way to the cave, but slapped a hand across her nose and mouth as soon as she stepped within it. The scent of sulfur was heavy in the air. With a muffled groan, she lifted her lantern and dutifully followed her tutor to the pools.

Koria set her lantern near the edge of one of the bubbling pools and turned up the wick. From the deep pocket of her cloak she pulled a small wooden bowl and a ladle. The tutor dipped a bit of water from the pool and dribbled it into the bowl. "Hand me the skin of powder, please."

Koria mixed the hot, smelly water with a small amount of the even *more* putrid powder until it made a paste.

"What a scowl you wear!" Koria laughed. "It's not that bad."

"It is, actually," Rose argued, but she laid down on the rock, allowing her head to rest on the edge of the pool above the water.

Koria's eyes watered as she mixed the ingredients. "Ah, that should do it. Are you ready?"

"Never." Rose plugged her nose with her thumb and fore-finger and closed her eyes. "Not that that's ever stopped you."

No matter how tightly she closed her eyes, the fumes were too close. Oh, how it burned. Within seconds, tears streamed from her eyes and fire raced down the back of her throat.

"Ach, stop!"

"You know I can't."

"I know," Rose growled. "But this is truly awful, Koria. It almost makes me wish to regain my own wretched hair color."

"Your wretched hair, as you call it, is the most beautiful I've ever seen."

"You only saw it once. And barely long enough to draw that sort of comparison!" Rose protested. "And if Rowlen hadn't decided to teach me to swim in a pond fed by a mineral spring, you'd not have suffered even that."

"Suffered? Hardly. I'd never admit it to your uncle, but I'm glad the minerals dissolved the dye that day. I'd always wondered . . ." her voice trailed off. She sighed. "I'll never forget it, Rose. Like a living flame, it was." She paused and then laughed. "Did you hear that? I've been here so long I'm beginning to sound like one of the Veetrish."

Rose chuckled, but when her scalp and eyebrows began to tingle, sending pinprick itches through her skin, her mind wandered back to her conversation with Mrs. Scyles.

"Koria, I've been in Veetri for eight years and my father's not sent a single message."

"Did he send messages to you when you lived with Sir Drinius?"

"Not directly," Rose admitted. "Uncle Drinius or Sir Gladiel would tell me things he'd said." She paused. "But I haven't seen Sir Gladiel in years. Even Uncle Drinius has stopped visiting." Her voice dropped. "And he promised to come as often as he was able."

"The rest of E'veria does not enjoy the same peace the bog affords Veetri. I'm sure your uncle has a very good reason for his absence. I've no doubt Kinley and other knights could tell you stories of—" Koria dabbed a cloth on Rose's brow. "Ah! I think we're ready to rinse."

"Finally."

With great care, Koria wiped the paste from her charge's eyebrows and then dipped the cloth in the hot spring. She carefully scrubbed away all traces of the blackening powder from Rose's face.

"Koria, last night you said that it's illegal to possess ebonswarth," Rose began. "Are you sure we're not breaking the law? I've no desire to meet one of the King's jailers."

Koria laughed. "Oh, we'd not stay in the jailer's company for long. Knowledgeable possession of ebonswarth is considered treasonous. And treason is a capital offense."

"A capital offense?" Rose gasped. "We could be executed?"

"I'm sure Sir Drinius would not let that happen. I didn't mean to worry you."

"But Mrs. Scyles—"

"Let me worry about Mrs. Scyles." Koria's tone darkened. "You just stay out of her way as much as possible." Koria paused. "Aspera has suffered much in her life, Rose. And although her dislike of you is misguided, it is sourced from a deep well of pain."

"Her husband left her for a black-haired witch."

Koria stilled. "She told you that?"

"Yes."

"Her pain does not excuse her hatred, but it does help to explain it, does it not?" Koria sighed. "Showing compassion to her, even in the face of her scorn, will not only help guard your own secrets, but will help to grow you into a more empathetic woman. Now close your eyes and I'll rinse out the dye."

Rose waited for her to say more about Mrs. Scyles, but when silence persisted, she knew the subject was closed.

"Did you bring the basil oil or the lemongrass to ease the scent this time?" Rose asked, hoping for lemongrass.

"Neither." Even with her eyes closed Rose could sense the smile in her tutor's voice. "Remember when we distilled roses for a natural science lesson last year?"

"Yes. I gave the rose oil to Lady Whittier. For her birthday."

"Not all of it. You gave her the oil from the pink roses. I put the other oils aside for a special occasion." Koria smiled. "I believe a girl's sixteenth birthday qualifies as a special occasion." She laughed. "If Sir Kinley's friends are any indication of the amount of attention you will receive at Lady Whittier's party, I think we can safely assume that many a young man will have his nose near enough your hair to benefit from a thorough application."

Rose laughed and inhaled deeply of the rich, spicy floral oil Koria massaged through the length of her black waves. "That's the one from the dark red roses, isn't it?"

"So you *were* paying attention!" Koria laughed. "It's potent, but we'll be sure to apply a few more drops each day to mask the dye's stench."

Koria pulled a length of towel from another pocket and placed it over Rose's head as she sat up. Sulfur still scented the air around the hot spring, but the spicy rose scent was an effective combatant.

"I'll coil your hair and then we'll go home."

"What about the lesson?" As soon as she had spoken Rose wished she had kept her mouth shut.

"The Shepherd's Staff will be in sight as we walk and I will tell you of it while we make our way back to Mirthan Hall." Koria paused. "And in case you are wont to daydream about any of the handsome young knights who've taken so much of your time today," she said with a smile, "keep in mind that I will be testing you on the lesson tomorrow."

Rose issued a groan, but couldn't help the grin that followed closely on its heels. "They are a rather handsome lot, aren't they?"

S I X

$\mathscr{T}$he snow-covered lawn glittered in the light of dozens of lamps. From Rose's third-floor window the walkway looked like a swirling path of stars. In all her years at Mirthan Hall the duke and duchess had never hosted so many guests nor planned so grand a gathering as this.

"Isn't it beautiful, Tinna?" Rose spoke to the maid waiting to arrange her hair—an unusual pleasure, since Rose generally saw to her own hair. "Have you ever seen anything like it?"

"Yes, Mistress Rose. I've seen this very view before. Years ago the duke and duchess hosted many a merry gathering. When the children came they entertained less of course, as is right and proper for a young Veetrish family. But now that you are near to grown I should imagine we'll see scores of parties again at Mirthan Hall. Shall we see to your hair now?"

It took a bit of time to manipulate Rose's thick, stubborn curls, but finally they seemed secure.

"There's a different scent about your hair tonight," Tinna said. "Like the flower you were named for, but with a lingering hint of your usual tonic."

Rose grimaced. "Is it awful?"

"Oh no, mistress. Quite the opposite! How did you achieve it?"

Rose swallowed. "Koria offered to add a bit of rose oil to my . . . hair tonic. She said she'd saved it for a special occasion."

"And it is that, indeed!" Tinna exclaimed. With just a few deft movements and mother-of-pearl pins, Tinna secured Rose's upswept black curls. "Is it too tight? Do any of the pins poke at you?"

"No." Rose stood and walked to the full-length looking glass in the corner of the room and smiled at the elegant young lady staring back at her. "It's perfect."

Rose smoothed her hands over the gown Lady Whittier had commissioned in secret when they had measured Rose for her winter wardrobe. Richly tailored in light blue velvet embroidered with a swirling pattern of shimmering white thread, its square neckline and fitted bodice flattered the curves that had blossomed on Rose's tall figure over the past several years. Three-quarter-length sleeves, edged in a delicately crocheted lace, added a touch of whimsy to the sophisticated design, seeming to give the slightest nod to Rose's retreating girlhood among the louder proclamation that she was now, indeed, a young lady.

Rose twirled in front of the mirror and laughed as the skirt flared out. "Oh, Tinna, isn't it grand?"

The maid smiled. "It's beautiful. Shall I help you with your slippers?" She had just finished fastening the blue velvet slippers to Rose's feet when Lord Whittier's knock announced he had come to escort his ward downstairs.

"Are you ready, mistress?"

Rose nodded and Tinna answered the door.

The duke strode into Rose's bedchamber. "Our guests should begin arriving any moment, Rose, so we'd best—" His words halted as his jaw went slack. "Well, my heart," he said with a smile. *"As sunrise awaketh the bluebird to song, mine eyes doth rejoice on the ones that I love."*

As a Master Storyteller, Lord Whittier's habit of reciting verse mid-conversation was hardly unusual, but the tears that misted his eyes were, indeed, a rare sight.

"Rose, my dear," he said finally, "you are absolutely stunning."

"Thank you." Rose dipped a small curtsy. "And might I say, my lord, that you cut quite a dashing figure yourself."

The duke offered Rose his arm and escorted her down the stairs. At the bottom, two men stood flanking the duchess. The shorter of the men stepped forward.

"Happy birthday, Rose, if a thrice late."

"Thank you, Lewys." Rose's actual birthday had passed three days earlier, and although Sir Kiggon's company had arrived the night before, between Rose's responsibilities in helping Lady Whittier ready the house for the party and Lewys's squire duties to Sir Kiggon, she'd barely had a chance for more than a brief greeting with Lord Whittier's middle son.

She gave Lewys a quick hug. "Did Sir Kiggon release you from your stable mucking a bit early tonight, then?" she teased. "I do hope he gave you time enough to bathe. I will not bear your company if you smell like a stall."

"Age may have allowed your height to surpass mine," Lewys said, seeming neither surprised nor offended by the admission, "but it hasn't yet tamed your tongue." He grinned. "Careful, girl, or I'll pick you up, carry you out, and dump you in what I mucked from yon stable!"

"You wouldn't dare."

"Wouldn't I?" Lewys took a step forward.

"No, you wouldn't!" Lady Whittier intervened, but Rose just laughed.

A man stepped from behind the door. The shape of his beard identified him as a knight, but the amount of silver threaded through it proved him much older than Kinley. "Hello, Rose."

Rose blinked. *"Uncle Drinius?"*

He opened his arms. "Happy birthday."

Seeing her uncle after so long and hearing his deep voice and cultured Stoenian accent, so different from the Veetrish brogue she had grown accustomed to, had a curious effect on Rose. Her throat tightened and tears burned her eyes. After a moment of hesitation, she stepped into his embrace.

"When Lady Whittier wrote to tell me of her plans for your birthday, I wasn't sure I would be able to come," he said. "But the closer the date grew, the more I knew I couldn't stay away. I've missed you so, dear one."

He missed me. The knight's admission lodged in her throat with sweet relief. She buried her face in his shoulder.

Sir Drinius chuckled. "The duchess will not thank me if I crush the gown she's waited so long to see upon you." Sir Drinius released his hold and stepped back. "I know the young men will be clamoring for your company, but might this old knight have the honor of escorting you into the grand hall?"

Rose's smile wobbled. She ducked her head. "Of course."

"You are right to attend her now, Sir Drinius. Our Rose has quite intrigued the young knights who arrived with Kinley," Lord Whittier said with a chuckle. "And Sir Kiggon brought a score and a quarter more with him, not to mention more than a dozen eager squires."

Rose grinned, but felt the heat of their flattery upon her cheeks.

A butler announced the first guests' arrival and Sir Drinius excused himself while the family moved to the doors.

"I'll be back to escort you in, Rose," he said. "We have much to discuss."

"Sir Drinius, it's a party!" Lady Whittier chastised him by tapping her fan against his broad chest. "Tonight is for revelry and merriment! Any serious matters can surely wait until the morrow."

His eyes clouded a bit. "Yes, my lady, I suppose they shall."

When the family finally joined the rest of their guests it took all Rose's strength to avoid staring. She had helped place many of the decorations, but she hadn't realized how different the grand hall would look filled with guests. Panels of light blue velvet hung over the tapestries and ribbons of white wrapped around the columns leading out to the snow-covered rear gardens. Through the large windows and doors she could see the many lanterns and lamps hung about outdoors, sparkling against the snow. But it was the guests' smiles and laughter and the women's gowns, glimmering like jewels upon the stone floor, which brought the room to life. It was an enchanting sight.

"It's like I've been transported into another world," she whispered.

In the corner, a group of three young men began to play a lively tune.

"Lady Whittier's letter didn't say this was to be a ball," Sir Drinius's deep voice arrested her wonder.

"It's not."

"And yet it appears we may be required to dance." He nodded to the couples nearest the musicians.

"You make dancing sound like a chore," Rose laughed. "But why should one abstain from dancing at a gathering? It is a most natural expression of joy."

Drinius smiled. "The ways of Veetri have become your own, I see."

She looked away and her voice was much smaller when she replied, "How could they not?"

Around them the others conversed happily, but Rose found she didn't know what to say to her uncle. Yes, she was happy to see him, to hear that he had missed her. She wanted to talk to him about so many things, but . . . how to begin? Small talk was too trite. But a party was hardly the time to broach a weighty subject such as Mrs. Scyles's accusations, so she said nothing.

"Shall we round the hall, perhaps?" Drinius said at last. She nodded, and with a hand to her elbow he guided her through the crowd, stopping here and there when he was greeted or someone offered birthday wishes to Rose. As their steps took them nearer the banquet tables she noticed Mrs. Scyles hovering nearby, and any enthusiasm she might have had for her reunion with her uncle retreated.

She caught a glimpse of their reflection in the grand hall's many silver-framed mirrors. As much as she tried to ignore the impulse, she couldn't help but compare Sir Drinius's features to her own, but other than the blackness of the hair upon their heads, there was none. And even that was false.

But then again, she thought, he had told her many times how she looked like her mother.

The silence between them stretched.

"You are staying healthy, I assume?" Drinius's voice broke into her thoughts.

"Yes, thanks. I've been blessed with a hardy constitution. And you?"

Their conversation was awkward, stilted by the questions to which Rose was afraid to give voice and filled with words that mattered little.

He said he missed me, but did he miss me as one misses a niece . . . or as one misses a daughter? And if I am not his daughter, then whose daughter am I? She was more than relieved to accept Lord Whittier's hand for a dance.

As the evening wore on, Rose relaxed in the care of many eager young men. With some she danced, but others seemed content to share anecdotes or to bring her a cup of punch. As she became more comfortable she began to feel graceful, almost as if she was a moving decoration in the room, her dress just another extension of the lovely décor.

"Have you a suitor, Mistress Rose?" Lord Channing, Duke of Ruchon, oversaw the dukedom just west of Glenhume. But, as with most of the guests present, Rose had never met him before.

"No, Your Grace."

"I've a comfortable home and three daughters who are near enough your age that they might be more friends than children to you."

"Your Grace?" Rose blinked at him and almost stumbled. Surely he wasn't suggesting—

"I've yet to have a son," he continued. "My wife, Rynloeft rest her, has been gone these five years past."

"I'm sorry for your loss."

He nodded. "I would welcome marriage again, Mistress Rose. Would you welcome my suit?"

Rose was glad when a young man bumped into her. His stammered apology gave her a moment's reprieve that helped cool her heated face.

"I am honored you would consider me," she spoke carefully when the young man moved on, "however, I've elected to refrain from commitments at this time."

To her dismay, the Duke of Ruchon wasn't the only man present with courtship on his mind, but they all received a similar, gentle rebuke. But as no one pressed her after its receipt, she had a most wonderful time.

The musicians took a break and those dancing moved to the edges of the room. Several young men offered to procure refreshment for Rose, but before she could accept any of their offers a slender young man arrived at her side, a goblet already in his hand.

His topaz eyes sparkled beneath hair the color of heavily milked dandelion tea. "Pardon me for arriving so late to your party. As an apology, I would offer my lady a birthday gift, would she but accept."

It was all Rose could do to refrain from shrieking with glee, but she remembered the crowd just in time to tamp down her excitement. "I have received the pleasure of your gifting in the past, Apprentice Rowlen. I daresay I could not accept such an offering unless you allow me to share it with all who may partake of its wonders."

"Very well." The young man let out a long-suffering sigh. "If my lady commands it."

Rowlen turned on his heel and moved to the center of the room. Upon reaching his destination he sent a grin and a waggle of his pale eyebrows in Rose's direction.

Rose hadn't noticed Lewys's arrival at her side until he spoke. "Rowlen is such a peacock," he said with a quiet snort. "Always has to be the center of attention, that one."

"Shh!" Rose jabbed an elbow in her middle brother's ribs, but grinned at the note of affection in his voice. "Rowlen has promised me a story and I don't want to miss it!"

SEVEN

"**A** story!" Rowlen de Whittier announced to the crowd. "For the sister of my heart, the lovely Mistress Rose de Whittier!"

Rose's cheeks bloomed with pleasure as she met Lord Whittier's beaming smile across the room. Rowlen had publicly proclaimed her a sister—had even bestowed his father's name upon her—and the duke approved!

Her smile wavered a bit when she noticed Sir Drinius's frown. But Rowlen's voice carried above the crowd in the way that only a true Veetrish Storyteller's could, and Rose couldn't help but turn her attention back to him.

"To celebrate her sixteenth birthday," the young Storyteller proclaimed, "and . . . something about some knight." Rowlen paused to roll his eyes. Laughter filtered through the room from those who recognized the Storyteller as Sir Kinley's brother. "It is my great pleasure to share the story of Lady Anya, a young woman whose bravery and spirit of adventure reminds me of our honored one." He held up a hand. "And

I mean Rose, of course, not you, Kinley." He winked at his brother. Another round of laughter circled the room.

"Rose," Rowlen addressed her, "did you know that it was at the same age we celebrate you achieving tonight that the clever actions of our Kingdom's greatest heroine sent the dreaded Cobelds into hiding?"

Rose nodded. "Indeed."

"Then I shall begin." Rowlen's gaze swept the hall. "Ladies and gentlemen, pray forgive me if my version of Lady Anya looks a wee bit familiar." A smile quirked the left side of his mouth upward. "As loath as I am to admit it, I've never actually met the woman."

"Hard to meet someone who's been dead for two hundred years, Storyteller!" A laughing voice called from the crowd.

"Exactly!" Rowlen snapped his fingers. "Therefore, I hope you will indulge me as I test my sister's modesty by giving the heroine of this story her face."

Rowlen opened his palm with a flourish and blew a puff of air across it. A shimmer of onyx and sapphire trailed through his fingers and on to the floor, forming into a translucent young woman with black hair and startling blue eyes that very closely resembled Rose.

Rose had seen both Lord Whittier and Rowlen tell the story of Lady Anya many times, but never had they created a character that looked so much like her. In fact, Lord Whittier's version of the tale showed the famous heroine as quite petite, with long, blond hair.

It was passing odd, she thought, seeing this translucent version of herself breathed into being across her brother's palm.

Suddenly, Rose gasped. Always, both breath *and* words preceded the appearance of the Story People, but the figure had arrived before Rowlen had even uttered a word!

Lewys leaned toward her ear. "It's quite rare that a Storyteller can do that," he whispered, "even among the Masters."

Rose's already wide eyes grew rounder.

"Lady Anya grew up in the Great Wood, the daughter of the Regent of Mynissbyr," Rowlen began. "Even then, the Great Wood was inhabited by strange and mysterious creatures. And perhaps it was that untamed wood that fashioned Lady Anya into the perfect weapon to fight the Cobelds." Another breath across his palm produced a shimmering green trail and placed the girl within a copse of evergreens.

Mesmerized, Rose's thoughts drifted along with the story.

"When a Cobeld's curse afflicted her father and brothers, eventually killing them, Lady Anya took it upon herself to avenge her family." Rowlen lifted his other hand and breathed across it, creating another scene even as the first faded away. "Using the resources of the forest, she disguised herself as a Cobeld."

Rose winced as the Story Anya, wearing a face so similar to her own, smeared mud on her arms, face, and neck, and then pressed moss over it, giving herself a hideous, goblin-like appearance.

"Every creature of the forest shared the loss of their Regent and offered their friendship and assistance to Lady Anya's scheme. Even the smallest creatures banded together to help design her disguise."

The Story Anya lifted her hand to a limb and a collective gasp rounded the ballroom as a flurry of eight-legged creatures crawled up her arm and onto her mossy green face. Lengths of white webbing soon extended from her chin and cheeks.

"A Cobeld's beard is, of course, its greatest weapon. And the spiders were more than happy to provide a suitable beard for young Lady Anya."

"Are you well, Rose?" Lewys's whisper held a chuckle, for he well knew his sister's aversion to spiders. How many times had he tortured her with the threat of them?

"That is the most disgusting thing I have ever seen." Rose shuddered and touched her chin to make sure it was spider-free.

"Look at my mother," Lewys whispered. "I'm not sure whether she's going to laugh or faint."

Rose peeked over at Lady Whittier, whose cheeks had bloomed with color. Her fan moved at a furious pace.

Rowlen clasped his hands together. "And her disguise was complete."

Whether Rowlen was oblivious to his audience's reaction or delighting in it, Rose couldn't be sure. She was only too glad that this part of his story was over when the spiders returned to the tree from whence they had come.

The Story Anya turned a full circle, showing the entire room that she no longer looked like Rose, but a monster, instead. And truly monstrous, she was.

I may have nightmares of this, Rose thought with a shudder.

Rowlen's story continued with each scene as vivid as the last, but thankfully none quite as disturbing as the beard-weaving spiders. Rose watched as the disguised Lady Anya snuck into a camp of Cobelds and listened to their plans.

"Months later, Lady Anya returned to the Great Wood. Sending her father's bravest messengers to the far reaches of the Wood, Lady Anya begged assistance from the most reclusive—and most fearsome—of all the Wood's creatures: the Bear-men of Mynissbyr."

As much as she loved Rowlen, Rose barely noticed the Storyteller anymore. What his breath had produced completely ensnared her attention.

The Bear-men of Mynissbyr were huge creatures. Golden brown fur covered their bodies; their faces were large and human-like, a hideous mix of man and bear. But when they opened their jaws, long, jagged teeth and fangs stole humanity from their mouths, though they spoke as men.

Rose shrank back from the creatures and felt something a bit too soft to be floor beneath the heel of her slipper. A hand immediately caught her elbow as she lost her balance. As soon as she righted herself Rose turned to apologize, but laughed instead when she met Kinley's eyes.

"I'll forgive you this time." Kinley's eyes sparkled as he whispered a reply. "It was, after all, the fearsome Bear-men of Mynissbyr that caused your misstep."

Rose grinned. "I appreciate your indulgence."

"Just don't get used to it. You may be sixteen now, but you're still my baby sister."

"Kinley," Lewys whispered, "have you not noticed how she's being fawned over? It's unseemly!"

"It's the way of things, Lewys," Kinley chuckled under his breath. "Our little Rose is growing up."

"Indeed." She lifted her chin. "I've even received a proposal or two."

"Proposals?" The set of Lewys's jaw was almost comical. "Tell me who and I will set the louts straight."

"I will not." Rose laughed. "Besides, I'm perfectly capable of refusing them myself. And I have. Now hush. I'm missing Rowlen's tale!"

When she refocused her attention the tale was almost at its end.

Of course, she knew the story well. She knew that Lady Anya would lead the Bear-men on an attack against the Cobelds that would, at its end, send them into hiding for the next two hundred years. But it was still odd to see this particular version of the famed heroine of old, which appeared so much like the image that greeted Rose in her looking glass each morning. Rose allowed herself a little laugh, for there the similarity ended. She had certainly never brandished a sword or led a military charge like Lady Anya!

"And so the Cobelds were defeated and Lady Anya retired to her home in the Great Wood, taking to husband a young Bear-man who had proven himself on the battlefield to be worthy of her love."

Rose laughed out loud, as did several other members of the audience, when a not-quite-as-animal-looking Bear-man bent on one knee and took Lady Anya's hand.

"They were very happy together," Rowlen said. "And although Lady Anya and her hairy husband rarely received invitations from her peers within the realm, they were content to remain in the Wood. And their descendents, most of whom were lucky enough to take after their more human ancestress, may yet be glimpsed among the trees by those brave enough to enter the Great Wood of Mynissbyr."

Rowlen gave a wide, sweeping bow and the vision of Lady Anya began to fade. As he straightened, he caught Rose's eye and, with a sly wink in her direction, blew one slight puff of air across his hand.

Just before the vision disappeared completely, a burst of orange erupted like a halo above the Lady Anya, showering over her and changing her hair from the inky black it had been to that of a flame opened by a burst of wind.

Story Anya turned to Rose and winked as well, her eyes a much brighter blue than they had been a moment ago, before disappearing in a flash of golden light.

Rose sucked in a breath, feeling suddenly naked in the crowd, but her gasp was drowned by the audience's applause.

Rowlen gave a second bow. As he straightened, his grin found Rose. His eyes narrowed. He cocked his head, but turned suddenly when someone grasped his arm.

"Rose?" Lewys placed his hand on her arm. "Rose, what's wrong?"

"Nothing!" Rose's voice squeaked. She tried for a smile. "It was amazing, wasn't it? His talent has developed so much!"

Rose scanned the crowd, but no one seemed confused or concerned. Indeed, it seemed as if not a soul in the room had taken any special note of the last, brief view of Lady Anya. "Would you excuse me, Lewys?" She looked at him finally. "I need to find Rowlen and thank him for the story." Immediately she moved away, but when her eyes sought the Storyteller, he was moving toward the doors, prodded along none-too-gently by Sir Drinius de Wyte.

EIGHT

*R*ose pushed her way through the crowd and slipped out on to the terrace just in time to hear her uncle's low, angry voice.

"What was the meaning of that, Storyteller?" His hand rested on the hilt of his sword. "I demand you tell me how you know about—"

"Uncle Drinius, wait." Rose pulled the door shut behind her and rushed forward. The look of cold fury set upon the knight's face could not bode well for her brother. "You remember Rowlen, don't you? Lord Whittier's youngest son?"

Drinius did not spare a glance at Rose. Instead he took a step closer to Rowlen until there was barely space between them. "Answer me, Storyteller."

Rowlen did not cower. "It was just a story, Sir Drinius. I assure you I meant no harm."

"No harm?" Drinius growled, leaning until his nose was but an inch from Rowlen's. "No harm?"

Rose slid between the two men, placed a hand on each of their chests, and pushed them apart. Rowlen stepped back. Drinius, however, was like a deep-rooted oak.

She faced the knight. "Don't be so quick to blame Rowlen," she said. "It's my fault he knows the truth. And speaking of which." She spun to face Rowlen. "How *could* you spill my secret like that? You promised!"

"Rose, it was a story about Lady Anya, not you. No one will—"

"She looked just like me! And at the end you—urrgh! *Rowlen!*" she growled and, splaying two hands on his chest, shoved him back another two steps. "But why stop there?" Her whisper was as violent with sarcasm as if she had shouted instead. "Perhaps next time you should have her sing a song glorifying the benefits of ebonswarth root powder!"

"Rose, quiet! Hold. He knows about the powder?" Sir Drinius put a hand on her shoulder but she was too busy glaring at her brother to turn around. "Rose, you have no idea—"

"Maybe I know more than you think I do." She whirled to face Drinius. Her voice was low, but carried a thickness, a fury, that didn't need volume to be conveyed. "I know it's poison. I know it's illegal for me to have it." She paused. "But it certainly isn't because *you* told me!"

"The powder." Sir Drinius ignored her, looking instead to Rowlen. "How did you learn of it?"

"It was when we were children," Rowlen explained. "We were swimming and—"

"It was an accident," Rose snapped. When the knight's eyes widened, she took a breath and let it out slowly, allowing some of the anger out with it. "It was an accident," she repeated in a gentler voice. Then, in whispered tones she told him about her disastrous first swimming lesson.

"Who else knows of this?"

"Well, Koria," Rowlen said, "but—"

"She's always known." Drinius ran a hand through his graying black hair. "Rose, your safety depends upon your identity remaining hidden."

"So you say." Rose blew a quick, hot breath through her nose and crossed her arms at her chest. "And perhaps I would take your warnings more seriously if I knew *why* you persist in giving them!"

"I wish I could tell you, but I cannot." Drinius paced four steps away and back. "There are enemies infiltrating every area of the Kingdom, Rose. There are even rumors that the Cobelds are planning to cross the Veetrish Bog. If they found out about you, even something so seemingly simple as the color of your hair could make you a target."

"Cobelds?" A chill rode the length of Rose's spine as she pictured the muddy, mossy goblins from Rowlen's tale.

"Don't worry, Rose." Rowlen patted her arm. "Cobelds have never crossed the bog. It's kept them at bay for hundreds of years."

"It may not stay them much longer." Drinius shook his head. "Rowlen, you must never, *never* tell that story again. At least not with a vision of Rose at its core." With a staccato grunt, he paced again. "You must take more care, Rose," he said when he came to a stop. "We don't know what might betray your location."

"I hardly think my story could reveal her identity." Rowlen crossed his arms and arched one pale brow. "Especially considering no one seems to know it but *you*."

Sir Drinius mirrored the Storyteller's expression, but the glare brooked less argument upon his stony face than it did on Rowlen's.

"And that is the way it must stay," Drinius said. "If the Cobelds or their allies knew of Rose's true identity she would be in the gravest danger."

"That's ridiculous," Rowlen scoffed. "The only person the Cobelds have reason to fear is the—"

"*Silence!*"

Rose almost missed the look of alarm that passed over the knight's face, so quickly was it replaced by something much more fearsome.

"Rowlen, you must swear, on pain of death, that you will never reveal what you know of this."

"Indeed. Though I know nothing but the true color of her hair." Rowlen's look was shrewd. "Sir Drinius, my brothers and I want nothing more than to protect Rose from anyone who might cause her harm, be they Cobeld demons," he said, taking a step toward the knight, "or indifferent uncles who only rarely deign to visit."

Rose paled as the skin at Drinius's collar turned an instant shade of red. "You would *dare* accuse *me* of being *indifferent*?"

"Stop it!" Rose's hands pressed against each man's chest again. "Both of you." She sighed. "Rowlen, for love of Rynloeft, don't push him. He's a *knight*. And Uncle Drinius," she said, turning toward the knight, "I consider the duke's sons as brothers, and they, in turn, have accepted me. Rowlen is trustworthy, Uncle Drinius. I would trust him—or Lewys or Kinley, for that matter—with my life."

"And it appears you have." Sir Drinius's look was grave. His gaze speared Rowlen over Rose's head. "Do I have your oath, Rowlen? Not a word? Not to . . ." he paused and his eyes glanced quickly at Rose before lighting once again on the Storyteller, "*anyone*. Understood?"

Rose stepped to the side so she could see both of them again. A line had appeared between Rowlen's pale brows as his eyes locked with hers a moment, and then, with a nod, he looked at the knight. "You have my word."

Rose jumped when the terrace door creaked open. "Rose?" Lewys stepped outside, "Oh! You're with Sir Drinius and Rowlen. Good." He greeted the knight and smiled at Rose. "I was worried when you didn't return. Mother was asking after you."

"You worry too much Lewys." She gave him a warm smile. "I'm in fine company, as you can see."

"Brother!" Rowlen slapped an arm around Lewys's shoulders. "I'm parched. Shall we go find that delicious punch for which Cook is so famous?"

Lewys looked to Rose. "Are you . . . ?"

"I'll be in shortly," she assured him.

After her brothers left the balcony, Rose turned to her uncle. "I should go inside."

"Come then." Sir Drinius nodded and led her to the door. "But do be wary, Rose. In the wrong hands your secret could prove deadly."

Rose's mind was still spinning with a mixture of anger and confusion when she crossed the threshold of the grand hall.

"Pardon me, Mistress Rose." Mrs. Scyles ducked her head. "My apologies, Sir Drinius. I did not see you there. I only just now came to see if there were any guests on the terrace who might require a fire built. Will you be returning outside, Sir Drinius? Mistress Rose? Should I call for someone to light a fire?"

Rose suppressed a grimace. "The other guests might appreciate it," she answered swiftly, "but I will not be in need of it."

There was something almost triumphant in Mrs. Scyles's steady gaze that caused Rose to wonder: how close had she been, really? And had she heard any of Rose's conversation with Rowlen and Drinius? But she had no time to ponder it, for a moment later Rose was surrounded by young men, vying for her favor.

NINE

Three days after the party, Rose nibbled a piece of toast at the breakfast table while Sir Kiggon, Uncle Drinius, Lord Whittier, and Kinley discussed the state of affairs in the rest of the Kingdom. Youth had allowed her to recover from the loss of an entire night's sleep given over to the revelry of the gathering much more quickly than the older generation, who sat stirring honey into very strong tea, and who were still, three days later, stifling the occasional yawn.

"We haven't seen the violence yet in Sengarra that they've experienced in Stoen, Shireya, and Dynwatre," Sir Kiggon said. "Insulated as we are by the Great Wood on one side and the southern sea on the other, we are fairly protected from the Cobelds. But if the rumors are true and Dwons has fallen—"

Lord Whittier cleared his throat and lifted his chin toward the far end of the table where Rose sat near Lady Whittier. He stood. "Perhaps we should adjourn to my study, gentlemen."

"I will plan to join you later," Drinius said as he pushed back his chair. "My exhaustion has allowed me to neglect both my horse and my niece these past two days. If Rose is willing, I think a good, long ride is in order. Rose?"

"Of course." An idea suddenly lit her mind. "Lord Whittier?"

"Yes?"

"Sir Drinius's horse is a large animal and I fear he won't be exercised as thoroughly if he is forced to keep pace with my mare. Might I be allowed to—"

Lord Whittier interrupted her with a resounding laugh. "Yes, you may take Falcon, Rose." Chuckling, he shook his head. "But just this once, dear one," he said with a wink, "lest he become more fond of you than me. Besides, we wouldn't want your old mare to become neglected, would we?"

"Thank you!"

"Mind that you're back in time for Sir Kiggon's departure," Lady Whittier added. "I'm sure Lewys will want to tell you good-bye."

Rose hadn't been alone with her uncle since he had arrived, and considering how stilted their conversations had been, she couldn't help but be a little nervous as they collected their horses. Drinius raised an eyebrow when Falcon was brought out, but he didn't gainsay Lord Whittier's decision, for which she was glad.

After the animals' muscles were sufficiently warmed, Rose suggested a race. Finally, when they were more than a mile from Mirthan Hall, Drinius slowed his mount and she followed suit.

"Whittier said you were a fine horsewoman. He was right."

Rose glowed with pleasure. "Thank you. I do love to ride."

"You always did. I remember when you borrowed my horse once," he chuckled. "How you got him saddled, I'll never know. In the dark, no less! How old were you then? Five? Six?"

"I was nearly eight. It wasn't long before you brought me here."

"Ah." He nodded. "Time has a way of creating a gulf in the memory. I wish—" he sighed. "I wish we'd had more than just eight years with you."

They both fell silent for a few minutes. Finally, when the horses paused to nose around in the snow, Drinius said, "Shall we walk a bit?"

They strolled in silence, but for the occasional snuffle of a horse. Finally, after a deep breath and a long, drawn out sigh, Sir Drinius spoke. "You are safe in Veetri for the time being, but I expect you will soon have to leave Mirthan Hall."

"But this is my home."

"No." He shook his head and looked away. "It is not."

"It has been for years."

"I know. And I'm sorry to have to take you from here, but Gladiel and I plan to come for you before your next birthday."

An argument rested on the tip of her tongue, but his tone made her swallow it whole. *A year,* she thought. *I may still have a year.* "Where will you take me?"

"I'm not sure of the exact location yet, but if all goes as planned you will be able to be with Alaine and Lily again."

Just the mention of Uncle Drinius's family caused Mrs. Scyles's accusations to burn in her mind. "Are you sure that plan will meet with Lady Drinius's approval? I wouldn't want to impose on her hospitality."

Drinius laughed. "Impose on her hospitality?" His laughter faded into a mild frown when he glanced at Rose's face. "I forget, sometimes, how fleet time truly is." His smile returned. "You needn't fear that time has lessened your hold on Alaine's heart. She will welcome you with open arms."

"Indeed?" Rose's words were bitter, but softly spoken. "Why would a refined Stoenian woman like Lady Drinius want one such as me under her roof?"

"One such as you? Whatever do you mean?"

"A young woman of questionable birth," she said, looking toward the horizon. "A pariah of society. A girl whose father is so ashamed of her that he would distance himself entirely from her association, even to the point of denying her his name. Need I go on?"

Drinius stared at her in silence. "Is that what you think, Rose?" he asked finally. "That you are ill-born or . . . unwanted?"

"What else am I to think?" She threw up her hands and let them fall back to her sides. "I've been told my mother is dead, but never her name or station. My father imposes my care on others for years at a time without giving me the benefit of his name—or even the knowledge of it!—only to rip me away from those I've come to love at his whim."

The volume of her voice increased with each statement, but her anger refused to censure it.

"I've been instructed to apply poison to my hair—poison that if discovered to be in my possession could send me to the gallows as a witch!—to avoid anyone connecting me to my dead mother or my mysterious father! So I ask you, Sir Drinius," she clenched her teeth, "what else am I to think but that my very existence is the product of disgrace?"

The Asp's accusations stretched the air taut between them. Lifting her chin and silently cursing the tears that burned her eyes, Rose pressed on, desperate to know the truth.

"Who am I, Sir Drinius? Am I the unfortunate result of your own shame? Is that why my presence was so painful for Lady Drinius to endure? Is that why you sent me here? If it is," the pitch of her voice rose, "then let me stay! I'm sure the duke and his family will look after me and you need not concern yourself even to visit."

The knight's face paled. The look of shock in his eyes seemed to confirm Rose's worst fears, but still he did not respond.

Rose's eyes threatened to spill over. Her voice fell to that just above a whisper. "Do you deny it, Sir Drinius?" she asked. "Can you look me in the eye and tell me you are not my father?"

Drinius ran a hand over his face. "Yes."

"Yes, you can deny it?" she asked, her voice trembling. "Or yes, you are my father?"

The grim set of his jaw registered a grief-laden defeat that made Rose's heart, even angry as she was, ache. Drinius drew a shaky breath, but when he met her eyes, his gaze was solid and sure.

"From the day you were born," he said, "I have loved you as if you were my own child. But, no. I am not your father." His voice was rough with emotion. "Lily is the only child I have ever fathered. You are not of my blood."

"I'm not of your blood?" she asked. "You are not even," the tears that had threatened finally spilled over Rose's lashes, "my uncle?"

"Oh, but I am!" Sir Drinius's eyes brightened and he smiled. "That, my dear, is an honor I can claim, though not by blood. It is through my wife's relation to you that I am your uncle."

"Aunt Alaine is my true-blood aunt?"

"Yes." He smiled, but then his brows drew together. "Well, no, actually." The smile did not completely leave his face, though it lost a bit of its sparkle. "Alaine is not your aunt by blood."

"But how . . . ?"

"Though I cannot tell you all, I will tell you enough to try and ease your mind." Drinius paused. "Your mother was orphaned at a young age," he said. "Alaine's parents adopted her into their family, much as the duke and duchess have taken you as their own. Alaine and—" He cleared his throat. "Alaine and your mother were, indeed, true sisters. Not by blood, perhaps, but by the bonds of love."

Rose brightened again, some of her hope restored. "She did not resent the care of me?"

"Never," Sir Drinius stated. "She has missed you most grievously these last years. As has your cousin, Lily. Believe me, Rose," he said with a sad smile, "if we are, as I hope, able to reunite you with them soon, they will rejoice with such fervor that the Cobelds will quail from the force of it."

"Speaking of Cobelds," Rose wrinkled her nose, picturing the hideous creatures from Rowlen's story. "Why are you so concerned they will find me? Why would they even care about me? I'm no one."

"There is an old . . . poem, I guess you could call it," Drinius began. He spoke haltingly, carefully, as if he was giving thought to each word before he allowed it to be voiced. "It was written in the time of Lady Anya. It describes a young woman who is quite powerful. Powerful enough to defeat the Cobelds."

"What has that to do with me?"

"Without the ebonswarth dye, you greatly resemble the description of that lady."

"I resemble a character from an old poem?" Rose blinked twice and then laughed.

"A powerful character in a story the Kingdom desperately needs to come true."

Rose laughed again, though the sound was a bit less enthusiastic when faced with her uncle's stern expression.

"Well, that alone disqualifies me. The only thing powerful about me is the smell of my hair."

"Be that as it may be," Drinius said, scowling up at the sky before meeting her eyes again, "if the Cobelds knew of your existence they would stop at nothing to kill you. Every red-haired girl in E'veria is in danger. Many have already been killed by the Cobelds, which is one reason why your father insists you use the dye." He shook his head sadly. "Your mother's hair was red, Rose. As red as yours would be without the dye." He paused. "And it was a Cobeld's curse that took her life."

"My mother was . . . murdered?"

Drinius nodded. "Yes. She died shortly after you were delivered. To protect you, your father claimed you had died as well."

That her mother was dead had never been kept a secret from Rose, but she had been led to believe her mother had died due to the complications of childbirth. "I—" Rose blinked. "Did they kill her because of me? Because of the poem?"

"I would be lying if I said no," Drinius said. "But there's a lot more to it than that. More that I cannot, as of yet, allow you to know. I'm sorry. But even what I've told you today must be kept close. Tell no one."

Rose paced a little bit away and he gave her the distance. When she returned it was with a slower step.

"Uncle Drinius, I'm sorry if my questions offended you. It was not my wish to hurt you. I would never have thought those things of you if not for Mrs. Scyles."

The knight's eyes narrowed. "The housekeeper? Why would she have reason, or opportunity even, to bend your thoughts that way?"

"She has a rather strong dislike of me," Rose stated. "And after she discovered the ebonswarth powder, she—"

"She knows about the powder? By my sword, Rose! You said only Rowlen knew!"

"I'm sorry! She only recently discovered it. The other night I was so worried about you hurting Rowlen that it skipped my mind."

"How long has she known?"

"Not long. Only a matter of a week or so."

This time it was Sir Drinius who paced away, but he returned much more swiftly. "And how did you discover she had found it?"

"She told me."

"She knew what it was?"

Rose nodded. "She's from Dwons. She feared I intended to bewitch Kinley."

"I see." Drinius rubbed a hand over his bearded chin. "Your father will not be happy with this development. Of that I am sure." He paced away again and back. "How did you convince Mrs. Scyles you would not use the powder for ill gain?"

"I didn't. She accused me of being the baseborn daughter of a witch and—" Rose paused as her cheeks flamed, "a knight."

"Me."

Rose nodded. "She assumed that, since you were the one who delivered me here, you were my father."

"She assumed, did she?" Sir Drinius's voice had taken on a deadly calm that made the skin on the back of Rose's neck tingle. "And where, might I ask, was the duke in all of this? You are under his protection, are you not? That he has allowed this woman to remain in his employ does not bode well for my plan to leave you here."

Rose shook her head. "The duke and duchess know nothing of this. Nothing at all. Mrs. Scyles acts differently toward me when no one is around. She always has."

Drinius tilted his head. His eyes narrowed. "Rose, how long has this been going on?"

Rose dropped her hand and looked at the ground, her mind going back to when she had first arrived at Mirthan Hall and the contempt with which Mrs. Scyles had looked at her in private even then.

"If I really think about it," she said finally, "her dislike of me began as soon as I arrived. But her disdain has grown progressively more . . ." she searched for the right word, "*direct*, I guess you could say, recently. She's prejudiced herself against me, I think, because of an evil committed against her by a woman with black hair."

"Ridiculous." A huff of breath clouded the air. "Rose, you have suffered this woman's scorn for far too long. But no more." He nodded, as if confirming his own course of action. "I will speak to Lord Whittier about this as soon as we return. I will see this put to rights, Rose, and that wicked woman will be turned out before the end of the day."

Rose bit her lip. Could he really do that? She had to ask.

"Your well-being is my utmost priority. If I must force her out the door at the tip of my sword, I will see it done today."

$\mathcal{T}$ E N

The early morning hours slipped away while Rose and Drinius talked and they had to hurry back to Mirthan Hall. When they returned, Drinius immediately went in search of Lord Whittier while Rose sought Lewys. After a hurried and tearful good-bye to her middle brother, she headed to the house where the midday meal was just being laid out in the dining room.

Lunch was a sober affair. Sirs Kile, Elden, and Worth had elected to leave for Salderyn with Sir Kiggon's company, which left only Rose, Drinius, Kinley, and Lord and Lady Whittier at the table. After an entirely-too-long stretch of time filled only with Lady Whittier's sniffles and the random, dainty clink of silver against stone, Rose was almost relieved when Lord Whittier stood and asked the small group to join him in his private study.

Lord Whittier faced the window for a long moment. Finally, he expelled a deep breath, turned around, and took the chair behind his desk.

"It has come to my attention," he began, looking at Rose with sorrow in his eyes, "that a longtime member of our staff has betrayed our trust and has wounded your spirit with lies and evil manipulation."

Kinley's eyes shot to Rose. "The Asp?"

She swallowed hard and nodded.

"You knew of this, Kinley?" Lord Whittier rose from his chair. "And you didn't inform me?"

"In truth, I did not know," Kinley said. "But who else could it be?"

"The fault of this rests with me." Lord Whittier sank back down in his chair. "Lewys came to me years ago with his suspicions. Knowing Mrs. Scyles to be of a rather surly disposition and knowing Lewys's tendency toward being overprotective of Rose, I shrugged him off." He let out a long sigh. "Can you ever forgive me, Rose?"

"Forgive you?" Rose blinked. "It's not your fault. I should have come to you myself."

"Why didn't you, Rose?" Lady Whittier's voice was strained.

"For a long time it was because there was nothing of substance to tell. Just a feeling I got from her tone of voice."

"But clearly, Rose," Lord Whittier said, his brows drawing nearer together, "she has threatened you now."

"Only recently. When she discovered—"

Drinius cleared his throat.

"When she was in my room one night," Rose rephrased her answer, "she implied that if you knew the truth of certain things about me that you would disown me. I wasn't willing to take the chance."

"Disown you?" Lady Whittier rose and rushed to her side. "Dear, dear girl," she said, wrapping Rose in her embrace, "nothing could ever make us love you less!"

Sir Drinius stood. "Rose holds no ill will toward this family and neither do I. This family's love and care of her has done a great service to both of us." He sat back down. "But Mrs. Scyles is still under your employ and your authority," he said to Lord Whittier. "I'd like to know what you plan to do with her."

"Kinley," Lord Whittier addressed his son, "please fetch Mrs. Scyles."

Rose looked back and forth between Lord Whittier and Sir Drinius, not sure who was in charge of the unfolding scene, but positive that she did not want to be around to witness it. "May I be excused?"

Sir Drinius shook his head. "No, Rose. As uncomfortable as it may be for you, E'verian law gives Mrs. Scyles the right to confront her accuser."

"I should think she's confronted her plenty!" Lady Whittier stood. Her hands balled into fists. "To put Rose through any further—"

"Do *you* need to be excused, Capricia?" Lord Whittier lifted an eyebrow.

Lady Whittier lifted her chin and sniffed before sitting down and arranging her skirts. "If Rose must stay, I will certainly not abandon her."

Rose was glad for the comfort offered, especially when Aspera Scyles entered the room.

Kinley closed the door but remained in front of it. Standing with his feet firmly planted and his arms crossed at his chest, Rose thought that if she didn't know him she might have been intimidated by the young knight's formidable appearance.

"You sent for me, my lord?"

Rose looked at her uncle. Drinius's eyes, trained as they were on the housekeeper, could have frozen a live coal.

"Aspera Scyles," Lord Whittier's tone was the darkest Rose had ever heard from the normally jovial Storyteller, "charges have been brought against you by Sir Drinius and his niece."

"If there is a problem with one of the maids or servants assigned to them," Mrs. Scyles said, "I will see it put to rights immediately."

Whittier's look was hard. "The problem, Mrs. Scyles, is not with one of the staff. The problem is *you*. The charges include, among other things, misconduct and slander. Rose has charged that for the past eight years you have denigrated her position in this home, most recently with vicious lies concerning her parentage. She claims you have threatened her, and furthermore, you have sullied the name of her guardian, Sir Drinius de Wyte, with falsehoods of your own design. What say you to these charges?"

"I say nay, my lord!" Mrs. Scyles pressed a hand to her heart with a look of disbelief on her face. "I have always tried to serve Mistress Rose as if she were a child of your own issue. Often, when no one else was around, she has bragged to me that the knight is, indeed, not her uncle, but her father instead."

"Liar!" Rose gasped. "I never—"

"Hold, Rose," Drinius whispered. "You must let her finish."

"As I was saying," Mrs. Scyles continued, her lies trailing like syrup and leaving sticky, poisonous marks across Rose's ears, "Mistress Rose has bragged to me of her connection to the knight as if it were a grand joke played upon Your Grace's charity. She's said many times, although I told her it was an unseemly thing to be proud of, that she herself was the product of an unblessed union between Sir Drinius and," her voice dropped to a whisper, "a red-haired harlot!"

Red? Rose tilted her head. Hadn't Mrs. Scyles been betrayed by a woman with black hair? How did she know . . . ?

Suddenly, Rose remembered how she had almost run into Mrs. Scyles coming into the Grand Hall. Had she overheard the conversation between Rowlen and Uncle Drinius?

Sir Drinius was on his feet now, his hand on the hilt of his sword and the ice even more pronounced in his gaze.

"These are not my words, Sir Drinius!" Mrs. Scyles's poise broke for a moment, as evidenced by the sudden screech in her voice. "I only repeat what I've been told." She lifted her chin and seemed to regain her earlier calm. "I know my place, and it pains me to break confidence with one whom I've been instructed to treat as a child of this house. But I fear the time has finally come when my duty to His Grace and Her Grace will allow me to do nothing less."

Mrs. Scyles turned to Lady Whittier. "My lady, you should know that the girl is in possession of ebonswarth powder, an illegal substance. I believe she used it to drug Masters Lewys and Rowlen on several occasions while they were still in residence and that, had I not found it, she would likely have used it to bewitch Sir Kinley or his friends."

"What, in the name of Veetri's green hills," Lord Whittier boomed, "are you talking about, woman?"

Mrs. Scyles faced the duke, her face paler, but her back straight. "Ebonswarth is a powerful substance found in my home province of Dwons. It has many uses, and among them is the practice of," she paused, lowering her voice, "*witchcraft!*"

Lady Whittier gasped and laid her free hand atop Rose's, which already clasped her other hand. "Mrs. Scyles! Surely you are not implying that our Rose could be involved in anything so contemptible!"

"I wish it were not so, my lady." She shook her head. "But I fear that it is true. The girl is as evil and manipulative as the harlot who birthed her!"

Drinius rose from his seat in a blur. At the same time, Kinley moved from his position at the door. A ringing buzz of metal seared the air as the two knights' swords left their scabbards. The blades' motion stilled less than an inch away from either side of The Asp's neck.

"Still your tongue, woman," Drinius growled, "before my blade stills it for all time."

With mortal terror in her eyes, Mrs. Scyles entreated Lord Whittier, "My lord?"

Drinius's blade followed her. The point of Kinley's sword rested between her shoulder blades.

"My lord," she begged, "you cannot let this evil live in your home! You must—"

The study door opened and Koria entered. "My lord," she said, "Rose is no witch." She came in and flicked her hand toward the door. It closed even though she hadn't touched it.

"Witchcraft!" Mrs. Scyles screamed and the undiluted horror of the sound made Rose's heart pound against her ribcage.

Koria flicked the same hand toward Mrs. Scyles. "Be still!"

The Asp was immediately silent, though her lips kept moving. Her hands grasped at her throat, grazing Sir Drinius's blade on their way up. A red line opened across her knuckles.

"Koria?" Rose heard the shock, the fear, in her own voice. "Did you . . . do that?"

"The door? Yes. Her silence? Thankfully, yes. But the injury is of her own making by way of Sir Drinius's blade." Koria ignored Mrs. Scyles's frantic gestures and bleeding hand. "Her outrageous lies had become tiresome, had they not?"

"Well, yes," Lord Whittier admitted, but his expression was clouded with questions and dread.

"Lord Whittier," Koria's voice was gentle. "I am not one of the deluded, power-hungry herbalists who claim the title of witch. And neither is Rose. I am Andoven. And much like the gifts of the Storytellers, my abilities are inborn, not acquired for evil gain by the use of substances and powders."

Rose straightened. Most Andoven lived on the island province of Tirandov. They were a people revered throughout the Kingdom of E'veria for their wisdom and their unique ability to communicate without speaking. They were also well known, Rose had learned, for a general disdain of Veetrish customs, and, more specifically, Veetrish Storytellers.

Rose stared at the tutor she thought she had known well before this moment. *Koria is Andoven?* She could hardly believe it. Why would an Andoven teacher volunteer to be a tutor in the home of a Master Storyteller?

"All these years," Lady Whittier's voice was filled with awe, "we've had an Andoven teacher in our home? I never even suspected!" She blinked. "Koria, however did you get them to allow you to come to Veetri?"

"Them?" Koria angled her head. "Oh. You mean the Andoven Elders?" She smiled when Lady Whittier nodded. "Trust me when I tell you that not everything you've heard about the Andoven is true." She bowed her head. "I am your friend, my lady, as always."

Lady Whittier turned to Drinius. "Did *you* know she was Andoven?"

"Yes." Drinius nodded, but his eyes never left Mrs. Scyles.

He did? Rose blinked. Koria had taught Rose about the Andoven in her lessons. Why had she never admitted to being one of them? Rose's mind spun with mixed feelings of wonder and betrayal. A sudden memory surfaced—a piece of old information that had seemed insignificant until now.

Aunt Alaine was part Andoven. Perhaps that is how Drinius knew Koria.

"So . . ." Lord Whittier shook his head as if expelling a bit of oddness from between his ears. "You have come to offer your assistance, Koria?"

"Yes, my lord." She bobbed her head. "You were speaking about the powder Rose keeps in her room, yes?" When Lord Whittier nodded, she continued. "Rose, of course, does not use the powder for any evil reason. I know this to be true because I have helped her with its safe application these eight years."

"But, Rose," Lady Whittier's voice trembled, "if it's illegal, why *do* you have it?"

Rose looked to her uncle who closed his eyes for the briefest moment before nodding his consent. "It's clear from Mrs. Scyles's accusations," he said, "that she already knows your secret. No one else in this room would harm you with it."

Rose nodded, closed her eyes, and took a deep breath. "I use it to dye my hair," she said. With the truth out in the open Rose felt as if a huge, black weight had been lifted from her soul. "Each new moon Koria helps me to apply the powder. It makes it stay black. Otherwise, it would be red." She wrinkled her nose. "Well, closer to orange, I guess."

"Like the vision of you at the end of Rowlen's story," Lord Whittier mused.

Rose nodded. "Rowlen discovered my secret years ago, but he never told anyone."

"Ahh." Lord Whittier nodded. "I asked Rowlen to explain why he made Lady Anya's appearance change at the end, but he refused to tell me, spouting some nonsense about 'symbolism' and whatnot. I had no idea he was keeping a secret." He scowled. "Or *not* keeping it, as it would appear."

"Your hair is red?" Lady Whittier ran her hand over one of Rose's wayward curls. "I can hardly believe it."

Rose shrugged. "It's true."

"I think I could count on one hand the number of red-haired women I've met." Lady Whittier said. "It's quite unusual, you know. Whyever do you dye it? You're such a lovely girl, Rose. I can only imagine you would be even more stunning if you let it be as Rynloeft intended."

"Mother." Kinley didn't take his sword from the Asp's back, nor did he take his eyes from the woman as he spoke. "Elsewhere in E'veria, a girl with red hair is considered unlucky, to put it lightly. In recent years the Cobelds have been known to curse girls as young as five years simply because they have red hair. Someone of Rose's age would be . . ." He trailed off. His brow furrowed and his eyes met those of Sir Drinius. "Someone of Rose's age could be the—"

Again, Rose noticed her uncle give a slight shake to his head. Kinley's nod was even subtler, but she saw it.

Lord Whittier inhaled sharply. "The prophecy," he whispered. *"Eyes the hue of jeweled sky—"* He broke off. Leaning back in his chair, he stared at Rose. Suddenly, the duke flew to his feet. *"Cobeld's whiskers*, Drinius!"

Rose gasped at the profanity she had never heard used outside the stables. And certainly never from Lord Whittier's lips.

For a long moment no one moved, not even to breathe. Finally, Drinius spoke again, his words softer now but his tone carrying as much warning, perhaps more, than before.

"As Kinley said a moment ago, it is a cruel fate for a girl to be born with red hair in E'veria," he said. "The bog isolates Veetri from much of the violence we see in other areas of the Kingdom, but increasingly these past years, young red-haired women are being hunted and killed by Cobelds, simply because they resemble the description of a woman in an ancient poem."

Rose reached up and touched her hair.

"I will not let that fate befall my niece," Drinius stated. "That is why, all those years ago, I obtained the powder and ordered Koria to dye her hair."

Rose noticed Mrs. Scyles's expression and it sent a shiver of dread across her scalp. Her uncle seemed to have noted it, as well. The muscle in Drinius's jaw twitched and the tip of his blade pressed up under Mrs. Scyles's chin.

"I believe your smile is unwarranted, Mrs. Scyles, considering the precariousness of the position your slanderous lips placed you before Koria so efficiently closed them."

Without moving the position of his blade, Drinius stepped forward and leaned down until his nose was within a breath of hers. "You are under arrest." Then, with a grunt of disgust, Drinius sheathed his sword.

"Pardon me, Drinius, I don't question your authority," Lord Whittier cleared his throat. "But what are the charges?"

"Slander," the knight began. "False testimony. Theft of personal property."

"Theft?" Whittier looked confused.

Drinius turned back to Mrs. Scyles. "Did you or did you not," he asked, "steal a wineskin from Mistress Rose's bedchamber?"

Still unable to speak, the Asp's expression hardened, but then she nodded the affirmative.

"That should do for now," Drinius said. "Sir Kinley de Whittier, as my fellow knight, you bear witness to her confession."

Kinley nodded. "I do. Would you like me to take her into custody?"

"No." Drinius glanced at Rose. "I have another task for you. Lord Whittier, I trust you can spare a guard or two to transport Mrs. Scyles into the custody of the jailor in . . . Delna? I think that would be a suitable place for her to await her trial."

"Delna? That's at least a four-day ride. We have a small jail in Glenhume that would suit."

"No. I prefer to have her a bit farther from Rose, if you don't mind."

Whittier stood and exited the room to see to Drinius's request.

"Hear me, woman," the knight growled when the door was shut, "in or out of jail, if you repeat what you have learned of Rose, and thus endanger my niece's safety, your life is forfeit and I will have no qualms about personally carrying out your sentence. Am I understood?"

Mrs. Scyles swallowed and nodded fervently.

"Sir Kinley will stand guard while you collect your things. You will leave within the hour and you will never return to Glenhume again. Understood?"

Again, she nodded, but when Kinley opened the door, Mrs. Scyles squinted at Koria with a curse and a question in her eyes.

"I will watch you leave Mirthan Hall, Aspera Scyles," Koria said, "and I will restore your voice when you cross its gate for the last time. But should you use it to endanger or even disparage the character of this child it will be my pleasure to lead this knight directly to whatever hovel you cower within."

Rose's eyes widened. Could Koria use her abilities to do that?

"Kinley," Drinius said, "please escort Mrs. Scyles to her room. And see to it that her final moments at Mirthan Hall are well supervised."

In less than the time given, Aspera Scyles was packed and away from Mirthan Hall. Before exiting, she paused in the doorway only to turn her head back and spit on the polished floor.

At Mrs. Scyles's childish gesture, the tension of days— no, *years*—erupted within Rose with a shout of laughter that completely overtook her. Burying her head in her hands, she collapsed at the foot of the stairs, still laughing, until her hysteria gave way to violent sobs that wracked her frame.

Lord Whittier pulled Rose gently into the cradle of his arms, much as he had when she was a little girl awaking from a horrible nightmare. "It's all right now, Rose. She's gone."

A steady stream of tears flowed down Lady Whittier's cheeks as she sat next to her husband on the stairs and stroked Rose's hair. When Rose had cried herself into exhaustion, Sir Drinius carried her up the stairs to her bed where Lady Whittier held her hand and sat by her side through the night.

$\mathcal{E}$ LEVEN

$\mathcal{I}$t was a bit later than normal when the exhausted family gathered for breakfast the next morning. The mood was one of false cheer and stilted conversation. Finally, after one exceedingly long silence, Rose realized a member of their party was missing.

"Where's Kinley?"

The adults at the table exchanged looks with one another. Rose set her fork down. "He's gone, isn't he?"

"Don't be cross with him, dear," Lady Whittier said.

"When will he be back?"

Whittier exchanged another glance with Drinius. Drinius cleared his throat. "I sent him to deliver a message for me. From there, I assume he will continue on to his new post."

"So it could be . . . years." Rose's shoulders slumped.

"Sir Drinius." Lady Whittier's voice shook the tiniest bit. "Do you foresee any complications concerning Mrs. Scyles?"

Drinius gave a slow nod. "I do. Although the housekeeper herself may not know this as of yet, the Scyles clan has recently declared independence from both the Regency of Dwons and the Kingdom of E'veria. They have allied with the Cobelds in hopes of gaining independence from E'verian rule."

"The Scyles clan?" Rose paled. "There is an entire clan named after her?"

Drinius gave her a small smile. "I believe it is the other way around, but yes. There is a Scyles clan. And if she finds a way to them while she awaits trial . . ." He shrugged.

"Oh, I don't think that's likely." Lady Whittier worried a crust of bread until it was little more than crumbs. "She came to Veetri because of a falling out with her clan. I don't think she'd go back. Do you, Whittier?"

"Clearly, she is not the person I thought her to be." Lord Whittier's voice was grave. "Drinius, what would you recommend I do to ensure Rose's safety?"

"Gladiel and I have been working on a plan. With these new developments, however, we will need to speed it up." Drinius paused. "As soon as possible, we will come for Rose. If even the slightest possibility exists that Mrs. Scyles will tell what little she knows to the wrong people, Rose could be in danger."

A small stifled sob came from behind the hand that rested at Lady Whittier's lips.

"You will have her yet a bit longer, my lady," Sir Drinius said, giving the duchess a gentle smile, "while we ready a secure location."

The evidence of Lady Whittier's affection brought tears to Rose's eyes. She dug her fingernails into her palms to steady her voice. "Does it matter that I would prefer to stay here?"

"I'm afraid not." Drinius's tone set Rose's teeth to grinding. "But," his stony voice softened, "I take no joy in removing you from those you love."

Rose knew her uncle's concern was sincere and that he regretted the pain his actions would cause her, but that didn't make the idea of leaving Mirthan Hall any easier to digest. As Lady Whittier deftly steered the conversation to more cheerful topics, Rose stared at her plate, silently cursing the red hair that had dictated her fate, and broken her heart, time and again.

It wasn't easy for Rose to tell her uncle good-bye a few days later. It had been so long since his last visit, and so much had transpired during this one, that she felt as if she was just getting to know him again when he rode away. Although he promised an adventure to come, the thought of his return was more bitter than sweet.

TWELVE

Drinius had been gone a fortnight when the men assigned to escort Aspera Scyles to the jailor returned. Lord Whittier had promised Rose a story after dinner, but as soon as the men entered, those plans disappeared.

The guards were filthy and haggard. Though young, both seemed to have aged ten years since they had left. They hung their heads, unspeaking. Finally, Lord Whittier prompted them. "Well? Were you successful?"

"No," the first guard answered, his voice raw.

The second guard spoke up, "She escaped, my lord."

Lord Whittier flew to his feet. "She what?" With a glance toward Rose and then his wife, he said, "Come with me."

The bedraggled guards followed Lord Whittier into his study and they remained within for the better part of an hour.

Lady Whittier wrung her hands, pacing, while Rose stared out the window.

Mrs. Scyles had escaped? How? She was no match for two guards. It made no sense.

Finally, Whittier came out and excused the guards with instructions to rest and recover.

"Rose, have you noticed any of your, ah, powder, missing?"

She shook her head. "The new moon isn't until next week. I haven't looked."

"Would you?"

She nodded, grabbed her skirts, and fled up the stairs. Koria met her at the top of the stairs. "Rose, is something amiss?"

"Mrs. Scyles escaped. The guards returned. They look . . . terrible. Haunted." Rose suppressed a shiver. "Lord Whittier sent me to check the powder."

Rose retrieved the wineskin, but neither she nor Koria could gauge if any of the fine powder was missing. "Do you think she poisoned them?"

"Less than a pinch could ruin a man's mind for months." Koria's hand trembled at her throat. "Oh, those poor men."

"But Kinley supervised her packing! He would've never let her come into my room."

"I can only assume she must have hidden a bit away when she found it in your room." Koria's eyes slid shut. She took a deep breath. "I'll go to the spring and bring back sulfur water for the men. Without treatment, they may still be influenced by whatever lies she told them."

It took several weeks before the two guards were back to normal, and although Lord Whittier sent out a search party to apprehend Mrs. Scyles, they could not locate the fugitive. Finally admitting defeat, he sent a messenger to Sir Drinius and doubled the guard surrounding Mirthan Hall.

An early spring hurried the onset of summer and the mildness of that Veetrish season lazed its way into autumn with no sign of mischief from Mrs. Scyles, nor any word from Sir Drinius. But plenty of troubling rumors circulated among the staff and in the village of Glenhume. As the trees began to turn color and lose their foliage, Rose, by order of Lord Whittier, stayed within the gates of Mirthan Hall, which now remained closed and guarded when not in use.

When the first snow came, Rose packed two saddle bags and kept them at the foot of her bed in readiness for her uncle's arrival. When her seventeenth birthday passed with no word from Sir Drinius, however, Rose began to worry that things were far worse on the other side of the Veetrish bog than even the gossip of the staff could imagine.

Rose's emotions vacillated between sorrow and excitement. Daily, she wrestled with anger and hope. She hated the thought of leaving Mirthan Hall, but she couldn't help but experience a little thrill thinking about what might come next.

THIRTEEN

Just east of the Stoen border in the province of Dwons, the Cobeld waited for the woman sitting across the table from him to speak. The dim lamplight of the wayside inn revealed her as a most pathetic creature, but he doubted even the noonday sun would make her less so. Thinner even than her cloak—and it was in sad shape, indeed!—the woman's fear was written in the shadowed creases at the corners of her down-tilting eyes. And fearful she should be, when addressing a Cobeld.

The inn was busy tonight, full of Dwonsil warriors who had allied with his kind against the tyranny of E'veria's King. Still, they kept their distance. Despite the advantage of their stature, they were no threat to him. Pawns, all of them: expendable fools, just like the young clansman who had contacted him, knees knocking, to arrange a meeting with the beggar woman before him now.

The woman pressed a hand to her stomach in an attempt to quell the rumble of emptiness within, but his keen ears caught the sound. It would be cruel, he thought, to let her live.

Perhaps he should.

For the moment, however, he decided it would please him to know her name.

"Scyles," she said. "Aspera Scyles."

"Ah. You are of the clan?"

"I was." Aspera nodded. "I've been away for years."

She spoke haltingly, telling her story as if the words themselves were painful to press past her lips. He had no interest in the details of her wretched life, of course, but her discomfort pleased him. He let her ramble on.

She had left her home province for a better life in Veetri, she said. After more than twenty years of faithful service, however, her fresh start had soured. With no reference to show for her employment and no prospects, Aspera Scyles was now desperate enough to betray her former employer.

"Not them," she amended her tale. "*Her.*"

"Yours is a sad story," the Cobeld attempted a guise of compassion. "But what has it to do with me?"

"It's the girl they've fostered these last nine years. She matches the description in," her voice dropped to a whisper, "*the prophecy.*"

He felt his pupils dilate, not that she would see a difference in the blackness of his eyes. "I am listening."

Her eyes darted to his beard and she scooted her chair the tiniest bit back. "H-how much are you willing to pay?"

"Tell me what you know," he said slowly, "and I'll tell you what I'll pay."

He leaned back from the table and prepared to wait. If she was truly of the Scyles clan, she would bargain.

"Assure my safety and make me an offer." Aspera crossed her arms. "You won't find her without my help. She hides her identity behind a witch's poison."

He chuckled. "You think *I* am afraid of a little poison?"

"No," she lifted her chin, but still it quivered. "But you are afraid of *her*."

Anger rose hot and red from the ancient place it simmered within him. He pressed it down. *Not yet, not yet.* As he regained perspective, he tilted his head, feeling an instant of what could only be called admiration. It was a risk for her to be so bold with one of his kind, and although her hands shook, she had taken the risk. He would remember to be more wary when dealing with the females among his new allies.

After a long moment he reached into the pocket of his cloak, pulled out a small pouch, and set it on the table. He then produced a flask and uncorked it, but he did not tip to drink.

"This bag contains fifteen gold rounds." He relished the way her eyes widened at the sum. "I will give you six now, in good faith." He counted out six of the shining coins and pushed them toward her. "Consider them yours. If your information pleases me, you will receive the other nine coins."

As soon as he released the coins, she swiped them off the table and into the pocket of her threadbare cloak.

"Tell me what you know," he said, tilting the bag toward her, "and you will have wealth enough to see you comfortably through five winters without a moment of employment."

"Her hair is black, but unnaturally so." The woman spoke quickly, her words slurred by desperation and greed. "When untouched by the powder of ebonswarth, I believe her hair is red. Like the color of an oak leaf in autumn."

"And her eyes?"

"The darkest, oddest shade of blue you'll ever see."

His mouth twitched, sending a quiver through the thick silver and gray hairs of his beard. "And where might I find this odd young woman?"

"In Veetri. She lives with the—"

"Well? Speak, woman!"

She swallowed. "If I tell you her location will you give me your word that none shall be harmed but the girl?"

His smile was slow, but wide. "And why would I want to harm even her? I only wish to find her. After all, she may not be the one I seek." He tilted his head. "But why do you seek to protect the very ones who threw you out to starve?"

Her jaw worked on the answer awhile before she spoke it aloud. "I had a happy home there until she turned them all against me. I don't care what you do to the girl, but you must promise not to harm the family. Or me," she added, her eyes darting again to his beard. "Otherwise I will tell you naught."

"Your loyalty is admirable. And you will, most certainly, have my word." He took a sip from the flask.

"Good." Aspera Scyles expelled a sigh of relief. "She answers to the name of Rose." The woman's facial muscles contracted as if speaking the girl's name filled her mouth with bile. She idly rubbed at a scar on her knuckles. "She lives at Mirthan Hall under the protection of Lord Whittier de Barden, Duke of Glenhume."

The Cobeld reached into his pocket and pulled out a fresh piece of twine. Humming a tuneless whisper of a melody, he tied it around the mouth of the pouch and slid it across the table.

The woman reached for it, but her hand paused mid-air. "I have your word?"

He nodded, and just before her skin made contact with the specially twisted twine, he whispered a word in his native tongue.

She paused for only a moment, her eyes meeting his as if to say, "Pardon?" but her hand, propelled by greed, was unable to stop its forward motion.

Shock widened her eyes. Even without the cold spark of light that flashed in his beard, he knew when her skin made contact with the one particular fiber he had twisted into the piece of twine.

"You asked me to give you my word, Aspera Scyles, and now you have it." His grin was menacing as her head lolled, but its threat had already been carried out. "My word for you is *death*."

By the time he finished speaking, a hazy film had covered her eyes. With one hand he swiped the loose coins from her pocket while the other retrieved the pouch from her limp and quickly cooling hand.

Feeling generous, he left one gold coin on the table for the innkeeper's trouble, and then he walked away, whistling.

ℱOURTEEN

Well past the hour most Veetrish girls were fast asleep, Rose struck her pillow again. But just like the first ten times she had assaulted its feathers, the sleep she longed for didn't come. She wondered if she was ill, but a hand to her forehead found it to be neither hot nor cold.

Rose pressed her fingers to her temples and groaned, but just as she was about to roll over in an attempt to find a more comfortable position that might lure her body to rest, a faint, repetitive sound drew her to the window. Clouds hid the waxing moon and anything it might reveal, but as the sound grew louder, she recognized it. *A horse!* And one in quite a hurry, if the rhythm of the hoofbeats could be trusted.

A moment later her tutor was at her door. "Rose," Koria whispered, "it's time."

Rose's breath quickened with a ripple of fear, a quiet pulse of grief, and an impending sense of something that felt like . . . destiny. She pulled a dark riding costume from the wardrobe and slipped it over her head, pausing only long enough to allow Koria to help with the buttons. Next, she added sturdy boots. Her warmest cloak. The dagger she had spent such long hours learning how to send to its mark.

Grabbing her comb from where it sat beneath the mirrored chest, Rose paused at her reflection. It had been over two weeks since she and Koria had last trekked to the sulfur springs. Leaning in, she examined her scalp and eyebrows, relieved to find that the dye held firm. The blackened roots of her hair would not yet give away their ruse.

Rose gathered a few more items and placed them inside the already-stuffed saddlebags waiting at the foot of her bed. She had coiled her hair around her head before going to bed. All that was left was to put on her hat and mittens and . . . to say good-bye.

"Rose?" Accompanied by the slightest knock on her door, the smooth, mellow tenor of the duke's voice caused her heart to clench. "Rose?" The duke's voice came again. "Are you about?"

She took a deep breath and opened the door. "I'm ready." But as soon as she met the duke's glimmering gaze, she knew she *wasn't* ready. Her lower lip quivered. She bit down to still it.

Lord Whittier reached for Rose and held her in his firm embrace for a long moment before he spoke in a strained voice, "Sir Gladiel is here."

"Sir Gladiel?" Rose blinked, pulling back a bit. "But I thought—"

"Your uncle was detained." Lord Whittier released her and moved to gather her bags. "We must hurry. Stanza is being saddled as we speak. Capricia and Gladiel await us in the entry hall. Come quickly now."

"Rose?"

Rose turned to her tutor. Koria's eyes were moist, as well.

"I'll soon leave for Salderyn." Koria had taken a position as a teacher at the Academy there. Her departure would coincide with that of her student. "Perhaps our paths will cross again."

Rose couldn't speak. Her throat was too tight.

"Until then," Koria said, embracing her, "be of good courage and remember you are loved."

Rose hastily wiped her eyes as she stepped back. "Thank you for all your patience with me over the years. I will miss you." Before her emotions could betray her further, Rose turned and picked up one of her saddlebags. Without a word, Lord Whittier took the other and moved toward the wide, curving stair.

Each step seemed to be a mile, yet the two-story descent to the ground floor of Mirthan Hall was over much too quickly.

Rose left her saddlebag at the foot of the stairs and bobbed a curtsy. It had been years since she'd seen Sir Gladiel de Vonsar and, although his wavy black hair had turned all but white at the temples, she could easily recognize the knight by his unusual, bright green eyes.

"Hello, Sir Gladiel."

"Rose?" The knight's eyes widened as she approached. "My sword, but you've grown!"

"She recently passed her seventeenth birthday," Lady Capricia's voice quivered. "It hardly seems possible."

"Seventeen already?" Gladiel shook his head and gave a little bow. "And may I wish you a belated happy birthday, Rose?"

"Thank you, Sir Gladiel."

"Are you certain you cannot stay the night?" Capricia asked. "You could rest your horse, get a good breakfast . . ."

"We mustn't tarry." He turned to the duke. "We have reason to believe Rose's whereabouts have been made known to the Cobelds. Mirthan Hall must be evacuated as soon as possible."

Lord Whittier shook his head. "Cobelds have never crossed the bog."

"They have already breached the bog. They're on their way. Do not go back to bed. Wake the staff as soon as we've gone. You should be away by tomorrow at the latest."

Lady Whittier gasped. "Leave Mirthan Hall?"

"Evacuate all of Glenhume if you can."

Shock painted Lord Whittier's skin a pale hue. "The rumors are true?"

Sir Gladiel nodded. "They've been given assistance, and, if our fears prove correct, motivation to move in this direction."

Lord Whittier ground his teeth. "Mrs. Scyles."

Rose flinched.

Gladiel nodded. "We don't have direct proof that Mrs. Scyles betrayed Rose's location before she died, but—"

"She's . . . dead?" Rose swallowed.

"Yes," Gladiel said. "It appears she was the victim of a Cobeld curse, but that is only speculation." The knight's brow narrowed. "We have to assume the worst and take all necessary precautions."

"Why did no one send a messenger?" Lord Whittier's voice was indignant.

"By the time the news filtered down to us, there wasn't time. I came straightaway."

"But Uncle Drinius said he would come."

"And he would have, were he able," Gladiel smiled. "Drinius is nursing a sprained ankle. We decided I could travel here more swiftly alone. I suspect he'll be back to rights by the time we reach him."

"We will all travel together, then?" Lady Whittier asked.

"No." Gladiel turned to Lord Whittier. "You and your household are to go north to the Regent's palace. Rose goes with me."

Lady Capricia's voice quavered. "Where will you take her?"

"For your protection and hers, I cannot divulge that information." He turned his attention back to Rose and gestured to the bags Lord Whittier had set on the floor. "These are your things?"

Rose swallowed. "Yes."

The knight gave a curt nod and then scooped up the bags as if they weighed little more than a pair of kittens. "I will give you a few moments, Rose. Then we must go." He nodded to Lord Whittier. "I'll be outside." At that, he turned and went out the door.

Lady Whittier's hand flew to her mouth to cover the whimper that escaped as soon as the door closed behind Sir Gladiel.

"When the boys left, I gave them all a parting verse." Lord Whittier's voice was quiet and thick with emotion. "For you, it seems even more appropriate." He took a deep breath in through his nose and blew it out across his palm. But instead of falling to the floor, the glitter swirled up and around Rose in a spinning vortex of light as Lord Whittier quoted a verse of poetry. *"The soul of love is wonder met, the heart of family true. And when you find a lonely day, may memories comfort you."*

Within the vortex, faces appeared. First, the Storyteller's own, and then Lady Whittier and Koria. Finally, each of the boys blew Rose a glittering kiss. But as quickly as the vision had formed, it faded away.

"We love you, Rose," Lord Whittier said, and Lady Whittier's clutch on her hand confirmed it. "In our hearts, no matter what the future brings, you will always be Rose de Whittier, our daughter."

Tears flowed without restraint as Lord Whittier pulled Rose and Lady Whittier into his arms for a final, long embrace.

$\mathcal{F}$ I F T E E N

$\mathcal{T}$hree days away from Mirthan Hall, Rose awoke missing the softness of her bed almost as much as she missed her family. Rubbing the sleep from her eyes, she sat up and groaned.

"It was a hard ride yesterday." Sir Gladiel was already awake and stirring a pot hanging over the fire. "Stanza is a fine horse. Lord Whittier was wise to find you a competent mount. And you handle him well."

"Thank you." Rose had only had Stanza for a few weeks, but she was quite fond of the horse Lord Whittier had given her for her birthday. Stanza had been bred for both speed and endurance and he had demonstrated both traits these last few days.

Of course, little about the Veetrish landscape could be considered a hindrance to speed. Even covered with snow, the rolling hills and tree-dotted valleys were easily navigated. Each day they had ridden from dawn until several hours after the sun had set. Not once had they gone through a village. That, she assumed, was planned by Sir Gladiel, for she well knew that villages dotted the Veetrish countryside much like the sheep in a meadow they'd ridden through yesterday.

"The ride was the easy part," she said. "I think the bed, however, could be improved by a thaw."

"Indeed." Sir Gladiel returned her smile as he reached for a mug and poured a thick brown liquid from the pot. He handed the mug to Rose.

"Thank you, Uncle Gladiel." Rose ducked her head. "My apologies. I mean *Sir* Gladiel." She laughed. "But I suppose I've often thought of you in that way."

"I have no niece, but I certainly don't object to the address." He chuckled. "But just 'Gladiel' will suffice. We've no use for pesky formalities out here."

"Very well. Gladiel it is." She smiled and inhaled the aromatic steam coming up from the mug. "Mmm. What is this?"

"It's called *keola*."

"Kee-o-la." She tried out the word. "I've never heard of it."

"It's rare." He said and took a sip from his own mug. "And expensive." He chuckled. "Keola is imported from Eachan Isle."

"The pirate island?" Rose's eyebrows shot up. "It really exists?"

"As do the Seahorse pirates." Gladiel nodded. "But of course you would know that. Your first sea voyage was aboard one of their ships."

Rose frowned. "I've never been to sea."

"Ah, but you have. The very day you were born. Did Drinius never mention it?"

"No. I'm fairly certain I would remember something like that! You're certain?"

"Indeed." He nodded. "I was there with you."

Rose's brow creased, but a smile soon erased that line. Her head tilted back. "Ha! Rowlen would squeal with envy if he knew I'd been aboard a real pirate ship!"

"Envious of an adventure you don't even remember?"

"Hmm. That does present a bit of a problem." Rose sighed. "It is rather tragic that I don't remember. Pirates!" She shook her head in wonder. "And Seahorse pirates from Eachan Isle, no less." She drummed her fingertips against the sides of the mug. "I can hardly believe it's true."

"Ah, but it is."

"So you say. But you could tell me the pirate's ship was, in fact, a chariot pulled by giant seahorses, as the legend insists, and I would have no context from which to argue." She laughed, a deep but merry sound. "And now that I consider it, I do believe I like that version! Better yet, what if I came to be aboard their ship because I was a poor, orphaned mermaid who was plucked from the sea by great steeds of the deep? That would not only explain the mysterious circumstance of my birth," she said as her gaze travelled to Stanza, nosing around in the snow beyond the fire, "but also why I have such a love for their land-locked brothers."

Gladiel's laugh deepened the crinkles time had dug around his eyes. "You may not have been born to it, but I do believe you are every bit as Veetrish as your accent implies."

"I don't have an accent. *You* have an accent."

"Ah." His eyes laughed above his mug. "I suppose I would have an accent to your ears. And you, dear girl, most certainly carry the lilt of the Veetrish brogue to mine. You may not be able to make the Story People dance from your palm as Lord Whittier does, but you certainly have a gift for drafting a dramatic tale."

"Thank you." Rose dipped her head in an abbreviated version of the bow she had so often seen her foster father and brother give upon the completion of a tale. "But you were saying? About the . . . koeelo?"

"Keola," Gladiel corrected. "It is a mixture of dried beans, berries, and herbs that have been crushed into a fine powder. We steep the mixture in water, much like tea. You'll find that it suits well as a filling breakfast without the need for bread."

Rose took a tentative sip. The drink's warmth soothed her throat, sore from breathing the cold night air. Its flavor was rich and sweet with a spicy aftertaste that teased her tongue. She took another sip. "It's good!"

Sir Gladiel smiled. "I'm glad you think so. Many do not. My daughter, for one, absolutely hates it. But she drinks it every chance she gets."

"Why, if it's so costly and she doesn't even like it?"

"Erielle wants nothing more than to be a knight. She hopes, in time, she'll acclimate herself to it."

"A knight?" Rose was torn between shock and admiration. "There are female knights?"

"Not in E'veria," he said. "But Erielle argues the case at every turn. Drinking keola is just one of many ways she aims to prove that she's as worthy of knighthood as her brothers."

Rose tilted her head. "Your sons are knights?"

"Yes. They are both in Salderyn. Erielle is much younger." The affection in his voice pinched a soft place in Rose's heart. "She pines for them."

"I know how she feels." Rose took a long drink to soothe the tightness of her throat.

Gladiel's smile was gentle. "I can't tell you how thankful your father is that you found such a loving home in Veetri."

The tender feelings vanished in an instant. "Of course you can't." Rose couldn't disguise the bitterness in her tone. "You can't tell me *anything* about him."

"Rose, I—"

"No, it's fine. I'm sorry."

But her feelings concerning her father had never been "fine." They certainly were not "fine" right now, when she had been ordered to leave her family at Mirthan Hall and told to ride away with Sir Gladiel to who knows where.

Rose sat up straighter. Was she so used to her every move being dictated from afar that she hadn't even questioned her destination?

"Where are we going?" Her lips pressed together. "Or is that another one of my father's secrets?"

"We are going to Mynissbyr. Drinius is readying a home for you and his family in the Great Wood."

Rose's chin dropped. "The Great Wood?"

"Yes."

Rose remembered how Rowlen had described the mysterious creatures that inhabited the Great Wood of Mynissbyr. She suppressed a shiver. Soon she would live among them.

They started the horses at a walk to warm their muscles, but soon gave in to the restless animals' desire for a hard gallop. As the morning wore on Rose realized they'd stopped riding uphill. Instead, they were on a continuous but gentle decline. As Gladiel had predicted, they reached the bog just as the sun reached its high point.

"Sir Gladiel?" Rose hated the quiver in her voice. "If the Cobelds are in the bog, do you think it wise to enter it?"

"They crossed at the Stoenian border. This location is too far west and too close to the Great Wood for their comfort. They may have dug up the courage to cross the bog, Rose, but I do not believe they are yet brave enough to dare the Great Wood of Mynissbyr. I doubt they ever will be."

"And yet he thinks *I'm* brave enough to dare it?" Rose grumbled under her breath.

Gladiel turned. "Did you say something?"

"Nothing of consequence."

Veetri's pastoral ease had become gradually more populated with trees, but they were smaller specimens, and, in the dead of winter, seemed less healthy than the old oaks and giant sycamores that dotted Veetri's hills and valleys. But even though the freeze stole the scenic value of the marshland, it made crossing the bog much less difficult than it would have been in warmer weather. Although the frost-hardened ground was pitted, Rose imagined it would be much easier for the horses to navigate it now than after the spring thaw.

"How long will it take us to cross the bog?" Rose asked.

"Normally, I would expect to spend four or five days trudging through," Gladiel said. "But without the swampy hindrances of water and muck, we might cross the border into Mynissbyr in two days. Maybe three if we run into bad weather."

Two days later, the Great Wood's ancient evergreens rose in the distance like angry low clouds of a storm. A small, treeless plain, less than half a day's ride across, was all that separated Rose and Gladiel from the Great Wood of Mynissbyr.

"Once we breach the Wood," Gladiel said when they stopped to water the horses at a stream, "it should take us no more than four days to reach our destination."

To Rose's relief and consternation, Sir Gladiel shared none of her apprehension. In fact, the nearer they came to the mysterious forest, the faster he rode and the wider he smiled. After a while, his manner served only to tighten the tension in her shoulders.

Stretching many days' ride to each side, the immense wood tapered up to the point of their entrance. Gladiel didn't hesitate for even a second when he reached the tree line. Rose gritted her teeth and followed him into the trees.

She leaned forward in the saddle, her knuckles white on its pommel. The sun, which had been a bit too bright reflecting on the snow-covered plain, was much dimmer when filtered through the canopy of ancient evergreens. It took several minutes for her eyes to adjust, but when they did, she was less than impressed by the rough road that, in Rose's opinion, could barely be called a trail.

It must be seldom traveled. At that thought, she almost laughed. *And no wonder. Who would want to visit the Great Wood?*

After a few hours of tedious riding Rose's patience reached its end. Fear of the Wood fueled her growing annoyance and her clenched jaw had brought on a dull headache, compounding her irritation. Every time she glanced at the knight and noticed how relaxed—no, *happy*—he seemed, she wanted to pull her hair out.

"That tree is called a Mynokk. It only grows here in the Wood," he would say. Or, "Did you hear that bird call? That was a Great Wood Hawk. They're quite rare. Beautiful birds. The breast is almost silver and the wings are dark blue."

Gladiel acted as if they were on their way to a village faire, traversing some scenic byway rather than the ramshackle excuse for a trail they had actually taken. Without seeming to need a response from his companion, he kept up a cheerful monologue, naming the surrounding flora and fauna. When Rose finally let out the exasperated growl of breath she had been trying to hold in, he turned.

"Is something wrong?"

"One would think," Rose said, grinding her teeth as she urged Stanza to step around yet another fallen tree, "that the Regent of Mynissbyr would give a *little more consideration* to travelers in caring for the upkeep of his roads!"

Sir Gladiel's mouth dropped open. He looked back at the trail they had passed, ahead to where they would go, and then, to Rose's utter disgust, he grinned.

"Yes," he said with a chuckle. "I suppose he should!"

Rose ground her teeth again and refused to look at him.

"I'm sorry you find this road difficult, Rose, but its, er . . . *lack of care*," his lip twitched on the words, "serves our purposes much better than would a well-maintained road." The knight coughed, a sound Rose knew was an attempt to hide a laugh. He cleared his throat. "These trails are just one of the many reasons people steer clear of Mynissbyr. Be glad. You will be safer here because of the Regent's," he coughed again, "neglect."

After two or three hours passed there seemed to be a marked improvement in the condition of the trail. Rose hadn't realized what a blessing the poor trail had been. With less need for concentration, her mind wandered back to Rowlen's tale. She peered into the trees, jumping at the slightest sound, as if she expected some hideous creature to charge out of the woods and devour her, Sir Gladiel, and their horses.

They continued thus for several hours. Every muscle in Rose's body remained taut and her eyes were sore from darting about the suffocating surround of evergreen foliage. Finally, they reached a fork in the path.

Sir Gladiel turned to Rose. "From here we go east." His brow furrowed. He tilted his head. "Rose, you're so pale. Are you feeling ill?"

"No. I'm fine. Let's keep moving."

Suddenly, the branches overhead rustled and swayed, letting a shower of evergreen needles down. A small squeal escaped Rose's lips as she ducked.

Gladiel laughed. "I didn't take you for the type who'd be afraid of squirrels."

"It was a—? Oh." Rose's cheeks flamed. "I thought—" Her embarrassment refueled the frustration that had been weighing on her for hours. "The Storytellers in Veetri have many tales of the Great Wood, Sir Gladiel. Stories of strange beasts, and creatures that are half-man and half-bear."

"Indeed." Gladiel's smile disappeared. "Many legends have originated in these woods, Rose, and people fear Mynissbyr for that reason. For the most part, their fears are unfounded. But people tend to be quite stubborn when it comes to holding on to their superstitions." He tilted his head. "You experienced that firsthand with Lord Whittier's housekeeper, did you not?"

Rose swallowed and nodded. "When Mrs. Scyles found out I had ebonswarth powder she assumed I was a witch."

"Did you ever use the powder for evil gain?"

"Of course not! I only used it to dye my hair. You know that!"

"Exactly."

Rose opened her mouth to argue, but snapped it shut. "It's not the same."

"No, it isn't. Because of the widespread telling of tales about Mynissbyr Wood, the superstitions are much more prevalent than those of the rare few who are familiar with the uses of ebonswarth root powder. The Storytellers have embellished the legends of Mynissbyr, Rose. And no matter how much those of us who love the Great Wood speak against superstition, the people refuse to be swayed. But," his tone brightened suddenly, "as with these sadly neglected trails, this also will serve our particular purpose well."

"So the stories are not true?" she asked.

"Not as you have heard them, I'm sure. As with many stories told and retold over time, tales of the Great Wood have lost their way. The stories are rooted in truth, of course, but truth is no longer the focus of the tale."

"And the Bear-men?" Rose's gaze darted all around. "They still exist?"

"In a way, yes," he paused. "The legacy of the Bear-men of Mynissbyr is alive and well. But you, of all people, have nothing to fear from them."

"Me? But why not?"

Gladiel's eyes slid shut. "I'm sorry. I shouldn't have said that."

"But you did, so you might as well tell me."

"I can't."

"Why not?"

Gladiel's brow narrowed. "I would think by now you would know better than to ask."

"And *I* would think that by now *you* would know better than to make leading statements with no intention of explaining yourself!" Rose slapped a hand over her mouth. "Forgive me," she said as she lowered her hand and her eyes. "I should not have spoken so."

Gladiel lifted a hand to smooth his beard, but Rose knew he was only trying to hide a smile. After a moment, he lowered his hand. "Would it anger you more if I were to tell you that you reminded me of your father just then?"

Rose thought to deny it, but at the last second changed her mind. "Most likely, yes."

"In that case," Gladiel said with a wink that drained Rose's anger, "I will keep that thought to myself. But regardless of what strange tales you may have heard in Veetri, I can assure you there is nothing within Mynissbyr Wood from which my sword cannot protect you."

Rose looked up in the trees where the squirrel now scolded her presence and felt a little silly.

"We'll be going this way," Gladiel motioned to the eastern trail, "but only for about two miles. My brother Ayden's home is near. Tonight we will take our rest in real beds, with a warm meal in our bellies!"

"That sounds good."

"Our day will start early tomorrow and end late, so a good night's sleep will serve us well. The trail will become a bit more arduous as we near the river."

Rose lifted an eyebrow. "It gets worse?"

"You're a good rider. You're up to it," Gladiel smiled. "We'll need to camp in the Wood at least one night. But you needn't fear. We are better protected in Mynissbyr than practically anywhere else in E'veria. The enemy still fears the legends of these woods, and at least in that way we have some assurance of your safety." The sudden change in Gladiel's tone sent a shiver up her spine. "I do not exaggerate when I say that E'veria is entering her darkest days in many generations."

Rose fought her trepidation by offering a lighthearted comment. "It's a shame the stories aren't real. Otherwise, perhaps Lady Anya might step out of them and yet come to our aid."

Gladiel arched an eyebrow. "I said *most* of the Veetrish stories are exaggerated, Rose, but they are not entirely without redemptive merit. Lady Anya was a real person and the battle she fought in is one of the great triumphs of E'veria's history."

Rose's laugh startled Stanza and he whinnied. "Surely you don't expect me to believe that a young girl could rally an army of mythological beasts to win a war?"

"More wondrous things have happened in E'veria than a sixteen-year-old girl leading an army."

Rose laughed. "An army of Bear-men?"

"Yes."

Her smile fell. "You really believe the story?"

"Yes." Gladiel nodded. "But not as the Veetrish tell it." His smile went suddenly lopsided, giving him an almost boyish look, though the black beard surrounding it was salted with white. "The Bear-men are quite human. And although I consider myself quite knowledgeable on the subject, you would do well to ask my brother. Ayden is a scholar. A historian, if you will. He will be most glad for an ear to listen to the true, historically documented tale of Lady Anya. Shall we?"

Without waiting for her assent, Gladiel spurred his horse. Rose leaned forward in her saddle as Stanza raced to catch up.

S IXTEEN

$\mathcal{A}$yden de Vonsar's cottage rose from the clearing like a frozen giant. Made of logs stained grayish-brown by the weather, it fit into the surroundings as perfectly as if it had grown up among the trees. Above the second story, a thatched roof gave the home the appearance of a large bird's nest that had fallen from a mammoth tree. Gladiel rode straight to a small barn situated a short distance beyond the house. By the time Rose dismounted, he had already begun removing his horse's saddle.

At the scrape of a door, she turned her eyes toward the house. A man walked toward them with a smile as open as his arms.

"Welcome, welcome, weary travelers! It is so very nice to have—" He blinked. "Gladiel!" The men embraced. "What brings you to darken my door? And who might your lovely companion be?"

Rose blushed as Sir Gladiel introduced her. "May I present Lady Rose . . . de Whittier. Rose, this is my brother, Ayden de Vonsar."

Rose curtsied. "I'm pleased to make your acquaintance, Sir Ayden."

He bowed in return and smiled up at her, his hazel-green eyes twinkling. "There will be no *sirring* of me, my lady, for I am no knight. Too short, you see?"

Rose laughed. He wasn't what she would consider short, but neither did he possess the giant-like form of his brother.

"Gladiel may have received the bulk of the height in the family," he said, "but all was not lost to me, for I've inherited the vast majority of our family's intellect."

Gladiel snorted.

"Call me Ayden, if you please," he said, "for I cannot abide formality. And I'd wager you're not used to being held to it, either. You are Veetrish, yes?"

Rose didn't want to lie, so she phrased her answer carefully. "I come from Veetri, yes."

"Are you a Storyteller, perhaps?"

She shook her head.

"Ah, I didn't think so. You haven't the eyes for it. In fact," he said, peering closer at her face, "if I had to guess your origins based solely on your eyes, I would have to say you are—"

"Is Bess about?" Gladiel interrupted.

"Of course." He turned back to Rose. "Bess is my housekeeper. And I'll wager she'll be glad to see a feminine face as surely as I would guess you're ready for a good, hot meal and some, eh, *intelligent* conversation." Ayden chuckled and elbowed his brother's side.

"Don't worry, Rose," Gladiel said with a laugh, "I'll be along shortly to provide it."

Rose smiled and shook her head, feeling a pang of longing for the banter she shared with her own brothers. "Ayden, Sir Gladiel informs me that my Veetrish upbringing has not provided me with the most accurate information concerning this wood."

Ayden nodded. "Likely true."

"He also mentioned that you are an authority on the subject of Lady Anya. I must admit I'm curious to learn the real story behind the Storytellers' legends."

"A young lady searching for truth! How refreshing! Most people who pass this way simply want directions for the swiftest path out of Mynissbyr!" Ayden laughed as he removed Rose's saddlebags from Stanza. "I'm afraid my stable hand is gone for the next week. Off on a hunt."

"You don't employ a huntsman?"

"Oh yes, I do. But it just happens that my huntsman is also my gardener and my stable hand." He laughed. "I am more than capable of taking care of your horse, my lady."

"You two go on up to the house," Gladiel said. "I'll care for the horses and be along in a bit. These worthy beasts deserve a thorough rubdown and a large helping of oats after their journey, and I'm sure Rose will welcome a fresh conversationalist. Even if he is my *little* brother."

Rose took Ayden's offered arm and he led her to the house.

The dark log exterior belied the bright cheerfulness inside. Whitewashed walls and open shutters let sunshine rule the space. Crouched before a large, southern facing window was a monstrous table with just one leather-upholstered chair. Neatly arranged on the table were bottles of ink, labeled for their different pigments. Near the inkwells, artfully blown glass vases held a beautiful assortment of quills: some of metal, some with feathered tops, and some that looked to be encrusted with gems. Every other wall in the room was lined with bookcases, where hundreds of books and neatly rolled scrolls were stacked on well-organized shelves.

"This room gets the most daylight of any in the house, so I use it to do my work," Ayden explained. "We aren't really set up for visitors, but I think you'll find the accommodations acceptable. Mynissbyr Wood is not a popular destination." Ayden laughed at his own joke, and, weary of the trail's tension, Rose welcomed the sound.

"I'll show you to your room and send my housekeeper up to assist you." He led Rose upstairs to a room that overlooked the stable.

Ayden moved toward the bed. "If you pull this cord," he said, "it alerts Bess that you need her assistance." He demonstrated. Rose heard a distant tinkling sound from somewhere below.

While Ayden deposited the saddlebags near the armoire, Rose moved toward a looking glass that hung on the wall opposite the window. She pulled the woolen cap from her head, dismayed to see that many of her black curls had escaped their coils, snagging numerous leaf fragments and tiny twigs.

Rose gazed around the room and was pleased to discover a small but adequate bathtub that was near a strange contraption coming out of the floor. Curiosity drew her to it. "What is this?"

"Ah, yes!" Ayden's eyes sparkled with delight. "It's a rather simple device, but I'll admit it is something of a luxury. I have a large vat of water in a room just off the kitchen that is kept warm at all times. We have such a ready supply of wood, you see. When a bath is needed, the fire beneath the vat is increased, which builds a head of steam. Turning this handle," he said, pointing to a hexagonal knob, "opens a valve that allows the pressure of the steam to force the hot water up through the pipes. It takes a bit of work to get the fire hot enough, but not as much as it takes to heat and haul water up the stairs, one bucket at a time!" He paused as if it was just a trifling matter. "I installed a similar system at Fyrlean Manor not five summers ago, and shortly thereafter the King requested the plans. I believe they recently installed several of my designs in Castle Rynwyk as well as at Holiday Palace in Port Dyn." Ayden chuckled again, and sighed, "Gladiel assures me the design will be in high demand all over E'veria soon."

Rose eyed the engineering marvel, thinking how much time such a thing could have saved the maids in Lord Whittier's house the past few years. "It's ingenious."

"Thank you. It's nothing really. I just thought to lessen Bess's workload a bit." Ayden looked down at the floor until footsteps sounded on the stairs. "And there she is."

He turned to address the housekeeper. "Bess, this is Lady Rose . . . de Whittier, did you say?"

Rose nodded and willed the mist from her eyes. It wasn't her real name, of course, but it was the closest thing she had.

"Lady Rose is traveling with my brother."

"My lady," the short, gray-haired lady gave a small curtsy.

"I'll leave you, then." Ayden shut the door as he left.

"Would you like me to unpack your bags, mistress?"

"That won't be necessary. Sir Gladiel and I are just staying the night. We'll most likely leave before dawn." She looked at the tub. "I would dearly love to bathe, though, if it's not too much trouble?"

"Of course." Bess's smile widened. "The earl's invention takes all the trouble out of it."

"Ayden is an earl?"

"Well, naturally!" Bess walked to the tub and began cranking the strange knob. "Since Sir Gladiel is the Regent of Mynissbyr, it follows that Milord Ayden, being the younger son, would be the earl. You'd never know it, of course. None in that family put on airs like most of the nobility."

Rose dropped her hat. *Sir Gladiel is the Regent of Mynissbyr?* The memory of a comment she'd made earlier flushed her face. "I thought Sir Gladiel was a knight!"

Bess blinked in surprise. "Why, of course he's a knight! One of the most honored knights in the land, from what I understand."

"But you just said he is the Regent!"

"To be sure. There are hardly enough people in Mynissbyr to justify the Regent's constant presence. There are but a few hermits to govern within the Wood and most of us live under the idea that life itself is too tenuous to cause each other grief."

Rose stared at the tub without seeing it. *What have I done?* Each of the Kingdom's nine provinces was governed by a leader known as "Regent." In E'verian nobility, a Regent was ranked directly below the King. Rose groaned. The free tongue of her Veetrish upbringing had been sparring with a Regent—*a Regent!*—for days.

Rose swallowed. "Is His Grace's status a . . . secret?" She well knew the trouble of concealing one's identity. After all, she had done it her whole life.

"Oh, goodness, no!" Bess laughed. "It's no secret. The whole world knows Sir Gladiel is the Regent of Mynissbyr. Or, I thought it did." Her smile faded to a question. "Perhaps politics are not so popular a topic in Veetri?"

"No, they're not. At least not in my family." Rose paused. "How did you know I'm from Veetri?"

"Your accent is fairly telling." Bess resumed her action, turning the knob. Suddenly, steaming-hot water gushed out into the tub. "Now let's get you out of those clothes and you can have a nice long soak while I wash your dress. Do you need help with your hair?"

"Thank you, but I can manage."

In no time at all Bess had helped her undress, and after reminding Rose of the bell cord, she left with Rose's dress.

Rose luxuriated in the warmth of the tub, letting its heat spread through her still-chilled body as the sleepy smell of the rich, spicy soap released the tension of the ride.

She dunked under the water to get her hair wet and then scrubbed her scalp, rubbing the soap in her hands and in her hair until her head was covered in frothy lather. When she dunked under to rinse it, however, she was a bit disgusted to discover the soapsuds skimming the water had turned a dull gray color.

I must have been filthier than I thought.

When the bath began to cool she pulled the cork stopper and climbed out of the tub. Even with the fire blazing the room had not yet lost its chill. She reached for the towel and made quick work of drying off.

Rose removed a comb from her saddlebag, turned toward the mirrored door of the armoire, and gasped.

"No . . ." She touched the sodden mass of coppery orange curls that used to be black. "No! Oh no!" *Was it the soap? The water?*

Rose dropped her head into her hands. Was there anything she could do to fix this? Shivering, she pulled a clean dress from her saddlebag and wrenched it on. Sir Gladiel knew about the ebonswarth dye, so it wouldn't matter if he saw her. But what about Ayden and Bess? She shuffled through one of her saddlebags, but then stopped. Her hand flew to her mouth. She'd forgotten the skin of powder! It was still stowed in the back of her wardrobe at Mirthan Hall. But even if she had the powder it would be useless. She didn't have access to a hot sulfur spring.

Defeated, Rose returned to the mirror. She turned from side to side, testing the vision from every angle before facing herself straight on. It was as if she gazed at a stranger.

"So this is what you're supposed to look like," she whispered to her reflection, and then jumped when a knock sounded at the door.

"Just a moment!"

Struggling with shaking hands, she reached behind her to fasten as many of her buttons as she could. Using the mirror as a guide, Rose wrapped the towel around her head.

"Oh, look at you!" Bess exclaimed when Rose finally opened the door. "You've managed to get dressed on your own! Would you like me to comb out your hair?"

"No!" Rose answered a little too forcefully. "Er, thank you," she said a bit more softly and summoned a smile, "but I can manage." Rose touched the towel to make sure it covered the nape of her neck before she turned around. "Could you help me with these last few buttons?"

"Of course."

Rose bit her lip, praying the towel would stay in place. "I have a pressing matter I need to discuss with Sir Gladiel," she said when Bess fastened the final button. "Is he about?"

"I'll fetch him for you, shall I?" Bess smiled, gave Rose a quick curtsy, and left to fetch the knight.

Rose closed the door and rummaged through her saddlebags for something, *anything* that might help disguise her hair. As she searched, the towel fell from her head. Dark copper hair fell in thick, damp waves over her shoulders and down her back.

"Rose?" Gladiel's voice rumbled from the other side of the door.

Leaving the towel where it had fallen, Rose walked to the door. Without opening it, she whispered, "Is anyone else upstairs?"

"No," he replied. "Everyone else is below. Are you unwell?"

Taking a deep breath, Rose opened the door.

In the rush of a word she could not decipher, Gladiel's breath left him. His face blanched and he grabbed the doorframe as if he had lost his balance.

Rose reached for his arm, pulled him into the room, and shut the door. "It was the bathwater. Or the soap. I'm not sure which. But it—"

"Rose?" Gladiel's breathing was shallow, his face pasty. "It is you, isn't it?" He rubbed his eyes and leaned hard against the back of the door.

"Sir Gladiel? Are you ill?"

"Hardly. I just had a bit of a shock, I guess." A tinge of color returned to his cheeks. He gave her a feeble smile. "I thought I was seeing your mother again, Rynloeft rest her soul." He took a breath. "You look so much like her now that you're grown."

"Sir Gladiel, I don't know what to do!" She whispered. "In my haste I forgot to pack the ebonswarth powder. And I don't have any sulfur water, either!"

"Of course, of course." Gladiel slapped his hand against his forehead. He straightened. "There is nothing we can do, Rose. There are no sulfur springs in the province of Mynissbyr by which to secure the dye. It won't matter once we've reached the Bear's Rest, but Ayden and Bess mustn't see you like this. Not yet."

He began to pace. When it became clear his pacing would result in nothing of use, Rose used the time to comb out her hair. It had already begun to dry and she knew it would be a mass of tangles if she didn't get to it.

Sir Gladiel's pacing continued. Every few moments the knight would stop to scowl in her direction, only to resume his pacing.

Rose ripped the comb through the last tangle with such force that a large knot became a casualty of the fight. Irritated with Gladiel's silence, but mindful of his near-royal status as a Regent, Rose clenched her jaw to keep quiet. She had already embarrassed herself enough.

First she'd insulted a Regent, the highest-ranking official she had ever met, with disparaging remarks concerning the conditions of his roads. Then she'd managed to ruin a most effective disguise by simply washing her hair, causing a disturbing problem for that same Regent. She knew she should apologize, but how to frame it without embarrassing herself further?

Rose glanced at Gladiel, whose scowl was pensive enough to make her wonder if he would even hear her. Yes, an apology was needed, but now was not the time.

Her hair blissfully detangled, Rose moved a chair closer to the fire to speed its drying. An idea brought her to her feet almost as soon as she sat down. Rose's sudden movement broke Sir Gladiel's concentration. He stopped pacing and stared.

A faraway smile crept across his features. When he spoke, his voice was quiet. Almost reverent. *"Eyes the hue of jeweled sky,"* he whispered, *"and head ablaze with fire."*

Rose tilted her head. She had heard similar words, spoken by Lord Whittier the day Mrs. Scyles was dismissed. "That's part of the poem, isn't it?"

"Poem?" Gladiel's brow furrowed. "Er, yes. It's from a poem, I guess you could say. Pay me no mind. I was thinking aloud. Forgive me."

Rose blinked. She'd had an idea, but Gladiel's odd remark had temporarily blown it from her mind. She bit her lip, trying to remember. Finally, it dawned.

"For tonight at least, couldn't I just wear my woolen hat?"

"Your hat?" Sir Gladiel let out a breath that visibly relaxed his shoulders. "Yes. I suppose that might do. They may think it odd, but they will not question you for it."

With a nod, Rose quickly coiled braids around her head, affixed them with pins, and pulled the tight woolen hat over her head. Facing the mirror, she carefully tucked the few stray copper curls inside. The wool had been dyed black, and in the dim light of evening it mimicked her usual hair color. Rose frowned. Her eyebrows were still red.

Eyeing the candle on a nearby stand, she licked her index finger, rubbed her thumb against it, and snuffed the flame. She let go for just a moment and then, gritting her teeth against the heat, rubbed the wick. Moving back to the mirror, she carefully transferred the soot to her brow. Rose straightened, took a deep breath, and a sense of calm returned.

"Very good." Sir Gladiel nodded. "And once I deliver you to the Bear's Rest you'll be secluded enough that you won't need to worry about your hair anymore."

"*The Bear's Rest.*" Rose didn't like the sound of it. "You mentioned it before. What is it?"

"It's a hunting lodge deep in the heart of the Great Wood. Which could explain why it was abandoned!" He winked, but sobered at her look. "It was built nearly fifty years ago by an enterprising young man who wished to make it into a hunting lodge for the nobility. The legends and superstitions surrounding Mynissbyr's history brought him few guests, however, and he was forced to try his hand elsewhere." Gladiel rubbed his chin. "It has suffered some from neglect, of course, and Drinius and I have a few more adjustments to make before it is completely finished. But it is quite livable and will serve you well as a home for a while."

By the door, a bell Rose hadn't even noticed jingled.

"That would be Bess, calling us to dinner," Gladiel said. "Ayden rarely has visitors and is looking forward to our evening together."

"Your brother is delightful. For his sake I shall attempt to be at my most charming. But—"

"Yes?" Gladiel paused, his hand on the door.

"I fear that even at my most charming I might offend. It would appear I've grown quite adept at causing offense since leaving Veetri."

"Whatever do you mean?"

"Well, I spent most of the day crossing words with *the Regent of Mynissbyr*, didn't I?" She tilted her head.

He smiled. "Bess told you?"

She nodded.

"No need to trouble yourself. I have not been offended in the least and do not require an apology. Now, shall we go to table and see which of the culinary delights of my province Bess has seen fit to serve us tonight?"

SEVENTEEN

After a filling meal, the Regent, the earl, and Rose moved to a simply furnished sitting room. As with most of the ground floor of the house, the walls were lined with bookshelves. Rose walked around the room, taking note of familiar titles here and there, amazed at the sheer volume of texts.

They discussed a few of Rose's favorite books before Ayden remembered her request to learn about the Lady Anya.

"It's a shame her story has been relegated to the fantastic imaginations of Veetrish Storytellers. It was quite a good story even before they expanded the tale." Ayden paused for a moment. "Of course, truth needs no enhancement to provide beauty to a story."

Rose thought on his words for a moment before responding. "But truth is a rather incorporeal concept, don't you think? Its substance is tempered by the experience of its hearer."

"Hmm." Ayden nodded thoughtfully. "Go on."

"Each time a tale is retold," Rose said, "it takes on a bit of the personality of the Storyteller. It's the natural way of things."

Ayden smiled. "Natural to the Veetrish, perhaps."

"There is truth that is not subjective." Gladiel interjected. "Truth that is what it is. It needs no drama or humor or dancing Story People to improve upon. By definition, it is beyond improvement. Beyond argument."

"But argument leads to discovery and discovery to knowledge, correct?" Rose pointed out.

The men nodded, albeit a bit grudgingly.

"As I've been taught," she continued, "argument is the very basis of learning."

"Yes, yes." Ayden leaned forward. "Arguing has its merit. As a means to an end. As a step in a quest." He rubbed his bearded chin. Unlike the triangular knight's beard worn by his elder brother, Ayden's beard was closely cropped and stretched from ear to ear. "Take, for instance," he continued, "a subject such as mathematics or history. Some things cannot be argued. There is just one correct response to a question, one answer to an equation. One truth."

"You make a good point about mathematics. Although I tried many times arguing sums with my tutor, she was always able to point out my mistakes." Rose laughed. "But I disagree with you about history being inarguable." She paused, gathering her thoughts. "Wouldn't the truth of an event depend upon the point of view of the person who recorded it?"

"How so?"

"Well, if Lady Anya defeated the Cobelds, it would be recorded in E'veria's history as a wonderful victory."

"She *did* defeat them," Gladiel said, crossing his arms.

"And indeed," Ayden agreed, nodding, "it was a glorious victory."

"According to whom?"

"Well . . . everyone!" Ayden laughed.

"Ah-ah-ah!" Rose wagged a finger at the enthusiastic academic. "I doubt the Cobelds found Lady Anya's victory very glorious. If the *Cobelds* recorded that same event it would be viewed as a terrible defeat."

"I see. Yes." Ayden nodded. "But the accounts, if recorded accurately, would arrive at the same end."

"But not the same conclusion."

Ayden slapped his knee. Gladiel hooted with laughter.

"Perhaps, brother," the knight said finally, "you should proceed with the story you promised."

"Indeed! I believe you were interested in the *true* story of the brave Lady Anya of Fyrlean Manor and how she delivered E'veria from the traitorous Cobeld invaders, yes?"

"Please!"

Sitting back in his chair, Ayden began. Although he didn't describe Lady Anya physically, the action of the tale very nearly mirrored Rowlen's telling.

"But if the Cobelds' curses are stored inside the hairs of their beards," Rose asked, "shouldn't it be easy to avoid being cursed?" Rose wrinkled her nose. "Who would want to get close enough to touch a monster's beard?"

"The hair can be plucked out, Rose." Gladiel's voice was soft. "The curse remains upon it."

"Oh." Rose blinked. "Is that how my—"

"Yes." Gladiel cut off the rest of Rose's question before she could finish asking, *"Is that how my mother died?"*

Caught up in the story, she'd forgotten for a moment that Ayden believed her to be Lord and Lady Whittier's daughter. But now that her mind had turned toward her Veetrish family—while discussing Cobeld curses—her breath caught in her throat.

Surely the duke and duchess would be on their way to the Regent of Veetri's palace on the northern coast, wouldn't they? *Please be safe*, her heart whispered.

"Unfortunately, most of the curses come from plucked hairs rather than direct contact with one of the creatures' beards." Ayden shook his head.

"But if the Cobelds are plucking the hairs of their beards all the time to curse people," she asked, "doesn't the magic eventually run out?"

"One would hope, but that is not information we have at our disposal," Gladiel sighed. "We can only assume that, just like our own beards, they grow back."

"Oh." She took a breath. "Please go on with Lady Anya's tale, Ayden. I'm sorry to have gotten us off track."

"There is no tangent too wild when one is searching for truth," he said with a smile. "Now where was I? Ah, the prophecy."

"Prophecy?"

"Indeed. While disguised among the Cobelds, Lady Anya learned of an ancient prophecy that foretold of hideous beasts—creatures that were half-man and half-bear—that would someday rise up from Mynissbyr Wood and slaughter the Cobelds."

"But if Lady Anya lived in the Great Wood she must have already known about the Bear-men, right?"

"Patience. I'm getting to that." Ayden smiled. "Another thing Lady Anya learned during her time with the Cobelds was that somewhere near Mount Shireya a Remedy existed that would put an end to the Cobeld curse. Though she never learned where or even exactly what the Remedy was, the knowledge of its existence gave E'veria great hope for the future."

"There's a Remedy?" Rose sat up straighter. "Why is it not in use?"

Gladiel glanced at his brother before answering. "The Remedy has yet to be found."

"But—"

"Let Ayden tell the story, Rose."

She bit her lip. "Please, go on."

"Lady Anya was almost discovered the night she left the Cobeld camp, but she managed to sneak past the roving patrols and made it to a main road. It took her several weeks to travel to Salderyn, but when she was finally admitted to see the King, he and his knights went into action. Every bearskin rug and hunting trophy that could be made into a cloak was fashioned into a disguise of Anya's design."

"Wait." Rose held up a hand. "So you're telling me that the Bear-men were just men? Men wearing . . . rugs?"

"It's rather amusing, isn't it?" Ayden nodded, chuckling. "Though many Cobelds escaped, the power of their number was destroyed. Those who survived fled to the foothills of Mount Shireya, and until a few years ago, they'd remained in hiding there."

"Why did they come out of hiding?"

"Tell her what happened to Lady Anya." Gladiel said quickly. Turning to Rose, he gave her a wide smile that seemed a little less sincere, somehow. "I think you'll enjoy this part of the tale."

"Indeed!" Ayden grinned. "Anya was given great honors by the King and named her father's heir, the only female Regent in the history of E'veria. She eventually married, and her sons became knights to generations of Kings. Even now some of her descendants operate in that capacity."

"What of her daughters?"

"She had only sons," Ayden said. "In fact, until this most recent generation of Bear-men," he said with a smile toward his brother, "there were no direct descendants of Lady Anya who were female."

Rose looked at Gladiel. "Your daughter, Erielle."

"Indeed." The pride in his smile was both infectious and indulgent. "The first girl born to our family in two hundred years."

"Not a girl," Rose said with a grin. "A Bear-woman."

Ayden chuckled. "And she is that, to be sure. But sadly, the truth of our legacy is lost to most of E'veria, and the Bear-men have been relegated to scary legends told around fires on gloomy nights." Ayden winked. "And in Veetrish parlors every day of the year."

"Hear, hear!" Rose laughed.

A log let off a loud pop in the hearth as if joining in their laughter.

"My brother once told a rather entertaining version of the same tale," she said after a moment. "In Rowlen's story it was Lady Anya herself who led the army. After the battle she fell in love with one of the Bear-men and, in time, became the mother of many legendary beasts." Taking on an expression of mock dismay, she lowered her voice. "Sadly, the poor lady became ostracized from polite society for loving such a frightening brute."

Gladiel and Ayden roared with laughter. Tears rolled down Ayden's cheeks when he finally spoke. "Who knew Lady Anya's descendants," he gasped on another fit of laughter, "were such monsters!"

When their laughter died down, Gladiel stood. "It is growing late," he said. "And I'm afraid we have a very long day ahead of us tomorrow, Rose. As much as I wish we could continue this discussion through the night, I suggest we retire."

Ayden reached for Rose's hand and bent to kiss it. "A warm welcome will ever await you at my door, Lady Rose. Sleep well this night. May you have safe travels on the morrow."

EIGHTEEN

*G*ladiel and Rose departed just as the first rays of dawn filtered through the trees. For the first hour or two the lack of light impeded their vision and they were forced to travel slowly. As daylight increased, so did their speed. At least until they reached the Ursina River.

The river was partially frozen and the trail alongside it was a rocky, frost-hardened narrow that had likely been carved by elk or deer rather than man and horse. Bits of icy rock kept them at a cautious pace. Rose and Gladiel spoke little, but the cheerful birdsong and water gurgling between sheets of ice seemed noise enough. Soon, however, even those sounds were drowned out by the thundering pulse of the multi-leveled Brune Falls.

"It's going to get a bit difficult here!" Gladiel shouted over the roar of the falls. "Follow my path exactly!"

Rose nodded.

The spray of the falls misted the air and added a wet sheen to Rose's cloak as she carefully followed Gladiel down the steep incline.

"Whoa, boy. Whoa." Rose pulled the reins gently when her horse got a little too close to the rear end of Gladiel's. The last thing either of them needed was for Gladiel's mount to get irritated into kicking out at Stanza. Stanza braced his front legs to obey her command, but his hooves slid across a patch of ice.

Rose's stomach flipped as they neared the deadly ledge, but Stanza found his footing just in time. "It's all right, Stanza." She patted his side and clicked her tongue. "There's a good lad."

They finally reached the bottom, and when they got a bit farther away, Rose looked over her shoulder at the waterfall. Like the river above, the flow was a mixture of stillness and movement. Giant hanging icicles, thick and sparkling in the sun, held fast next to the rush of cold water, which was adding to the icicles' girth daily, inch by icy inch. It was beautiful from this side. But she hoped she never had to repeat the trip down again. Even the thought of it reminded her muscles of their fatigue. It would have been nice to take a break, to get off her horse and walk about a bit, but with only a spare glance or two back to make sure she still followed, Sir Gladiel continued on.

It was late afternoon when he finally reined in his horse. "Are you hungry, Rose?"

"Famished." Her stomach had let her know more than an hour earlier that midday was approaching, and even though her muscles had relaxed a bit, she was more than ready to stretch them.

"We're making very good time," Gladiel said as they ate the food Bess had packed for them. "We should reach the bridge by nightfall. We'll camp on this side tonight and cross it in the morning, following Fynnen Stream the rest of the way."

Rose's head swam with the unfamiliar landmarks. "The trail along the stream leads to the Bear's Rest?" Even saying the name of her new home made the hair stand up on her arms. Ayden's tale had helped her relax about the creatures inhabiting the Great Wood, but after being away from her aunt and cousin for nearly a decade, she was still decidedly nervous about the upcoming reunion.

"Unfortunately, there is nothing you might consider a trail, per se." Gladiel's slight smirk was the only tell that referenced Rose's comments from the previous day. "But the stream will lead us nearly to the door of your new home."

All too soon they had packed away the remnants of their meal. Rose couldn't help but groan a little as she pulled herself into the saddle.

"The trip down the falls is a bit taxing, isn't it?"

Rose arched an eyebrow. "A bit? My legs are still quivering." But her tone only held a trace of the sarcasm she might have used had Gladiel not been the Regent of Mynissbyr.

Still, he laughed. "Ah, but you're young. You'll recover much faster than these old bones will allow me."

He clicked his tongue at his horse and they were off again, riding swifter now that they had reached lower, more level ground. They stopped for another quick meal as the sun touched the trees on its downward journey, this time supplementing the remaining food from luncheon with mugs of keola. Before the light completely disappeared, the bridge came into sight.

Rose gaped at the arching log and stone structure that spanned the river at a narrow place. "It's a real bridge!"

Gladiel dismounted. "Indeed. What did you think it would be?"

Rose slid from Stanza's back. "I don't know. I suppose I thought that since I've had to reevaluate my definition of the word 'trail' while in Your Grace's province that the same might be true of what comprises a bridge in the Great Wood."

"Ah." Gladiel smiled. "So you were expecting a few slippery stones perhaps? Or a wide, rotting log?"

Rose laughed. "Something like that. But I must say I am impressed. Not only does it appear structurally sound, it paints quite a picturesque scene." She grinned. "My compliments to the Regent," she said and dipped her head.

Later that night, while Rose made her bed near the fire on the frozen ground, she missed Ayden's warm cottage. But sleep came quickly even then. When dawn once again opened her eyes, the happy chirping of birds was accompanied by lighthearted conversation and a sense of happy expectation as they crossed the bridge and made their way through the Wood toward Fynnen Stream.

Little more than a creek, Fynnen Stream was covered in a layer of ice, though it was thin enough in places that Rose could see bubbles of water moving beneath its glassy surface. They followed its southwesterly path for the rest of the day and half of the next as they gained ground toward their destination.

"There it is, Rose." Gladiel pointed to a sunny clearing and a dark shadow she could just see through the trees. "The Bear's Rest. Your new home."

Approaching the Bear's Rest from the rear, Rose was impressed with the size of the log structure. The roof, like Ayden's, was thatched, but sheltered a much larger building that rose higher than Ayden's by far at its peaks. There were three large dormers in the front and two in the rear. The peak of each dormer was adorned with a wooden carving that upon closer examination resembled said sleeping bear. Smoke poured from at least three of the several chimneys protruding from the roof, giving the promise of a warm welcome.

The front yard held a stable capable of housing several horses and a small barn with a few livestock. A man she vaguely recognized from her youth came out of the stable and nearly tripped when he saw Gladiel. After greeting the knight, he turned to her.

"So good to have you back, Miss—I mean, *Mistress* Rose," he pulled the woolen cap from his head.

His voice aided her memory. *Walen.* The stable master had been with Sir Drinius's family for years. It was Walen who had first taught her how to ride.

"It's good to be here, Walen," she smiled. "I trust," Rose paused as the woman's name escaped her, "your wife is well?"

He beamed. "My Eneth will be happy you remembered her," he said. "She's missed you so these years. We all have."

"Thank you." Rose said as a rush of nerves returned. She certainly hoped it was true. Although Uncle Drinius had assured her of Aunt Alaine's affection, memory of the doubts Mrs. Scyles had fostered caused Rose's stomach to wobble a bit as she dismounted and gave Stanza's reins and care into Walen's capable hands.

"And speaking of Eneth," Sir Gladiel said and offered Rose his arm, "shall we go see if she has a kettle on? I would welcome a cup of something warm."

Rose nodded, but bit her lip and brushed her hands down the skirts that had certainly seen cleaner days. "Do I look presentable?"

But Gladiel's reply was interrupted by a shout from the direction of the house.

"Rose!" A young woman raced across the porch and down the steps, her white-blond hair streaming out behind her. "Rose!" she called. "I can't believe it! You're finally here!"

"Lily?" Rose returned her cousin's enthusiastic hug, though it was slightly awkward due to the marked difference in their heights. "You're scarcely taller than when I left!" Though Lily was several months older, Rose was more than a head taller than her petite cousin.

"I thought I'd never see you again! It's so good you're here. The lodge is almost completely renovated. Father has done a miraculous job with the—well, hello, Sir Gladiel!"

Gladiel grinned. "Lily, I don't think I've ever heard that many words come out of your mouth at once." He laughed. "I might be led to believe that you've been storing them up all these years."

Lily took a step back from Rose. Her alabaster cheeks grew pink. "Well, yes. I imagine I have."

Rose's chest tightened when Uncle Drinius's deep, familiar voice called from the porch. She looked up, wondering if he would have shrunken or become diminished somehow from his injury, but he looked as hale as ever. And beside him, Aunt Alaine dabbed her eyes.

"I'm sure Rose and Gladiel are cold and tired, Lily," Drinius called. "Bring them in! You can talk inside."

Lily grasped Rose's hand and pulled her out of Gladiel's grasp, much as she had when they were children.

Although this time, Rose mused as she approached her aunt and uncle, *Lily is pulling me toward something rather than away from it.*

Memories of childhood assailed her then. Her penchant for mischief, a trait that had been not only encouraged but refined by her Veetrish brothers, had often been curtailed by the easily-prickled conscience of her meeker cousin. Regardless of Lily's exuberant welcome, Rose wondered if such a refined young noblewoman from Stoen would have anything in common with the Veetrish country girl who'd been deposited at her door once the newness of their reunion wore off.

Rose had little time to ponder the future of their friendship, however. Before she even realized her uncle had left the porch, she was engulfed in his embrace.

"I'm so sorry I couldn't come for you sooner."

"Sorry? Uncle Drinius, you were hurt!"

He squeezed her tighter before releasing her, "I'm nearly healed and you're here safely. All is well. Now come greet your aunt."

"Welcome, Rose."

Aunt Alaine was every bit as beautiful as Rose remembered. With porcelain skin and eyes the same pale blue as the winter sky, her hair was the color of sunlight on a cloud. A few small lines about her eyes betrayed the passage of time, but they did not mar her beauty.

Alaine opened her arms for an embrace. As she leaned down to accept it, Rose was almost worried that to hug her aunt would risk breaking her.

Next to Alaine's and Lily's wispy frames, Rose thought, *I am as cloddish as a giant.*

Drinius cleared his throat. "No sense standing out here all day. Come along now."

As Eneth readied the table, Lily gave Rose a tour of the lodge.

Though the Bear's Rest would have comfortably fit inside Mirthan Hall several times over, the lodge was more than adequate for their current needs and had a very cozy feel. Each room had its own stone fireplace, though they varied in size. There were six large bedrooms on the second floor, though not that many beds, and the ground level boasted a modest kitchen, an immense front room that served as both parlor and dining room, and two small bedrooms. A smaller parlor on the opposite side of the lodge's wide, open staircase had windows on two sides and it served quite nicely as a sewing room.

Though it couldn't rival Mirthan Hall in either size or charm, the interior of the Bear's Rest was sufficient. The tapestries and woven coverings on the beds and furniture made the space seem warm and snug. And Lily's company for the tour, while having matured as would be expected, felt blessedly familiar. Rose took a deep breath, and as she exhaled, the bulk of her nervousness fled. She missed her Veetrish family, but she had no doubt she would soon feel at home.

As she and Lily made their way back to the dining room, Rose paused to wonder how long her stay in this home would last . . . and if the legends of the Wood would be enough to keep the Cobelds away.

NINETEEN

The next year passed swiftly, and Rose, indeed, felt at home with Sir Drinius and his family. Gladiel had not stayed long after delivering Rose, but he made the occasional appearance, bringing bits of news and supplies, like fabric and spices, with him.

Happenings at the Bear's Rest were not the same lively sort Rose was used to in Veetri, but the members of the household were certainly industrious. Under Eneth's tutelage, Rose, Lily, and Alaine learned to garden from the abundance of seeds Drinius had brought from Stoen, and they also learned how to prepare simple meals, a task none of them had undertaken before. Rose often grew restless, but when Drinius learned of her proficiency with the dagger, he insisted she keep it up.

With the help of Walen, who had squired to a knight until a training accident took the thumb and two fingers from his sword arm, Rose fashioned men of straw to use as targets. Whenever the house seemed too confining, she escaped to practice marking them with the dagger.

Life moved at a steady if cloying pace, but practicing with her dagger and joining Drinius to exercise the horses gave Rose welcome and frequent breaks from the house-bound activities Aunt Alaine seemed determined she learn.

Having just returned from a ride with Sir Gladiel, who would soon leave again, Rose was running a curry comb over Stanza's hindquarters when her horse whinnied a greeting.

"Walen," she said without looking up, "as I've told you a hundred times, I like brushing Stanza. Now let me be."

"Rose."

"Uncle Drinius!" She laughed and turned. "I thought you were Walen, here to lecture me about doing his job."

He smiled, but it was weak. "A rider was here while you were out with Gladiel."

Rose reached a hand to her head. She still wore her woolen cap, but her hair was visible, plaited in a thick braid, hanging down her back. "Is he still here?" she whispered. She knew better than to be seen by anyone outside their small group.

"No. He didn't stay long." His lip twitched. "It seems he's not that fond of the Wood."

In the next stall, Gladiel chuckled. "What news, Drinius?"

"We've been summoned to Salderyn."

Rose blinked. "We have?" she asked at the same time Gladiel said, "All of us?"

Drinius shook his head. "Gladiel and I."

Rose gaped at her uncle. "You're leaving?" She hung up the curry comb and exited the stall.

He nodded, looking miserable.

"Ah, Rose." Gladiel stepped around the corner and wrinkled his nose. "You're safer in this wood than anywhere else in the world. Haven't I told you time and again?"

Drinius scowled. "I wish I were as confident as you, Gladiel. Or that we at least had some more ebonswarth powder."

"Well I certainly don't!" Rose vehemently shook her head, suppressing a shiver at the memory of the haunted faces of Lord Whittier's guards. "I don't ever want to be near that evil powder again."

"Walen will still be here," Gladiel said. "He has all the skills of a knight. Even with his weak arm, he's a force to be reckoned with."

"True, but it doesn't sit well that we should leave four defenseless women alone here in the Wood with only one man to protect them."

"I'm hardly defenseless." Rose lifted her chin.

"That's not the point, Rose! You don't know what sort of—"

"Drinius." Gladiel's voice stilled her uncle's tirade. "Friend." His tone softened. "I understand your reticence. I do. But we've been summoned. The Knight's Oath requires we obey."

"We've made other oaths, as well." Drinius ground the words through his teeth. "One does not undo the other."

"She'll be safe here. They all will."

Drinius pressed his lips together. "I don't like it."

"In truth, neither do I." Gladiel sighed.

"How long will you be away?" Rose asked.

The knights exchanged a look.

"We can't know for sure," Drinius hedged. "But I imagine we'll be back before the first sprouts in your garden come through the soil."

She groaned. "But we haven't even planted the seeds yet!"

"It's not a simple day's jaunt to Salderyn from here, Rose." Gladiel said. "We'll ride hard and be there in two weeks, maybe three if the weather turns bad again. After we attend to our business, whatever it may be, it will take the same amount of time to return."

"But what if someone finds us?"

"No one but me has sought the Bear's Rest since you arrived. Why would they now?"

Rose crossed her arms. "The messenger did!"

Gladiel's response was swift. Sure. "Only because he was sent."

"Well, what if he was followed?"

Gladiel laughed. "Who would brave the Bear-men and follow him into the Wood?"

"Errgh!" Rose growled. "You're impossible!"

"*Rose!*" Drinius's tone reminded her of Gladiel's status.

"My apologies, Your Grace." She ducked her head, but peeked at Gladiel out of the corner of her eye.

"Your apology is unnecessary, but I accept." He turned to Drinius. "We'll leave at first light, then?"

Drinius sighed. "Yes. We'll leave at first light."

TWENTY

The seeds sprouted and were eventually harvested, but the knights did not return. The trees began to turn and cooler weather descended upon the Wood. Just as they had during their first autumn at the Bear's Rest, Eneth, Alaine, Lily, and Rose picked, boiled, mashed, and preserved the apples and bright berries of the season. But neither Drinius nor Gladiel reappeared.

As had become her habit each evening, Rose paced between the window and the fireplace. With each step, her brow creased and her shoulders tensed a bit more. Something was wrong. She knew it in her bones. Something was dreadfully wrong. She stopped at the window. Caught by a twilight breeze, brittle leaves scattered and swirled over the dead, brown grass of the stable yard.

Rose lifted her eyes to the sky where a lone star bravely poked out from the dusky blue. "Where could they be?" she whispered.

Walen was in the barn, seeing to the evening chores. After clearing away the remnants of their simple meal, Eneth had appeared only to announce that the last of the leavening had been used in their dinner's bread, yet Lily and Alaine sat at the fire, knitting away as if the mittens they fashioned wouldn't be needed for years. Inwardly, Rose groaned. Did they not mark the change of the seasons, read the portents of the skies, or worry over Eneth's bleak announcement?

Rose paced again, her hands clenched at her side. Winter was coming and neither Gladiel nor Drinius had returned to bring them supplies. They had stored produce for the winter, but they had butchered the pig last spring. Walen had planned to get another when he rode for supplies. After the knights had returned.

But they hadn't returned. And the pork was gone.

They needed the cow for milk and the chickens for eggs. The hay was running low and the horses would need grain for feed to outlast the winter. Already, grazing was limited.

She stopped again at the window. "They should have been back months ago," she said.

"We'll be fine." Lily set her knitting aside and joined Rose at the window. "This waiting is not new for us. A knight's duty always comes first."

"He said he'd be back before summer. It's almost winter."

"When the King needs him elsewhere he must attend that first," Alaine spoke without breaking the rhythm of her needles. "Don't worry. He'll come back soon."

"Our food stores are nearly depleted."

"Walen is a good hunter and game in the Wood is plentiful," Lily reassured. "We have eggs from the chickens and milk from the cow. Don't worry, Rose. My father and Sir Gladiel would never leave us stranded."

"I'm sure they wouldn't mean to," Rose said. "But how are we to know if they even made it to Salderyn? Uncle Drinius promised to be back before your birthday last summer, Lily.

And now we're but weeks from mine. I could understand a little delay, but we've not had a word from him in nine months!"

"And who would get word to us, Rose?" Alaine asked. "Apart from your father, only Drinius and Gladiel know where we are."

The next evening the discussion repeated in the same fashion, but for the new, wet view from Rose's place at the window.

"Standing there every night isn't going to speed their journey home," Lily teased.

"I know." Rose sighed. "I'm afraid if I turn away, they'll appear through the trees and I will have missed it."

"Then by all means turn away!" Lily laughed.

Rose just smiled and resumed watching the rain. "It will only get worse," she said. "If the chill in the air is any indication of the season, I don't think it will stay just rain much longer. And once the snow comes we could be stranded. The animals' feed is getting low. I'll go myself before I allow the horses to starve."

"I forgot about feed for the animals." Lily sighed. "We can hardly expect for them to feed us if we don't feed them."

"Exactly." Rose angled her eyes upward. "The sky has the look of snow about it, don't you think? It even smells like snow."

"Really?" Lily laughed. "And what, dear cousin, does snow smell like?"

"Oh, you know." Rose shrugged, her eyes on the thick clouds above. "The air smells less of earth and more of air. It smells cold." Rose walked to the door, flung it open, and inhaled deeply through her nose. "Cold, clean, and," she said with a shiver, "heartless. Here, smell for yourself."

Lily took a long whiff. "I don't smell anything."

"Close the door, girls," Alaine scolded. "Our fire doesn't need to heat the stable yard as well as the house." She sighed. After several minutes with the clicking of knitting needles adding to the rapping of the rain, Alaine spoke. "I'm afraid there's nothing for it but to send Walen and Eneth for more supplies."

Lily's needles stilled. "It's beastly out there! And it's at least a four-day ride to the nearest village!"

Rose moved toward the fireplace. "I hate the thought of sending Eneth and Walen out in this weather," she said, "but it may only be a hint of what's to come."

"I will speak to them at dinner," Alaine said. "Rain or shine, they will depart in the morning."

But when the household arose the next morning, it was to a cloudless sky. Lily teased Rose about her dire weather prediction until the women stepped outside to bid the servants farewell. A thin crust of ice now topped the puddles left by yesterday's rain.

Rose and Lily took over Walen's chores while he was away. Their completion may not have been as precise, but none of the animals suffered for it. The kitchen became Alaine's responsibility, and even she seemed surprised on the rare occasions when the meals she prepared came out as good as Eneth's.

Eneth and Walen had been gone for a week when Rose was awakened in the middle of the night by a howling wind and the rapping of sleet against her window. Worried for the servants who had become so dear, Rose couldn't fall back asleep. Finally, she slipped her feet into woolen stockings, wrapped a blanket around her shoulders, and resumed her vigil at the front window.

"Dreadful weather, isn't it?"

With a little shriek, Rose spun toward the fireplace. "Aunt Alaine! I didn't see you there!"

"I'm sorry. I didn't mean to startle you." Alaine chuckled and scooted her chair closer to the fire. "I assumed you saw me when you came down the stairs."

"You couldn't sleep, either?"

"No." Alaine stared into the flames. "I awoke with the oddest feeling that someone was coming."

"Was it your Andoven gift?" Hope lit in Rose's chest.

"I thought so. At first. But now I'm not sure it wasn't just wishful thinking." She sighed. "I feel rather out of sorts tonight. I hoped it was Drinius, of course. I thought I'd wait here to welcome him." She sighed. "But it must have been a dream."

"Lily said you can always sense his approach." Rose moved to the opposite chair and tucked her feet beneath her. "She said that because your father was Andoven—"

"My father was only one-quarter Andoven," Alaine reminded her. "My own abilities are quite limited, I assure you. And Lily's blood is even more diluted than mine."

"But you can speak to each other without words," Rose said with a close following grin, "and if I remember correctly, Lily often gave my schemes away without knowing it when we were small."

Alaine chuckled. "Indeed. My gift may not be as impressive as some, certainly nothing so strong as your friend Koria's, but it is a comfort at times." She smiled. "As a child, you had a certain knack for finding trouble, dear one. If you'd been content to adventure alone it would have been much more difficult for me to curtail some of your more dangerous escapades. Since you almost always coerced Lily into joining you, I was able to intervene."

"Like when we lived at Argus Keep and I decided I would have a better chance of catching a falling star from the roof?"

"Oh, stop! How I've tried to forget that night!" Alaine laughed, but rubbed her arms as if they had been dusted with snow. "When I saw you scale that trellis, with Lily not far behind, I thought I would die from fear!"

"But you didn't. And I never did manage to catch a star, thanks to your Andoven interference." Rose tried to sound haughty, but failed miserably so she laughed instead.

"It was a blessing that you almost always ensnared Lily in your schemes. Because I could easily listen in to her thoughts I was able to more efficiently avert disaster." The words would have sounded harsh had they not been gentled by Alaine's affectionate smile. "A useful gift, but tonight I can't help but wish my Andoven blood was a tad thicker. Outside others of Andoven ancestry, Drinius is the only person whose approach I can identify with any certainty."

"Well, that is certainly more than I'll ever be able to do."

Alaine chuckled.

"What's so funny?"

Alaine sobered quickly. "Nothing." In an instant, the tone of her voice went from light to dark. "It is certainly *not* funny." When she didn't elaborate, Rose resumed her watch at the window.

"What a dreadful night!"

"Good fortune, Lily!" Rose squealed as she spun around toward the voice. "Where did you come from?"

Lily laughed. "I came from my bedroom, same as you."

"You're as stealthy as a Cobeld, you are!"

"Rose!" Alaine gasped. "Don't say such a thing!"

"She was only jesting, Mother. Rose wouldn't—"

"You must never, *never* compare anyone to one of those horrible creatures, Rose. Regardless of what liberties the Storytellers may take, I will *not* have that sort of language bandied about in my house. Do you understand?"

Rose swallowed hard and nodded. "I'm sorry, Aunt Alaine. And, Lily. Forgive me. I didn't mean to insult you."

"I know you didn't mean anything crude by it." Lily's tone was gentle. She joined Rose at the window. "It is nasty out there, isn't it? I can't imagine anyone could sleep through that racket. It's raining ice." She moved away from the window and took a seat on the footstool in front of her mother's chair. "Why don't you tell us a story, Rose?"

"You've heard all my stories."

"Then tell us one we already know. It will help to pass the—oh!" Lily was knocked from the footstool as Alaine sprang from her chair.

Rose rushed over to help Lily rise, but Alaine pushed past them both on her way to the window. "Are you all right?"

Lily nodded. "Do you think it's my father?" she whispered.

"I don't know." Rose whispered back. "I hope so."

"It's just one person, but it's not Drinius." Alaine glanced at the door and then toward the back of the house. Her eyes clouded with apprehension. "And it can't be Walen or Eneth. Not yet." She wrung her hands. "Whoever it is, they must need shelter from the storm."

"But . . . we're alone!" Lily whispered.

"The law of hospitality demands we invite the traveler in," Alaine said, her voice shaking.

"The law of hospitality?" Rose asked. "Is that a Stoenian law? It may not apply in this province."

"It is a law common to all nine provinces of E'veria," Lily explained. "You likely didn't hear it mentioned in Veetri since they have not the need for an enforceable edict. Hospitality comes naturally to the Veetrish."

"We must not divulge that there is not a man on the property,"Alaine said. "If necessary, we'll say he's gone to bed early . . . or is caring for the animals."

"You would have us lie?" Lily's voice held the incredulity Rose refrained from voicing. She could not imagine her aunt telling a lie.

"Deception is never a good choice," Alaine said. She looked at Rose, her gaze drenched in years. "But sometimes it is necessary to protect the ones we love." She looked back to the window. "If necessary, we will lie. Now," Alaine said as she moved toward the door, "you must do as I say. And quickly."

The girls nodded.

"Rose, move away from the windows. Put on your boots and cloak and pull the hood over your hair. As soon as you've done that, please go prepare the spare room off the kitchen for a guest. When that is done, go up to my room. The three of us will bed down together while the stranger is here."

"Shouldn't I prepare one of our rooms, then? They're better equipped for a guest."

Alaine's smile was weak. "I'm sure that is what Lord Whittier's family would do, were they in our predicament, but I do not relish the idea of a stranger that close to you girls. Now go, Rose. And do not allow yourself to be seen. You must stay hidden while our . . ." she paused, "while our *guest* is here."

"You want me to hide?" Rose was sure she had misunderstood.

"Yes. And make sure you have your dagger." Alaine twisted the ring on her finger. "I only hope you don't need it. Now go. And keep out of sight."

The look Rose gave her aunt was beyond incredulous. "I will not go and hide to leave you alone with a stranger in the house!" Rose folded her arms. "I am the only one of us who's been trained to use a dagger. I'm the best equipped to defend our home." Rose crossed her arms at her chest. "*You* go prepare the room, Aunt Alaine. Uncle Drinius would expect me to protect you."

Alaine spun around, her face bearing an expression so livid that Rose took a step back. "Drinius would expect no such thing!" Her cheeks flushed pink and her eyes narrowed on Rose. "Do not argue with me, child! There is too much that you do not know!"

At Alaine's outburst, Lily blanched and stumbled backward. Rose moved to steady her, but when Lily met her eyes, the look of sheer awe on her cousin's face was so disconcerting that she almost let Lily fall.

Lily stared at Rose. After a long silence, she spoke. "Go, Rose. Do as Mother says," she said weakly. "You . . . must."

"No. It's not—"

"Do as I say!" Alaine's fearful eyes bored into Rose's defiant glare. "And hurry!"

"Fine!" Rose grabbed her boots from their place by the fire and shoved her feet into them. "But be sure that I will not hesitate to come to your aid if I deem it necessary."

"Rose," Lily's eyes pled with her. "You *must* hide. We are in more danger if you *are* seen than if you are not."

"That's preposterous!"

"Think of the way you left Veetri!" Lily pleaded in a whisper. "Think of Lord and Lady Whittier."

Rose blanched. The Cobelds targeted Mirthan Hall because they thought she was there. She and her stupid red hair.

Her shoulders drooped. "I will stay out of sight," she said. But she would do everything she could to keep them safe.

Rose hurried to the guest room, opened the flue, and after several tries, managed to light the fire. She then lit the oil lamp that rested on the mantel and turned down the bed. She took a quick peek down the hall, only to find Lily and Alaine staring out at the storm.

Alaine turned. "Rose, your cloak! Cover your hair!"

Rose rushed to the kitchen, grabbed her cloak from the hook by the door, and put it on, still questioning the wisdom of her aunt's plan. After peeking down the hall to make sure Lily and Alaine weren't watching, she silently moved toward the kitchen's back door.

TWENTY-ONE

With one hand on the door knob, Rose slipped the other into the pocket of her cloak. Her fingers curled around her dagger's hilt and she silently thanked Lewys and Rowlen for seeing to it that she was proficient with the weapon. With renewed confidence, she pulled up the hood of her cloak and slipped out the back door.

The night was thick with heavy sleet that made the ground treacherous in the sloping yard. Rose inched her way around the side of the house, holding firmly to the hilt of her dagger. She was almost to the corner when her eye caught the light of the opening door reflected in the snow.

Rose moved around the corner of the lodge just into time to see a huge, beastly shadow rear up through the path of light.

A high-pitched gasp broke through the darkness as the form lurched toward Alaine. Rose's heart froze in her chest. But Alaine jumped back just in time to avoid being crushed. Her movement, however unintentional, bumped the door the rest of the way open and cleared the creature's path into the house.

Rose's dagger was up in an instant. She rushed forward, poised to throw, but just as she let the blade loose her right boot hit a patch of ice. Failing to find traction, she slipped on the frozen ground and lost her balance. The dagger left her grasp in that instant, its aim skewed by her sudden fall.

Sprawling sideways across the layer of ice that covered the yard, Rose watched in horror as the dagger grazed the assailant's forearm and just missed impaling Alaine's shoulder before imbedding itself in the doorframe.

The creature collapsed. What was it? A bear that hadn't yet found its place to sleep for the winter?

The corner of the front porch finally stopped Rose's slippery passage, but the impact jarred her shoulder and sent her sprawling to her backside.

"Is that you, Rose?"

"Uh-huh."

"I told you to hide!" Alaine scolded. "What are you doing out there?"

"Protecting you!" Rose cried. "Now stay back from that animal! It could hurt you!"

Grasping the porch's railing, Rose awkwardly gained her feet and moved as quickly up the steps as the sleet and ice would allow.

Collapsed in a heap, half-in and half-out of the house, the giant creature did not move, but she didn't know what it was, and therefore, didn't trust it. With a stealthy motion she hoped her aunt would not see, Rose pulled her dagger from the doorframe.

"Help us get him in the house, Rose."

"Get him in the house? No!" she cried as Alaine and Lily knelt at the creature's side. "Are you out of your minds? We can't possibly take a bear into the—"

Rose stopped short as her gaze travelled the length of the creature. She tilted her head. "Is this animal wearing . . ." she paused and blinked several times, "boots?"

Lily braced her feet and tugged one of the creature's arms, each syllable coming forth as more of a grunt than a word, "It's. Not. A. Bear."

If the situation had not been so ridiculously dangerous, Rose would have been tempted to laugh at the sight of her petite aunt and cousin so ineffectively pouring their full strength into moving the hulking lump of strangely booted fur.

"A little, *ugh*, help, please?" Lily grunted.

"Oh. Oh!" Rose knelt near the back of the creature. She gripped the dark brown fur with passing wonder at whether Rowlen's story about the Bear-men of Mynissbyr was, in fact, more accurate than Ayden's.

At her first shove, the heap of fur groaned what sounded like human speech but quieted at Alaine's gentle words. "It is all right now, you are safe. There are no Cobelds here, sir."

"*Cobelds*?!" Rose dropped the leg she was holding with a thud that produced another groan.

"Rose, please. A little care." An annoyed glance from her aunt propelled Rose back into action. Finally, the three women were able to get the gargantuan pile of fur into the house.

Rose's estimation of a bear at the door had not been far off. The man wore a huge bearskin cloak. Its hood was the head of the animal, complete with bared fangs and open eyes. Tiny icicles hung from the animal's useless ears and snout, making a mess of the floor as they melted within the warmth of the old lodge. Beneath the bearskin cloak he wore several other lighter layers, which made him seem even larger than he probably was. But one look at the stranger's face revealed a fur-like beard that contrasted golden against the brown fur of the bearskin, and it was clear he was, after all, human.

"Look at his scabbard!" Alaine gasped. "It carries the King's seal."

"He's a knight," Lily whispered. "He may have information about why Father has been delayed. Oh!" She pointed to his arm. "Mother, he's bleeding! Rose, help me apply pressure to the wound."

He's a knight? Guilt stained Rose's cheeks at the evidence of her dagger's path.

She pulled the cloak's hood from her head so she could better assist her cousin, tossing her unbound copper hair over one shoulder to get it out of the way.

If I hadn't slipped on the ice, she thought as she pressed the hem of her cloak against the wound, *I might have killed a knight!*

Aunt Alaine knelt next to the knight and gently touched his swollen and heavily bearded face. "You are among friends, sir. Open your eyes."

The knight's eyelids fluttered, but closed before focusing.

"Sir," Alaine continued, "as limited as our resources may be, we would offer you protection this night. But you must rouse yourself enough that we might move you without causing further injury."

The knight's eyes squeezed tightly shut, opened, and repeated the exercise several times. As his vision focused, he looked directly at Rose.

"How can it be that I am with you?" His voice was deep and raspy, as if he had been out in the cold for a very long time. Confusion clouded his features. "Is this a dream?"

Rose opened her mouth to speak, but her voice was arrested by the brilliant emerald hue of his eyes. The knight blinked again and his eyes cleared.

The shade of his eyes was a green so darkly brilliant that it could rival any shade of that color found in the Wood. *Beautiful.* The intensity of the trust on his face made it appear as if he had known her his whole life and was quite comfortable in her presence.

And indeed, Rose puzzled, there was something familiar about this knight. But she was quite sure she had never laid eyes on him before. If he was indeed a knight, and therefore no danger to them, why, then, did her stomach lurch so and her breath come faster to be caught in his gaze?

"I am dead, then?" He held Rose's gaze, speaking as if the prospect of death held no fear for him. "Did the Cobelds finish me?"

"You're not dead," she said finally and almost laughed. A sharp glance from her aunt stilled the bubble of sound from escaping. "Sir, if you are being pursued we cannot guarantee your life will not yet be forfeit." She frowned. "And if you are, in fact, being pursued by Cobelds, you have put us all in danger."

"Rose!"

"Honestly, Lily, it's the truth!"

"It is," Alaine agreed. "We must get him inside and out of sight."

Rose looked down and realized she held his hand, but his eyes never left her face. He seemed coherent enough to follow directions, but little more than that.

"Sir, I am passing tall, but I can't carry your weight myself and my friends do not share my height. I fear transporting you shall be quite awkward."

"My apologies, my lady."

"Are you able to stand at all?"

The knight gave a pained nod. "I am weak, but I will try."

Each movement evidenced his pain. With some effort he rolled to his side, and after a few moments, finally to his hands and knees.

"Lily." Rose locked an arm beneath his shoulder and motioned her cousin to do the same. Finally, the knight stood. "Lean on me," she said. "I'm more able to bear your weight."

With the cloak removed the knight was not nearly so monstrous. Although he was quite tall—at least as tall as Sir Gladiel in Rose's quick estimation—he was not as gigantic as he had looked with the bear's head resting atop his own. Suddenly, his body sagged.

"Stay with me." Rose placed his arm around her neck, her shoulder under his shoulder, and her arm about his waist. His steps slowed as his head lolled, then snapped back up. "You can do it," she said. "Just a little bit further, now."

While Lily and Rose were coaxing the knight to stand, Alaine lit another lamp and moved down the hall.

"I'll put a kettle to boil," Alaine said, moving to do just that.

Lily helped Rose guide the knight onto the one small bed in the room.

"It's cold now, but it's a small space and should warm quickly once we shut the door."

Lily nodded. "I think he's unconscious."

"It's probably just as well." Alaine sighed as she returned and hung a kettle over the fire. "Lily, Rose, stand watch in the hall while I check him for further injuries."

"He is ill. Feverish," Alaine said when she called the girls back in. "And I fear he may have suffered frostbite in addition to the more *recent* injury he's suffered."

"It was an accident, I didn't mean—"

"We should be glad your dagger did not hit the target it was meant for! Had you hit your mark you might have been tried for treason."

"Treason?" The word squeaked from Rose's throat. It didn't seem that long ago that the same charge had come forth from Koria's lips.

"This knight wears the emblem of King Jarryn," Lily said as she set a pitcher of water on a small table in the opposite corner from the bed. "To murder a knight of E'veria is an act of treason punishable by death." She placed her hand upon Rose's arm and gave her a small smile. "Thank Rynloeft your knife did not hit its target."

"We will take turns sitting with him," Alaine said. "I am sure he means us no harm."

"But—"

"I am going to take the first watch with him. I will shut the door to keep the heat from the fire within. Check in with me every hour."

"Two should stay in here."

"And leave only one person to watch from the front room? I think not, Rose." Alaine gave a stiff smile. "You and Lily keep watch together. And dear?"

"Yes?"

"Keep your hood over your hair and don't go outside again." With that, she shut the door.

Rose sent a glare through the door and stood thus for several minutes, seething.

At dawn, Lily took her mother's place and Rose fought sleep while Alaine dozed in her chair by the fire. That evening, it was Rose who sat by the knight's side. Lily and Alaine remained in the main room, but neither made a pretense of trying to stay awake. The threat that had seemed so imminent the night before had waned over the course of the uneventful day.

Rose startled when the knight groaned. She must have fallen asleep. She rose from her chair and laid her hand upon his forehead. Still feverish. Again he groaned, this time reaching his right hand toward the wound on his left arm, but he didn't regain consciousness.

Guilt assailed Rose. She had thrown the knife in hopes of protecting her aunt, but her motive didn't matter. She had injured an innocent man. A knight! And now his very life was her responsibility. She had to gather her wits. She had to ensure that he lived.

Rose's hands shook as she lifted the blood-soaked fabric Aunt Alaine had wrapped around the dagger wound. The wound was near enough the knight's elbow to ensure a painful recovery. Luckily, the cut was not terribly deep. Although it would be an uncomfortable process, healing should be swift if Rose could keep infection at bay.

But his skin was hot. So hot! Fever, too, could put him in death's grasp. Whatever illness or injury had weakened him before his arrival, it could not be allowed to claim his life.

Rose chastised herself as she gathered the items needed to clean and re-dress the knight's wound. If not for that fortuitous patch of ice, her strong will would have resulted in a more terrible outcome for the knight.

And a death sentence for her.

"Forgive me," she whispered. "I'm so sorry I hurt you."

The room was warm, but still the knight shivered. Rose pulled all the quilts from the foot of the bed and covered the knight, then added another log to the fire. She hung a kettle to heat. Even if the knight was not conscious enough to partake, Rose would certainly appreciate imbibing something warm before attempting to pass the rest of the night on the hard wooden floor.

As the two separate concoctions brewed, one medicinal, one not, Rose watched the knight. "Who are you?" she whispered. "Why are you here?" Other than an occasional grimace and the subtle rise and fall of the blankets at his broad chest, however, he gave no answer.

When the tea cooled just a touch, she soaked a clean bit of bandage and squeezed the liquid through his lips a bit at a time. Though he wasn't conscious, he seemed to swallow, at least intermittently, and she had some hope that the herbs' medicinal properties would soothe his fever and his pain. By the time his tea was gone her own had grown cold, but she drank it anyway and curled up in the chair.

Rose tried to close her eyes, but sleep eluded her. *Who was this knight? What brought him here? Did he know what dire thing had kept Drinius and Gladiel from returning to them?* Her stomach clenched, rebelling at the tepid tea and the thought of what the knight might have met on his way to them. *He mentioned Cobelds.* Were they, even now, on their way to the Bear's Rest?

And if he had been sent to the Bear's Rest, why?

Questions jumbled in her mind one over top the next. At some point Rose fell asleep, but a ragged moan from the knight sent her scrambling to her feet as if she hadn't even closed her eyes.

She put a hand to his cheek. If anything, the knight's fever had risen.

"I have to cool you down," she said. He shuddered as Rose ripped the blankets off. "I'm sorry. Forgive me, but I must let the heat escape."

As she placed a cool, damp cloth on his forehead, he flinched away. She persisted and finally he was too weak to fight. But it was then he began to speak. Just a jumble of syllables at first, but out of his delirium Rose caught one coherent phrase that erased any lingering doubt that he might be an enemy in disguise. She had heard Uncle Drinius, as well as Sir Gladiel, speak the same words with reverence in response to their duty as knights. She couldn't hear the solemn oath from this man and remain in fear of him.

"With all that I am," the knight mumbled, "and for all of my life."

TWENTY-TWO

After hearing him speak the Knight's Oath, Rose decided that the Bear-knight, as she had begun to call him in her mind, was likely a man of her uncle's acquaintance. The thick covering of his lustrous golden beard couldn't hide that this knight was quite a bit younger than Drinius or Gladiel, but perhaps they had served together at some point, somewhere.

Exhaustion pulled as Rose caught only spare snatches of sleep between the Bear-knight's bouts of fevered restlessness. In the moments when he was still, Rose dripped medicinal tea down his throat, and when the thrashing began again, she held his hand and spoke soft words while trying to keep him as still as possible.

Time stretched. Days passed. The women sat with him in shifts, engaging in the repetitive procedures of caring for the man and his wounds. Little by little, signs of healing became evident. No visible infection had taken root, yet he remained feverish, and for the most part, unconscious.

Rose gauged the hours she spent at his side by the amount of time the medicines took to wear off, and the Bear-knight resumed his fevered mumblings. When he was quiet, she filled the silence with stories she had seen Lord Whittier and Rowlen perform in Veetri, closing her eyes as she spoke and imagining the translucent Story People dancing across Rowlen's hand.

How he would laugh, her brother, if he saw her now, playing both nurse and Storyteller to a sleeping stranger. How he would tease her for slipping on the ice and nearly killing a knight.

Rose sighed. She would welcome Rowlen's teasing if he was here, helping her pass these hours.

"Mother and I fed the livestock," Lily whispered when she arrived to relieve Rose's vigil. Ever since the Bear-knight had arrived, Alaine had forbidden Rose from leaving the house.

Rose nodded. "And the knight's horse?"

"Not as fearsome as I first thought," Lily smiled. "He's a giant of a beast, but as gentle as a lamb."

"Do you think Aunt Alaine would let me go out and see him?"

Lily's expression was compassionate, but her words, unfortunately, were all too sure. "No. She doesn't want you outside the house. Just in case."

Rose pressed her lips together in frustration, nodded, and silently left the room. Her joints were stiff from the hours of inactivity. What she wouldn't give for a breath of fresh air, even if the air's freshness was marred by the chore of mucking out a horse's stall.

To keep her mind from lingering on her captivity, Rose took it upon herself to inventory their ever-dwindling supplies. Thankfully, there was kindling enough by the kitchen door to last a few more days without making a trip to the woodpile, but their cache of bread wouldn't last the day, and should the Bear-knight wake up, he would need to eat something gentler than bread.

"We need broth," Rose said, neither expecting nor receiving a reply.

"Has the knight awakened?"

Thinking she was alone, Rose jumped at Alaine's question. "No," she said when she caught her breath. "But when he does he'll need the sort of food an invalid might eat, won't he?"

Alaine nodded, her expression worried. "I have no idea how to butcher a chicken."

Rose shuddered. "Neither do I. And I don't intend to learn. What if we soaked a bit of the dried venison in water? Could it make a broth?"

"Perhaps." Alaine nodded. "Why don't you lie down and I'll experiment a bit." She sighed. "I never thought of myself as ignorant until the day Eneth and Walen left. If I ever get back to Stoen I will never again take our servants for granted."

Rose couldn't help the grin that pulled at her cheeks when Alaine reached for Eneth's ample apron and wrapped it around her middle—twice. "I do wonder what your friends at court would say if they saw you now!"

"I daresay they wouldn't even recognize me."

Feeling a tinge of responsibility for her aunt's melancholy tone, Rose turned away and went upstairs to her room.

———

"Rose?"

She startled awake at Lily's voice and bolted upright. The sun was bright in her window, her days and nights confused by the strange hours of caring for the sick.

"I'm sorry to wake you. Would you like me to take your shift with the knight so you can sleep?"

"Is it my turn already?"

Lily nodded. "But I don't mind."

"No, I'll go. Unless you'd rather I do the barn chores, of course."

A smile infected her cousin's words. "I know you'd rather, but Mother is quite insistent that you stay indoors."

Rose sighed and looked down to realize she hadn't even removed her shoes. "Has there been any change?"

"Not yet."

Rose bit her lip. "How long can one sustain a fever like that?"

Lily shook her head. "I don't know. I've prepared a medicinal tea for him, if you'd like to try to administer it."

"It hasn't seemed to make a difference yet, but we might as well."

Rose had little luck getting the knight to take the tea. Most of it ran through his beard. She used a damp cloth to wash his brow and sat at his side, willing him to awaken, entertaining herself with more of Rowlen's stories. Hours later, she brewed a fresh pot and began the process again.

This time, however, as she was attempting to drip the tea into the knight's mouth, his eyes blinked several times and then opened. Without warning, he grabbed at Rose's wrist, spilling the remaining tea on to her skirt.

"Please. No more. I need . . . wake up," he groaned. "Please. I don't want . . . to be . . . ugh." The fight left him with a shiver.

Rose felt his forehead. Where before it had been hot and dry, it was now cool and sweaty. Finally, his fever had broken. Setting the cup aside, Rose allowed herself to smile for the first time since she had entered the room.

When he awakened, he would need food. Something simple. A broth, perhaps, as she and Alaine had discussed. She went to the kitchen, but found that whatever Alaine had prepared in her experimentation had either been consumed or thrown out.

Rose unwrapped a portion of dried venison and put it in a pot. She reached for the pitcher of water, but there wasn't even enough left to brew one pot of tea. Rose groaned. It would be so easy to run to the stream and fill the pitcher. But she wasn't allowed outdoors.

With a huff, she set down the pitcher. She would have to send someone else.

Alaine was sound asleep upstairs, but Lily was nowhere to be found. Rose went to the window and scowled out toward the barn. Could she be tending the animals? Or had she taken a different pitcher the stream? If so, what was taking so long? Frustrated, Rose returned to the Bear-knight's side.

Several times over the next few hours, Rose went in search of Lily, to no avail. She knew the chores could take awhile, but this seemed excessive. Alaine still slept, even snoring the daintiest little bit, which made Rose worry that her aunt might be coming down with something. She didn't want to wake her, even when Lily's absence became so glaring that Rose worried for her cousin's safety.

Rose paced at the Bear-knight's side. If Lily was in danger, what could Alaine do? Nothing. She may be improving in the kitchen, but Alaine was hardly able to thwart a villain by boiling an egg. And Lily was nearly as helpless. Neither could mark the dagger. Neither had been brought up with brothers bent on teaching them to defend themselves.

But Rose had.

Rose looked at the Bear-knight. His color had returned, but without the flush of fever. Now he simply seemed to sleep. She knelt by his side and took his hand.

"I must go check on my cousin," she said. His eyes fluttered. "If you can hear me, if you understand me, can you tell me somehow?"

He opened his mouth, but no sound came out. His brow contracted as if he was trying to open his eyes, but couldn't.

Rose decided to believe he was responding to her voice. "My aunt is asleep upstairs and my cousin has been outside too long. I'm worried about her. I think she might have gone down to the stream."

When she said that, a dozen possible reasons for Lily's delay careened through her imagination—and none of them good. Had Lily slipped and fallen into the icy water? Had she tried to cross the stream and been caught by a current? Had she tripped over a root and even now was sitting in the cold snow, unable to walk back to the house? Had she met up with an enemy? Or had she simply become distracted by the Bear-knight's giant, gentle horse?

"Use . . . care, my . . . lady."

Rose gasped when the Bear-knight spoke. "You're awake?"

His eyes fluttered, then opened completely, capturing Rose in their brilliant, but watery green depths. He blinked as if his vision was blurred. "I'm not . . . sure. Where am I?"

"This is an old hunting lodge. It's called the Bear's Rest."

"I'm in the Great Wood?"

Rose smiled. "It's not as bad as the stories make it out to be."

"This I know." He smiled and closed his eyes again. "Still, there may be enemies about. Use caution, Lady . . . ?" He left the phrase dangling, as if hoping she would fill it.

"I'm Rose," she said.

"Lady Rose. I'm . . . Julien." The word came out as if forced. He winced and reached toward his arm. The arm Rose's dagger had torn.

"You're in pain. I'm sorry." Rose bit her lip. "You are a knight, aren't you?"

"Yes." He opened his eyes.

Rose's own eyes slid shut and she sent another word of thanks to Rynloeft that he had survived her dagger. "Please forgive me, Sir Julien, but I really must see to my cousin."

"Wait. I'll go—"

But before she could give it a second thought, Rose rushed from the room, grabbed her cloak from the peg by the back door, and put it on. She would check the stream first. If Lily had come to harm near or in the water, every second mattered. And since she was going that way, she might as well refill their water. Pitcher in hand, she slipped out the door.

Rose inhaled the fresh air and realized at once just how stale the air inside had become. The coolness of the breeze invigorated her spirit, renewing her energy. With each step closer to the stream, her hope that Lily was all right became surer.

Rose made a wide path up the stream and back, narrowing her search closer and closer to the water with each pass, but there was no sign of Lily but a few dainty footprints in the snow, going both to and from the stream. Frustrated but hopeful, she took off her mittens and knelt next to the water, cupping her hands to drink. Lily must have gotten distracted in the barn. Perhaps the cat had finally had those kittens Lily had been so anxious to see. That would explain her absence better than any sort of accident or act of an enemy.

Besides, Rose reminded herself, Alaine and Lily were part Andoven, and as mother and daughter, closely connected.

If Lily had come to harm, surely Aunt Alaine would have known, even in sleep.

With that realization, Rose relaxed. Lily was fine. She had to be.

The water was so cold that it made her hands ache, but the fresh taste more than made up for it. A beam of sunlight broke through the trees and warmth seeped through the hood of her cloak. Rose lowered her hood and lifted her face to the sun's caress. Closing her eyes, she basked in its warmth.

After a moment, she sighed and set about her task, dipping fresh water from the stream to fill the pitcher. Rose had just finished that job when a low, muffled cry sounded on the other side of the stream.

Rose closed her right hand around the hilt of her dagger and swung toward the sound. A slight movement beside a fallen log caught her eye. As she cautiously moved forward, Rose let out a sigh of relief. It was just an old man.

He was a hermit, most likely out hunting, one of the few brave souls who called the Great Wood their home. Harmless.

"Hello?"

Intent on some task involving a large fallen tree, the old man made no response to indicate that he had heard her. He did appear to be quite old. Perhaps he was deaf.

"Sir?" she said a bit louder. "Pardon me, sir," she nearly shouted. "Do you need help?"

The old man turned his head and . . . screamed.

Rose jumped and emitted a small yelp of her own.

"I didn't mean to startle you," she said. "Can I be of some help?"

"You are from . . . Veetri?"

"Yes."

The old hermit's accent was as strange to Rose as hers must have sounded to him in the middle of the Great Wood of Mynissbyr, but she was not well-traveled and her own speech was a perfect example of how many dialects prospered in the Kingdom of E'veria.

"Are you far from home as well?" she asked.

"Not so far as I don't know my way back."

"Oh."

A hermit, then, she decided. *And an ill-mannered one at that,* she thought when he added, "And for someone who offers help you're rather slow at providing it. At this rate I'll die in my old age before I see my home again."

"What do you need me to do?"

"Can't you see, stupid girl? My beard is stuck in this log!"

Rose ground her teeth to keep from replying with a matching insult. After all, a hermit had no need to develop great social skills. But she had been raised to be mannerly, and she had no excuse to be unkind.

"I'll find a place to cross and have a look."

Rose replaced the dagger in her pocket and pulled her mittens back on as she moved upstream. A slight drop in the stream left a few rocks protruding, and if she was careful, she could cross without getting her boots wet.

But for a near-slip on one of the rocks, Rose made it swiftly across the stream. She hurried over to the old man to examine his predicament.

The tip of his beard had been caught in a jagged crevice in the bark of a fallen log. By the look of things, he had been struggling to free himself for quite some time.

"Oh, you poor dear. Have you been here a while?"

"Long enough," he grumbled.

She pulled her dagger back out. "I'll have you free in a trice." she said. "Now hold still, if you will. I'll just trim that end piece off and you can be on your way."

"No you will not! I've spent my *lifetime* growing this beard!"

"It is just the tip," she said. "One swift pass of my knife and you'll be on your way."

"Do not cut my beard!"

The old man's vehemently hissed words made the hairs on Rose's neck tingle. She took a small step back. When she spoke again, she chose her words carefully.

"Are you one of the hermits of the Great Wood, sir? Or is your home further away?"

The old man's eyes narrowed. "What does it matter? I'll likely die attached to this log for all the help you're giving."

"It matters," Rose said, "because there are rumors of Cobelds in the Wood. And you, sir, have a rather unnatural attachment to that scraggly old beard of yours."

"Do I look like one of those Cobeld goblins?" Even with the growly accent his tone was layered with offense

A picture from Rowlen's tale of Lady Anya sprung to mind. "Well, no, but—"

"Didn't your mother teach you to respect your elders? To call someone a Cobeld is the greatest insult one E'verian can give another!"

A flush heated her cheeks. "My apologies, sir," she said. "But these are dangerous times. I meant no offense." She knelt by the log. "Please, let me cut just this little bit off your beard and we can part as friends."

"NO!"

Rose flinched, but her patience had met its end. "I daresay it will grow back," she snapped. "Now be still and I will cut it quickly so we can be done with it!"

He made a strangled sound and screamed at her. "Step away!"

"I have obligations I must return to," she said in a clipped voice. She'd already been gone longer than intended and had yet to locate Lily. She needed to get to the barn and make sure her cousin was safe before heading back to the Bear-knight—Sir Julien, rather—before Aunt Alaine awoke and panicked to find her gone.

"My honor will not allow me to leave you here to freeze or starve to death simply because you caught your ridiculous beard in a log! If you don't want me to cut it, what *exactly* do you suggest I do to help?"

She rose and walked around the log, stepping directly in his line of sight, making eye contact for the first time. "Well?"

"You could pull it out." His voice trembled, but something in the way his black eyes contracted as they connected with hers sent a shiver down her spine.

Ridiculous. Rose shook off the feeling. *He's just a poor old hermit. He's just scared. Like everyone else in E'veria.*

"I mean you no harm." She gave him a kind smile. "I would help if you'll let me."

"I'm an old man, and as you said, these are dangerous times." He gave a little cough. "Pardon me. Dry throat." He reached for the flask strapped at his waist. "I've been stuck here for some time and have worked up quite a thirst."

He uncorked the top and looked inside. "Ah. Just enough."

"I could refill it for you at the stream if you—"

"No!" He coughed. "Ah, thank you, but no. You're young and strong. Now why don't you try to pull on my beard and see if it comes loose."

The old man took a sip from his flask and whispered something under his breath.

"Pardon?" Rose paused.

He shook his head and gestured for her to continue.

Rose grabbed hold of his beard and tugged, but her mitten slipped and she lost her balance. She fell hard into the snow.

"That won't do, silly girl." His scathing tone returned. "You must use your bare hands to get a proper grip!"

Rose brushed the snow off of her backside. The return of his nasty temperament irritated her, but she conceded that he was right. Her hands were still a little numb from the cold water and she hated to take her woolen mittens off again, but if it would free the surly old hermit and get her back inside before Aunt Alaine found out she was gone, she supposed she could stand the cold.

Rose pulled off her mitten and tossed it on the ground.

The old man smiled. "There, now. That will do nicely."

Rose reached for his beard.

The blurred flight of a dagger just missed Rose's bare hand. A sound like that of a cat's claws sliding down a metal shield rent the air as the weapon cut through the old man's beard and impaled his throat.

Rose gasped and jumped back as the old man collapsed, dead upon the log. She spun around, pulling her own dagger from her pocket.

"Show yourself!" Rose stood, her hand poised to throw her dagger into the unknown assailant's heart. "What sort of villain are you, to kill a helpless old man?"

The first thing she saw was the bear's mouth, open as if in mid-roar. But just as her gaze lowered to the familiar human face directly beneath it, the Bear-knight collapsed, revealing Lily behind him, her face as white as the snow.

TWENTY-THREE

The dagger slid from Rose's fingers. "Lily?"

"How could you be so foolish?" Lily hissed as she knelt beside Sir Julien. "You could have been killed!"

"Me?" Rose blinked. "*Me?!* Lily, what's *wrong* with you? Sir Julien just murdered an innocent old man!" Rose's hand tingled in the cold bite of the winter air. She reached for her mitten.

"Stop!" Lily shouted. "Don't move. I'm coming over there."

Rose put her hands up and took a step back. "But my hands are freezing!"

"Please, Lady Rose," Sir Julien called, his voice gruff from disuse. "Listen to her."

The shock of the moment combined with Rose's frustration and her worry for her cousin's welfare. Hot, angry tears pooled in her eyes as she watched Lily navigate the same rocks she had moments ago.

"Rose." Lily approached her slowly, her glance straying to the old man. "Did your mitten touch his beard?"

"Well, yes. But his beard was stuck in the log, Lily! He wouldn't let me cut it and my mittens were slippery so I took them off and then he—" She hiccupped and then pointed at Sir Julien. "He *killed* the poor man!"

"Rose." Lily placed her hand gently on her cousin's shoulder. "That isn't some hermit of the Wood. And he certainly isn't some innocent old man. That is a Cobeld. And if Sir Julien hadn't been able to rouse when he did," a shudder moved through her delicate frame, "that Cobeld would have killed *you!*"

Rose glanced at the old man and then looked away from the gruesome sight. "He's a . . . Cobeld? But aren't they all wrinkly and green and—"

"No. That's the Storyteller's version." Lily shook her head. "I can't believe my father and Sir Gladiel never told you what to look for."

Rose sank down into the snow, not even feeling the cold as it seeped through her cloak.

"There could be hairs from his beard on your mitten, Rose," Lily said softly. "If you touch one of them you could die."

"What should we do with it?"

A shadow fell between them. Rose looked up to see her aunt's tear-streaked face.

"*You* aren't going to do anything but help Sir Julien back into the house." Alaine's voice shook with a combination of relief and anger. "When I awoke and found the house empty—" Her voice broke off in a little sob. She closed her eyes and took a breath.

"I'm sorry. I couldn't find Lily and I was worried about her."

"You should have awakened me!"

Rose could have argued her reasons for letting her aunt sleep, but instead she looked down at the ground. "I'm sorry."

Alaine took a deep breath. "Girls, you may return to the house. I will burn the mitten and join you shortly."

"But what if there are more of them?"

"We will pray there are not."

Rose shivered. "I'll help you. You shouldn't be alone out here."

"And you shouldn't be out here at all."

"Come on, Rose," Lily urged. "Sir Julien is weak. I need your help to get him inside."

"Return to the house and care for the knight," Alaine ordered. "He may be our only hope to get out of Mynissbyr alive." Her proclamation sent a chill through Rose's blood that was warmed by shame when she added, "And Rose? Do *not* leave the house again!"

Rose wiped her face and made her way back across the stream, Lily close behind. Sir Julien had lifted himself into a sitting position and sat propped against a tree, his eyes closed.

"Sir Julien?" Rose whispered.

Slowly, as if it took some effort, he opened his eyes. As they lit on her hair and then searched her face, they widened and then narrowed as if confused. "Your name is . . . Rose?"

The way he asked was almost as if he wanted to argue, as if he knew her, at least on some level, but by a different name.

"Yes." Perhaps he was thinking of whoever he had mistaken her for on the night of his arrival. "Can you stand?"

He gave a nod, retracted his knees, and pressed up to a standing position, using the tree for support. Rose and Lily moved to either side of the knight and together they trudged toward the Bear's Rest.

Once they had settled the exhausted knight in his bed, Lily went to retrieve the pitcher Rose had left by the stream and to see if her mother needed any assistance, leaving Rose and Sir Julien alone.

They stared at each other for many long moments, until the space between his blinks seemed to herald that sleep would soon claim him.

Rose swallowed. "Thank you for saving my life," she whispered.

His eyes opened again. "I'm glad to have gotten there in time." His eyes closed, but he spoke. "Lady Drinius is your aunt?"

"Yes."

Her answer seemed to trouble him, but his brow soon relaxed and she knew he was asleep.

With Sir Julien comfortably situated, Rose moved to put another log on the fire. She glanced at the knight. His eyes were closed, but he reached for his left arm and winced when his hand touched the bandage.

"It would seem I've acquired wounds with no memory of how they came to be," he said.

Heat prickled along Rose's scalp. "You were quite ill when you arrived." How could she admit the origin of that particular wound? *Better to wait,* she thought. *Talk of something else.*

"What brought you to the Wood?" she asked, trying to avoid the topic of her guilt. "We don't get many visitors."

"I was searching for my father. And . . . your uncle, as it turns out."

"You know my uncle?" Of course he did. He had already referred to Aunt Alaine by her title.

"Indeed. I've known Sir Drinius all my life."

Rose hung the kettle above the fire. "And your father is . . . ?"

"Gladiel de Vonsar."

If the kettle hadn't already been attached to the spit, she would have dropped it in the flames.

"Of course!" Rose silently called herself every kind of fool. "I should have known. Your eyes are the same green as his. Not that I've had the opportunity to see them open much, of course." She turned around to find those emerald eyes upon her. "Now that you're awake, however I—"

Her voice stilled at the look on the knight's face. "What is it, Sir Julien? Are you in pain?"

His eyelids drooped. "I thought it was a dream."

"You thought what was a dream?"

When he didn't answer, Rose moved toward the bed. "Asleep again," she whispered. A stray curl had fallen over his forehead. She brushed it back before it would have a chance to tickle his eyelashes open.

Oh, but his hair was beautiful. She had not considered it such while she cared for him. In truth, she hadn't considered it at all. But now that the fever had broken, now that she had spoken to him and learned his name . . . indeed, now that he had saved her life . . . she wondered why she hadn't noticed it before. Although it was matted from several days' and nights' tossing and turning and would benefit from a thorough washing, Sir Julien's hair was a beautiful shade of burnished blond, almost as if one of Rynloeft's messengers had dipped a comb in liquid gold and sent it through a baby Julien's curls just as he entered the world.

Her eyes traced the path of his strong jaw and tried to imagine what he might look like with less of that golden hair on his face. She stopped short of touching his face again, but her hand lingered just above his cheek for a long moment.

Though she didn't doubt his word, a part of her could hardly believe he was the Regent's son. Whereas Gladiel's eyes were widely set on a rectangular face with sharp angles, Julien's strong chin was the rounded point of a gentler oval. His forehead was narrower than his black-haired father's and his cheekbones were set at such an angle that she wondered if his cheeks would dimple when he smiled. Rose searched Julien's face for a feature to betray his relation to Gladiel, but with his eyes closed there was none, save the impressive height and muscular build that had made it so difficult for her and Lily to transport him.

As the events of the past few days, especially the last few hours, crowded in, fatigue descended upon Rose with the swiftness of a brass snuffer to a flame. With a sigh, Rose took off her boots and curled up in the chair to sleep.

TWENTY-FOUR

The crackling of the fire broke through Rose's dreams. Without opening her eyes, she listened as another spark popped and the pieces of kindling shifted. It was a normal, homey, comforting sound. She reveled in its commonness until the crick in her neck intruded. Yawning, she stretched, savoring the warmth of not-quite-wakefulness.

"Good morning, Lady Rose."

"Oh!" She startled violently at the deep voice. Her eyes flew open. "Ow." Rose wrinkled her nose at the tightness in her neck. She rubbed at the sharp pain and, as the cramp released, she regained her composure. The light from the fire was stronger than that from the window. "It's morning?"

"Evening, actually." At some point a second chair had been brought in and placed opposite hers and it was now occupied by Sir Julien. His smile had a hint of teasing at its corners. "But it's the common phrase used when people awaken, so I thought it appropriate."

"Oh." She tried to straighten in her chair, but groaned when the crick in her neck protested again. "Did you sleep well this afternoon?"

"Better than you, I fear." One corner of his mouth slid further up, but the beard was too thick on his cheeks to reveal a dimple. "I'm afraid, my lady, that you have not seen me at my chivalrous best."

Rose laughed and arched an eyebrow. "Perhaps chivalry is defined differently where you come from? You did, in fact, save my life."

He looked at the fire. "Had I roused but a moment or two later, however . . ." He shook his head. "May I ask how long I've been here?"

"The days have run together a bit," she admitted after a moment. "If I could wager a guess, I'd say four or five days." She paused. "If I may be so bold, Sir Julien, what happened to you? When you arrived you mentioned Cobelds."

"Did I?" He ran a hand over his beard. "I don't think I've run across any for a while. Well," he sent another twinkling smile her way, "at least not since this afternoon." He laughed. "It was probably the fever talking. I was already a bit ill when I ran into Dwonsil warriors near the Stoenian border. I managed to evade them and I wasn't wounded. At least not then." He paused, his right hand moving to the bandage on his arm. "But the weather certainly didn't help me regain my health. I don't remember much past getting into the Great Wood. I'm not at all sure how I made it to your door, other than the supreme intelligence of my horse." He winced and pressed his hand against the wound.

Rose's breath caught. His pain was her doing. At least the pain that seemed to bother him the most. "Do you need medicine, Sir Julien?"

"No, thank you. Not just now, in any case. It dulls my mind and I must have my wits about me to figure out what I shall do next." He sighed as he poked at the log in the stove. "You say you're Sir Drinius's niece?"

She nodded. "Yes."

"I know him well, but I can't say he's mentioned having family in Veetri."

Rose felt a moment of fear for his mind. "Sir Julien, we're not in Veetri. We're in Mynissbyr." Had he received a head injury they hadn't noted? "This lodge is located in the Great Wood." She bit her lip. "Perhaps you're up and about too soon?"

"Oh, I'm not quite that addled," he said with a chuckle. "I only meant to remark that your accent is decidedly Veetrish, my lady. And I well know Sir Drinius hails from Stoen."

She sighed. "The Duke of Glenhume was my guardian until your father brought me to live in Mynissbyr."

"The Duke of Glenhume?" His eyes brightened. "Lord Whittier de Barden?"

"Yes. Unless perchance you know of another Duke of Glenhume?" Rose teased. "I must say Lord Whittier will be quite shocked to hear of it, if 'tis so."

"I've never actually met the duke," Sir Julien said with a smile. "But his eldest son is one of my closest friends." He blinked. "Rose." He whispered. "*Rose.* You're *that* Rose? Kinley's Rose?"

"You know my brother?" Rose's throat tightened. Oh, how she missed her Veetrish family! "And how is Kinley adjusting to the knight's life in Salderyn? I've not seen him since just after my sixteenth birthday."

"Your . . . brother?"

"Not by blood, of course. But certainly by affection."

"Oh." Julien rested his elbows on the chair's arms, his fingers tented at his waist. His brow furrowed and his index fingers tapped together a few times.

"Sir Julien?"

He looked up. "Oh, I'm sorry. You asked after Kinley."

She nodded.

"He was quite well the last time I spoke with him. But it's been months, I'm afraid, since I've been to the capital." Sir Julien took a deep breath. "I was sent to find news of my father and Sir Drinius. They came this way last summer on a mission of utmost secrecy and were expected back in Salderyn before the harvest. I've searched for them for five months, chasing rumors as fruitless as the wind." He sighed heavily.

"Do you think they are still alive?" Rose's eyes stung.

"I dearly hope so." He took a deep breath. "Cobelds have infiltrated nearly every area of the Kingdom since the clans of Dwons have rallied to their cause. The legends of the Wood have kept the Cobelds at bay for a long time, but this afternoon proves that security false."

"So much about our knowledge of them is false!" Rose was suddenly incensed. "The Storytellers make the Cobelds out to be grotesque, fearsome creatures. I'd always believed they were monsters. Hideous and gruesome! I was certainly not expecting someone's *grandfather* to try and kill me!"

"It's a common misconception." Julien nodded gravely. "The legends confuse the design of their hearts with their physical appearance."

"Well, they shouldn't! It's dangerous. How many other people have been deceived by what seems to be an innocuous old man?"

"Too many."

His words were sobering. Rose worried the edge of one thumb against the other. "It's bad, isn't it, in the rest of the Kingdom?"

Julien nodded. "It is."

He gazed at the fire and then at his boots on the floor beside it. Suddenly, he looked up. "The King entrusted me with a message for Sir Drinius's wife should I be unable to locate his knights. In all the excitement of the day, I nearly forgot my duty."

"Shall I call her for you?" Rose asked.

The knight took a breath as if to speak, then paused. "In a moment, perhaps." He met her eyes as if carefully measuring his words before he let them free. Finally, he spoke.

"Lady Rose, what can you tell me of your connection to King Jarryn?"

"My *what*?" She laughed and wrinkled her nose. "I have no connection to the King. I've never even met him." She paused. "Of course, my father is a knight. Perhaps the King knows my father."

Julien's eyebrows rose. "Your father is a knight, you say? What is his name?"

Rose squirmed in her chair. "I don't actually know."

"Hmm." Julien nodded, but his eyes searched her face with an intensity that brought heat to her cheeks. "I don't mean to offend, but might I ask your age?"

"Is that an offensive question?"

"Not to me, but I've been told some ladies can be sensitive to it."

"Well, I'm not an old maid quite yet," she said and gave him a lopsided grin, "so I take no offense. How old are you?"

"Twenty-seven."

"Ah. You're Gladiel's eldest, then?"

He nodded.

"I've a birthday coming in just over a month and I'll mark my nineteenth year upon it," she said. "So I suppose I'm closer to that mark than the other."

"Nineteen." The knight's eyes slid shut. "Next month."

Rose almost feared he had fallen into unconsciousness again, but finally he spoke.

"The night I arrived at your door," he began softly, "I was very ill and mostly out of my head. I am not of a superstitious nature, Lady Rose, but when I first saw you I was certain I was seeing a ghost."

"You did ask me if you were dead," she gave him a half smile. "I can't say as I've ever been asked that before."

"It all makes sense now." Excitement danced in his eyes. "Of *course* the Cobeld would want you dead!" Sir Julien rubbed his bearded chin and then leaned forward, meaning to rest his forearms on his thighs, but a wince reminded them both of his wound. As he reclined back in the chair, his gaze intensified. "It's no wonder that the King is concerned for your well-being. You are very nearly the image of his dead wife, Queen Daithia. And, as such, the Cobelds' most feared adversary."

"You jest, sir."

"No." He shook his head. "I do not."

"So because I look like the dead queen, I'm the enemy? That's even more absurd than Drinius and Gladiel believing I'm in danger because I look like a character from an ancient poem."

"They told you that?"

"Yes. They said the Cobelds make a habit of killing girls with red hair. They believe the poem's a prophecy or some other such nonsense." She paused. "Did the queen have red hair?"

"Yes. Quite like yours."

"And she died in childbirth, didn't she? Just like . . . my mother."

"Yes." Julien nodded slowly as if willing her to understand his implication.

And she did glean his meaning. But it was an insane supposition.

Wasn't it?

Her voice came out as a whisper. "But everyone knows the Queen's baby died with her."

"That is what we have believed these past *nineteen* years, yes." She didn't miss the way he emphasized the number. "But now I must admit a certain curiosity."

Rose barked a laugh and quickly covered her mouth, embarrassed.

"I was only eight years old when Queen Daithia died," Julien said, "but I remember her well. She was very dear to me. But even if I did not recall her face, her portraits hang in Castle Rynwyk in Salderyn, as well as in Holiday Palace in Port Dyn. And the likeness you bear the Queen is quite remarkable. For all these years I've believed—" He drew in a sudden, quick breath. "It is of utmost importance that I deliver the King's message to Lady Drinius."

Rose stood. "I'll summon her. I—"

Rose jumped when a sound came from the direction of the door, but it wasn't the sound that had startled her, it was the flash of light—or was it color?—that followed.

TWENTY-FIVE

Julien attempted to rise as Aunt Alaine entered, but she stopped him. "You'll have plenty of opportunity for that when you're well."

"Lady Drinius, I have a message for you," Sir Julien said. "From the King."

Aunt Alaine's hand fluttered to her chest, her gaze flicking to Rose and then back to the knight.

Rose fought dizziness as she moved from the chair, but she only made it as far as the edge of the bed. She sat heavily upon it.

Alaine took her vacated chair. "Julien de Gladiel. It's been a long time since I've seen you, but not so long that I shouldn't have recognized you, even with that excess of fur on your face." She shook her head. "Now, what is this about a message? What news is so urgent that you should nearly die to deliver it?" Her hand moved to her chest again and her voice fell to a whisper. "Is it about Drinius?"

"I don't know. But neither do I know where your husband and my father have been these last months." Julien said.

"Where is the missive?"

"Between the soles of my right boot." Julien reached for the boot and used the fire poker to pry the leather loose. "I have not read it, nor could I even if I had tried. It was written in code in case it was taken from my person. The King said you would be able to read it." He removed the sole of the boot, withdrew an oilcloth that held a piece of parchment, and handed it to Alaine.

As she opened it, her eyes misted. "Yes," she said softly, "I can read this." Turning her eyes to Rose she said, "When your father and Drinius courted your mother and I they devised a code to send us secret messages. Love letters, as it were." Color dotted the apples of Alaine's cheeks. She sighed. "It has been a long time, but I think I can decipher this."

Giving the parchment her full concentration, she read through the message, resting her eyes for a moment before turning to Rose.

"Rose," she said as she looked up, "your uncle, Sir Gladiel, and I have shielded you from the past—and from the future—for as long as we could. It's time you know the truth." She gave a pained little laugh. "But I find I don't even know where to begin."

"If I may be so bold, Lady Drinius," Sir Julien said softly, "perhaps a direct approach would be best."

After taking a deep breath Alaine sat up straighter. She opened her mouth to speak, but her eyes filled and her hand lifted to her lips.

Rose glanced over at Julien to find his eyes locked on her face. His jaw was set, his gaze intent upon her. Then, without the slightest movement of his mouth, the light of a smile brightened his eyes, encompassing every degree of that expression within their sparkling emerald depths. Suddenly, the smile parted his lips, imbuing his face with so many emotions that she couldn't pinpoint just one.

Heat spread up the back of her neck, accompanied by a strange sort of comfort she could not define.

"As you know, your mother was an orphan, adopted by my parents when she was small," Lady Drinius said, stealing Rose's attention from the knight. "What you don't know, is that shortly after she married your father, she became Queen."

Rose clutched the arms of her chair, feeling as if the bottom had just dropped out of the world through her stomach.

"Drinius was with the King and Queen at Holiday Palace when your mother's pains began," Alaine continued. "He had just assigned a fresh patrol and was on his way to join Gladiel in guarding the royal chambers when he discovered a lone Cobeld had breached the palace. They fought and Drinius inflicted a mortal wound, but the Cobeld was slow to die. Its final words revealed the curse it had delivered, through a hair of its beard dropped in the very cup that was bound for your mother's lips. Drinius tried to reach Daithia in time to warn her, but—"

Alaine's voice caught on a shard of memory. A moment later she took a deep, shaking breath and continued. "The labor was unexpectedly fast for the birth of her first child and you were already delivered and being cleaned and swaddled by the physician when the cup reached Daithia's hands." She took a breath. "Daithia saw the hair before she took her first sip. When she reached in the cup to remove it, her skin touched the hair of the Cobeld's beard and she received the curse."

Rose swallowed. Her mind spun. If Queen Daithia was her mother, that meant . . .

When she spoke, her words came out as if lamed by a punch to the gut. "She died."

"Yes, but not right away as the rumors have claimed." Alaine took another breath. "Cobeld curses are specific in their intent. Daithia was supposed to have ingested the curse through the tea. In that way, the Cobeld intended for her to pass it to the child within her womb, allowing one cursed hair of his beard to kill both the Queen and the heir. In that specificity, the curse was foiled. She didn't drink the tea, but the curse touched her, and for Daithia, the end result was the same. She did not die instantly, but she did die. You survived because the curse never touched you."

Tears rolled down Alaine's cheeks as if from a bottomless fount.

But what should I be feeling? Rose wondered. *Grief? Wonder? Relief?* Numbed by shock, she could lay claim to no emotion of her own but sympathy—and that for her aunt's distress.

Alaine wiped her eyes. "King Jarryn gave orders and within a matter of hours you were aboard a ship on your way to me. Your father believed the only way to keep you safe was to make the Cobelds believe you perished from the curse. To accomplish that, he hid you away. But that decision has had its own consequences."

Rose blinked. "What do you mean?"

"Other than the grief you've both suffered from being apart? The Cobelds target young women with red hair. And it weighs heavily on your father's heart."

"But it's not his—" She paused to swallow. "He's not the one who wrote that poem, is he?"

"No," Julien spoke up. "Lady Anya recorded the prophecy. The Cobelds fear the King will remarry and they don't want to take a chance on another red-haired queen, and eventually, an heir."

Rose's mind swirled. There was too much about this conversation she wasn't yet able to digest.

"You have waited a long time to know the truth," Alaine said softly. "And I must admit that it is a relief to finally tell it. All that's left," she said slowly, "is for you to accept who you are."

All her life, Rose had longed to know who her father was, but now that she had been told, could she believe it?

"It's true." Alaine nodded. "Your father is King Jarryn. Your mother was Queen Daithia." She paused for a breath. "And you, my precious girl, are Princess Rynnaia E'veri."

Rose sat as if frozen, staring at her aunt, weighing this new information against her known history.

It was absurd, wasn't it? Yet it made perfect sense.

The taste of truth was entirely new to her experience. A fresh feeling sizzled through her blood, like that of a waif on the verge of starvation, who for years had been given only food enough to sustain life, but was now seated at a banquet.

"Rynnaia," she whispered. "My name is Rynnaia . . . E'veri?"

An explosion of color and light stole her vision. It coursed through her blood, unlocking something in her mind that had teased her senses, unknown, for the whole of her life. She felt its release as surely as she knew it had been waiting within her all along.

Vibrant color overwhelmed her thoughts. Deep patterns washed over her being like a thick, warm wave. The very air surrounding her became embodied with a richer texture and a sweeter aroma. Even the silence of the room held layered planes of newness within it.

Gradually her vision cleared, though she knew nothing would ever look the same to her again.

"My name isn't Rose."

Alaine shook her head.

"My father is . . ." She squeezed her eyes shut. "No. This is wrong."

"It's the truth," Alaine repeated. "Your father is King Jarryn and you, my dear, are the Ryn."

"The Ryn?" Rose had never heard the word before, but something about it rang within her soul.

Rose looked from her aunt to the knight. Julien's face was pale, but his expression held something more than shock. Was it . . . hope?

A giddy sort of laughter built within her chest, the kind that results from too little sleep and too much grief. She shook her head. Blinked. And, with barely enough breath to accomplish it, she barked out a laugh. "My father is the King of E'veria." She pulled in a breath, and then she laughed and laughed until the sound drew nearer to panic than relief.

Tears coursed down her cheeks, and just as suddenly as the hysteria had come upon her, she stilled. Her voice dropped to a whisper. "My father is the King of E'veria." And with that statement, that . . . *acceptance* . . . she found her voice.

"My name is not Rose. My name is Rynnaia E'veri."

PART II: RYNNAIA

TWENTY-SIX

*I*t may have been shock that allowed me to sit so still and silent as I digested the knowledge I'd craved for so long.

"Rynnaia E'veri." I tasted the foreignness of the name. Amidst the fear clawing in my chest, I savored the way that saying it, even in a whisper, made my vision swirl in a cacophony of color.

It was my name now. It had *always* been my name. But even though something deep within me exulted to finally receive it as my own, a big part of me—my entire history, in fact—was, in that instant, lost.

Who am I? Panic strangled my breath. *I'm not Rose. I'm not a cast-off. I'm . . . a princess?*

It was laughable, really. Me? The daughter of the King?

I'd been told that my father was a knight and therefore had always thought of him in those terms. To me, he was a nameless stranger, an indifferent knight who dictated my life from afar. *But he's not just some mysterious knight. He's the King!*

Rynnaia. The name rolled around in my brain, seeking a foothold. *Not Rose. Rynnaia.* Color after color assaulted my mind, clearer than they'd ever been. *This is real,* I thought. *This is who I am. This is true.* The intensity of colors shocked and dizzied me to the point that I was barely aware of Aunt Alaine and Sir Julien's presence in the room, yet the colors brought with them a sort of calming assurance.

I am Rynnaia E'veri. Somehow I knew that I had to claim that name as my own. I had to step away from the familiar and into the role appointed to me.

Suddenly, the room felt bigger, as if the whole world had shrunk to fit within it. My knees trembled as I stood. "My name is not Rose," I said. "My name is Rynnaia E'veri!"

The name felt strangely right on my tongue. Entirely mine, as if to call myself "Rose" again would be an error of taxonomy. The shift overwhelmed me, yet left me undeniably pacified. The colors settled to a more comfortable state in my mind and I became, once again, aware of my surroundings.

It wasn't until a sob released from my throat that I realized I was crying.

I could not stop the tears, and as I looked through bleary eyes at Aunt Alaine I felt *her* pain, as fresh and raw as if her sister had just died. I had to look away, overcome by the grief emanating from my aunt's eyes, so that I might allow myself to claim the grief this knowledge had made mine.

Aunt Alaine moved to sit beside me. She pulled me into her embrace.

"I made a vow to my King," she said. "It was my sister's dying request." Her voice was just above a whisper. "Even though it was for your own good, the weight of this deception has been such a burden upon you. Upon all of us." She took a shaking breath. "I never dreamed it would carry on this long. Please forgive me."

"Of course," I said. How could I hold it against her? Would I expect her to gainsay the order of the King?

Aunt Alaine released her hold on me and took a step back. "Oh!" Her hand fluttered to her lips. "Oh, of course."

I turned to follow the direction of her gaze. All I could see through my tears was the glimmer of firelight reflected on a shiny surface. I wiped my eyes and blinked away the moisture.

The shiny surface was Sir Julien's sword, laid flat across his palms. And directly behind it was the knight himself, kneeling and offering it to me.

"Julien?" I croaked. "What are you doing?"

"By charge of Rynloeft," he said, "and by my sworn duty as a knight of E'veria, I vow my sword, my fealty, and my service to you, Princess Rynnaia, with all that I am and for all of my life."

The Knight's Oath.

I'd heard the vow spoken before, but never had it sent such a crackling of truth through my blood. With a motion I could hardly claim as my own, I took Julien's sword and raised it above my head.

"Julien de Gladiel, I accept your sword, your fealty, and your service. On behalf of my fallen mother, my father, King Jarryn, and the Kingdom of E'veria, I thank you for your sacrifice and the honor you give me by the words of this vow."

Where did that come from? The words were not my own and the action was equally as foreign, but somewhere deep within me I knew it was *exactly* right.

Who was this person—this *princess*—who knew the right thing to do and the correct words to say? The answer came like a thought, a whisper breathed upon my soul:

You are the Ryn.

As I lowered the sword back into Julien's outstretched hands, I looked deeply into his emerald eyes. Were they greener than they'd been but a moment ago? Or were they simply more beautiful now for the hope that surged within them?

Julien took his sword and returned it to its sheath, but remained on one knee. "Your Highness, I pledge to you my friendship, as well," he said, "as it has flowed between our families for generations."

"And I mine, to you."

Again, words came from whence I knew not, but I meant them, just the same. A strange stirring at my breast increased the speed at which the edges of the room began closing in. The last thing I remembered was the floor rising up to meet me.

TWENTY-SEVEN

"Wake up, Rose!" Lily's impatient voice swept through my troubled dreams. "Come awake, now. Your first official day as the Crown Princess of E'veria and you faint in a heap!" She laughed.

It wasn't a dream.

Assaulted by smelling salts, I gagged and pushed my cousin's hand away from my face. "Ach! Stop. I'm awake. Ohhh," I groaned and held my aching head, "but I wish I wasn't."

"I brought breakfast." Her singsong voice grated against my skull, but my stomach rumbled in response to the announcement. "You slept all through the evening and night."

I pushed myself into a sitting position, surprised to find myself in bed.

Across the room, Sir Julien sat by the fire, a small looking glass propped on the table against a stack of books and a razor blade in his hand. He turned and I couldn't stop the sharp intake of breath from sounding.

The long, full beard was gone, leaving only a triangle of short-trimmed dark blond whiskers around his lips and covering his chin.

When Julien smiled, I almost wondered if Lily would need to use the smelling salts on me again.

"Perhaps I should introduce myself, since this is the first time you've actually seen my face." He chuckled and stood. "Sir Julien de Gladiel." He bowed. "At your service, Your Highness."

Behind me, Lily giggled.

"Princess Rynnaia," he said, "I am pleased to report that I've just completed my first act of valor in your honor."

I almost flinched at the way he addressed me, but his tone was formal to the point of being ridiculous, and the humor of it, accentuated by the light that danced in his eyes, would not allow me to dwell on the strangeness of my new name.

"Speak then, knight," I exaggerated my aunt's careful elocution. "I will hear your report."

"As you can see by peering in this cask of dishonor," Julien said, gesturing to a bucket that was filled with the dark blonde fluff and whiskery remains of that which had covered his face, "I have vanquished the beast that dared to impose upon your hospitality."

"A beast, you say?" Our repartee released a deep tension I hadn't even felt building since leaving Mirthan Hall. Although Lily was quick to laugh when I teased, neither she nor Aunt Alaine ever instigated a jest. Now engaged in such sport with Julien, I realized just how sorely I'd missed the affectionate words of play that had been a daily, if not hourly occurrence in Veetri.

"Indeed," he nodded gravely. "A most foul beast."

I wasn't sure how to answer. Julien had been handsome even with the full beard. But without it he was utterly . . .

"He doesn't look like a bear so much now, does he, Princess?" Lily's voice came from behind me, where she had moved to fluff the pillows. "And you're quite right. He is, indeed, even more handsome without the beard."

"Li-*ly!*" I gasped.

She'd never admitted to being able to see into my thoughts before. Had she been able to all along? And why had she never told me?

"I can't believe you never told me you could see my thoughts! So you sneak into my head without permission? Is that not bad enough? Must you comment on my thoughts as well?" With every sentence the volume of my voice increased. "If I'd wanted Julien to know I thought him handsome, I would have told him myself!"

Lily moved in front of me, grabbed my shoulders, and looked into my eyes. Although her mouth did not open, I heard her laugh. *I'll stay out of your head if you stay out of mine! I'm not the one saying embarrassing things aloud! You are.*

I gasped and scooted away from her. "What is happening to me?"

"Princess Rynnaia?" Julien took a step forward. "Lady Lily?"

Lily's hand softly touched my shoulder. Her look of mirth turned instantly to one of compassion.

"Rose, I'm so sorry," she spoke aloud. "This is a lot for you to take in all at once. The Bear-knight, the Cobeld, the truth of who you are, and the release of your Andoven abilities . . . it would overwhelm anyone!"

"What do you mean, my *Andoven abilities*?" I asked. "I'm not Andoven!"

"Well, of course you are!" Lily sat down beside me. "Mother didn't tell you?" I shook my head. "Oh. Well, I suppose there was quite a lot to tell. And you did faint, after all. She must not have had time."

"Well?"

"In addition to being the Ryn, you're Andoven, too. Your abilities are much stronger than mine or my mother's. There are Andoven ties on both sides of your family."

"But—"

"You see colors now, right?"

"Yes, but—"

"That's part of it. Mother says your parents put a guard of sorts on you. They somehow cloaked your Andoven abilities so they couldn't be released until you knew your true name."

"How?"

"I don't know. I don't think my mother does, either. But then again, like we've told you before, our Andoven abilities are weak. We've never been trained to use our own abilities, other than the knowledge that's passed down from parent to child. Each generation's gifts are a bit weaker than the one before. We're not like you. We've never even visited Tirandov Isle."

"And you think I have?"

"Not yet, but I bet you will someday. Mother says your father visits the Andoven at Tirandov at least once a year." Lily paused. "You know, I always thought it a bit odd. Although Mother and I share our thoughts fairly easily, I could *never* read her thoughts about you. She always kept her guard up, but it slipped the night Sir Julien came."

"What do you mean, her guard slipped?"

"Hmm. How to explain . . ." Lily squinted at the wall, as if the answer were written there. "We see colors, and in them, are able to interpret emotion. By focusing our minds on one particular color, that which lacks color—"

"Black?"

"No," Lily shook her head. "More like gray, I'd say. By pulling the gray to us, around our thoughts, we can block them from each other's Andoven abilities."

"Oh."

"But in that moment, when my mother's guard dropped and the grayness slipped away, the truth was revealed and I knew that you were not just my cousin, but, in fact, the Ryn. It was quite a shock," she admitted, "but when it was your turn to sit with Sir Julien, Mother told me everything that I might assist her in keeping you safe."

She took a step toward the door. "I should leave you to break your fast."

Lily exited the bedroom. When she was out of sight, her voice found my mind as clearly as if she were standing at my side. *If you need anything, I'm here.*

I was glad Julien's back was turned, because I startled a bit violently. *I'm sorry!* Lily said. *You'll adapt to your abilities soon. I'm sure of it.*

While his back was turned, I threw off the blanket and found my feet. I closed my eyes and took a deep breath. When I looked up, Julien was holding one of the chairs for me. I moved to take a seat.

"Are you feeling better?" he asked.

"Yes, thank you."

"Are you hungry?"

"Very." He was choosing to ignore my embarrassing outburst and I was grateful. "You?"

"Very." He sat down. We stared at each other. He was the first to look away. "At Castle Rynwyk," he said finally, "it is customary that no one partakes until the King has taken his first bite."

"Oh." I thought about that for a moment, and then dropped my head into my hands and groaned. "He's going to hate me."

Julien's brow furrowed. "Who?"

Even though it was just one word, it was spoken almost like a threat. Not to me, but to whomever would have the audacity to hate me.

"The *King*!" I said. "I don't know anything about being a princess."

"He won't hate you." Julien's features relaxed. "I've always found King Jarryn very easy to please. Now eat."

"Go ahead. I'm too miserable." The growl of my stomach argued with my words.

Julien's lip twitched. "You'll feel better about it after you eat something."

All of a sudden, his chosen topic of conversation made sense. "I'm supposed to eat first, aren't I?"

A slow smile spread across his face. He nodded.

I laughed. "You could've just told me, you know." I picked a cube of cheese, popped it in my mouth, quickly chewed, and swallowed. "There. Satisfied?"

To answer, he tore one of the eggs in half, wrapped it around a cube of cheese, and popped it in his mouth.

TWENTY-EIGHT

With the release of my Andoven abilities, my perception of everything changed. Even confined to the house, the world seemed brighter and more colorful.

Aunt Alaine brought a fresh salve that seemed to speed up the healing in Julien's arm. And, after a rather uncomfortable confession, I apologized for being the cause of it.

Every day Julien's health and stamina improved. When I complained of missing my daily rides since Walen and Eneth had left for supplies, Julien endeavored to teach me the series of exercises he'd been doing to alleviate the stiffness in his limbs. This system of controlled movements, devised to keep a knight strong if taken prisoner, was not as easy as he made it look. But it was effective. The exercises not only helped to pass the time, but strengthened my body and provided a bit of much-needed laughter when my long skirts would get in the way and I would lose my balance.

I spent more time with Julien than anyone else. It was an unspoken understanding that, being the Ryn, I was safest in his company. But at least once a day, Aunt Alaine took me aside to try and tutor me in the skills necessary to have at least some control over my newfound Andoven abilities. The most precious of these lessons, at least to me, whose innermost thoughts were now exposed to my aunt and cousin, was learning how to reach for the gray amidst the colors in my mind to hide my thoughts from my Andoven companions.

It wasn't an easy skill to learn. And there were challenges. For example, the better I got to know Julien, the more I relaxed in his company I became, and when I relaxed, the cognitive swirls of gray I'd so painstakingly reached for—the gray that hid my thoughts from Lily and Aunt Alaine—slipped away. I never realized they were gone until Aunt Alaine would pop into the room. When she sat with us I was more aware not only of myself, but of Julien somehow, of his maleness, as well as his beauty. And those were the hardest thoughts to hide.

Beauty seemed too feminine a term for a knight, but I could find no other within my vocabulary to describe his form, the curl of his hair, the emerald green of his eyes . . . Why the attraction didn't occur to me as much when we were alone, I could only guess had to do with the comfort of our growing friendship. But I was glad for the many hours of comfort, because when my aunt and cousin were about, it was with the lacking grace of a newborn foal that I could even meet his eyes.

"It really is remarkable," Julien said one evening. "The resemblance, I mean."

He'd offered to tend the animals earlier and the fresh air seemed to have invigorated him. After Aunt Alaine and Lily found their beds, we sat by the fire, playing a game of dice.

"Your height, the rich blue of your eyes . . . that alone is so unusual that anyone who'd met Queen Daithia would suspect you a relation. The blue is so deep. Pure as an autumn sky, but with the jeweled tones of a dark sapphire stone."

His eyes roved over my features. "The set of your cheek-bones is a bit stronger than hers, though. And your chin. You inherited that from your father. Your lips are a bit fuller, per-haps . . ." Julien's voice drifted off, but his eyes lingered on my mouth for a moment. Suddenly, he blinked, cleared his throat, and looked back to the fire. "And your hair, of course, is very like hers. Like flame itself."

I was glad his gaze was averted, sure that by now my face was glowing brighter than the kindling.

Julien kept his gaze on the fire, and after clearing his throat again, his voice took on a less personal tone. "Perhaps your hair is a shade or two deeper than the Queen's," he ad-mitted. "But when the light hits it just right you look very much as I remember her. I can hardly believe no one made the connection all these years."

"My hair used to be black."

"Black?" His gaze swiveled back toward me. "How is that possible?"

"Ebonswarth root powder."

He took a moment to digest that information. "You used it as a dye?"

"Yes. Mixed with water from a sulfur spring."

"Ah. That would nullify its poisonous properties." His brow furrowed and the corner of his mouth turned down. "Did you know that possession of that powder is a capital offense?"

"I do *now*," I said dryly. "When I first learned of its ques-tionable legality I was not quite sixteen . . . and more than a little concerned about keeping my head, regardless of its col-or! But my tutor presumed Uncle Drinius had received some sort of special permission, and since Gladiel knew about it, too, I can only assume she was right. At least I hope so. I like my head where it is, thank you."

"As do I."

The warmth in his tone made my stomach flip.

"Though, considering who your father is," he said with a quirk of a smile, "I imagine that dispensation was fairly easy to come by." He tilted his head, squinted, and then shook his head. "Princess Rynnaia with black hair. I cannot even imagine it."

"I wasn't Princess Rynnaia then. I was just Rose."

"I have a hard time believing you've ever been 'just' anything."

Heat moved up the back of my neck. I looked at the floor. "Do you know him well? The King?"

"I can't remember a time when I didn't know the King," he said. "I visited Castle Rynwyk in Salderyn so often as a young boy that I considered it a second home. When my younger brother Gerrias was small and my mother was engaged in caring for him, the Queen took me under her wing." He smiled. "Queen Daithia was a merry, imaginative soul and she loved children. She would have been a wonderful mother if she'd lived."

My throat tightened. "At least she got to mother you a bit."

He nodded. "I believe the Queen had a lot to do with King Jarryn's decision to take me on as a page at such a tender age."

"How old were you?"

"Six."

"Six?" I was shocked. "So young? Kinley and Lewys were never pages. And they didn't even leave to become squires until they were fourteen!"

"Well, the Veetrish are a bit unusual that way," he smiled. "Even for a boy from Mynissbyr, six was young. But the Queen was ever my champion. It was thanks to her that I was given the great honor of such close tutelage with the King. He became almost a second father to me."

A pang of jealousy stung near the region of my heart, but I shoved it away. It wasn't Julien's fault that my father had sent me away.

"When the Queen died . . ."

A sharp stab of sadness tinged the bright green I had learned to associate with Julien's thoughts. Regardless of the mixed feelings I had for my father, Julien's affection for him moved me. My eyes filled as sorrow filtered through his thoughts and into mine. I reached over and placed my hand on his, touched by the affection and grief he felt for my mother.

Julien looked at my hand a long moment before lifting his face. When our eyes met, something strange passed between us. It was a thought of sorts, an unfamiliar *knowing* I couldn't put a name to. My mind filled with starbursts of burnished gold and emerald green. The colors flowed hot and true, dashing the sadness of the moment away and my breath with it. Where our hands touched, our pulses thrummed in a perfect, galloping rhythm.

Suddenly, Julien pushed his chair back and stood. He turned to face the flames, his back to me.

"The healing of my arm is nearing its completion, Princess Rynnaia." His words carried a breathless sense, yet his tone was formal. "We should be able to depart soon."

He clasped his hands behind his back and took a deep breath as if to expel the charge in the air between us. The warmth that had coated his thoughts mere moments ago slid away so quickly I shivered. My head swam at the contradiction.

"Wait. Why are we leaving?" It just occurred to me that I'd never asked. "Since you're here, aren't we safe now to stay at the Bear's Rest?"

He blinked. "Why would you think you are safe here?"

"Your father was most assured of it," I said, remembering that my uncle was not as confident. "Besides, you're a knight!"

"There was a Cobeld," he said slowly, "in the Wood. You could have died."

"You were ill, then. But now you're better."

"I am but one knight," he said, adding, "you are the Ryn." He paused. "And even if I was able to ensure your safety here, your father has other plans for you. Since my strength has returned we will be able to go to Fyrlean Manor."

"Fyrlean Manor?" I grabbed at the familiar landmark. "Lady Anya's home?"

"Lady Anya? Indeed." He smiled. "It's as safe a place as we'll find in E'veria and I've no doubt our presence will be welcomed." He sighed. "It's been much too long since I've seen my mother and sister."

"You expect your family to be there?"

"It's our home."

"Of course." I shook my head, disgusted with myself. "I have a tendency to forget your father is a Regent," I said and then grinned. "And a Bear-man."

Julien laughed. "I can understand why. This Regency isn't as formal as some." He stood. "I want to show you something. Wait here."

Julien retrieved his sword from his chamber and held it so that it caught the light. "See this design on the hilt of my sword? It's our family crest. It honors the Lady Anya and alludes to the legend of the Bear-men."

I peered at the blade, its seal so different from that on his scabbard. Beautifully wrought scrollwork wound around a shield, and on the shield, a circle with a diamond shape at its center was topped by the fierce face of a roaring bear.

I laughed. "I called you 'Bear-knight' because I didn't know your name. But that's exactly what you are."

"Yes," he grinned, "I suppose I am."

We turned our attention back to the game, but it wasn't long before Julien's expression grew serious.

"I would like for us to leave tomorrow night."

I nodded, but reached to rub my temple as a strange, new set of colors flooded my mind.

"What is it?" Julien was immediately at my side.

"I don't know." Just then, a woman's face flashed through my mind. "Eneth?" I stood.

"Your aunt's housekeeper?"

I nodded. The colors were stronger now, and there was both an urgency and a vagueness to them, but I couldn't discern the meaning. I closed my eyes, straining to focus on the new colors and to glean some meaning from them. Suddenly I stood. "She's almost here," I said. "I think she's . . . hurt."

Julien strapped his scabbard around his waist. "Which way?"

I shook my head. "I don't know. But Julien, she's not . . . Andoven." I blinked. "How can I . . . ?"

"Bar the door. Let no one in save me."

And with that, he was gone.

I pulled the wooden bar down, set it in its latch, and paced. After several minutes, I ran upstairs and woke my aunt and cousin, who hurriedly dressed and joined me in the front room.

"Aunt Alaine, is Eneth part Andoven?"

"No."

Then how could I sense her presence? Was it just my wishful thinking that she and Walen would return that had sent Julien out into the cold, dark night? Or was she really out there?

"Your mother comes from strong Andoven lines, Rynnaia," Aunt Alaine said when I resumed my pacing.

She must have seen my thoughts. But then again, I hadn't even tried to pull the gray around them.

"Daithia could both see and speak into the thoughts of those not of Andoven blood almost as easily as she could mine or Jarryn's."

"And the King? Can he as well?"

"I don't think so. His gifts are strong, but I think his communication, like mine, is limited to those of Andoven blood. If you've inherited that gift, it would be from Daithia's side of the family. I've been told it is an unusual gift, even among the strong lineages."

"I can see Julien's colors," I mused. "And his thoughts, too, sometimes. But I hadn't really considered it—"

A step sounded on the porch, drawing Lily to the window. "It's Sir Julien. He's carrying . . . Oh dear! It's Eneth!"

I ran to unbar and open the door. Julien came in, a sodden lump of Eneth in his arms. "She's injured," he said. "I think she may be in shock."

"Her chamber is the door just beyond yours. The one closest to the kitchen." Aunt Alaine rushed after him.

"I'll heat some water," Lily said, rushing to the kitchen. I followed her.

"I'll light the fire in her room," I said, grabbing kindling and two sturdy logs from the dwindling pile just inside the door before racing to Eneth's bedchamber.

"He's dead, Lady Drinius," Eneth wailed. "My Walen is dead! Struck down by a cursed clansman!"

I gasped. Walen? The man who had taught me to ride as a child, who had good-naturedly fought me for the right to care for my own horse ever since I'd arrived at the Bear's Rest, was dead?

Eneth's injuries were not severe, but now that the urgency to reach us had passed, her grief was incapacitating. Aunt Alaine held her while she sobbed.

Julien turned to me, his voice low. "Where were they?"

"They went to the village of Otley. On the Sengarra border."

"West, then." He nodded. "Good. But if there are Dwonsil warriors in the Wood," he said, "or even near the Sengarra-Mynissbyr border, we must head east to Fyrlean Manor as soon as possible."

TWENTY-NINE

Eneth fell into a sleep that lasted well into the next day, but hers was the only stillness in the house.

"We need provisions for one night's journey," Julien had instructed us that morning. "It will be a hard ride. We will stop once to allow the horses a brief rest. Eneth will be fit for travel?"

"Fit enough," Aunt Alaine replied. "Rynnaia's safety is more pressing."

"Indeed."

I wanted to argue, but neither had invited me into their discussion.

"I will ready my horse and three of yours at dusk," Julien continued. "The princess rides with me. We must travel with all deliberate speed to make it to Fyrlean Manor before dawn. Everyone should wear an extra cloak, if you have one. Our speed will only increase the chill."

I could stay silent no longer. "Stanza is fast," I said. "We would travel more efficiently if I was on my own horse."

Julien cocked his head. "Princess, I assure you that your presence will be no burden to Salvador. My horse is strong and I can better protect you if you're close to me."

"He speaks modestly, Rynnaia." Aunt Alaine laughed. "The horse is a monster!" She laughed and turned to Julien. "But he has not suffered in our care. I'm afraid my daughter has grown quite fond of your horse. She now refers to him as her overgrown lamb."

Julien laughed. "It's a good moniker. Salvador is unswervingly loyal and docile with those he loves. But I daresay Lady Lily would not recognize her 'lamb' on the battlefield."

Eneth awoke just past the midday mark and took a bit of food. She was still a bit shaky and prone to tears, as could be expected, but she was as anxious as any of us, if not more so, to reach the safety of Fyrlean Manor.

The afternoon was spent in a bustle of preparations and Lily shed not a few tears when she went out to say her good-byes to the animals she would be releasing to fend for themselves in the Wood. Aunt Alaine was with Eneth, coaxing her to take a bit of venison broth, leaving Julien and I in the front room alone.

Julien knelt beside his saddlebags, rearranging the contents. The deep brown color of his shirt and trousers brought out streaks of gold and bronze in his slightly curly, golden-blond hair. He didn't notice my silent appraisal. Not meaning to, but still unaccustomed to the Andoven gifts that were now such a part of me, I picked up my name scuttling across his thoughts. In the tumult of information that had assaulted me since the day I learned my identity, I had nearly forgotten Aunt Alaine's letter from the King. But it was clearly on Julien's mind now, and in it, the plans for my future.

"May I see the King's letter, Julien?"

"Of course." He rose and handed me the folded parchment. "Lady Drinius mentioned you might like to read it, but

I'd forgotten you hadn't yet." He smiled. "Other than your parents, I've rarely been in close contact with the Andoven. It's going to take some getting used to, being around someone who can so easily see the direction of my thoughts."

"I'm sorry. It wasn't intentional. I just don't always remember to block you out." I bit my lip. "I'll try to do better."

"Not to worry, Princess," he said with a smile. "You can't help who you are and you shouldn't be ashamed of your gifts." He returned to his packing, freeing me to look at the parchment in my hands. The characters on the page were entirely foreign to me.

"I forgot it was written in code." I sat down, frowning at the page. "Why would Aunt Alaine think I could read this?"

"One of Queen Daithia's Andoven gifts was the ability to decipher unknown languages. Perhaps Lady Drinius assumed you inherited that gift?"

I looked at the parchment. It was of a language I did not know, comprised of an alphabet I'd never seen. I was just about to give it back to Julien when the shapes on the page seemed to take on motion. I stifled a gasp and peered closer. As my eyes adjusted to the odd, strained feeling it produced, a queasy sense of dizziness assailed my mind, but I was too curious to stop.

As I concentrated on the foreign shapes, they rearranged themselves into readable print. "This is a strange bit of magic," I whispered. Moving to a chair, I sat down and focused, surprised to find the page suddenly quite easy to read.

Dear Alaine,

I pray you receive this letter while safety yet holds you.

I have become aware of certain scrolls that, once deemed lost, have been recovered. Gladiel and Drinius were sent to retrieve them from Fyrlean Manor and, from there, they were to collect Rynnaia and transport her to Tirandov Isle to be trained in the use of her gifts. If you are receiving this message, Drinius and Gladiel never reached their destination and Rynnaia does not yet know who she is. Deception has been our guard until now, but my daughter's existence and location may soon be discovered. The time has finally come that Rynnaia's safety depends upon truth, however difficult it might be for her to hear it.

Sir Julien will accompany you and your household to Fyrlean Manor, collect the scrolls, and take Rynnaia on to Port Dyn where my most learned scribe and dear old friend, Dyfnel, hastens now to escort them to Tirandov Isle.

Though I would much rather have Rynnaia at Castle Rynwyk with me, Dyfnel assures me that she must be tutored at Tirandov before becoming known. Though it pains me, I trust his judgment. Dyfnel will translate the scrolls while Rynnaia is engaged in her Andoven studies and we will then know what steps must be taken next in this war against the Cobelds.

You must travel with the utmost speed using every precaution. E'veria is no longer the safe land of our youth. Lady Gladiel will be glad of your company at Fyrlean Manor, and you and Lily may stay there at your leisure until I send for you. Gladiel's home is well fortified. You and Lily shall be safe within its walls.

My heart goes out to you and to Gladiel's family. I pray my friends are merely delayed. I can never repay the debt of service and love I owe to your family and to the family de Whittier. I long for the day I can, in person, express the overflow of my grateful heart. I now look forward to finally knowing the daughter I have been forced to love at a distance for so long and to protecting Rynnaia under my own roof in her true home.

Please give Rynnaia the assurance of my love, though she may doubt it, and know that your King and friend remains forever in your debt and at your service.

I hold on to the Hope I have carried these many years. May
that same Hope strengthen you in the difficult days ahead.
  Please allow Rynnaia to read this missive when she is ready.
What follows is for her:
  Rynnaia, remember.

It was as if the words were a command to the deepest recesses of my mind. Of their own accord, my eyes closed and a
scene appeared to me as if from a dream.

I was in my bedroom at Argus Keep, the last place I'd lived
with Uncle Drinius's family before he'd taken me to Veetri. I
was in my bed, the window dark with night, but the wick of
the bedside lamp turned up bright. Aunt Alaine stood beside
the bed, wringing her hands. Across the room I caught my
reflection in the looking glass.

I was still a little girl. A little girl with freckles and curly
red hair.

The wooden door shuddered. Aunt Alaine hurried to answer the knock. My breath caught in my throat as the man
entered my room.

He wore dark, close-fitting riding breeches and a matching hip-length tunic was open, revealing a white shirt beneath.
A short-trimmed moustache met the telltale triangular beard
that identified him as a knight.

"Are you my father?" My own lips utter the question, but
my voice was every bit as young as I'd appeared in the mirror.

"Yes."

"You're tall."

He smiled. "As, I've been told, are you."

But he did not share my coloring. This knight had dark
hair. It was hard to tell if it was brown or black, but it was
certainly not the same flaming hue as mine.

Aunt Alaine quietly exited the bedchamber, shutting the door behind her. The knight hesitated just inside the door as his eyes adjusted to the dimness. When he approached the bed his step faltered. Inhaling sharply, he whispered a word I hadn't recognized then, but I did now.

"*Daithia.*"

"What did you say?"

"Your mother's name." He pulled a chair next to the bed. "Sir Drinius told me you resembled her, but I had no idea it was such a striking comparison."

He reached forward to stroke my cheek and I flinched. An emotion crossed his face that reminded me of physical pain. "Eight years is too long for a man to be separated from his daughter," he said as he dropped his hand, but his eyes caressed my face as if memorizing each feature.

"Am I to go with you now?"

"Not yet, love," he sighed. "Not yet. Your safety is the most important thing in the world to me and I have instructed Sir Drinius to keep you hidden in order to ensure that safety." He paused. "But I believe I have devised a way by which you may be seen by more than just this household. I've made arrangements for you to live in Veetri."

"Veetri?" The youthful heart within me leapt. "Where the Story People dance in the hands of the Storytellers?"

My father chuckled. "Yes, the very same. And I've no doubt you will see be able to watch them dance whenever you'd like. I have it on good authority that a Master Storyteller resides at the very house in which you will live!"

I clasped my hands at my chest. "Lily will be so excited! We've read of the Storytellers in our lessons!"

His smile fell. "I'm afraid Lily will not be accompanying you. When the time comes, your uncle and Sir Gladiel will be delivering you to the home of the Duke and Duchess of Glenhume and you will stay with their family."

"Without Lily and Aunt Alaine?"

"I'm sorry, love. It will be difficult, but I believe it's the right path for you. At least for now."

His tender tone broke my thin, young reserve. Tears welled in my eyes, blurring my vision. A moment later, strong arms surrounded me and pulled me into his lap. His arms felt warm and safe around me, and the soft fabric of his tunic absorbed my tears as he murmured words of comfort and love.

"Believe me, child. If there was another way, I would find it." He increased the strength of his embrace. "If I could have you with me, I would move the Sacred Mountain itself to see it done."

A light knock on the door turned both our heads toward it.

"I have already stayed longer than I should have," he said, "and I do not wish to compromise you or this household, further. Please know you have always had my love and you always will." He paused and put his finger under my chin, lifting it so he could look directly into my eyes. "With all that I am and for all of my life, I love you."

My father placed his right hand on my head but kept the other arm wrapped around me. I watched, wide-eyed, as he angled his face toward the ceiling. "Loeftryn de Rynloeft," he petitioned. "*Embral e' Veria.*" He spoke several more words in a language I couldn't understand, but I knew he spoke a blessing over me. "I commit this child to you. Please wrap my daughter in your care in the days to come and give her the comfort and peace that she can only find in you, our Mighty First King."

He took a deep breath and kissed the top of my head. "I love you," he said. "You will not remember my love for a long time, but it is forever yours."

He stood and placed me gently back in my bed, almost as if he had tucked me in every night of my life. When he spoke, his voice was layered with pain.

"Guard this night deep within your heart," he whispered. He touched his hand gently to my forehead. "But do not recall it until you've gained the truth of who you are and I've given permission."

At once, swirls of gray invaded my mind and he disappeared within them.

I opened my eyes. The letter in my hands—my full-grown hands—was signed simply, *Jarryn.*

"He's my father," I whispered. "King Jarryn really is my father."

The sweetness of the hidden memory from my childhood lingered, tightening like a fist around my heart. I was suddenly overcome with a desire to make some connection with the man within it. Like a child calling out in the night after awakening from an unsettling dream, I whispered the word that was so unfamiliar to my upbringing.

"*Father.*"

That one whispered word loosed wave after wave of color over my mind. I closed my eyes and lost all perception of where I was. Outdoor scenery moved past my eyes as fleet as quicksilver across my consciousness.

It was as if I was flying through Mynissbyr Wood and across the plains of the Stoen province at an alarming speed. I passed over villages, through a large city, and into a massive building in the space of time it would take to draw a deep breath. I had only *seen* the movement, however. I'd not felt even the slightest breeze through my hair. A vague awareness told me that my body remained still, but a part of my consciousness had traveled far away.

My travel halted. Directly before my line of vision, a man sat at an ornately carved desk, writing on parchment. His russet-brown hair was tinged with silver at the temples and his knight's beard was salted with a few silver-white whiskers as well. Across his forehead a simple circlet of gold rested. He looked up and I was arrested by the bright blue of his eyes.

Something deep within me recognized his face and traces of mine within it. Our eyes locked and I felt the truth of his love and the grief that gave him such profound fear for me.

The intensity of that moment was stronger than anything I'd felt in my life. My mind and my heart were barraged with such a powerful rush of feeling that I could barely take it in. It was as if I was there, with him. My father! But I was *not* there. Not really.

The King blinked. *"Rynnaia . . . ?"*

The surprise in his voice made me think he could actually *see* me. I gasped and felt as if my body was thrown back, but I knew I had not moved. His eyes captivated me. Intense in the depth of their blueness, the King's eyes were not quite as bright as my own, but nearly. *Andoven eyes,* I thought with surprise. But as clear as they were, I detected a cloudiness of sorts. Though I couldn't give it a name, there was something in his eyes, something just as strong, just as true as our kinship, but it was hidden from my view.

A sudden rush of gray swirled and fogged until I could see little else but flecks of the colors that, for a moment, had been so bright.

It is intentional, I realized, not knowing from where my knowledge came. *He's hiding something from me. Something dangerous. Something . . . important.*

The fog cleared, but before I could see past it and into the secret he still kept, a tidal wave of brilliant, undiluted love poured from the King.

As if a battering ram assaulted my gut, I hurtled backward. With a loud noise the air was knocked out of me as if I'd been punched in the stomach and landed, many feet away, on my back.

I opened my eyes to find that I was, in fact, on my back. The chair had tipped over. Above me, Julien's face was drawn with concern.

"Julien?" I blinked. "What happened? Where's my father? He was just over . . ." The desk, the chair, the King . . . they were all gone. "Where am I?"

"You're at the Bear's Rest."

"Oh." I blinked. "Of course I am. I'm sorry."

"Do you feel as if you can rise?"

I nodded. Worry marked his handsome face as he lifted the chair, with me in it, and set us both upright. "You were reading the missive from the King," he said. His brow furrowed. "I'm not sure what happened. You fainted, I think. And rather violently."

I could not address the questions in his eyes. My mind was too overwhelmed to put words together.

"Perhaps you should lie down for a bit."

I tried to stand, but my legs gave out. Catching me before I hit the ground, Julien picked me up as if I was as tiny as Lily and took me up the stairs to my bedchamber.

"I'm so . . . tired." I couldn't even thank him, so heavy were my eyelids. Too exhausted to move or think, I slept.

*T*HIRTY

"*P*rincess Rynnaia."

Could it be morning already? No. Hadn't I just gone to sleep?

The room was cold, as if someone had let the fire go out. I tried to burrow deeper under the blankets, but even though a part of me knew I should get up and see to the fire, it would have to stay unlit. I was too tired to care about the cold.

"Princess Rynnaia."

I pulled the pillow over my head and wished that whoever the man was talking to would answer him so I could sleep in peace.

Someone forcibly removed the pillow from my grip.

"Princess Rynnaia." The man spoke again. He cleared his throat. "Ah . . . Rose?"

I opened my eyes. Julien's face was just inches from my own. I reached my hand to his cheek and brushed a golden curl from his forehead. "Good morning, Bear-knight."

"It's not morning." he straightened. "It's time to leave. You must rally yourself, Princess. You need to eat something quickly. The others await us by the stream."

Aunt Alaine. Lily. Eneth. The stream.

Fyrlean Manor.

I shook my head. The last thing I remembered was reading my father's letter. And that had happened in the morning hours. "I thought you wanted to travel at night."

"It is night. You were asleep for some time. The King's letter had a rather profound effect."

I sat up and ripped off the blanket as I swiveled my legs to the edge of the bed. I stood up a little too quickly and my knees revolted by turning to mush.

Julien's hand was there to steady me. And it was a good thing. It was as if I had no strength in my body at all. "Julien, I don't think I can . . ."

He settled me into a chair and handed me a piece of bread with butter and jam on it. "Eat, Princess. I will carry you if necessary."

I managed to eat the bread only by giving it my full concentration. When I finished, I looked up—and screamed.

Julien quickly lowered the hood of the Bear-cloak. "I'm sorry. I thought you saw me put it on."

I waved a hand to silence his apology, feeling terribly foolish for forgetting about the cloak. I was unable to focus my mind clearly enough to dwell on my embarrassment for long, however, because a moment later Julien had me in my boots and cloak.

"Julien, what's wrong with me? I feel so—"

Before he could answer, my mind filled with a swirling tornado of gray and black flecked with gold. Somehow I knew that Julien had picked me up and was carrying me, but I could barely feel him. I was lost in the swirl.

Cold air assaulted my face. I opened eyes I hadn't even realized were closed. Pinpricks of starlight seemed almost blinding to my overindulged mind. I turned my face toward Julien's chest, but felt dizzy nonetheless.

Julien said, "The princess is not well." The next moment I was high on a saddle with him behind me. "Don't look down," he said a moment too late. I started to fall, but he caught me and I was gone again, amid the black and gray and gold, not even feeling the horse beneath me.

I awoke some hours later. My head had cleared and my sense of balance was restored enough to realize I was no longer on horseback. A moment of panic choked me when I was unable to move, so tightly was I bound. I squirmed and the hold loosened, but did not allow me to sit up.

"Julien . . . your cloak." The bear-cloak was wound tightly around me, cushioning my body from the hard, frozen ground. The knight was immediately by my side. The moon was high, and even through the branches of the trees it gave enough light that I was able to see the worry etched on his face.

"I'm better now," I assured him. "Thank you." Without the fur, the raw cold of the air bit through my cloak, but as Julien wore no cloak at all, I was glad to relinquish it.

We were deep within the Wood but appeared to be on a trail of sorts. I cautiously took to my feet as Aunt Alaine came toward me.

"I am so sorry. I had no idea how powerful your father's words would be! I assumed you would be able to read the code, of course. Your mother's Andoven abilities were so strong. But I didn't know it would affect you so terribly." She wrapped her arms around me. "I am a poor teacher, I'm afraid."

"I'm feeling much better now." I returned her hug. "It was strange, Aunt Alaine, as if I stood in the same room with him!

He looked at me and said my name, my *real* name, and it held so many powerful emotions. So much . . ." I paused, searching for a different word but could find none, "truth."

"I don't know what this means." Aunt Alaine gazed at me with a strange, bewildered expression. "But now I understand why you must go to Tirandov Isle. The Andoven will be able to explain it. They will help you, Rose." She faltered. "I suppose I should get used to calling you by your *real* name, shouldn't I?"

"Perhaps not yet." My laugh seemed to release a well of pent-up emotion. "No one even knows I exist!"

Eneth's familiar chuckle, deep and throaty, came from where she hobbled out from behind a tree. Her face bore half-healed scratches and she wore her grief about her shoulders, stooping her to a position much older than her fifty-some years. A lump formed in my throat as I remembered the loss of Walen, who had served Uncle Drinius's family for longer than I had been alive.

Julien shrugged on the bear-cloak and retrieved the horses from where they nosed through the snow to graze.

"Oh, Julien!" I breathed. "He's beautiful!"

Salvador's white mane and silver-gray coat reflected the moonlight and snow as if they were working together to camouflage his giant form. Many hands taller than Stanza and much more muscular, Salvador was, quite easily, the largest horse I had ever seen.

I walked the short distance to the huge animal. "So this is your overgrown lamb."

Salvador looked down at me, strength and intelligence clearly visible in his greenish-gray eyes. He took a step forward and made a soft, whinnying sound. I held my hand up to caress his muzzle, the bottom of which was above my head.

For such size, he appeared to have an almost regal grace about him.

Salvador sniffed my wrist as I touched his nose and startled me by moving suddenly closer and lowering his massive head to rest on my shoulder.

With a gentle, steady motion, Salvador moved his head from one of my shoulders to the other before retreating two steps back. I moved to approach him, but Julien stopped me with a hand to my arm.

"Wait."

Salvador extended his left foreleg while bending the right. He lowered his head.

"He knows who you are," Julien said softly. "He is offering his fealty."

It was a beautiful thing to see. Reverent. My hand fluttered to my chest. "Even discounting his size," I whispered, "he is not a normal horse, is he?"

"No," I could hear the smile in his voice, "he is not. He is Alvarro."

"Alvarro? That is a breed?"

"The Alvarro are quite rare. When they bond to a human, it is an intense bond. They are a very special breed."

I couldn't argue with that. I walked over to the majestic creature and gently touched his head. He arose and nuzzled my face with his. Closing my eyes, I leaned into the massive head, pleased with the ease at which I could sense his thoughts.

Salvador was more than a horse. He was, for lack of a better term, a knight in his own way, a sentient, emotive animal whose commitment to duty was clear, though in a more primitive, straightforward form than I had yet seen in the thoughts of another.

I sighed, resting my head against Salvador's neck. "Sir Julien, I do believe I love your horse."

Julien grinned and patted Salvador's flank. "It appears the feeling is mutual. Are you ready to ride?"

Salvador's head bobbed. I laughed. "I supposed that settles it! Let's go."

We started at a fast canter and gradually increased to a light, steady gallop. I passed the time attuning myself to the way the horses reasoned as we traversed the Wood. When I'd learned I was Andoven, I hadn't even considered that my abilities to communicate without audible words would stretch beyond humanity, but the discovery was beyond fascinating.

I stiffened when a sudden tension and alertness came from Salvador. Julien slowed down enough to veer off the trail and Salvador took us down an incline out of sight of the path. The other horses followed his lead and my gift picked up the first prickling colors of fear from my companions.

Julien slid off the mount and put his finger to his lips. He pointed at me, tapped his ear, and placed two fingers on his forehead, giving me permission to listen in on his thoughts.

Lily and Aunt Alaine leaned into their mounts and stroked their necks to keep them still. Eneth copied their behavior. I stayed in the saddle, but Julien crept up the incline the way we had come. He'd almost reached the trail when I heard the horses. A moment later my head ached from the cacophony of thoughts of their riders.

Focus on Sir Julien, Lily's voice broke through my dizziness. *Only him.*

I concentrated on picturing his face and let the vision of the gold of his hair and the emerald of his eyes draw me into his thoughts. As soon as I was able to separate Julien's colors from those of my immediate companions and the oncoming riders, I mentally reached for the strands of gray Lily and Aunt

Alaine had taught me to seek. A foggy sort of ripple coated my mind, bringing with it a clarity that could, with a bit of effort, selectively block other distractions and help me to focus on what I sought. *Julien.* The chaos in my mind gradually faded.

The riders made no attempt at subtly as they approached. Salvador stood still as death. For a moment I kindled the thought that it was a regiment of the King's men, sent to escort us. But one clear message from Julien quenched my hope.

Enemies! His thought shouted. *Stay hidden!*

It seemed an eternity before the sound of the horses died away and Julien returned, his expression grave.

"Dwonsil warriors," he reported. "We must stay off the road."

Like his father the Regent, Julien thought of what we'd been traveling on as a "road"? Unbelievable.

"Don't worry." In the darkness he misinterpreted my sigh. "Salvador knows the way." He paused, looking off through the dark trees. "It will be a lesser distance, but a harder ride. We're not far from Fyrlean Manor now and should arrive in about two hours' time."

Julien mounted and spoke softly in my ear. "I had hoped to stay to the road a while longer for the sake of the others, but this way is faster and much safer."

I couldn't help myself. "You and your father have a rather broad definition of the word 'road,' don't you think?"

His silent laugh vibrated against my back and the breath of it tickled my ear as he grabbed the reins. "Home, Salvador."

It was slow going at times, making our way through the bracken and bramble of the Wood, and although it was no challenge for Salvador or Stanza, we kept to a slower pace for the benefit of Aunt Alaine's and Eneth's much smaller horses.

As the first hint of dawn appeared ahead of us, I entwined my fingers in Salvador's silky mane. At my touch he seemed to add a bounce to his step. I giggled and turned my smile to Julien. His eyes reflected my mirth as he leaned his head toward my ear.

"Salvador is no doubt anxious for his comfortable stall and the groom who knows his fondness for a certain variety of oats!"

We paused on the crest of a hill and I had my first glimpse of Fyrlean Manor in the early morning sun. In my limited experience I would have called it a castle, though Julien assured me later that it was not. Whatever it was, it was breathtaking. Built of a warm, reddish-brown stone that reached three stories, each corner was marked by a square turret and I could just make out the forms of guards, pacing on high.

The huge manor house and other buildings of the keep were surrounded by a high and heavily guarded wall made of the same stone as the structures. The gates were of iron.

"It's beautiful."

Julien's pleasure was evident as he took in the scene before him. I could tell he appreciated my reaction to it. His eyes turned more serious as he said, "Many who guard and serve within Fyrlean Manor have spent time in service to the King. Even those who did not meet Queen Daithia have seen her portrait in Castle Rynwyk. They are loyal to the crown, but I don't think the time is right to reveal you just yet."

I nodded and pulled my hood further down in front of my face. Then, as if he could not wait a moment longer, Salvador led us down the hill and to the western gates.

The guards recognized Julien and Salvador.

"Sir Julien approaches!" A shout announced the arrival of the Regent's son and the guards bowed as they opened the gates. Julien nodded, and without a word we rode around to the front of the manor where three grooms already awaited us. We left the horses with them.

As we approached the house, the front door burst open and a boy ran down the steps. With a whoop, he vaulted over a side railing to speed his passage toward us.

As he came closer, I noticed a long, blond braid bouncing off his back. *Odd.* On closer inspection, however, I realized that the feminine features on the youth belonged not to a lad, but instead, to a petite young woman.

Julien laughed, picked her up, and swung her around. "What have you done with my sister, little squire?"

"Oh, Julien! Quit your teasing."

When she punched his arm I could barely contain my grin. *So this is Erielle, Gladiel's adventurous daughter!*

I watched their reunion from a short distance away, suddenly homesick for my brothers in Veetri. But my reverie was broken by a shout.

"Julien!" I turned toward the woman's cry. "Julien!"

Julien embraced the woman and swiftly turned to us. "Mother, Erielle, may I present Lady Drinius, her daughter Lily, and her ward," he faltered just a moment, "Rose."

My head was covered and my face was shadowed by the hood of my cloak, but still I kept my eyes to the ground as I bobbed a curtsy.

"Ladies, this is my mother, Willo al Gladiel, and my sister, Erielle."

Erielle curtsied, not in the least bit impeded by her masculine attire. Lady Gladiel greeted both Lily and me before moving forward to embrace Aunt Alaine.

"Alaine," she said. "It has been much too long. Come in now and refresh yourselves. I would imagine you've had quite a ride!" With her arm around my aunt's shoulders, Julien's mother ushered us inside.

THIRTY-ONE

Lady Gladiel led us up an impressive brown marble staircase and into a large chamber.

"You may wait here while I see that rooms are readied for you." She turned to go, but Julien followed.

"Mother, might I have a word?"

"Of course." Lady Gladiel turned to her boyishly dressed daughter. "Erielle, would you alert the staff to see to refreshments?"

Julien returned moments later. "Lady Drinius, Lady Lily, you are welcome at Fyrlean Manor for as long as you desire to stay." He turned to me. "We'll rest for a few days and make preparations for our journey."

"Sir Julien," Aunt Alaine stepped forward and took my hand. "What route do you plan to take to reach Tirandov Isle?"

"From here we'll ride east until we hit Dynwey Road," he said. "We'll follow it all the way to Port Dyn and await the King's scribe there."

"Wouldn't it be faster," I said, thinking back to the collection of maps Koria had forced me to study at length, "if we traveled through Shireya's foothills?"

"It's too dangerous." Julien shook his head. "The King's men patrol Dynwey Road and most of the villages along it." His brow furrowed. "Our departure may be delayed a bit while we try to devise some sort of disguise for you." He rubbed his chin with his thumb and forefinger. His face suddenly brightened, but his tone was dry when he said, "I may seek my sister's help with the matter. Erielle has been known to disguise herself in the past. And I must say she is quite . . . creative."

I sensed there was a story there, but a maid entered with a tray that made my stomach remember how long it had been since we'd eaten.

After we partook of the refreshments offered, the maid led us to our rooms where deep and fragrant tubs of steaming water awaited us. I could not suppress my grin when I noticed the hot-water apparatus that Sir Gladiel's brother Ayden had designed.

"If you leave your garments on the bed," the maid curtsied, "I will pick them up and have them cleaned for you." She pulled the drapes closed. "Would you like me to stay and assist you with your hair?"

"No, thank you."

With another quick curtsy the maid excused herself, leaving the door ajar. Julien was still in the hall, speaking with two armed guards. He motioned for me to join him.

"Lady Rose, these men will be posted outside your door. Should you need anything, or have any fear, they will be at the ready. My chamber adjoins your own, so do not hesitate to call upon me."

"Thank you." I curtsied to the guards, careful to keep the hood over my face, and turned to enter the chamber.

Once inside, I locked the door and leaned against it, sighing with the pleasure of being alone. My chamber was furnished with rich mahogany pieces, some covered with up-holsteries patterned in gold and emerald green. It reminded me of the colors that kissed my mind each time I thought of Julien. But of course it should be like him. This was his home.

Home.

The word brought both fondness and pain. As I undressed and lowered my aching limbs into the warm water, my mind lingered on the images it recalled. Home had been with Uncle Drinius, Aunt Alaine, and Lily until my father ordered me to Veetri. But Veetri had become my home as well, as had the Bear's Rest, even though it would never claim the same fond-ness in my heart as Mirthan Hall.

Suddenly, I felt lost. My father's parchment had called Castle Rynwyk my true home, but I'd never been there. How would a Veetrish country girl like me ever fit in at the castle of the King?

As I scrubbed my hair I recalled the look upon Julien's face when we were on the ridge overlooking Fyrlean Manor. Was there a place for which I might someday have that same pride, that same sense of belonging?

I rinsed the soap from my hair, and with a heavy sigh I climbed out of the tub.

After I dressed I dug through my saddlebag until I found a brush and comb and began the long process of untangling my hair. When I finished with that dreaded chore I repositioned a chair closer to the fire and draped my hair over its back, toward the heat. I must have dozed, because when Julien's knock on the door adjoining our rooms awakened me, my hair was nearly dry.

Oh. My breath caught in my throat and my hand stole up to the place where it waited. *Oh, my.*

Gone were the heavy garments necessary for winter travel, replaced with an ivory and gold embroidered vest over a simple beige shirt and fawn-colored breeches. His hair had been trimmed, but it was still a bit damp and had begun to curl around the nape of his neck. Standing on the threshold between our rooms, his manner exuded confidence. He seemed taller, almost as if being in his own home had increased his already impressive stature.

I dropped my eyes, but I didn't blush until I realized that he had been appraising me as well.

"If you're hungry," he said finally, "I've a table laid out in my chamber."

The refreshments we'd had upon our arrival had satisfied me for a little while, but the bath and nap had reinvigorated my need for something more substantial.

Julien's chamber was the exact opposite of mine. Instead of mahogany, the wood was a golden oak and the upholstery was a whitish gold with hints of green. Open curtains let in the bright sunshine of a late-morning sky and it danced in dots of light across the walls as it reflected on a glimmering chandelier that was somehow elegant and masculine at the same time.

Julien held a chair for me.

"At Fyrlean Manor, as in Castle Rynwyk," he explained as he took the chair across from mine, "we speak a blessing over our food before we partake of it. In my condition of late, I fell out of the habit. But if you don't mind . . . ?"

"Please." I was no stranger to the practice, although it was a ritual irregularly performed before meals at Mirthan Hall—and even less frequently at the Bear's Rest after Uncle Drinius left us. Tradition dictated I should close my eyes and lift my face as Julien did. But when he closed his eyes I couldn't seem to tear my gaze from his face.

"We are grateful for the protection that saw us safely home," he began. His words were simple, but he was beautiful saying them. As he spoke it was as if he'd been transported elsewhere, carried to a place of affection I could not follow, but if allowed within, I would find utterly serene.

It gave me cause to wonder, but not for long. As soon as he finished the blessing he filled my plate first and then his own.

I quickly took my first bite so he wouldn't have to wait. The food was wonderful, but Julien seemed preoccupied.

"Is something amiss? You're quieter than usual."

"Am I? I'm sorry." He paused. "Being here with you makes everything seem so much more real than it did at the Bear's Rest."

"What do you mean?"

"I suppose it's a number of things. For one thing, your hair is . . ." he paused, as if searching for the right word, "different."

"Different how?" I laughed, well knowing the answer. "I believe the word you are looking for, most gallant knight, is *clean*."

He grinned. "Well, that certainly doesn't hurt." He chuckled. "But unbound, cascading as it is, it catches the light and I can see more of that hint of flame you've inherited from the Queen. It's truly lovely."

He took another bite, but by the way his brow furrowed again I could tell he was chewing on more than food.

"Your resemblance to the Queen does present a bit of a problem," he said. "We must endeavor to keep you out of sight while you are here."

"Even from your mother and sister?" I asked.

"They understand the nature of discretion," he said, "but it would be a big shock for them to learn the truth."

"Oh." I nodded. I should have expected as much. "Of course."

"They would, however, be given much hope by seeing you." Julien took a bite, chewed, and swallowed. "I will speak to Lady Alaine. If she agrees, perhaps you may meet them later, if that would please you."

"Yes!" I exclaimed. "Very much!"

He smiled and set his napkin over his now empty plate. "If you'll excuse me then, Your Highness, I'll see to it at once."

I made a face. "I thought we were letting off with that."

"Pardon me, *Lady Rose.*" He winked and left me to finish my meal alone.

With little else to occupy me while Julien spoke with Aunt Alaine, and hopefully, his mother and sister, I returned to my own chamber and paced. After examining the curtains, the furniture, even the beams of the ceiling, my eyes caught on a tapestry. I stepped closer to examine it more thoroughly.

The design was one of the most intricate I'd ever seen. I couldn't imagine the hours spent creating such a masterpiece. In the center of a multihued green background, a bear stood on its hind legs. Embroidered in shades of bronze and brown and gold, it looked so real that I almost took a step back. Instead, I stepped closer.

The enraged bruin's face held an unexpected trace of humanity. *A Bear-man,* I realized. Not only had Ayden explained the story of Lady Anya and the Bear-men, but I'd seen one of the cloaks in use. Still, I shuddered as the fierce gaze of the Bear-man followed me across the room and back. The bear's green eyes bored into me, as if daring me to push the curtain aside and see what treasure was guarded behind his deadly, piercing gaze.

I never could refuse a direct challenge, even if it came from an inanimate object.

I pulled the tapestry aside to find it protected not an arsenal of weapons or a trove of jewels, but books.

Books! That would certainly help me while away the hours. Locating a tieback, I secured the tapestry out of the way in order to examine the collection.

I'd enjoyed unrestricted access to the extensive library at Mirthan Hall, and this shelf held many familiar tomes. Mostly philosophy and folktales, the golden-etched titles called to me like old friends. I smiled and ran my hand over their wrinkled spines. The books revealed signs of wear, but few showed any great love for the words within until I picked up an unusually small volume of poetry.

Carefully sliding it out from between two larger books, I ran my hand across its oft-repaired binding. The leather cover was softened, like a lady's favorite kidskin glove, and the edges of the pages uneven, without a sharp edge among them. As I opened the cover, the scent confirmed the manuscript as very old indeed, but neither an author nor a title for the work was listed.

The nondescript pages lacked the scrollwork I was accustomed to in scribe-copied texts, consisting instead of simple, yet feminine penmanship, with an occasional smear of ink marring a page here and there. I moved to a chair by the fire and began to read a rhyming versed account of Lady Anya's time among the Cobelds.

Dizziness crept up from my torso to my fingertips, much as when I'd read the King's letter. I did not welcome the sensation, but I could no more deny my curiosity to finish the poem than I could deny the boredom that would ensue should I decide to stop reading.

Unlike the coded letter, this poetry was written in my own language. Other than compensating for the fade of time upon the parchment, my eyes did not have to strain. I took a deep breath and pressed on, but with each line of poetry the dizziness increased. My stomach seemed to tumble forward and back, but even that discomfort could not quench my desire to find out where my strange, new Andoven gifts would take me next.

The book in my hands gradually faded from my conscious view, and although I knew my physical body remained in the chair, I had the odd sensation of being in two places at once. I knew I hadn't moved, but a part of my consciousness stood behind an occupied desk, looking over the shoulder of a poet who wasn't really there, as words flowed on to the parchment from the quill in her hand.

Of slight build, her hair was coal black and plaited in one thick braid down her back. She dipped her quill into the inkpot and set it on the paper. I read the words as they appeared beneath her hand:

Beyond the rim of firelight, he stood as in a trance.
The prophesying creature spoke, death's shadow in his glance.
"With sky-jeweled eyes and mane of fire," the withered creature cried,
"The Ryn Lady E'veria will Cobeld's curse exile."
From all around, the Cobelds let a panicked, outraged cry
They did not know deception's beard disguised a ready spy.
Away she crept, through darkened night. Alone, but armed with hope
The Great Wood birthed a servanthood 'til vanquished be the foe.

The poet paused and a drop of ink dripped just beside the last word. She blotted it with a piece of cloth, set the quill on a stand, and turned slowly in her chair to face me.

Her eyes widened. She stood. "Ryn Naia." She pronounced my name strangely, as if it was comprised of two separate words, but she dipped her head as if she knew exactly who I was and had been expecting my arrival for quite some time.

Wispy black tendrils had escaped their bonds, framing her heart-shaped face and bringing out the deep green color of her eyes. Their familiar emerald brightness held such intelligence, courage, and purpose that I immediately knew who she was, though a part of me knew it to be impossible. Wasn't it?

"Lady Anya." I greeted her, my voice barely above a whisper.

"Time is short." She placed her hand upon my arm and spoke quickly, almost as if she expected to be interrupted. "Assemble those who will best help you quest for the Remedy. But locating the Remedy is only the beginning, Ryn Naia. You must—"

A soft noise, like a hand slapping the surface of water, interrupted Lady Anya and arrested the attention of us both for a moment. When she spoke again the cadence of her words increased.

"This much I have translated," Lady Anya said. "Listen carefully. *Nine marks stand guard to guide the way. Three tasks upon the Ryn will prey. Death stalks the path with fierce desire, a counsel of four will strike the pyre.*" She paused and repeated the rhyme twice before prompting me to say it back to her.

I did. "What does it mean?"

"I cannot be certain, but—"

Another noise jarred us both. I followed the direction of her gaze to the door adjoining my chamber to Julien's. My stomach dropped, like the sensation of falling in a dream, and the part of me that realized I'd never left the chair felt the book of poetry slide from my hands.

When I turned back toward Lady Anya, her presence was filmy, fading. "Let truth be your guard, Ryn Naia," her words faded as she disappeared, the last bit barely above a whisper, "and I pray he will reveal the rest."

"Who?" I asked. "Julien?" But she was gone.

A wave of nausea washed over me.

The noise repeated. Knocking! It was louder this time and accompanied by a voice, but I could not respond. Instead, I concentrated on the rhythm of my breaths as if they were the steps of a dance that would bring the two halves of me back together. *In two-three, and out two-three, and in two-three, and out two-three.*

The door burst open just as my mind rejoined itself. I gasped at the shock of being fully present.

"Princess?" Julien's voice was strained, almost angry. "Did you not hear me knocking?"

"I did, but I didn't know ... Don't worry. I'm ... back."

"Back? From where?"

"From ... here, I think." I winced and rubbed my temples. "Oh, my head."

"You're hurt?" Julien sheathed his sword so swiftly it sang against the scabbard. The sound was like ice scraping under my skull. "Did someone enter your chamber?"

"No. Er, yes, I mean. But ... no. And yes." I blinked up at him, knowing my words were as jumbled as my vision. "It was just Lady Anya. No one dangerous. Oh! You have her eyes."

Julien knelt in front of me. "Rynnaia, did you fall? Hit your head?"

"No. I was ... reading, I think."

Was I? Yes. The poetry.

"It was like before. With the King's letter!" I struggled to put the pieces together and then into words. "I was sitting right here, but I was also standing behind the desk over there

. . ." I looked toward the window. A trunk sat beneath it, but there was no desk, no quill or parchment. "Well, it was there a moment ago."

I bent over to pick up the volume and groaned as pain shot through my skull. Julien followed the direction of my reach and placed the book into my hands.

I leaned back into the chair. "I'm sorry I dropped it. I'm sure it's quite precious." I ran my hand over the soft leather cover. "Lady Anya was lovely. In quite a hurry, of course, but—" Even to my own ears my words seemed more than a tad idiotic. But I couldn't seem to contain them. "You do have her eyes, you know. Such a bright green. Like a Veetrish hill on a cloudy summer day."

Julien took the book from my hands, his gaze troubled. "I've read this poem many times, Princess Rynnaia, and I don't recall it ever mentioning that Lady Anya had green eyes."

"She does." I scowled and shook my head. "Er, she did, rather. I saw her. It was like when I read the King's letter. But gentler, somehow. She wasn't—"

She wasn't trying to hide something from me, like the King was. Like he always has.

I shook my head to clear away the sudden resentment. "I saw her writing the poem, Julien. She spoke to me."

Julien stared at me for a long moment and then moved to sit in the large winged chair across from mine.

"In the future," he began slowly, "I would appreciate it if you would inform me of your intentions *before* you start reading anything that might—well, anything at all, I guess." He sighed, but his gaze warmed. "Are you feeling better?"

"I am." I was surprised by the admission, but the pain and dizziness had evaporated. "It was easier this time."

"Good. Can I get you anything? Something to drink?"

"I'm fine, thank you. Really." I held out the book. "You've read this?"

"Many times." Julien took the book from my hands. "It has been the belief of so-called experts that this story was penned by a scribe, or even a Storyteller. But I have often wondered, and my sister has always been convinced, that Lady Anya herself was the poet."

"I saw the words form beneath her quill, Julien." The thrill of my experience raced through my torso and out of my mouth. "I, for one, am certainly convinced." I laughed and it felt good to do so. "Lady Anya looked at me and she spoke to me. And although she pronounced it oddly, she called me by name! I don't understand all of what she said, but it appears I am supposed to find the Remedy and then stop the Cobelds."

"The poem alludes to that," he nodded. "But this experience of yours is beyond me. Perhaps someone you meet on Tirandov Isle shares this ability and will be able to explain it."

"Lady Anya said 'time is short,'" I said, relating the whole of my unwritten message from Lady Anya's poem. "Julien, if time was short in her day, it must be infinitely more so now."

"Indeed." Julien pressed the balls of his hands to his temples and then down his jawline before resting them in his lap. "I've heard it said that no one can find Tirandov Isle without the assistance of an Andoven guide."

"That must be why the King has sent his scribe to Port Dyn! He must be searching for a guide while awaiting our arrival."

He nodded. "It's likely."

"Certainly the Andoven would come if the King ordered it, wouldn't they?"

He snorted a laugh. "One would hope. The Andoven's relationship with the crown is . . . unique."

A soft knock came from the direction of his chamber's door. "Do you feel well enough to meet my mother and sister? I could tell them to come back later."

"I'm fine."

He studied my face for a long moment and then, with a nod he stood. "The maids will ready the table and I will come for you as soon as Erielle and my mother arrive."

He paused to look at me again before crossing back into his chamber and closing the door between us.

Nervousness fluttered through my midsection. Julien's mother was a Regent's wife, yet I had never even been to court! I wanted Lady Gladiel and Erielle to like me. To approve of me. But how could I possibly meet their expectations of what a "princess" was supposed to be?

THIRTY-TWO

My nerves had not settled in the least before Julien reappeared and led me through the door. As nervous as I was, it didn't occur to me that I should block my mind. As soon as I crossed the threshold a rush of images assaulted me.

A woman, looking much like me—smiling.

A huge portrait of that same woman, hanging on a stone wall.

The King.

Lady Gladiel gasped. Her hand went to her throat.

"Sky-jeweled eyes," Erielle whispered as her face split into a grin, "and head ablaze . . ."

The force of their reaction caused me to take a step backward.

"Forgive us, Your Highness," Lady Gladiel curtsied. "I did not doubt my son's word when he told me who you were, but even if I had, what I see before me now puts all to right. Queen Daithia was a dear friend and—" Her hand moved to her mouth as a tiny sob escaped. "Forgive me. It's such a shock."

I bit my lip and looked to Julien.

"Mother, Erielle," Julien lightly squeezed my elbow. His voice was soft so that it wouldn't carry beyond the room, but jubilant and strangely reverent at the same time. "May I present Her Royal Highness, Princess Rynnaia E'veri, our long-hidden heir to the E'verian throne."

"Ryn Naia!" Erielle whispered, pronouncing my name just as Lady Anya had. "Well it's about time, Your Highness!" She laughed. "And might I say that it's grand to finally meet you!"

"Erielle!" Lady Gladiel gasped. "That was impertinent. Remember to whom you are speaking!"

"But we've been waiting two hundred years for her! Lady Anya—"

"A little respect, Erielle. Please." Lady Gladiel shushed her daughter. "Princess Rynnaia is *the Ryn*, for goodness sake."

"The what?" All eyes turned to me. I turned mine to Julien. "You've said it. Aunt Alaine's said it, the voi—" I was about to say, *the voice in my head said it*, but thought better of it. "But . . . what is it, really? What does it mean?"

Julien opened his mouth and closed it. He took a breath. "The Ryn," he explained slowly, "is the title given to the first-born child of the ruling family. When the child is named, the word is added to another word of ancient significance and given as a name to the heir to the E'verian throne."

"*Naia* means 'lady.'" Erielle supplied.

The Ryn Lady E'veria will Cobeld's curse exile.

"The title is incorporated into the given name of each heir to the throne," Julien continued. "Your father is King Jar*ryn*. His father was King *Ryn*itel. You are *Ryn*naia and will some-day be Queen." He smiled. "You are the Ryn."

"Not just the Ryn!" Erielle let out a little squeak. "The *Ryn Naia*! The Ryn of the prophecy!" She winced and looked toward her mother. "Sorry." She bit her lip. "Forgive me, Your

Highness. Sometimes I get excited and my manners cease to exist."

I couldn't help but like Julien's exuberant sister, but her words gave me pause. "What prophecy? Do you mean the poem?"

But as soon as I asked the question I knew the answer. That was it! Lady Anya's book was the reason the Cobelds hunted down red-haired girls. The reason they hunted *me*. "The poem is the prophecy, isn't it?"

"Yes!" Erielle looked at her mother who sighed and nodded permission to continue. *"With sky-jeweled eyes and mane of fire, the withered creature cried, the Ryn lady E'veria will Cobeld's curse exile."*

"Yes. I've read it." I forced a smile, hoping the dizziness of earlier would not accompany my memory of reading it. "Why do you call it a prophecy?"

"It was penned by the Oracle Scribe, Your Highness," she said. "Lady Anya herself."

"She was an oracle?" For all the education I'd received, all the stories I'd been told in Veetri, this was entirely new information. Although considering what I'd just experienced reading her poetry, I felt rather like a dolt for not figuring it out earlier.

Julien came to my rescue. "Princess Rynnaia has lived away from court with no knowledge of her identity until very recently. Certain information was omitted from her upbringing for her own protection."

Erielle's eyes widened. "I can't imagine growing up without knowing about Lady Anya."

"Oh, I knew the stories," I corrected. "I just didn't know she was considered an oracle."

"Oh, she would never have called herself that," Erielle said. "And no one else did while she lived. It wasn't until she died that her grandchildren discovered her diary. In the diary she confided that she had no memory of writing the poetry or the scrolls. So, technically, she was only recording prophesies, not speaking them. That's why we call her the Oracle Scribe."

"Prophesies?" I asked. "There are more?"

"Yes. The book of poetry is only the beginning. Her diary also spoke of several scrolls that she'd given into the care of a trusted friend."

"Who?"

"No one knows," Lady Gladiel said. "She never confided, at least not in the diary, to whom they were given or where they were stored."

"But she did write other things," Erielle said.

"Like what?"

"Well, she mentioned having seen the Ryn Naia in a vision when she was young."

I turned my head and Julien met my gaze. His thought was as clear as if he had spoken. *And now it has come to pass.*

My mind spun. Had it happened then, or now? Or had we both somehow stepped out of time to meet? I didn't realize Julien's hand was still on my elbow until he gave it a slight squeeze. Regardless of when, it had happened.

"Shall we sit?" Lady Gladiel broke the silence and gestured to the beautifully set table.

Julien's mother put me at ease with her genuine care and gentle smile. "Julien tells us you grew up in Veetri?"

I nodded, but I wasn't ready to give up the subject yet. "Growing up in a Storyteller's home, I have, of course, heard many stories of the Lady Anya," I began, "but not that she was a poet or a prophet."

"Her poetry prophesied your birth, and here you are," Erielle said. She seemed as eager as I to continue the discussion. "When I found the scrolls and they matched the handwriting in Lady Anya's diary and poetry, I was discouraged because we had no Ryn. Not even a Queen to produce one."

"Erielle," her mother warned.

"But," Erielle's voice calmed, but only for a moment, "since you aren't dead, like we thought, and since you have the right hair and eyes, well! It's only a matter of time until the Cobelds are gone forever!"

Julien's lip twitched. "I have a feeling it won't be as easy to vanquish our foe as you seem to think, Erielle." His smile dimmed. "Not at all."

A shiver traveled up my spine. "These scrolls you found," I said. "What do they say?"

"I don't know. None of us can read them."

"Weren't they written by Lady Anya?"

"It's possible," Julien said. "They look old, to be sure. But they couldn't have survived where they were hidden for two hundred years."

"Don't listen to him," Erielle said and wrinkled her nose. "It has to be her. The handwriting is identical."

"Then why can't you read it?"

"Almost all of it is written in the Ancient Voice," Erielle explained. "Few are able to translate it. For all we know it could also be encoded somehow, though I can't imagine why."

I'd read the King's letter, which was encoded. *Perhaps . . .* "Maybe I could—"

"No." Julien shook his head. "Absolutely not."

"Julien." Lady Gladiel's brow arched to match the warning in her tone. "Before you issue an order to our lovely guest you may want to consider that you do so to the Ryn."

"Indeed." Erielle grinned. "Indeed you should consider that, big brother."

Julien's lips pressed together. His eyes narrowed on his mother and sister. A moment later, he turned. "My apologies, Princess Rynnaia," he said finally. "I only have your safety in mind. I meant no offense."

"And none was received," I assured them all. "This is all so new to me. Please, tell me more about the scrolls."

"There isn't much more to tell." Erielle said. "She wrote them. I found them. You're taking them to Tirandov Isle." She shrugged. "I guess we just have to hope the Andoven are able to figure out the translation." She sighed. "I wish I could come with you," she said under her breath, but I caught each word as surely as did the other members of our party.

"A little over a hundred years ago there was a terrible fire at Fyrlean Manor," Lady Gladiel picked up the subject. "No copies of the scrolls had ever been made and there was no record of their existence other than family lore. The scrolls were believed to have been destroyed. Erielle, however, discovered their existence on one of her recent excursions."

"Excursions?" Julien snorted, but his eyes twinkled with warmth. "I believe *exploits* would be a more appropriate word." He turned toward me. "My sister refuses to play the part society has assigned her. She's a trouble-finder, make no mistake. It is mischief itself that calls her from her bed each morning."

"And it is most excellent that I have the habit of answering, don't you agree, Princess?" Erielle grinned. "Being as my mischief-making resulted in discovering the scrolls."

I laughed. "Indeed." Julien acquiesced with a nod.

"I was blessed with two wonderful knights for brothers," Erielle said. "They indulged me enough in my youth that I am not often content to be idly lady-fying my way through life."

"In your youth?" I laughed. "How old are you now?"

Her chin lifted slightly. "I will pass my seventeenth birthday midsummer."

"I meant no offense. After all, I'm not that much older than you. I'll mark my nineteenth birthday next month." An idea suddenly sprang to mind. "Erielle, when I first saw you I thought you were a boy."

A subtle shift in her jaw was the only tell that revealed her offense. I hurriedly added, "But as soon as I saw your face I was disabused of the notion. You're much too pretty to be a boy."

She flushed, but her pleasure at the compliment seemed guarded. *Odd.*

"But it is thanks to your happy disregard of convention that I have an idea that might help to safeguard my passage to Dynwatre."

Julien sat forward in his chair.

I took a breath and addressed them all. "Would you be opposed to disguising a princess as a boy if it would help to ensure her safety?"

They all looked at me, silent, with expressions caught somewhere between thoughtful and appalled.

"The Ryn *Lady* is the Cobeld's enemy, correct?" I added. "Wouldn't they be less likely to attack a boy?"

"No one is safe these days," Julien said grimly.

"But I'd be a mite safer without that pesky prophecy hanging over my head, wouldn't I?"

"You sound like a Storyteller." Erielle giggled. "But it's a good idea."

"Do you really think *she* could pass as a *boy*?" Julien's look was as incredulous as his tone. "Look at her! She's—"

"Yes, Julien?" Erielle prodded, a smile pulling the corner of her mouth up. "She's . . . ?"

"Well, she's . . . a princess!" He sputtered.

"I suppose Gerrias might have some old breeches we could take in." Lady Gladiel tapped her finger against the rim of her cup.

"I don't think it will work." Julien shook his head.

Erielle wrinkled her nose. "I do it all the time!"

"*Exactly!*"

The sound that ushered forth from Erielle's mouth was full of offense. "And what, dear brother, is *that* supposed to mean?"

"Erielle. Julien," Lady Gladiel interrupted. "Manners, please. We have a guest."

When color flushed Julien's cheeks I had to bite my tongue to keep from laughing.

"My apologies again, Princess Rynnaia."

"Mine as well," Erielle said with a sigh. "Forgive us?"

"Of course. But to be truthful, your banter only makes me feel more at home. Such was the way of things at Mirthan Hall, when my brothers were home."

We talked then for some time about my years in Veetri, but too soon our time came to an end.

Before she took her leave Erielle promised to search out some of her brother's old clothing. "I don't know what we will do to alter it, since we can't allow the staff to see you," she said. "This is the first time that I ever wished I had learned to sew!"

"I may not yet know how to wield a sword," I answered, "but I am reasonably adept at wielding a needle and thread. I don't doubt that I can sufficiently alter a pair of breeches, though I will need help with the measuring, if you don't mind."

"By your leave then, Your Highness," she said with a wink and a curtsy.

"I look forward to your return."

Aunt Alaine and Lily ate supper with me that night and, afterward, they assisted me with the alterations to the clothes Erielle had delivered.

Erielle returned in the morning and I sought her opinion on the altered shirt and breeches.

Her eyes clouded a bit as she looked at me. "You're built much more womanly than I am." She gestured to the subtlety of her own curves. "Maybe Julien was right. Even with boys' clothes it's quite obvious you're female."

I turned to the looking glass and scowled. "We'll just have to find a way to camouflage that, I guess. Then all we have to worry about is my hair."

"I have an idea about that." Erielle's gaze moved from my head to my feet and back to my face. "But your eyes will be remembered by anyone who looks your direction." She paused and set down the small box she had carried in with her. "This is my mother's," she said. She opened the box and withdrew something black. "It's a hairpiece."

"It's black." I tried to picture it on Lady Gladiel with her fair hair and olive complexion.

"Yes. And it looks absolutely wretched on her. You, however," Erielle squinted at me, "could probably make it work."

"Why would your mother buy a black hairpiece?"

Erielle shrugged. "Who knows? But she was happy to donate it to your cause. It's never been worn outside Fyrlean Manor." Her eyes sparkled. "Well, not by my mother, anyway."

My eyebrows lifted.

"I may have found the occasion to borrow it once or twice."

I laughed. "Help me pin up my hair and we'll try it out. I used to have black hair, so it will probably work."

"You used to have black hair?" One blonde eyebrow arched severely upward. "How is that?"

I groaned. "It's a long story." While we worked on my hair, I gave her the short version.

Finally, I pulled the hairpiece over my braids and looked in the glass. "Well, the problem of my hair is sorted." I slipped a squire's cap over my head. "From the neck up, I look like a boy. But what can we do about," I looked down at my chest and hips, "this?"

Erielle pursed her lips. She paced to the tub and came back with a grin . . . and a towel. "I have an idea."

She wrapped the thick towel tightly around my chest and torso, doubling it over around my waist region to give the allusion of thickness. Using the chalk we had employed when measuring the pants for alteration, she made marks at various locations where fasteners would need to be sown to hold the towel in place. Tucking the end of the towel into itself, Erielle helped me put the breeches and shirt back on over the improvised camouflage.

She stepped back. "Excellent!" Then she scowled. "Except for one thing. Wait here." Gathering her skirts, Erielle ran out of my chamber through Julien's adjoining room. Within a few moments she returned, holding a pair of spectacles.

"Put these on," she said. "I've been saving these to use for one of my own adventures, but you need them more than I do."

When I placed them on my nose I was surprised that I was able to see out of them clearly.

"I had the lenses replaced with a slightly gray tinted glass the last time I was in Salderyn," she explained. The room did look slightly darker.

A knock sounded on the door between my room and Julien's.

"He said it couldn't be done." A mischievous spark lit her eyes.

"There's only one way to find out if we've succeeded!" I grinned. "Hide!"

After having spent so much time together I thought it unlikely that Julien would be fooled by my disguise, especially since this was my room. After all, who else would be here?

But I was Veetrish enough that I was unable to pass up the opportunity for a good prank.

The knock came more insistently. I wasn't sure what to do. If I answered, I would spoil the ruse, so I stayed silent.

The handle turned and the door began to open. "Princess? You aren't reading, are you?"

Julien peered into the room. His eyes widened, and before I could speak, his sword was drawn and my back was pressed against the wall.

THIRTY-THREE

Julien's left arm pressed against my neck, lifting my chin. His blade rested between us at my ribs.

Erielle stepped out from behind the drapery, already laughing. "Julien, it's *her*. Now put your sword down. You've scared poor Rynnaia half to death!"

"Rynnaia?" A hairsbreadth of a moment later the blade was swept away from my person and he stepped back.

I couldn't speak. My mouth was dry and my pulse had returned at a furious clip. I pulled the cap and hairpiece from my head, wincing as the pins fought against me. Lastly I whipped the spectacles from my face.

Julien exhaled and I felt the release of his anger the moment it transferred its focus to his sister.

"*What* were you *thinking*?" he hissed. "Attempting something like this without warning me? How could you be so foolish? She is *the Ryn*, Erielle. *The Ryn!*" He sheathed his sword with such force that I flinched. "I could have killed her!"

The color drained from Erielle's face. "I'm sorry. I didn't think—"

"Exactly!" He growled. "You didn't *think*! As usual, you did whatever your impulsive nature led you to without first calculating the risk."

Erielle's eyes pooled with tears. Her shoulders drooped. She lowered her head and a drop of wetness splashed on to her shirt.

"Julien, this is my fault." I rested my hand on his arm. "I-I thought it might be fun to surprise you. I didn't think the disguise would fool you, but—"

But it *had* fooled him.

It had *one-hundred percent* fooled him!

I couldn't contain my smile. "But it did. It worked! And if it worked on you, it will work on anyone!"

Julien's exhale sounded as if he'd been holding his breath for a week. He ran one hand through the thickness of his blond curls, but remained silent. The moments stretched with him neither speaking nor meeting my eyes.

Finally, I moved my gaze back to Erielle, but her eyes were riveted on my hands. A slow smile transferred the dread on her face to a grin.

I looked down.

Both my hands now rested between Julien's. "Please, Princess Rynnaia," his voice was low. Soft. Almost pained. "Please do not attempt to surprise me again. It nearly cost you your life." He paused and the tiniest bit of light lifted the corner of his mouth by way of his eyes. "And I have no wish to die at the tip of your father's sword."

His eyes closed for a moment then turned to his sister. "Erielle, I'm sorry. You were trying to help the princess and I hurt you. Please forgive me."

"Of course." Erielle pressed her lips together as if trying to suppress laughter. "I have to go. Excuse me." She dipped the fastest curtsy I had ever seen and ran out of the room.

Our hands separated without losing contact. Instead, they shifted as he stepped back so that my left was in his right, my right in his left. Our fingers curved, remaining connected as he appraised my costume.

"It was dangerous to surprise me like that," he said as a smile tugged at one corner of his mouth, "so please don't do it again. But you and my rapscallion of a sister have managed to solve the biggest obstacle to our course."

When he released my fingers they tingled at the loss.

"I hadn't thought to take on a squire yet," he said, "but now that I have, I must endeavor to name him." Amusement colored his words. "What shall we call you, boy? It must be something befitting a future knight, but also something that does justice to your remarkable transformation."

"And something that, should you accidentally call me by the wrong name, will be easily covered over," I added.

"That makes it more difficult," he said. "Any name with the word 'ryn' in it would be a dead giveaway. By ancient law, none but an E'veri heir can claim that word."

Julien clasped his hands behind his back and walked to the bookshelf. He pulled down a thick volume and rifled through it. "Ah-ha!" he exclaimed after a few moments. "Since your Veetrish accent becomes more pronounced when you are being pranksome and impish," he said, "then you must hail from Veetri. You shall be known as Rozen de Morphys!"

I laughed. The story Julien cited was a rarely told tale, but one that I, having lived with a Master Storyteller for a good portion of my life, knew well. In the story, Morphio the Mage transformed a young prince into an ugly caterpillar as punishment for his extreme vanity. After several brushes with both death and disgust, the prince learned his lesson, and with a little help from the mage, turned into a beautiful butterfly before resuming his natural form.

"Well, it's not a variation of your real name, but you might answer to it better."

"You flatter me, Sir Julien," I said with another laugh. "For this wormish creature before you could not be confused with a butterfly."

"I agree that the comparison is less than accurate." Julien closed the book and returned it to its place on the shelf. "But not for that reason."

When he turned back to me, the warmth of his smile— nay, the heat of it—reached the core of my being.

"Indeed, Princess Rynnaia," he said, "I've never seen a butterfly that could hope to match your beauty."

I ducked my head as color burned hot on my cheeks.

Julien covered the distance between us, and placing two fingers gently under my chin, tilted my face upward. "You are unaccustomed to compliments," he said. "Perhaps you've been secluded from male company for too long. You are unaware of how lovely you are."

The familiar emerald and gold of his thoughts caressed my own. His fingers dropped from my chin and he stepped back. His colors faded from my mind as his tone grew more formal. "Therefore, I must endeavor to ready you for the onslaught of admirers that will, no doubt, darken your father's door after he presents you to the court."

"An onslaught?" I laughed. "You make it sound as if I'll be set upon by bandits."

"It may very well be bandits who seek your favor, though they won't appear as such at court. Princess," he paused, looking both slightly uncomfortable and entirely ferocious at the sound of his own words, "there could be many men who, upon hearing of your survival, will seek to be the next King."

I wrinkled my nose. "My father is the King by the nature of his birth. Surely my identity being revealed will not put him at risk for losing the throne."

"No. But you are his only child. You are the Ryn, the heir." Light flashed in Julien's eyes. "Someday you will marry. And when you rule as Queen, your husband will also have power. And men greedy for power will do most anything to achieve their end." Several faces flew through his thoughts.

"So many?"

"Likely more than I can even guess." He ran his hand over his beard again, a gesture I had learned to expect when he was thinking about something that troubled him on a deep level. "Being Andoven, of course, you have an advantage." His features relaxed into a smile, erasing the lines that had darkened them. "Your abilities will allow you to see through any false motives your suitors may have for seeking your hand."

"Ugh," I groaned and crossed my arms over the binding at my chest. I gave Julien a sardonic smile. "I haven't even met my father yet, and already you're trying to marry me off to some foppish usurper?"

He smiled back at me, but the light of it did not quite reach his eyes. "I just want you to know what may await you when—" He paused. "When this business with the Cobelds has reached its end. You don't need to worry about it yet, though. You are still unknown, and shall remain so for at least a little while. Especially," he added with a grin, "in that costume."

He shook his head, as he appraised my outfit again. "We may be able to leave sooner than I thought. Could you be ready to leave for Port Dyn the day after tomorrow?"

I took a moment to calculate the distance and probable traveling time from our location in southeastern Mynissbyr to the southern coastal cliffs of the Dynwatre province. "I will need to have Lily and Aunt Alaine help me alter a few more items tomorrow, but I'm sure that with their help I will be ready. But—" I paused, embarrassed.

"What is it?"

"It's a bit difficult to dress myself," I said, not meeting his eyes. "There are, um, bindings, you see, that are necessary for me to appear more, ah," I swallowed, "boyish."

His eyes narrowed, but he didn't respond. Frustrated again at the heat creeping up my neck and into my face, my words came out more clipped than I intended.

"Regardless of the fealty you've sworn, it would be most improper to have *you* assist me, Sir Julien." Had I been able to think at all, I would have kept my mouth shut rather than to suffer the embarrassment it drew to my face.

When I'd regained enough composure to risk a glance at Julien his expression was vague. As much as I wanted to, I refrained from seeing his thoughts without permission.

"I may have a solution for that problem," he said. "I will go and speak to my mother about the matter and then I will join you for dinner." He turned toward the door but swiveled back, smirking. "Should I expect my new squire at table tonight, Rozen?" he asked, his eyes alight with humor. "Or will the princess be joining me?"

"The princess has informed me that she would very much enjoy dining with you this evening, Sir Julien."

"Very well," he said. "I was hoping that she would. She has much better manners than my squire."

Thirty-Four

The sun had not yet appeared above the eastern tree line when Erielle entered my chamber two mornings later. Wearing breeches and a heavy linen shirt, she stood just inside the door between Julien's room and mine.

"You're about rather early," I said. "But I'm glad I got to see you one last time before we have to leave."

"One last time? Oh, don't be so maudlin. I'm here to help you dress for your trip, Princess." She winked and leaned in toward my ear. "And to serve you thus all the way to Port Dyn!"

With a squeal I reached out to hug her. We danced a little circle around the room. "I am so relieved!" I laughed. "I was afraid Julien had forgotten about that particular problem."

"You think so little of my memory, Princess?" Julien chuckled from behind Erielle. His chamber had only one lamp lit and I hadn't noticed him there.

"Certainly not," I said. "But you hadn't mentioned it again."

"Perhaps I wanted to *surprise* you," he said. Even though I couldn't see his eyes, I knew they held the merriment of teasing.

I held the lamp to my face. "Get a good look then, Knight," I said boldly, "for this *butterfly* will disappear momentarily and you will be left with naught but a wormy squire in her place."

"May it be so," he laughed.

Erielle flashed a grin. "Begone, knave," she said, pushing him back into his room, "we've a bit of wormifying to attend to."

With Erielle's help it took hardly any time to become Rozen the squire. As I finished pinning the hairpiece in place I voiced a question that had troubled my dreams. "Erielle, has your brother spoken for a lady at court?"

I was probably breaking a hundred rules of propriety by asking. But the more time I spent with Julien, the more time I wanted to spend with him. Even though I was as sure of the answer to my question, and just as sure that confirming it was bound to hurt me, I was afraid if I entertained my dreams any longer it would make the pain of crushing them even worse.

"Julien?" She laughed. "No."

"*No?*" That was not the answer I had expected. "But someone like Julien must receive a fair amount of female attention," I mused. Perhaps she had misunderstood my question. "Surely there is some lady that has earned his favor."

"Being the heir to the Regency, my brother is, of course, quite sought after as a dancing partner," Erielle admitted. She searched my face for a long moment. "But to my knowledge he's never shown particular favor to any lady of his acquaintance."

"Hmm."

The flicker of a smile crossed her face as she turned away, and had she not turned I would have had to hide my own.

I pulled the gray squire's cap over my black hairpiece and slid the spectacles onto my face. Rynnaia was gone. Black-haired Rose, even, had disappeared. For the next several weeks I would be Rozen de Morphys, squire to Sir Julien de Gladiel.

"You look very wormy indeed, Squire Rozen," Erielle said when she examined my costume. "Now it's my turn." Stepping up to the looking glass, she pulled a blond hairpiece over her tightly coiled hair. "I'd thought to cut my hair years ago, but my father forbade it." She cocked a smile as she added a dark brown cap to her ensemble. "In retrospect, I'm glad. Short hair on a young lady might draw scorn at a ball and I do so love to dance."

The metamorphosis was complete, each of us a contradiction. Standing side by side at the mirror, we grinned at our boyish reflections.

"I'm Rozen, but what should I call you?" I asked her. "I can't call you Erielle!"

"Erril de Skyzer, at your service!" She bowed.

"Surely you jest!" I laughed. "Isn't *disguiser* a bit, well, obvious?"

She frowned, sighing. "You're right, of course. What do you suggest?"

I thought for a moment before the perfect name came to me. "You are descended from the Bear-men, so . . . how about de Bruin?"

"Erril de Bruin," she tried the name out. "I like it!"

I gathered my saddlebags while Erielle doused the candles and shrugged into her cloak. We knocked on Julien's door, but when he didn't answer we went on through. Erielle grabbed her bags and we headed downstairs. I hadn't seen much of Fyrlean Manor during my stay, having been confined between my room and Julien's, and it didn't appear that I'd be seeing any more of it now. We quietly left the house and headed for the stables.

"Rozen," Erielle whispered. I turned and grinned at her, answering to my new name for the first time. Her face, lit by the lamp she carried, held a serious expression.

"What?" I asked, concerned.

She grabbed my arm and whispered in my ear. "You've got to try to walk more like a boy!"

Oh dear. This was going to be harder than I thought.

Stanza whinnied as I approached. It seemed he'd forgiven me for riding Salvador the night we came to Fyrlean Manor. I lowered my voice and spoke softly as I saddled my horse, trying to do it in a less-girlish fashion than I would have normally. He cocked his ears and danced a few steps away, so I leaned in to him and sent him my thoughts instead. He relaxed and allowed me to continue. I attached the saddlebags with ease, glad that at least my horsemanship was above reproach.

Julien approached with two knights. "This is my squire, Rozen de Morphys, late of Veetri."

Although the lilting accent I had acquired during my years in Veetri had faded quite a bit since coming to Mynissbyr, I allowed myself to fall back into my old manner of speech. Julien quirked an eyebrow, but the intensity of my brogue must have convinced Sir Alek and Sir Rylin. Each gave me a slight nod, which I returned as boyishly as I could manage. Which was, in all likelihood, still rather girlish.

"Rozen will ride in front with me. Alek, Rylin, you take the rear and Erielle will stay between us." He turned to Erielle. "You *will*," he repeated, "stay between us."

At that Erielle told him that her name was now Errill de Bruin, *not* Erielle, and it would do him well to remember it.

Julien laughed at the last name and I had to turn away to hide my smile. Sir Alek and Sir Rylin only chuckled, clearly used to Erielle's saucy remarks.

As we left the stables I sensed Lily and Alaine watching from a window. I could not turn and wave without giving myself away, but I could use my Andoven abilities to tell them good-bye. I was glad the Regent's knights were at my back and did not note the sniffles that accompanied those farewells.

For two days we rode hard through Mynissbyr Wood, often in single file with Julien in the lead. We crossed the icy Ursina River at a large stone bridge, but other than that, we kept away from the main trails, camping within the cover of the trees and sleeping as close to the fire as we dared.

I was afraid of acting too feminine, so I didn't speak to Erielle unless she first spoke to me. Sir Alek and Sir Rylin, however, were good at drawing me into their conversations.

"Stanza's a rather odd name for a horse, isn't it, Rozen?"

"Odd how?" I asked. "His name was inspired by a poem."

"Aach!" Sir Rylin laughed. "You Veetrish! Must everything be," he made his voice go higher, mimicking mine, "inspired?"

"Not everything." I'd quickly adapted to the knights' teasing. "But Stanza is a rather remarkable horse, I think. He deserved to be given a name that would do him justice."

"So, what's the story, Rozen?" Erielle prodded. "How did Stanza get his name?"

I smiled, thinking back to my seventeenth birthday, before Gladiel came to Mirthan Hall to deliver me to the Bear's Rest. "As you no doubt know," I said, "in Veetri it is our habit to use verse to express emotion. When I noted that white mark upon his forehead and how it stood out against the black, a poem came to mind."

"A *poem* came to mind," Rylin mocked, but he patted my back to let me know his scorn was in jest.

"What poem?" Erielle leaned forward.

I leaned forward, and when I lowered my voice, my companions leaned in as well. *"A ripple 'cross the inky black celestial-studded night. A glimmer's trace for just a breath, thus ends its path of light."*

"That's beautiful," Erielle said.

"Aww, you Veetrish." Sir Alek echoed Rylin's guffaw. "Always spouting off some verse or other."

"Oh hush, you silly knights," Erielle scolded. "Let Rozen tell the tale."

I shrugged. "That's about it, I'm afraid."

"But I don't understand." Erielle wrinkled her nose. "The poem is about a shooting star."

"Lady—er—my mother wanted to name him Glimmer, after the poem." I glanced at Julien, who wore a strange expression on his face. But Rylin stopped me from commenting on it.

"That's a rather feminine name for a stallion."

"That's exactly what I said." I nodded to Rylin. "So we tossed around some ideas and finally landed on Stanza because, although there is quite a bit more to the poem, I only recited one wee little stanza of it."

"Well," Alek chuckled, "what a very Veetrish thing to do."

I shrugged. "No matter where I call home, a big piece of my heart will always be in Veetri."

"As it should be." Rylin nodded. "You're a good lad," he said, and then added with a wink, "and I imagine once you've had a few years of Sir Julien's tutelage under your Veetrish belt, you'll make a fine squire as well."

Julien rose. "I'll take the first watch. You should all get some sleep."

"Sir Julien?" I stood. "Might I have a word?"

"Come."

I followed him away from the fire, away from the listening ears of those who thought me nothing more than Sir Julien's clueless Veetrish squire. He stopped so suddenly that I almost ran into him.

"Sorry."

"You needed a word?"

"Yes." I swallowed. "I—" What was it I wanted to speak with him about? Faced with the stone face of a knight speaking to his squire, I drew a blank. "We are near the province line?"

"Yes. We'll cross into Stoen tomorrow and angle down to Dynwey Road. We should reach it by nightfall. Was there anything else?"

Yes, I thought, *there is something else.* I looked at the ground. *I miss the old Julien. The courteous Julien. The Julien who remembered I was a girl.* I kicked the dirt and sighed. "There was, but I forgot. I'll . . . go." I turned to leave.

"Wait." His whisper made me turn back around. "Please." His expression softened. "I know your disguise is necessary, but it troubles me when you speak of the duke and duchess as your parents. They are not your parents."

Anger flared within me so suddenly, it took my breath. To listen to the knights' teasing as they insulted the Veetrish was one thing. To have Julien disparage Lord and Lady Whittier was quite another.

"How are they not my parents?" I whispered through my teeth, each syllable clenching my jaw a bit tighter than the last. "They are more my parents than some stranger who sits on a throne and is willing to cast off his only child for nineteen years!"

"King Jarryn didn't—"

I lifted a hand to stop his words. "Do you have any idea what it's like to grow up feeling like there must be something wrong with you because your father doesn't want to claim you? To have a father who won't even tell you his name, or your own name even, lest you be associated with him? Of course you don't! Your father loves you! He was proud to be seen with you and to call you his son. My father won't even admit I *exist*!"

"Your father loves you. Everything he did was to protect—"

"To protect me? Or to keep me alive so I can fulfill some prophecy?" My hands fisted at my sides and my elbows locked in place. "Don't defend him, Julien. I don't care if he is King. He's a liar," I hissed. "A liar!"

"Shh. Quiet." Julien stepped to the side, pushed me behind him, and silently drew his sword.

"Rozen? Are you about—oh." Erielle paused, then smirked when she saw Julien's sword. "A bit jumpy, aren't we, Julien?"

"You should know better than to sneak up on me in the dark, Erielle."

"It's Erril, remember? And I wasn't sneaking. In fact, I made so much noise coming over here that I probably woke up the guard at Castle Rynwyk."

Her mention of the King's home only deepened my scowl. "I'm going back to the camp." I stepped around Julien.

"Wait. Please." He placed a hand on my arm, but I shook it off. Had Rylin or Alek been present, he would have been forced to discipline me in some way. A squire was never allowed to behave so disrespectfully toward a knight. But Rylin and Alek were not present. And I was *not* Julien's squire.

I barely slept that night, though I did a fare job of convincing my campmates otherwise. But when dawn greeted us with the winter birds' song, the ground was not the only thing covered with frost.

If Alek and Rylin felt the tension in the air, they did not comment on it. And I, determined to be every inch a squire, obeyed Julien's commands with superb efficiency, but little enthusiasm.

Finally, we left Mynissbyr and entered the province of Stoen. Salderyn, E'veria's capital city, and Castle Rynwyk, the home of the King, were in Stoen, just a week or two's ride to the east. For me, the bitter taste of deception flavored even the air of the entire province. And all the years of longing to know my father were tainted by anger.

Beside me, Julien was silent as a stone, his back rigid in the saddle. Every so often he would glance at me as if he had something to say, but each time he met my icy gaze, he sighed and turned away.

By the time we stopped to make camp that night I was exhausted. After caring for Stanza and brushing down Salvador, a duty any proper squire would perform for his mentor, I devoured the sparse but filling meal Rylin had prepared over the fire.

"I will take the first watch," Julien said. "And Rozen?"

I lifted my head from the hard, flavorless biscuit that was the staple of every meal I'd had since leaving Fyrlean Manor. "Yes?"

"When you've finished eating, see to it that the horses are each given an apple from the bag. They've ridden hard and deserve a treat." That was certainly true. "Then come and join me for the watch."

Dread, and not a little twinge of guilt, assailed me. But if I was to maintain the role of a squire I could not disobey. "Yes, Sir Julien. Right away."

I popped the last bite of the biscuit into my mouth as Julien strode away. There were just enough apples left for each of our five horses to get one. I could tell from the feel of them that they would be mealy and mildly unpleasant should we have eaten them ourselves, but the horses wouldn't mind.

Salvador was uncharacteristically fidgety as he ate the apple. His eyes darted to me and away, much like Julien's had all day during our ride. I leaned my head into his neck. As soon as my mind connected to his, I gasped, overcome with the mighty beast's confusion. He worried that he'd displeased me and didn't know how or why.

"You are such a good, beautiful boy," I cooed, quietly enough that no one except Salvador, and possibly Stanza, could hear. "You've done nothing wrong."

Julien's face suddenly flashed into my mind amidst a swirl of muted green and gold. His scent—something I'd never noticed before, but knew to be uniquely him, overcame the scent of horse and apple. It spoke of evergreen needles and leather, linen and steel. I was seeing—er, *smelling* Julien as Salvador saw him.

"Oh, I see." Salvador was confused about me because Julien was confused about me. Their bond was much deeper, I realized, than mine with Stanza. "I'm sorry, Salvador," I whispered. "I'll try to make it right."

Salvador's whinny ended with a snort, almost as if to say, *"It's about time, Princess."*

"You'd best move faster, squire," Rylin warned from his place by the fire. "Sir Julien does not like to be kept waiting."

"Sorry." Quickly distributing the rest of the apples, I went in search of Julien. He was easy to find.

"Sir Julien."

"We are alone?"

I nodded. "The others are at the fire."

"Walk with me."

I fell into step beside him.

"I've thought about what you said yesterday," he said. His voice was low enough that I had to strain to hear it. "And I want you to know that, although I will defend my

King as is my sworn duty, I think I can understand why you feel as you do. I apologize if anything I said added to your pain."

I sighed. "I'm sorry, too." I hated being the last to apologize. "It was wrong of me to attack you in place of him. You didn't do anything." I stopped. "I suppose I'm exhausted with living a ruse. Even now I'm forced to disguise myself from Rylin and Alek."

He stopped and scanned a full circle around us before turning to face me. "You may not want to hear this, but King Jarryn is a good man. An honorable man. What other sort of man would, when evil tore his Queen from him, choose to deny himself the joy of watching his daughter grow up in order to keep her safe?"

My throat tightened. I'd never thought about it from the King's point of view. My father had always been an abstract concept to me, a cold presence, dictating my life from afar. My mind swam through every emotion, through all the years without so much as a note letting me know he cared.

The memory I had recovered reading my father's letter to Aunt Alaine, however, indicated something else, something other than what I'd believed of him all these years. And, after all, Julien knew him far better than I did. If he believed the King's motivation was pure, it likely was.

That didn't mean I had to like it.

But none of this was Julien's fault.

"Forgive me," I said finally. "My behavior toward you was undeserved and unkind."

"There is nothing to forgive."

"Nothing but a full day of throwing daggers at you with my eyes," I mumbled.

The corner of his mouth twitched. "It was a long day," he admitted. "And of course you are forgiven."

By the time Alek took the second watch, Julien and I had fallen back into a comfortable companionship. When I crawled into my bedroll I fell into a dead sleep, barely even aware of the cold until I awoke stiff and aching with the rise of the sun.

By the second week of our journey, my body began to toughen up. As I grew stronger, new muscles developed in my legs and I gained more stamina and slept better, my aches and pains minimized by routine.

The knights' cautiousness increased as the days wore on, and a strange, prickling fear crept through my mind at unexpected moments. Colors I didn't recognize would creep into my mind without warning, causing me to tense in a way that irritated my horse. Salvador, I noticed, seemed agitated as well.

When we stopped for our noon meal one day, I couldn't shake the sense of trepidation that had plagued me off and on all morning. With a little maneuvering, I managed to find Julien alone before we took to the saddle again.

"Sir Julien," I whispered formally just in case someone would overhear, "something doesn't feel right."

He put a hand on my shoulder. "I know. Salvador knows. Stay close to me and be on your guard at all times."

We ate quickly and quietly. The knights absently checked their swords, almost as if they knew they would soon be called upon to use them. Fueled by an increased urgency to reach the well-guarded towns and villages along Dynwey Road, Julien set a rigid pace for most of the afternoon.

We had been back on the road for about two hours when, suddenly, my skin prickled from head to toe, as if an ice-blue blast of wind had permeated my many layers of clothing. Movement at the periphery of my vision turned my head.

In the distance, no less than fifteen—no, at least *twenty* horses galloped toward us. Though I had never before seen this type of cavalry, somehow I knew who they were.

"Dwonsil warriors!" Rylin's shout confirmed my suspicion. The swords of my fellow riders left their scabbards. "Do we fight, Sir Julien?" Rylin called from the rear.

"No!" Julien hollered back. "We're grossly outnumbered! We ride!"

I looked toward the approaching riders. Their trajectory had shifted and there seemed no doubt that they would intercept us. I frantically scanned every direction, trying to figure out the best way of escape, but there was none, not even a patch of trees in which to hide. I glanced back toward the approaching enemy. Their bows were drawn and aimed at us. They were in range. We couldn't possibly escape.

Almost as one, they drew their bows back and . . .

"No!" I gasped. Leaning into Stanza's neck, I squeezed my eyes shut, expecting an arrow to pierce through my cloak at any second. When no pain arose I ventured to open my eyes and check the condition of my friends.

No one was hurt. In fact, when I turned to look at the Dwonsil warriors I saw nothing but a cloud of dust and a flurry of flailing hooves. Arrows careened in every direction but toward us.

My mouth dropped open. I could not imagine what might have caused disaster to befall the warriors, thereby allowing us to escape. There must have been some hazard or trap set, unbeknownst to the enemy. What else could explain twenty-plus horses and riders suddenly collapsing on the Stoenian plains?

"Don't slow down!" Julien yelled at me. "Keep moving!"

I dug my heels into Stanza's sides. Whatever had happened to the Dwonsil warriors, I only hoped a similar accident did not await us further down the trail.

My heart pounded so frantically I feared it would be heard over the sound of the horses' hooves. We rode as hard as we could until sundown, but there was no sign of pursuit. When we finally felt safe enough to set up camp, Sir Alek's comment expressed my own thoughts.

"If someone told me that story," he said with a shake of his head, "I don't think I would believe it."

"Indeed." Julien added. "The First King himself must have been between us and our enemies today."

Everyone else nodded agreement, but it seemed an odd remark to me. All my life I had heard the stories of Loeftryn de Rynloeft, E'veria's First King. But that was ancient history. The thought of a dead king interceding in our modern time was one I chewed on with almost as much effort as I needed to send my teeth through the flavorless biscuit that accompanied my meager dinner. Finally, I let it go, deciding that perhaps Julien's comment was one born of knight lore that had never made it to Veetri.

Everyone else seemed as pensive as I, and without the usual conversation around the fire, my eyelids drooped much earlier than usual. As soon as I finished my chores I spread my bedroll. As the excitement of the day worked its way out of my blood, exhaustion claimed my brain, and with one last look toward Julien, I sighed and let sleep claim me.

THIRTY-FIVE

Sixteen days after leaving Fyrlean Manor, we finally reached Dynwey Road. Julien sent Alek and Rylin ahead to make sure the nearby village was still secure, and if so, to arrange rooms for us at the inn.

Julien spoke quietly enough that no one would hear. "As my squire, it is expected that you will share my room, but Erielle will have a room adjoining mine. When we retire you will join her and no one will be the wiser."

At the inn, Julien ordered baths for all of us. Once the innkeeper realized his guest was a future Regent, he was more than happy to oblige.

Every speck of dirt and every drop of dried sweat on my body itched as if it was a living thing. On the trail I'd felt dirty. Off, I *knew* I was disgusting. I'd never gone this long without bathing and I could hardly wait for my turn. As the highest ranking member of our party—as far as the innkeepers knew, anyway—Julien got the first bath. He might have hurried, but as I sat in my own filth, it felt like forever.

Finally, Julien appeared, dressed in freshly pressed clothes—the innkeeper had insisted—and shortly thereafter the knights were shown to the small but steamy tubs that awaited them in their rooms. Once they'd departed, Julien took Erielle and me upstairs and stood guard outside the door while we bathed.

The tub was the tiniest I'd ever bent my body into, but the wonder of washing the grime and stench from my body was worth the awkward contortions I had to make to get myself clean. I couldn't help but notice that the body in this tub was much changed from that of the girl who had left Fyrlean Manor just over two weeks ago. I had never carried extra weight, but the strenuous trail had created a new leanness to my frame and had sculpted muscles that had, before this time, been hidden among my bones. I was glad for the small sewing kit stowed among my things. I needed to make a few alterations to my clothes before morning.

As I helped Erielle comb a particularly difficult knot out of her fine, wet hair, Julien came in.

"Erielle, I brought your—" He paused in the doorway between the two rooms, a food-laden tray in his hands. As his eyes traveled the length of my hair, a warm current tingled up my spine, almost as if his hand had touched it instead.

"*Rynnaia.*" His whisper was so soft, I wasn't sure if he had spoken my name or thought it. But regardless of whence it came, it moved over my ears like liquid silk. The caress of his gaze turned apologetic. "I wish I could bring you a tray, but the knights would wonder."

"It can't be helped." I returned my attention to Erielle's hair, but something about his discomfort at seeing me as a woman again pleased me.

Julien cleared his throat. "I've accustomed myself to seeing you as a squire, but seeing you now, I can't imagine how you ever passed for a boy. I wonder what your father would say if he knew about all this."

"I know what he would say," Erielle spoke through the golden veil of hair covering her face. "He would say, *Julien, my boy,*" she lowered her voice, *"what a brilliant disguise! I'd wager your highly intelligent sister had a part in its design!"*

"And so she did," I laughed.

My hairpiece was almost dry by the time I finished combing out Erielle's mass of tangles. I braided and coiled my still-damp hair, pinned the black hairpiece in place, and topped it all with the squire's cap.

"I'm ready. Are you sure you want to stay up here, Erielle?"

"More than sure. My head needs to breathe." She grimaced. "Sorry. That was a rather thoughtless thing to say since you have to go below."

"Shall we?" Julien held out his arm and I laughed. "I very much appreciate your chivalry, Sir Julien, but as your squire I cannot accept such an invitation."

Julien let his arm drop and scowled. "It goes against everything within me to treat you this way."

"You can make it up to me when I'm a girl again," I said with a grin. "But for now I must admit that I am hungry. After you, my liege." His brows drew together, but he preceded me out the door.

The dining room was crowded, but Alek and Rylin had already claimed a table for the four of us. No sooner had we sat down than we were served. Julien's status afforded us a most attentive staff, and we feasted on a hearty beef and vegetable stew, warm, buttered rolls, and baked apple tarts.

"I've heard there's a Storyteller here tonight," Rylin commented as we finished our meal.

I had to contain the squeal of delight that threatened to burst out of my throat at the prospect of seeing a real Veetrish Storyteller again.

"I was planning to make an early night of it," he said, "but it's been a long while since I've seen the Story People dance. Anyone care to join me?"

"Aye," agreed Alek, nodding. "I've a mind to stay up for it. What say you, Rozen?"

"You have to ask?"

Julien grinned behind his mug. "Mayhap we could make an exception to our schedule and leave a little later in the morning than we planned. I'll go upstairs and get Erielle . . . *Erril*, I mean," he laughed. "I'm sure the little scamp would enjoy the evening's entertainment as well."

Julien appeared a short while later with *Erril* in tow. When the supper dishes were cleared away everyone pitched in to push back the tables and make a space in the center of the room. The space was almost clear when a large man bumped into me from the side. I lost my balance and fell hard on to the floor.

The impact knocked the spectacles from my face. They skidded across the room out of sight. Worried about the rest of my disguise, I reached up to feel my head. My hairpiece and cap had held fast . . . but where were my spectacles? Keeping my eyes as downcast as possible, I pushed myself into a kneeling position and scanned the floor for my missing eyewear.

There they were! I cringed, but a hand reached down to pick them up just in time to avoid them being trod upon by a large man's boot. I let out a sigh of relief and moved my gaze upward to identify who held my spectacles in case I should lose him in the crowd.

I couldn't stop his name from forming on my lips, even though there was no sound coming forth from my mouth. *"Rowlen?"*

My brother had filled out considerably in the three years since last I had seen him. His tall form was lean and strong and his long, gleaming blond hair was pulled back and tied in a queue at the nape of his neck. At the gathering celebrating my sixteenth birthday, there were still bits of the boy I'd grown up with lingering about my Storyteller brother, but there was no denying now that he was a man.

Rowlen held the spectacles for a moment and looked around the room for a possible owner. As he met my gaze, his eyes widened in surprise, then delight.

He's here! My smile surely matched his own as my heart leapt with joy. *My brother is here!*

"Oy, Rozen!" Rylin's voice stole my attention from the Storyteller. "That was a nasty fall you took."

I took his offered hand to rise. "Thank you." I avoided the knight's gaze as I pushed myself up. "My spectacles . . ."

"Sir Julien is retrieving them. Can you see without them?"

"Enough." I looked back toward Rowlen, who was in the process of handing the spectacles over to Julien. When he looked back at me, confusion reigned on his face.

I bit my lip. *Oh, Rowlen!*

I wanted to cry. I wanted to run to him. But I couldn't. I was Rozen de Morphys now and he . . . wouldn't understand.

A spark of light stole my gaze from his face. A smattering of applause began near him, and as the rest of the room caught on to who he was, they joined in. Rowlen looked down at his hand. He almost seemed surprised to see the bright, translucent plant growing from his palm. He pursed his lips and blew the smallest stream of air toward it. A bud formed and opened, revealing a copper-colored rose.

No! My thought was violent, immediate. *You promised!* The rose shattered into hundreds of tiny, glittering pieces that fell to the floor and disappeared into the dust motes.

A look of utter surprise flew across the Storyteller's face as he looked at his palm. He turned his hand over, as if searching for the rose. The crowd clapped again, and with a troubled glance in my direction, he smiled and offered them a bow.

Homesickness crushed my chest, battling with the fear that he would call me out and ruin Julien's carefully laid plans.

"I need some air. I'm going to check on Stanza." I pushed passed Rylin, keeping my eyes downcast as I made my way outside.

I ran all the way to the stables and climbed into Stanza's stall. My heart beat a furious pace as I leaned my head into my horse's neck. The next stall over, Salvador whinnied, seeming to sense my unease. I knew I couldn't hide there forever, but I couldn't go back in and risk being found out.

Seeing Rowlen opened a wound that seemed to be incapable of healing and ignited a heavy, wrenching homesickness for Veetri. For Mirthan Hall. For my family. I'd denied it as well as I could while at the Bear's Rest. But I could deny it no longer. Just across the way, a most-beloved brother, one of the dear ones I had not seen in years, was entertaining a crowd. That I could not even acknowledge I knew him tore at my heart, and I'd never felt more alone.

I sank down into the straw and pounded my fist into its scratchy depths. Stifling a sob, I sat back against the wooden wall, drew my knees up, and buried my head in my arms.

A torrent of emotion shook my frame, though I made no sound other than taking an occasional, gasping breath.

I just want to see my brother! my heart cried. Shaking, I ground my fists into the straw over and over, not even noticing when the dry skin on my knuckles began to crack and bleed.

"Rozen?" The call was soft, but urgent. "Oh, there you are." I looked up as Julien arrived at Stanza's stall. When he saw my tears his eyes widened. A moment later, he was in the stall with me, the gate latched behind him.

"Where's your cloak?"

I tried to answer, but bit my tongue. I could not stop shaking. My body trembled from crown to toe. Julien removed his tunic and placed it around my shoulders. My teeth began to chatter as hot tears coursed down my cold cheeks.

"Are you hurt?" he whispered, even though there was no one else in the stables. "Were you injured when you fell?" His eyes roved over my form as if he expected to see a blackened eye or a series of gaping wounds. I shook my head no, still unable to speak while my body convulsed so.

He knelt beside me and lifted my hands, concern furrowing his brow as he examined bleeding knuckles that had just started to sting. After another look at my tear-streaked face, he pulled me to him, crushing me against his chest. His heart thundered against my cheek.

"I couldn't find you." His whisper was ragged. Had I been unable to make out the quiet syllables, however, his thoughts would have been strong enough to pierce the night. "You fell and then you just . . . disappeared."

Julien loosened his hold and I was able to breathe easier. "Finally, Rylin told me that you had left to check the horses," he said. "Why would you do that? You know what a risk it is for you to be running about on your own!"

His tone was rough, but I felt the worry that fed his chastisement. His body, pressed so close to mine, imparted warmth and comfort. He held me until I was able to speak.

"Rowlen recognized me," I whispered, choking back a sob. "I was in the same room as—as my br-brother, b-but I couldn't even talk to him!" A fresh wave of tears soaked Julien's shirtfront.

"The Storyteller is Rowlen de Whittier?" Julien ran his hand over my head and under my jaw to lift my chin. "He certainly doesn't resemble Kinley."

"Their eyes are the same."

"The rose," Julien whispered as understanding dawned. "That was for you."

I nodded.

He ran a hand through his hair. "I can't protect you if I'm not with you."

"I know. I'm sorry." I reached into Stanza's watering trough and splashed some of its cold water on my face, knowing my eyes were swollen and my face was most likely red and blotchy from tears. I handed Julien back his tunic and dried my face with my sleeve. He withdrew my spectacles from his pocket and placed them on my face.

"It really is a convincing disguise." He frowned. "You look nothing like yourself." He shook his head. "How did he recognize you, dressed as you?"

"Remember when I told you about the ebonswarth powder?"

He nodded.

"My hair was black in Veetri. Without the spectacles, the only thing about my appearance that would strike Rowlen as odd would be my clothing. The orange rose was his way of saying he knew the real me."

"He knows about you?"

"He knows about my hair, nothing more. The dye washed out once when we were young. It was my first swimming lesson. Rowlen was my teacher. No one else saw."

"You and Rowlen were quite close, I gather?"

I nodded.

Julien rubbed his beard. "Do you think he will seek you out?"

I thought about it for a moment. "If he saw me leave, then I'm surprised he's still indoors."

"Let's get you inside," he said. "I will speak to Rowlen after his performance. Perhaps I can arrange a way for you to see him."

"Truly?" I clasped my hands together in an entirely un-squire-like way.

Julien's chuckle warmed me better than his cloak. "I will try."

(Thirty-Six

I nearly wore a path in the floor of my room as I waited for the Storyteller's performance to end. It was excruciating. Intermittent bouts of raucous laughter and thunderous applause came up through the floorboards from the crowded dining room below. I wished I could see Rowlen's performance. His skill had improved so much by my sixteenth birthday party that I could only imagine how much more amazing it would be to watch him now.

Finally, Julien and Erielle returned, but Rowlen was not with them. I tried to quell my disappointment as Erielle, her face alight with pleasure from the entertainment, chastised me for missing the Storyteller's performance. When Julien explained my absence, however, she apologized.

"Oh, that's awful, Rynnaia. If you need to talk . . ."

I shook my head. "I'll be fine. You go on to bed. I'll be there . . . in a bit."

Erielle had just shut the door between our room and her brother's when a firm knock sounded on Julien's door.

"That would be Rowlen." Julien smiled at me and opened the door.

My brother's face no longer bore the jovial smile of a Storyteller. It was, instead, set with an unveiled hostility of which I'd never seen the like. Before Julien had fastened the lock on the door, Rowlen strode to my side.

"Is this knight your husband?"

I opened my mouth in surprise only to snap it shut again before speaking. "No! Of course not!"

He spun around. "You dare to sully my sister's honor?"

"No, I do not."

"It does not flatter the King when one of his knights dallies with the affections of a maid and convinces her to share his bedchamber!" Rowlen's voice was low and laced with deadly menace, "I demand you explain yourself!"

"Rowlen, I—"

"Quiet, Rose!" Rowlen's hand slashed the air. "I will handle this."

Julien leaned against the doorframe, seeming quite relaxed, even slightly amused. "I think you may be surprised when you learn the truth of our arrangement."

"Your *arrangement*?" Rowlen hissed. "This lady is considered a daughter of the Duke of Glenhume and is under his protection whether she dwells beneath his roof or not!"

Rowlen put an arm around my shoulder. His voice was tight, but gentler as he addressed me. "Gather your things, Rose. We're leaving." The tone of his command was firm enough and the angry fire in his eyes so compelling that I started to move toward the door where my saddlebags, and Erielle, rested.

Julien cleared his throat, drawing my eyes to his face. He tilted his head, a bemused smile dancing upon his face. I bit the corner of my lip, unsure of what to do.

Rowlen squeezed my shoulder. "Now, Rose."

"Calm yourself, Storyteller." Julien's amusement at my discomfiture was hardly masked by his tone. "The lady will not be leaving these rooms again tonight."

"My sister," Rowlen growled, "will not be disgraced!"

"I should say not," Julien chuckled and turned his gaze to me. "Would you care to explain our arrangement to your most protective brother before that vein in his forehead explodes?"

"All of it?"

"Is he trustworthy?"

I nodded.

Julien's voice lowered even more, "Speak quietly then, Princess. These walls are thin."

"Princess?" Rowlen sputtered, wrinkling his nose in disgust. "A vain endearment, spoken by an errant knave! The King shall hear of this!"

"Hmm," Julien mused with a subtle nod, "I suppose he shall."

At that, I giggled. Rowlen shot me a look, but I had already removed the squire's cap and was disengaging the pins that secured the hairpiece to my head. "I've no doubt the King would approve of Sir Julien's behavior," I said.

"Then you do not know the King."

"Not yet," I admitted, pulling the hairpiece free. "But I don't think I can put it off forever. He is, after all, my father."

"He's your . . . father?" Rowlen blinked.

I nodded. "I know it's hard to believe, but—"

"No, it's not." He shook his head and the beginnings of a smile tugged at his lips. "Not at all. In fact, it makes perfect sense." He laughed, but the sound was strained as he turned to Julien. "That's why you called her Princess."

Julien smiled and gave a nod.

Rowlen shook his head. "Honestly, Rose. This is—"

"My name isn't Rose."

"Oh," he said, tilting his head. "Well, of course not. So what is it?"

"Rynnaia," I whispered. "Rynnaia E'veri."

We stood for a moment, staring at each other. Finally, Rowlen waggled his eyebrows. "My sister's a princess," he whispered. I jumped when he tilted his head back and let out a shout of laughter.

Rowlen pulled me into a hug and spun a circle, squeezing me so tightly that I feared my ribs would bruise. When he released me, he put an arm around my shoulder and turned to Julien.

"You have my apologies, Sir Julien." His smile faded. "I do, however, still question the propriety of the sleeping arrangements."

The door to Erielle's adjoining room creaked and she stepped through, still dressed in Erril's clothes, but looking completely feminine with her blond hair streaming down her back. "I don't mean to interrupt," she said, "but perhaps I can help to ease your mind, Master Rowlen."

For the first time since we'd met, I saw Erielle de Gladiel blush.

"I've been traveling with Rozen. Er, Rose, I mean." The color of her cheeks deepened, "Ah . . . the princess, rather. As a chaperone of sorts. She'll sleep in the other room. With me," she explained. "My brother is an honorable knight, Master Rowlen. He would never do anything to damage her reputation."

"My lady," Rowlen stepped forward, reached for Erielle's hand, and placed a kiss upon her knuckles. "You do me and the entire Dukedom of Glenhume a great service. I thank you." Erielle's eyes could have rivaled a new ball of yarn for size by the time he arose from the deep bow he gave her.

Julien stepped forward and cleared his throat. "Master Rowlen de Whittier." *Was he gritting his teeth?* "May I present *my* sister, Erielle de Gladiel?"

"You are the Regent's daughter? From Mynissbyr?" Rowlen ignored Julien.

"Yes."

"Thank you, Erielle." Julien interrupted any further conversation between our siblings. I couldn't help but note the color that had crept up his neck. "We appreciate your help in clarifying the situation, but your presence is no longer required. Try to get some sleep, now. We must be off early in the morning."

I couldn't suppress a giggle. The bounds of brotherly protection had been crossed again.

Rowlen kissed Erielle's hand again. "Goodnight, Lady Erielle."

"Goodnight, Master Rowlen. Goodnight, Rozen—er, Princess." Without a word to her brother, she went back to our room.

As soon as the door closed, Rowlen turned to me. "All right, Rose. Tell me everything."

I sighed. "We may as well sit down." I moved to a chair by the fire. "This could take awhile."

I explained to Rowlen all that I had learned in the past few weeks: the letter from my father, the release of my Andoven abilities, and what I had seen in Lady Anya's poetry. He was captivated by my story, and even though he was clearly uncomfortable with the idea of me traveling cross-country with only a young girl as a chaperone, he was at last satisfied that I was in no danger of losing my virtue.

"People see what they expect to see." He winked. "Unless, of course, they are watching one of my stories for the first time." He laughed, but held a question in his eyes. "And that brings me to another question. Did you destroy my rose?"

"Did I *what*?"

"When I saw you downstairs you took me by surprise. It must have triggered the appearance of the rose and then it—well, it exploded! I wasn't intending to make it in the first place but sometimes my thoughts just take on a life of their own."

Rowlen held his hands out to his sides and shrugged. I giggled when a tiny trail of shimmer fell from his fingertips. He smiled. "You see? Like that. So, did you do it?" He asked. "Did you destroy my rose?"

"How could I?" I wrinkled my nose. "I don't have the Storyteller's Gift."

Rowlen tilted his head. "But you are at least *part* Andoven." He made a face. "And I know *I* didn't do it. Nothing like that has ever happened before. It almost upended my performance!"

"Well, don't ask me to explain it, Rowlen." I rolled my eyes, secretly enjoying the feeling of being involved in a sibling spat again, even if it wasn't an argument I could win. "Oh! Erielle called you Master Rowlen, didn't she?" The title was one of great significance in Veetri. "You've completed your apprenticeship, then?"

"Yes. And my time traveling with the guild. Almost a year ago."

"So soon?"

"I bribed the examiner."

"Rowlen de Whittier!" I gasped and smacked his shoulder. "You did not!"

"Ow! No, I didn't." He laughed. "But I may have considered it once or twice. The examinations were quite rigorous. Only one other apprentice made it through with me."

"I want to hear all about it."

It was late when we said our good-byes, and I did not try to hide my tears. Rowlen's eyes were moist as well, but as he left, he kissed my forehead.

"I travel widely, Rose. Er, Rynnaia." He shook his head. "That will take some getting used to! But I'm sure our paths will cross again soon. And someday, after you've completed your quest and E'veria is allowed to finally love her princess, I will spread the most wonderful tales about our brave and beautiful future Queen, who traipsed through the countryside disguised as a lowly squire. Until then." He held out his hand and offered me a daisy.

When I reached for the flower, it disappeared.

"Still falling for my oldest tricks." Rowlen *tsked* and shook his head. "I love you, Rose."

I didn't correct him. "I love you, too."

After he gave me one last, lingering embrace he left. And I was left wondering at his confidence that I would, in fact, complete the quest assigned me by that pesky prophetic poem.

THIRTY-SEVEN

"Do you smell it, Rozen?" Erielle called from behind me. Even on Dynwey Road, we'd kept our original formation in the days since leaving the inn.

I took a deep breath in through my nose. An unfamiliar scent floated on the southerly breeze. "What is it?"

Erielle inhaled loudly enough that I could hear the breath. "That, my dear squire, is the beautiful scent of the Southern Sea!"

We hadn't passed another company of travelers for a good hour. Although the lack of people gave me cause to wonder about enemy activity in the area, it did help to relax our conversation.

"My sister has more than a passing fondness for the sea," Julien chuckled. "If it was up to her, we'd leave the Great Wood behind and live upon a ship."

"Not true," she argued. "I'd be quite content living in Holiday Palace *by* the sea and taking the occasional months'-long excursion." She closed her eyes and took another deep breath through her nose. The look on her face was one of rapture.

"Indeed," Julien laughed. Turning back to me, he pointed ahead. "You see that hill? Port Dyn is just beyond it."

Finally. In the week since we had left Rowlen at the inn, the road had seemed to stretch, each day a bit longer than the last. But at last, we were almost there.

By late morning we had entered the bustling city. Skin in every shade met my eyes and unfamiliar lilts of tongue caressed my ears in a mad cacophony of sound as we neared the docks. I'd never been in a city before. I found it fascinating—and a little bit frightening.

Looking eastward along the coast, my eyes trailed upward to a bright, white-stone palace sitting atop a cliff. Flags of moss green and white waved from each of the numerous turreted towers, catching the breeze off the sea, waving, as if welcoming me home.

Holiday Palace, I thought. *That's where I was born.*

The structure was immense, yet graceful. Grand, and yet somehow inviting. "It's beautiful."

"It is." Julien nodded. "You'll not find a more stunning example of architectural vision anywhere in E'veria."

As entranced by the palace as I was, Port Dyn soon stole my attention. I'd never seen so many buildings so close together or so many people of such diverse appearance. It was an amazing place with conveniences of which I'd never dreamed. Every corner found a new sort of shop to capture my fancy. Bakeries, butcheries, millineries, and dress shops were plentiful, as were shops dedicated to sweets, jewelry, and other luxuries. One shop we passed seemed to specialize in soap. Soap! I couldn't imagine such a thing! But the mixed perfumes that greeted my nose birthed a desire to darken its door as soon as possible.

"I will send Erielle on to the palace with Rylin, Alek, and the horses," Julien said as he dismounted. We'd discussed this before, so it wasn't news to me, but as I slid from Stanza's back my heart clenched a bit at the thought of being away from my new friends, let alone Stanza and Salvador. But they were not to accompany us to Tirandov Isle and, as soon as Julien could arrange for a guide and passage, we would depart.

We said our good-byes, restrained as they were since I was still playing the part of Sir Julien's squire, and then Julien and I walked to a pleasant-looking inn and he arranged for a suite of rooms.

Our suite was a wonder. Luxurious and secure, Julien explained that it was reserved for visiting dignitaries and members of the E'verian nobility who had not made arrangements to stay at Holiday Palace. A sitting room divided the bedrooms and each bedroom had its own separate bathing chamber. I was disappointed that it lacked Ayden's inventive tub-filling apparatus, but Julien assured me a bath would be drawn for me posthaste. A procession of maids soon had tubs filled in both our chambers and when they finally finished the chore, Julien locked the door and turned his warm, relaxed smile on me.

"Wait here."

He hurried into his chamber. When he came back, he held a piece of fabric, tightly rolled and tied with twine. The color was a feminine shade of lavender, the texture of the fabric familiar. "Is that . . . mine?"

He nodded. "I thought perhaps you were ready to be done with Rozen for a while." He smiled. "I had your aunt choose a dress to pack among my things before we left Fyrlean Manor."

"Thank you." My eyes misted. "It's one of my favorites. That was very kind of you."

"This inn is secure and a guard detail is always assigned to the rooms when nobility visits, so you will be well guarded. After I've bathed I have a few errands I need to attend. Will you be all right?"

I nodded. Even though I would be locked in a suite with guards outside the door, I couldn't deny the appeal of a few moments of solitude.

"I won't be gone long. If there is a knock, ignore it. I've alerted the staff that you are not to be disturbed."

As I took the dress from his hands I was almost giddy at the prospect of becoming a girl again.

In my chamber, I unrolled the dress, touched to find several sprigs of dried lavender and rosemary tucked within the folds of material. I had expected my dress to be full of mustiness and the scent of horses, but instead it smelled almost freshly laundered and slightly perfumed.

Although it had been necessary to alter my boyish clothes, I did not realize exactly how much my *body* had been altered during our journey until I put on my dress. The sleeves were uncomfortably tight where my arm muscles had developed, but the lower part of the bodice and the waist hung loosely on my leaner frame.

When Julien returned, I asked after his errands.

"I took the liberty of asking a local dressmaker to come here for a fitting. You'll have need of a few more items before we leave for Tirandov Isle." His brow furrowed. "You should probably wear the hairpiece, however. It won't do to have rumors of Queen Daithia's look-alike creeping up all over town. Especially since the King is still at Castle Rynwyk in Salderyn and unable to answer them."

I hadn't even thought of the need to have more clothes, but less than an hour after our meal a dressmaker had measured me and promised to deliver a new gown by morning. I was amazed that it could be accomplished with such speed but she assured me that, in a busy city like Port Dyn, she was used to working under a tight schedule. I figured it didn't hurt that the request had come from a Regent's son.

Tired of wearing the hairpiece, I was content to stay within the confines of our rooms while we waited for word from Erielle as to whether or not the King's promised scribe had yet arrived at Holiday Palace.

The sun had set and we had just finished our dinner when Julien answered a knock on the door. Not wishing to don the hairpiece again, I retreated to my bedroom, but soon Julien appeared in the doorway.

"It's Dyfnel, the scribe sent by your father. He wants to meet you."

I'm not sure why Julien thought Dyfnel wanted to meet me. The hunched-over, bespectacled old man barely looked at me when I entered the room, even though my hair was hanging freely down my back. With a cursory glance in my direction and a little grunt, he handed a parchment to Julien.

"You have the scrolls?" His rough voice scratched against my ears.

"Yes. Right here." Julien handed Dyfnel the oilskin pouch containing the scrolls Erielle had discovered.

"Very good." The old man gave me a quick nod and headed toward the door.

I stared at the back of the door when it closed. "Well," I said, "that was certainly not what I expected."

Julien nodded. "He's an odd old fellow, but the King knows what he's about." He paused to unroll the scroll Dyfnel had given him and quickly scanned its contents. "News certainly travels fast," he said with a chuckle. "It appears the Regent of Dynwatre is hosting a ball at Holiday Palace the night after next, and as the son of the Regent of Mynissbyr, I have been invited. If you would like to go it might be a nice diversion while we await our escort to Tirandov Isle."

"A ball?" I looked down at the coarse fabric of my ill-fitting gown. "I couldn't possibly!" I laughed. "Even if I could suitably disguise myself, I have nothing appropriate to wear to a formal ball!"

"There is a shop that specializes in hairpieces like yours," he said. "As well as longer styles for women." He grinned. "I've always thought it a vain, foolish expense. But in this case?" He shrugged. "I'll run out and see if I can find something to suit."

"But my eyes," I reminded him.

"With Rozen's spectacles no one will recognize you. And since the dressmaker already has your measurements, I'm sure she would be able to create a gown for you if you would like to attend the ball."

A ball gown? The closest to a ball gown I'd ever had was still tucked away in my closet in Veetri. I bit my lower lip. "But Julien, I don't have any way to pay for such an extravagance. Being anonymous does have its drawbacks."

"I'll take care of it," he said with a shrug. "Consider it a birthday gift."

"A what?"

The corner of Julien's mouth turned up. "You may have forgotten your calendar during our journey, Princess Rynnaia, but I have not. Tomorrow you will celebrate your nineteenth birthday. Consider the gown my gift to you."

"I couldn't possibly accept such an expensive gift! You're a knight."

He arched an eyebrow. "I'm not a *poor* knight, Princess. We may have lived rather roughly these past few weeks, but I trust you do remember visiting my home?"

I blushed. He was the heir to a Regency. Of course he could afford it.

"I want to do this for you." He crossed his arms at his chest. "I *will* do this for you. I'm tired of Rozen hanging about. I want my princess back."

My princess. My pulse accelerated at his words.

"Very well," I sighed. "If you insist."

"I do." He jumped up and moved toward the door. "I'll go now to speak to the dressmaker and then I'll find you a new hairpiece." He threw a grin my way that was almost boyish in its enthusiasm. "Lock the door behind me."

I did as I was told, but my hand shook a little from the tumult of unexpected emotions his words had stirred in me, not to mention from the anticipation of being held in his arms, if only for even one dance.

THIRTY-EIGHT

The morning of my birthday I awoke feeling much older than my nineteen years. Less than a full day out of the saddle and my body had already stiffened in protestation of the lack of activity. I slipped out of bed and toward the window where the sun had just crept above the horizon. Its eastern light glinted off the sea, giving the waves a golden glow.

I had never seen the sea before, but something about it drew me. I could have stood at the window for hours, but a ship moved into the harbor, its deck bustling with activity. With a small sigh I stepped away from the window and went about brushing my hair. When the tangles had been tamed, I decided to forego the ill-fitting dress in favor of Rozen's more comfortable wardrobe.

I pulled a bouquet of flowers from the vase on the bedside table and perched the black hairpiece Julien had procured for me upon it. Much more elaborate than my simple squire's style, it consisted of thick, corkscrew curls, pulled back to the crown but for a few which would frame my face. I couldn't wait to try it on. I quickly braided my hair and coiled it around my head and then pulled the tight cap sewn beneath the glossy black hair over my head.

Gazing in the mirror, the years dropped away. It was as if I was back in Veetri, so familiar was my reflection. When the knock sounded at my bedroom door, I almost expected to hear Lord Whittier's voice on the other side.

"Come in."

Julien came in, bearing what could only be a gown, but it was so wrapped in muslin that I couldn't see it.

"Ah, so you tried it on. I prefer your natural color, of course," he said, "but that hairpiece will do nicely for the ball. The style is very becoming, Princess."

"Thank you."

Julien laid the parcel on my bed and unwrapped it to reveal a simply fashioned but attractive gray dress, as well as a new, lighter-weight cloak, stockings, and shoes. "Oh, Julien . . . thank you! This is wonderful!"

"It would be my honor, Princess Rynnaia, to escort you to breakfast and on a stroll afterward, if you are so inclined."

"I am," I replied. "I am *very* inclined! But," I added, "you should probably leave off with calling me princess, don't you think?"

"Indeed." He chuckled. "I will leave you then, to put Rozen to rest and turn back into a butterfly. Or should I say a *flower*, my Lady Rose?"

The new dress was simple, but charming. Flattering lines, sewn exactly to my new measurements, allowed me freedom of movement that my other dress had not. It was good to be entirely female again.

Julien guided me to an eating establishment not far from the inn where we enjoyed a light breakfast before strolling among the nearby shops. The whole morning was a novelty to me, having been so secluded all my life. I'd never been in want, for the duke and duchess provided me with more than enough of anything my heart desired, but I had never shopped beyond the village of Glenhume. There was so much to see. Jewelers, dress shops, bakeries, and oh! That entire shop devoted to soaps! Julien bought me three bars in scents that appealed to me.

We stopped at a flower cart where Julien purchased a small nosegay of hothouse flowers. "Happy birthday, Rynnaia," he whispered as he handed them to me. He had referred to me as "Lady Rose" all morning, but hearing my real name, spoken so intimately in my ear, was wonderful.

We continued our walk near the docks, my hand resting comfortably in the crook of my escort's arm. I raised my eyes toward the Holiday Palace. Black banners had replaced the green and white flags I'd noticed the day before. Curious, I questioned Julien about the change.

His eyes followed my gaze. "E'veria mourns her Queen today."

Of course. The day of my birth also marked the anniversary of my mother's death. *How stupid*, I thought. How *selfish* of me, to forget something so important.

Although I had a vague sense of loss, it was hard to conjure much emotion. How could I mourn someone I had never met? Instead, I thought of the King. I wondered if this day still caused him pain so many years after the Queen's death.

"Your father must have very mixed emotions about this day," Julien spoke as if he'd read my thoughts. "Although I'm sure he mourns the loss of his wife," he leaned in and spoke in a low voice that none but me would hear, "he must be thrilled with the anticipation of finally being reunited with his daughter."

A sense of winged creatures fluttering within my chest accompanied my question, "And when will that be?"

Julien was silent for a moment. "I must admit surprise that he was not here to meet us," he said. "Perhaps he thought it would be difficult to allow you to go off to Tirandov Isle without him so soon after your reunion. I can only guess that I will receive orders to escort you to Castle Rynwyk when your Andoven training is complete."

I nodded and the winged creatures went on their merry way.

The mood of the city was subdued, which I attributed to the remembrance of the Queen, but Julien made a concerted effort to make the day special for me. After lunch he took me by the dressmaker's shop to check on the progress of my ball gown. "We're a little early. Shall we see if they're ready for you?"

Much to my amazement, they were. My fitting went well, and for the rest of the day, Julien acted as if I was the only person in the world. We stayed up talking late into the night and I crawled into bed happy but exhausted.

It was nearly afternoon when I awoke, and only a few hours later the dressmaker herself arrived to help me ready for the ball.

The gown had a wide v-neckline that repeated on the back of the dress. Beneath it, what seemed like hundreds of tiny pearl buttons traced angled paths down the ruby-pink silk. Set at the tips of my shoulders, the long sleeves were encircled with more of the tiny pearl buttons at the cuffs. Other than the buttons, the rosy silk was without adornment, but the styling and quality of the fabric was of such richness that any added decoration would have been superfluous. Pearl-colored slippers slid on to my feet and a pink silk ribbon, complete with a dangling teardrop-shaped pearl, was fastened at my neck as a choker to complete the ensemble.

"All finished," the dressmaker said as she stepped back to admire her handiwork. "I'll fetch Sir Julien."

She returned a moment later. "The color is lovely on her, don't you think?" She addressed the future Regent. "She looks as beautiful as a princess."

"I would have to agree," Julien spoke from the open doorway. "Thank you, Clara."

The dressmaker curtsied and Julien showed her to the door. He returned shortly.

"I have something for you."

I turned, a bit embarrassed to have been caught admiring myself in the mirror. But in his finery, Julien took my mind completely from my own appearance. Wearing a white shirt under a silk tunic of powdery blue, Julien cut a dashing figure. His boots were polished to an ebony shine and they rested just below his knees overtop dark-blue dress breeches. The white sash across the front of his tunic bore his family crest, symbolic of his status as the future Regent of Mynissbyr.

"Would you like to see what it is?"

"Pardon?"

His eyes sparkled. I'd been caught staring.

"I have something for you," he repeated. "A late birthday gift."

"You've been more than generous with your gifts already!" I laughed and twirled around so that he could see the finished gown. "Thank you for the gown. It's beautiful."

"But it is, I'm afraid, incomplete." Walking forward, he reached for my hand and turned the palm up. Pulling something from his pocket, he dropped two small objects into my hand.

Two dangling, teardrop-shaped pearls, each topped by a glittering gem that was nearly the same color as my dress, rested in my hand. "Earrings?"

He nodded.

"They're perfect!" I quickly put them on.

"Now the gown is complete." He smiled. "You look beautiful, Princess Rynnaia." He reached and brushed a curl back from my shoulder, leaving a path of tingles where his fingers touched my skin.

"Thank you." Even slipping on the gray-tinted spectacles couldn't quench the happy feelings swirling around in my mind. I took Julien's offered arm and he led me down the stairs where a hired coach waited to take us to Holiday Palace.

The road up to the palace was not difficult to traverse. It was a wide path that had been cut into the cliffs, winding upward at an easy grade. Julien was recognized at the well-guarded gate and we were easily admitted. I tried not to look like a naïve country girl as we approached the beautiful white structure, illumined orange and pink by the setting sun, but I knew my eyes were as wide as the wheels of our carriage.

Once inside, however, my mouth made a perfect "Oh!" that couldn't hope to match the scope of grandeur. The first thing that caught my eye was the oversized portrait, hanging at a landing of the wide staircase at the end of the bright, cavernous entry hall.

"Is that . . ." I almost said "me?" before I realized the portrait was, in fact, Queen Daithia, my mother. But with other guests arriving and following our same path, I wasn't allowed time to study it.

A lush, moss-green carpet covered the center of the marble steps, making our procession entirely noiseless. Hanging from long chains anchored to the ceiling, metal-worked silver chandeliers sparkled with what appeared to be, but couldn't possibly be . . .

"Are those *diamonds*?"

"No," Julien smiled. "They're made of blown glass, and most date back to when the palace was first constructed, over a century ago." He said. "Among the large staff there is a team of ten men whose only job is to see that the chandeliers in the palace are kept clean."

"Only ten?" I laughed, taking in the brightness of the castle, achieved with an abundance of like chandeliers and similarly styled sconces. "I would think it would take an army!"

White seemed to be the prevalent color throughout the palace, but green touches stole the coldness from the space, imbuing it instead with a sense of life and ease that made it feel both elegant and welcoming.

Just before we reached a copse of trees sculptured from white marble, Julien paused. "You will be introduced as Rose de Whittier, daughter of the Duke of Glenhume."

"But what if—?"

"No one will question me."

Julien was the son and heir of a Regent, and as such, considered by many to be a branch of royalty. Of course his word would be accepted.

He led me though the "trees" which arched over our heads, framing the path into the Grand Hall, where we were announced.

"His Grace, the future Regent of Mynissbyr, Sir Julien de Gladiel," a herald announced, "and the Lady Rose de Whittier, daughter of His Lordship Whittier de Barden, Duke of Glenhume."

Curious eyes followed our entrance, and before I thought to block my mind from the onslaught of gossiping thoughts that accompanied our appearance, it became clear that, while Sir Julien de Gladiel was a favorite dancing partner of many ladies in attendance, other than his sister, he had never before escorted a young lady to a ball.

My smile widened, even as I stretched my mind to find the swirls of gray necessary to dim the noise in my head.

Larger than the Great Hall we had passed as we came in, the Grand Hall was as green as the rest of the palace was white. Here, even the marble of the floor was green, veined with white, which was the exact opposite of the floors I had crossed elsewhere in the palace. Rimmed with round tables, the space was no less than six times larger than where my sixteenth birthday had taken place at Mirthan Hall. The Grand Hall was well lit, but dimmer than the rest of the castle due in part to the darkness of the green stone, paneled walls, and rich velvet curtains. The dimness gave the large space a sense of intimacy, if not a touch of mystery. On a raised dais in the center of the space a group of musicians sat on gilded chairs and accompanied the dancers already in motion around them.

"You're here!" Erielle found us in the crowd and crushed me in a hug. Gone was the wily young squire, almost as if he had never existed. Before me stood a most elegant and lovely young lady.

Wearing a gold gown embroidered with black and liberally studded with black crystals, Erielle de Gladiel exuded elegance and youthful splendor. Her transformation was truly breathtaking and I was certainly not the only person to note her beauty. We had barely exchanged words before a young man whisked her away to dance.

"Might I have the honor?" Julien let go of my elbow and offered his hand.

"I do enjoy dancing with you, Julien," I said after our fourth turn about the floor, "but aren't you worried that people will talk if the Regent's son continues to dance with the same lady all night?"

"Let them talk." He grinned, but his smile fell when a man tapped on his shoulder.

"Might I cut in?" The young man's question was directed at Julien, but his eyes were on me.

I looked to Julien, who scowled, but gave a slight nod and passed my hand into the newcomer's grasp. "Lady Rose, may I present Daws de Wallis? De Wallis, this is Lady Rose. I believe you've met her brother, Sir Kinley de Whittier, yes?"

"Indeed."

"Mind her toes then, Daws." Julien's tone was light, but his eyes as steely as his sword. "I'd hate for you to have to explain to Sir Kinley why his sister suffers a limp."

Inwardly I winced, wondering if my new partner was, in fact, as clumsy as Julien seemed to imply, but I almost giggled when I perceived Julien's subtle threat of a second knight who would be willing to avenge me should this young man prove to be an unskilled dancing partner.

"I'll be near." Julien speared the young man with a look that made my new dancing partner pale.

As it turned out, Daws de Wallis was a fine dancer, as were most of the men who claimed my hand as the evening progressed.

"You're Kinley de Whittier's sister, yes?" A middle-aged knight asked when one of the group dances landed us as partners for a short time.

I nodded.

"A pity about Glenhume," he said. "Such a loss. But I'm sure your father will set it to rights."

I made a small sound in my throat that I hoped passed for confirmation, but my thoughts spun as tightly as my heart clenched. What had happened to Lord Whittier's dukedom? And when?

"You've been to Glenhume?" I asked, wondering how to draw the information from him without giving myself away. "Recently?"

"Not for years. But rumors, you know." His eyebrows narrowed, but with concern rather than censure. "Were you away before the attack?"

"Yes." My answer came out as a whisper and I had to blink rapidly to dispel the mist in my eyes.

"I'm so sorry to have mentioned it, Lady Rose. I'm sure it's a painful subject. Please forgive me."

I forced a smile. "Your concern is well met, sir. And I thank you for it."

The steps of the dance switched our partners again, and although I managed to smile, my heart was heavy.

"Something is bothering you," Julien said as he took my hand for the final dance of the evening.

"Is it that obvious?"

"Only to me." His hand on the small of my back felt safe. *Right.*

"Someone asked me about Glenhume," I began. "They said it was . . . attacked." I bit my lip to stop it from quivering.

He squeezed the hand he held. "It was. About two years ago."

"You never said." I wasn't accusing, I just didn't understand.

"I'm sorry. I—"

"And Rowlen!" I said. Julien's omission was understandable. But my brother's? Hardly. "When I asked after Lord and Lady Whittier, he acted as if all was well."

"Lord and Lady Whittier are well. They and their household were away before the attack," Julien said. "In fact, nearly everyone was away. They'd been warned."

"By your father," I said. "When he came to get me."

"Ah." Julien nodded. "That fits the timeline."

"You said *nearly* everyone was away."

"There was very little loss of life."

"But some."

"Yes," he said. "Not everyone heeded the warning. When the village was razed—"

"Razed?"

He hesitated before answering. "Destroyed. It was burned. And several small farms, as well."

I almost couldn't bear to ask, but I had to know. "And Mirthan Hall?"

"The same," he said softly. "But last I heard, it was nearly rebuilt."

I could barely breathe, imagining the cheerful home of my childhood in ruins. "Why would Rowlen not have told me?"

"You've said that all your brothers are overprotective. Perhaps it was his way of protecting you."

I nodded. He was probably right. *But still.* Mirthan Hall. Glenhume. Gone. It was hard to reconcile such a thing, and even harder to know that those who had committed this villainy had been drawn there because of me.

A tear traced its path down my cheek. Julien brought our clasped hands close and used his thumb to wipe it away. "There's nothing you could have done to stop it."

Julien was quiet as he led me through the more intricate steps of the dance. When the bridge was over and the tempo slowed again he leaned into my ear.

"While you were dancing with Sir Risson, I spoke with Dyfnel, the scribe."

Sir Risson. I searched my mind for a face to put with the name, but there had been too many new faces over the course of the night. And now there was too much weight on my heart to put effort into identifying one among them. "And?"

"Our passage is secured," he whispered. "We'll leave for Tirandov Isle in the morning."

When the dance finished, he led me to Erielle to convey our plans.

"May Rynloeft speed your journey," she whispered, returning my embrace.

"Thank you, Erielle," I whispered as well, but it was due more to the emotions caused by leaving my friend than a desire for secrecy. "I will miss you."

"As I will you, my friend." When she pulled away, she dabbed at the corner of her eyes. "It has been the greatest honor of my life to serve you."

Thirty-Nine

The ball left little time for rest before our early morning departure, but even so, my nervousness about meeting the Andoven and my grief over the happenings in Veetri stole the quality from even the spare amount of sleep I was able to claim. After sleeping less than two full hours I awoke to the sharp sort of headache that can only result from such emotions.

By the time Julien knocked on my door to awaken me, I was already dressed and ready to go, but the new shoes I'd worn to the ball had left my feet swollen and blistered. Forced into my boots, they throbbed in silent protest.

The sky showed little sign of the approaching dawn when Dyfnel arrived to escort us to the docks. Julien's bloodshot eyes served as evidence of his own restless night, but heedless to our discomfort, Dyfnel chattered as amiably as if it were midday rather than this uncivilized predawn hour.

The fog was so thick I could barely see my hand in front of my face—not that I'd take my hands out of my pockets if I could help it. Perhaps it was the early hour and the sluggish way my blood seemed to be moving, but the air seemed much colder than I'd expected after enjoying such temperate days in Port Dyn. Wearing the new gray dress, I was glad for the additional warmth of my cloak. Rather than pin the hairpiece on to my aching head I'd opted to hide my hair beneath the cloak's ample hood. But I had to wonder if I'd done the right thing. I might welcome the hairpiece's warmth if the sun failed to warm us when it rose.

"Hurry now," Dyfnel said. "The ship I've arranged isn't the sort of vessel that likes to pass time in busy harbors."

"Has the Andoven guide already arrived?"

"Indeed," Dyfnel said with a slight chuckle. "Indeed."

Oil lamps hung at the edge of the walkway, dimly lighting our murky path along the nearly deserted dock. By the time Dyfnel stopped it felt like we had walked a thousand miles and ended up in a foreign land.

"How will the captain be able to leave the bay without crashing into another ship?" I whispered the question to Julien, but Dyfnel answered.

"No need to worry. Our captain is a gifted sailor."

The old man stopped so abruptly then that I almost ran into him. He lifted the cane, and with a spry flick of his wrist, tossed it into the water. Standing up straighter than I had deemed possible, Dyfnel looked almost a foot taller than he had appeared a moment earlier. He removed his spectacles and pierced me with his gaze.

His eyes were bright blue. Brighter than even my own. He spoke a greeting into my thoughts.

I gasped. "You're Andoven?"

"Dyfnel de Arturen, at your service. It is my honor to be your guide to Tirandov. But truth be told," he added, "on this particular ship you have no need of me." He bowed first to me

324

and then to Julien with a youthful flexibility I would not have guessed him able to achieve mere seconds earlier.

A gray film of which I had not even been aware lifted from his thoughts, reminding me to cover my own.

I scowled at him, realizing the deception of his appearance was not the only thing he'd kept from us.

"You are not the King's scribe."

Julien's hand moved to his sword.

"At ease, knight." Dyfnel smiled. "You are correct. I am not a scribe as you have been led to believe, though I am capable of that position. I am a physician."

"A physician?"

"Yes." He stretched again before he continued. "I was at Castle Rynwyk when you were born and my friendship with your mother dates back many years before that." His eyes took on a watery sheen. "However, now is not the time to dwell on the past. You have much to learn and Tirandov awaits! Shall we?"

We hurried to follow the Andoven man up a wide boarding plank and onto the ship. As soon as our feet hit the deck, a sailor plucked up the plank and stowed it away.

"Welcome aboard, Princess."

I jumped when a man whispered in my ear.

"Try to remain as silent as possible until we're in the open water. We wouldn't want to raise the alarm, aye?"

I nodded and turned, but whoever owned the voice had already disappeared in the fog. Dyfnel ushered us to a private area on deck and we settled on benches a bit away from the crew.

I wasn't sure I liked the motion of the ship. It made my insides feel displaced, somehow, and the fog, as thick as it was, strained my eyes even more than the dark.

My hands balled into fists, expecting us to crash into another vessel at any moment. "I hope they know what they're doing," I whispered to Julien.

He squeezed my shoulder. "They do."

The minutes stretched and Julien invited me to use him as a back rest. He was positioned in a corner and, when he lifted his left arm and rested it on the rail, it made the perfect place for me to cozy in. "Thank you."

Dancing with him last evening had brought fully awake the feelings I'd been forced to contain while traveling as his squire. Snuggled into the safety of his warmth brought a sense of comfort that put me so at ease I didn't even know I'd dozed off until a shout roused me.

I sat up, disoriented.

"Did you have a nice nap, Your Highness?"

The voice was stained with a smile I didn't quite trust, and when I saw to whom it belonged, I thought my suspicion justified.

In the dim light of encroaching dawn, a young man grinned at me from his place atop a barrel. Beneath a tightly tied blue sash, his black hair hung about his shoulders in loose curls. A spare patch of beard grew just below his lower lip, but stopped shy of his chin, and a jagged white scar traced a path across his left cheek. Bronzed from the sun, his skin bore the sheen of youth, but his eyes, his startling, ice-blue eyes, seemed much older than the rest of him.

"Who are you?" I scooted closer to Julien.

"I'm known hereabout as Cazien de Pollis, Your Highness, and I'm the captain of this fine ship. Welcome aboard."

"Captain?" I blinked. "But you're so—"

"Handsome? Yes. Quite. But I promise my good looks will not impede my ability to transport you safely to Tirandov Isle."

"I was going to say *young*." Heat scalded my cheeks. He *was* handsome, but in a very dangerous sort of way.

"Some would say *vain* is a more apt description." Julien's dry voice rumbled behind me. "But young is certainly as true. Cazien is barely older than you, Princess Rynnaia. But he is our captain and has much more experience than you might expect in one of his years."

"You know each other?"

"I've had the occasion to sail with him before and, although many might disagree, I assure you he's quite harmless."

"Harmless? Ach! You wound me, knight." Cazien shook his head. "To call a pirate harmless is the gravest of insults."

"And I trust you will bear it with the restraint and aplomb for which your men are so famous."

Their repartee, spoken clearly as words between friends, was so fast I almost missed an important detail. "Did you say *pirate*?"

"A pirate? Me? Of course not," Cazien answered with a wink. As he raised his voice he added a rhythmic sort of music to his words. "No sailor here would dare lay claim to being such a rogue."

A chorus of off-tune voices joined their much younger captain in his impromptu song, "*Unless he be a pirate of the Seahorse fleet!*"

"You're Seahorse pirates?" My jaw must have dropped a foot. "Like in the stories?"

Cazien jumped off his barrel. As he made a low, sweeping bow, a silver chain and pendant caught the light. "Ever at your service, Your Highness." He rose and winked. "When it pleases me to be, of course."

I blinked. *When it pleases him?* "How do you know who I am?"

"Apart from the title your loyal knight used to address you?" He laughed. "Ah, I heard of you long ago from my mother. More recently, however, from King Jarryn's own lips. In a manner of speaking." He rapped his knuckles against his head. "The Andoven connection, you know. It comes in handy for the King when he wishes to order me about. And occasionally," he laughed and waggled his eyebrows, "I even choose to comply."

"You're Andoven?"

"A bit."

"More than a bit, I'd say." Dyfnel followed his hrrumph by mumbling, "Among other things."

I turned to Julien. "Does the King know our captain is a pirate?"

Julien nodded as laughter filled the deck. I blushed to the roots of my hidden red hair.

"Oh, he knows," Cazien replied. "His Majesty happens to be my cousin. A distant cousin, of course," he said with a grin, "but a cousin nonetheless. That makes us family, Princess, whether you like it or not."

Family. Two months ago I didn't even know my real name. Now I had a king for a father and a pirate for a cousin? I turned to Julien. "Rowlen is going to go absolutely mad with jealousy when he hears about this."

Julien smiled. "Perhaps you should keep it to yourself, then?"

I shook my head. "Not possible."

He laughed.

"Come, cousin." Cazien stood and offered his hand. "Let me show you the sunrise."

I slipped my hand into my cousin's and allowed him to lead me away from Julien's warmth. Standing at the bow of the ship with pirates—*pirates!*—all around me, I watched a spectacular dance of color streak the sky with orange, pink, purple, and gold. I had never seen such an amazing dawn and said as much.

"I never tire of watching the sun rise from the sea," Cazien sighed. "The sight alone is worth the early hour. So what fair task has my friend Jarryn devised that requires you to keep company with the stodgy old Andoven?"

"It wasn't just him," I said, pausing to cover a yawn. "Lady Anya told me to seek the Andoven and that they would help me on my quest. Whatever that means." I bit my lip and turned to Julien, who, of course, had followed us. "Should I not have said that?"

"Your father puts great trust in Cazien and the Seahorse fleet. I don't think he would mind."

Cazien's lip twitched. "But perhaps you do, Julien?"

When Julien smiled but refrained from answering, the pirate simply laughed and turned back to me. "Not everyone shares your father's fondness for my family's way of life," he said with a wink. "But I want to hear more of this business with Lady Anya." Cazien made a face that seemed to question my sanity and poke fun at the same time. "How did she give you this grand bit of instruction? It is my understanding that Lady Anya has long since passed from this world."

"Well I guess she left a bit of herself behind." I glared at him. "Because one moment I was reading her poetry and the next I was watching her write it."

The laughter faded from the pirate's eyes. "If that is true," he said slowly, darkly, "then you are gifted beyond what your lineage prescribes."

Dyfnel grinned and slapped Cazien on the back. "Of course she is!" He turned back to me. "I was not told of this news! You must have seen an original copy, Princess! Imagine, Cazien! The first written copy of the prophecy, written in the prophet's own hand! Remarkable!"

"Remarkable, indeed," the pirate mumbled.

I looked back and forth between the two men. "What does that have to do with it?"

"For a poet," Dyfnel began, "truth flows out from the imagination, through the hand, and on to parchment as ink. But when it is copied by another hand, a hand not so invested in the telling, it is diluted."

He looked at me as if waiting for a reply, but when he got none, he continued. "As an Andoven, especially an Andoven of your unique gifting, you are able to see all of the emotion and truth as the author herself saw it! May I ask where you came across this ancient volume?"

"Yes." Cazien rubbed his chin, seeming to assess me in a different light. "Do tell, Princess."

My eyes narrowed on the pirate. Did he think me a liar? "I came across the book in Mynissbyr."

The pirate's expression never changed, but something briefly lit in his eyes, almost as if he had foreknowledge of my answer. "And you found this book . . . where?"

"At Fyrlean Manor."

"And what about the scrolls?" He tilted his head as if that wasn't the answer he had expected. "Were they also *inside* the manor?"

"Did you think the Regent's family would store them out-doors?" I laughed.

"Of course not. I just wondered how the scrolls came to be in their possession."

"Why does it matter?"

"It doesn't." When he smiled his face was clear of decep-tion, yet I knew he was hiding something. Something that made me think that, for Cazien de Pollis, the answer to that question meant very much indeed, but that he would not, per-haps even upon pain of death, reveal why.

Even though it felt wrong to attempt to read another's thoughts without permission, I couldn't help myself. I had to know what my pirate cousin was hiding—and if the information I'd thoughtlessly imparted was safe in his hands.

When we locked eyes, the ice-blue determination in his gaze nearly froze me to the spot. But I couldn't get so much as a swirl of gray from his thoughts.

Nice try, Princess.

I gasped to find Cazien's voice in my head, but its tone exactly matched the amused smirk on his face. What sort of Andoven was he, anyway?

No kind you'll likely come across again. But I'll not betray you.

Dyfnel spoke then and I was forced to move my attention back to the older man.

"I've no doubt it is you the prophecy speaks of." Dyfnel rubbed his hands together. "Physically, you match the description. Blue eyes, red hair. You were born the Ryn. You're female. Besides, only the one of whom it was written would have been able to so clearly see the intent, the truth the author most wanted to convey."

I thought back to the conversation I'd had with the poet. "I guess Lady Anya wanted to convey instructions, then?"

"Yes, you would see it that way." Dyfnel pulled on his long gray beard. "The King will be mightily disappointed that your education did not delve into the deeper studies. The skills you receive on Tirandov Isle will be of little use to you until you acknowledge their source."

My defenses rose at his insult to my upbringing. "The Duke of Glenhume saw to it that my education was quite thorough."

"I meant no disrespect, Princess Rynnaia." Dyfnel sighed. "Sadly, the Andoven are mostly to blame. For far too long we have taken our position as Protectors of Truth so literally that we have failed to see that the only way to truly keep it as the light it was meant to be is to make it known." He paused. "And the attitude of the Elders toward the Storytellers does not hasten the propagation of truth in that province." Dyfnel sighed. "But truth is not something to be learned by education, Princess Rynnaia. It is revealed to the heart."

I turned and stared out at the sea. "I may not know much about being Andoven, but I believe what I saw at Fyrlean Manor. I saw Lady Anya write the words and I heard her speak to me."

"Sometimes prophets speak in riddle and metaphor and we can only know the meaning of their words after the event has come to pass."

"Enough." Cazien clapped his hands together. "You'll have plenty of time for boring conversations among the Andoven, Princess. You're aboard *Meredith* now. And I for one cannot abide the bleak mood that has descended upon us."

He winked and a wave of relief swept over me.

"I believe Jayma has saved back a pint or two of eachanberries," he said, "and I see no reason why we should let them spoil." The pirate offered his arm, and without thinking, I took it. "Have you ever tasted the berries of Eachan Isle, Rynnaia?"

"No. Of course not."

"Tragic, that is," he tsked. "But a tragedy that shall soon be averted. Come along."

When he lifted my hand and twirled me as if to dance, I had to laugh. Somewhere, a sailor began to sing a lively tune, and as the rest of the crew joined in, their young captain danced me across the deck. Suddenly a sharp, green, metallic *fwwing* flew through my mind, stabbing our merry crossing.

"Don't mind him. He's just jealous," Cazien whispered in my ear as he angled his head toward Julien. "And can you blame him, really? Even when compared next to the King's favorite knight I am *quite* a catch. Your knight worries you might rethink where you've cast your net."

"Indeed?" I almost tripped spinning back into his arms. "I don't recall casting a net."

"Ah, but you have. And I fear Sir Julien is well tangled within it." The tenderness in his softly spoken words surprised me. "But even if you cast in a more seaward direction," he added dryly, "I'm afraid your net, as beautiful as it is, could not hold me." His tone took on that tinge of mystery that told me I needn't bother trying to see into his thoughts. "A pity that," he said, regaining his former humor, "for I think you might have made a fine pirate."

"Not that you would admit to being one, of course."

"Me? A pirate?" He grinned. "Of course not."

FORTY

Later that afternoon Cazien asked me if I would like to hold the wheel. He didn't have to ask twice. I could hardly resist, could I? Rowlen wanted a rousing adventure about my journey to becoming a princess and he would get it! What could be more thrilling than steering the wheel of a Seahorse pirate's ship?

After giving me cursory instructions, Cazien sat down by the railing with a board in his lap and a collection of thin, charcoal pencils. I assumed he was doing something captainish, like drawing charts or navigating, or whatever it was pirates did when they weren't pillaging a ship, but I couldn't have been more wrong.

"That grin you're wearing is positively devilish, Rynnaia."

Sometime during breakfast Cazien had quit addressing me by my title and reduced it to my first name. I didn't mind. He was still something of a mystery, but whatever distrust I'd felt for him in the beginning had melted as we spent more time together. He was, after all, family.

In contrast, Julien, who'd spoken to Cazien like an old friend when we'd first come aboard, had grown increasingly unfriendly as the day went on. If the scowl upon his face was any indication, the affection Julien seemed to hold for the young pirate when we arrived had waned considerably.

The motion of the water ceased to bother me after breakfast, and standing at the wheel of the ship with the wind in my face and the sun reflecting off the waves was exhilarating. There was something so freeing about being on the sea. The hood had long since blown from my head and my hair had refused to remain bound by its coils. Yet as it waved behind me, looking, I imagined, like a wind-blown flame, it felt as if something within me had been released. Not so violently as when I learned my name, but a more comfortable freedom. There were no secrets here—at least not concerning me. I had no reason to hide.

"I think I could get used to this!" I laughed.

"You hear that, lads?" Cazien called out. "The sea has claimed herself another victim!"

"And a beautiful victim she be!" a sailor called back.

"Huzzah!" Cazien shouted. The cheer echoed back to him from all around. Julien's scowl deepened.

"You disagree with the assessment, de Gladiel?"

I shot Cazien a look with a clear message: *Don't bait him.*

"Of course not," Julien replied. "I am caused to wonder, though, if the men of this ship would speak so freely if the King were here."

"Of course they would!" Cazien laughed. "It's not as if Jarryn's our King, you know."

I spun around. "He's *not*?"

"Try not to turn the wheel when you spin around like that, Rynnaia. And no, he's not. Eachan Isle is its own monarchy. We're not under E'verian rule."

"Oh." I carefully straightened the wheel. "So who is the monarch of Eachan Isle?"

"Uh . . ."

I turned my head again, careful not to move the wheel as I did so.

Cazien picked up a new piece of charcoal, turned his attention back to the parchment, and mumbled something.

"What did you say?"

Cazien didn't look up, nor did his lips move, but I clearly heard his reluctant answer to my question in my mind.

"*I am.*"

"Oh." My eyes widened. "Oh. But you're so—"

"Handsome? I know," he sighed dramatically. "My curse."

Julien snorted.

The skies had been clear since morning, but without any forewarning, a bright fog appeared directly in our path.

"Cazien?" I couldn't disguise the quiver in my voice. "I think you should—"

"Princess? What is it?" Julien was at my side in an instant.

I pointed. "There."

"Ah!" Cazien stepped to my other side. "You've found it."

"Found what?"

"Tirandov Isle, of course!"

I squinted. "I don't see an island."

"No one ever does."

I turned and put my hands on my hips. "Could you *be* a little more cryptic?"

"Of course I could." Cazien grabbed for a spindle before the wheel could spin too far. "But before I demonstrate that particular gift, I do believe I shall regain control of my ship."

"Oh! Sorry!" My eyes caught on the board Cazien had set aside. "What is that?"

"A sketch," he grinned, "of Princess Rynnaia E'veri, playing the role of a pirate."

"May I see it?"

"Of course."

I walked over and picked it up, the fog forgotten for a moment as I marveled at the realism of the image Cazien had drawn.

He had caught me from the side. I could almost trace the path of the wind through my hair and could almost hear my laughter.

"You're quite talented, Captain."

"I like to draw." The moment of boyish honesty lasted only a breath before the now-familiar smirk took its place. "I'd rather be slitting throats or commandeering ships, you understand, but when none of those amusements are available, it helps to pass the time."

I rolled my eyes. He was worse than Rowlen.

Dyfnel appeared from wherever he'd spent the afternoon. "From here we take oars, my friends," he said. "Are you coming ashore, Captain?"

"Not this time," Cazien replied. "I have business in Luce." A cloud passed over his features.

Dyfnel nodded. "Of course. Give my regards to your brother."

"Indeed I will if he's not yet turned tail. I've heard rumors of Dwonsil warriors infiltrating the harbor."

Concern marred Julien's brow. "Does the duke have enough troops to keep it from falling?"

"Yes," Cazien nodded, "I believe he does. The better question is if he has the fortitude to command them." He turned to me and winked. "But Luce won't fall. Not if the Seahorse fleet gets there in time." He turned back to Dyfnel. "You will contact me when Rynnaia needs to return?"

"Indeed I will."

Cazien nodded. As he led us to the longboat, I whispered to Julien. "I have another cousin? In Luce?"

"No. Roeg is Cazien's *half*-brother," he said. "And even more of a scoundrel. But he's no relation to you."

Between the growl in Julien's voice and the hardness of Cazien's glare, I decided not to question either man further.

Three burly sailors reached over the rail and gave the longboat a shove outward. When it came back, they grabbed it and held it steady while another two sailors fastened ropes to the longboat and the rail.

Julien got in the longboat first and turned to offer me his hand. I was just about to take it when Cazien stopped me.

"Rynnaia, wait."

I turned around. "Yes?"

"Don't let the Andoven intimidate you," he said softly. "Remember you are the Ryn. There is no dilution of purpose, only of blood. Truth of purpose strengthens a person's character deeper than the purest blood can reach."

"Well, at least I know you aren't a liar," I said, arching an eyebrow, "you *can* be more cryptic. And now you're a philosopher, as well?"

He smiled, but without the smirk. "Be strong. Take hold of your legacy, Cousin. Be the Ryn. E'veria needs you."

His words were a warning that nearly stole my composure—nearly made me beg to stay aboard *Meredith*—but I leaned over to kiss his cheek. "It was a pleasure to meet you, Captain."

Getting into the longboat was not an experience I looked forward to repeating, but the water was strangely calm beneath us. As the boat was lowered I noticed that the current between the fog and our sailing vessel rippled rather than waved, almost as if a light breeze was crossing a small pond rather than wind across the ocean. As I looked down the side of the larger vessel, though, I noticed the rest of the sea contained normal-sized swells.

"I've never been on the sea, Julien. Is this typical?"

"Only here."

When the boat finally settled on the water I reached for an oar, but Julien just smiled and took it from my hands. "You're not Rozen the Squire anymore." His smile faltered. "And you're certainly not some pirate's muse. You are the Crown Princess of E'veria."

He was jealous? *Of Cazien?*

"I should accustom myself to it, I suppose," he sighed. "You'll receive much such attention, I'm sure, after you're made known."

He *was* jealous! I sat down and let the men row, ducking my head to disguise my pleasure.

It wasn't long before the fog enveloped our little boat completely. "Dyfnel? Are you sure you know the way?"

"It knows me," Dyfnel chuckled. "You may stop rowing now, Sir Julien."

I cautiously peered over the side of the boat. The water was barely visible, so thick was the fog. Driven forward by an invisible current, we moved quickly, but I felt no breeze upon my face. The morning air was cool but not chilling, and though it seemed to have no motion, neither was it stagnant. We waited within an otherworldly calm for what felt like hours with no sound other than our breathing. Even the movement of the longboat was silent in the water.

The fog took on a pinkish glow for a moment and then, suddenly, we were out of it.

Stretching before us, the white sand of Tirandov Isle shone with glimmering flecks of pinks, blues, and greens, almost as if crushed jewels had been sprinkled upon the shore.

Beyond the shimmering, shallow beach was a beautifully manicured lawn with the most lush, brightest green grass I had ever seen.

Sections of the lawn were joined together by pathways forming diamond shapes. At the center of each diamond, small circular fountains, statuary, or carved seating beckoned further study. These, too, seemed to have a pastel glow. Although, as my gaze moved up, I realized the glow might be nothing more than a reflection of the singular mountain before us. Or was it a castle? It seemed as if the structure had literally been carved out of the opalescent rock that made up the center of the island.

The castle was immense, but the island itself appeared to be quite narrow. Although I couldn't see past the castle to judge the isle's length, I estimated that a moderate stroll to the east or west would quickly reach the water.

"I almost don't believe it's real."

"Well then, Princess, let's go ashore and prove your eyes correct!" Dyfnel seemed to have regained his cheerfulness. "Are you hungry? I believe my wife has a meal laid out for us."

"Your wife? You never mentioned . . . oh! Do you see that, Julien?" I found it hard to finish a sentence, so taken was I by the beauty around me. The boat docked—by itself, it appeared—and we disembarked in the sand without even getting our feet wet.

"Where shall I tie up the boat?" Clearly as awestruck as I, Julien was trying harder to hide it. "I don't see a—"

"It is not necessary to tie the boat, Good Knight. It will wait for us, should we have need of it again."

Julien and I exchanged a glance. I raised my hands in a "your guess is as good as mine" sort-of way and we followed Dyfnel toward the towering opalescent structure.

The long pathway was built at a gentle incline, but even so it was quite a walk to the elegant, imposing castle. Multiple arched doors graced its front. I chanced a look up and was dizzied at the sheer height of the building.

Two levels up from the ground, a curtain shifted and a feminine face peered down at us, smiling. Our eyes met and she bowed her head in greeting.

Dyfnel waved his hand and one of the monstrous doors began to open.

"How did you—?" I began, but Dyfnel was already inside. I turned to Julien. "Did you see that?"

He nodded. "The Andoven have many diverse gifts."

Inside, the castle was at least as bright as the outside of the building, if not more so, but there were no lanterns or lamps about. The walls themselves seemed to glow.

"You are very astute, Princess," a voice commented from my left.

I turned and faced a young man wearing a robe the color of mint, embroidered with silver thread. His light brown hair was cut short and his bright blue eyes held a forced sort of seriousness that made me almost sad.

"The stone is called tirandite," he said, "and is thought to be unique to our island. During the day our stone walls absorb the heat of the sun and convert it to light. We are rarely in need of candles here, though the stone forces us to hang tapestries in our sleeping chambers to provide the necessary darkness for sleep."

"It's . . . nice."

He moved forward and bowed. "I am called Edru. Refreshments await you in the dining room. After you have eaten you will be introduced in the Great Hall."

"Are you to be one of my teachers here, Edru?"

"Yes. Your lessons with me will begin yet today. Until then, Your Highness." At that he bowed slightly and exited the entry hall through an ornately carved wooden door.

I winced. Would all the Andoven be so formal? As Veetrish as I was, the thought did not bode well for us getting on smoothly.

"Edru is a good man," Dyfnel said with a twinkle in his eye. "You will learn much from him. Perhaps, you might even teach him a few things! He tends to be overly serious at times and a bit of a pessimist. He is usually a bit friendlier, but I believe he is rather irritated with me right now."

"Why?" I bit my lip. "Not that it's any of my business."

"I was bound to secrecy concerning your existence, Princess. Even at Tirandov. The Andoven are not fond of secrets." His step hitched as he paused. "Well, not unless they are the ones keeping them, that is."

"But couldn't they have seen your thoughts and known about me?"

"No."

He didn't elaborate. While we snacked on fruit, spicy tea, and the most delicate little pastries I had ever had the pleasure of consuming, Dyfnel explained to me that, although I would interact with many of the Andoven while on Tirandov Isle, the bulk of my visit would be spent in lessons with Edru and with a woman named Celyse, who happened to be Dyfnel's daughter.

Of course, I had no idea what that would entail, but the dry, circumspect way Dyfnel explained it made it sound like it would not only be extremely taxing, but possibly monotonous at times. Oh, well. In that way I supposed it wasn't any different than any other schooling I'd had.

As soon as we had finished eating, Dyfnel led us through several corridors and down a wide hall before turning a corner that opened into an immense room—the Great Hall.

The ceiling rose in a series of overlapping arches that repeated, in smaller form, at the edges of the room, forming a gallery of sorts beyond. The center of the room was without furniture of any kind, but filled to capacity with people looking quite severe to my eyes, each attired in a robe similar to that worn by the young Andoven man Edru I'd met earlier.

"Dyfnel . . . ?"

"All of Tirandov has assembled to meet you, Princess. Are you ready?"

All of Tirandov? "They expect me to—to address them?"

He laughed. "Indeed. It would be most appropriate, don't you think?"

Appropriate, yes. I supposed so. But it was also petrifying.

$\mathcal{F}$ORTY-$\mathcal{O}$NE

$\mathcal{T}$hrough the lower glowing arches ringing the center assembly, more people stood in the galleries. Dressed more in tune to the style to which I was accustomed on the mainland, they stood apart from the robed figures that filled the center of the hall.

"Who are they, Dyfnel?" I whispered, indicating those in the galleries. "Why are they dressed differently? And why do they stay back?"

"Those are the wives, husbands, and children of the Andoven who are not Andoven themselves. There are many bloodlines present, and a few of strong Andoven ancestry. *Some* of our Elders believe that the others should not be here at all."

Something inside of me rebelled at the arrangement of this gathering, but I had little time to think about its implications as Dyfnel urged me forward and introduced me.

Having never spoken in front of a crowd, I assumed my insecurities would cripple my ability to speak. But for some reason, as I stood before this crowd of my father's subjects,

I felt nothing of the sort. Instead I felt . . . *exactly right.* Comfortable. Completely at ease.

"Her Royal Highness, Rynnaia, Princess of E'veria," Dyfnel announced, and then stepped back.

I stepped forward.

"Thank you for allowing me to visit Tirandov Isle. I look forward to the lessons I will receive in this exalted place." I paused, my eyes drawn back toward the outer borders of the room. Those people were not in the gallery by choice. They were placed there—kept on the edges of this elite society. As my gaze moved back to the bulk of the assemblage, I was somewhat taken aback by the smug expressions on a few of the faces before me.

Cazien's cryptic warning echoed through my brain: *Don't let them intimidate you.*

I took a breath. "I'm sure the news of my survival has been a shock to many of you. Learning my identity has been something of a shock to me, as well. Until recently I had no knowledge of my status as the Ryn, nor did I know that Andoven blood flowed in my veins. And while I do appreciate the effort you make to welcome me, and look forward to the knowledge I will gain from your tutelage, I must make it clear that I have no intention of recognizing a division of import among you."

I took a deep breath. Feeling anger billow toward me from the center of the room, I addressed the gallery. "Thank you for your welcome. While it's true that I am the daughter of the King, I, like many of you, am not entirely Andoven. Indeed, as you might tell from my accent, much of my personality is informed by my Veetrish upbringing." I moved my gaze back to the center of the hall. "Therefore I must insist that I be treated no better than those considered the least of this beautiful isle."

Whispers rustled through the crowd.

Dyfnel placed a hand on my shoulder. "You do your father proud."

"Indeed," Julien's low voice spoke from behind me.

"*Tura hathami Ryn Naia!*" A shout came from the gallery.

"*Tura hathami Ryn Naia!*"

The words repeated around the gallery and scattered here and there, even throughout the robed figures in the middle of the room. "*Tura hathami Ryn Naia!*"

I angled my whisper at Dyfnel. "What does it mean?"

"Listen, Princess. Listen as you did to Lady Anya, and you will know."

I closed my eyes and let the words glide over my ears, through my consciousness, and into the Andoven gifts coming to life within me. Suddenly, I knew the exact meaning of the crowd's chant. My mind translated the thoughts of their hearts, even though it was verbalized in the Ancient Voice, a language I did not speak.

"*Long life to the Reigning Lady! Long live Princess Rynnaia!*"

Smiling, I held up my hand for quiet and continued. "Thank you. I certainly hope to achieve that."

There was a small tittering of laughter in the crowd. I squared my shoulders.

"I confess I am quite ignorant of Andoven ways. I appreciate your friendship and beg your patience as I seek the knowledge and skills necessary to exile the Cobeld curse and restore peace throughout E'veria."

I stepped back from the podium and a cheer broke out. In that moment, I realized what I meant to these unusually gifted people. Most of the residents of Tirandov Isle were untouched by the idea of a direct threat from the Cobelds. They were, however, committed to seeing prophecies interpreted and successfully carried out.

"Princess Rynnaia?" Edru, my young teacher, stood just to my left. "Shall we begin your first lesson?"

I took his offered arm and we left the Great Hall, Julien trailing behind us.

"Edru, do the Andoven leave Tirandov Isle often?"

"A few do. Most are content to stay here and see to the needs of our people and our studies."

"I've heard the Cobelds fear the sea," I said, "so I guess you're safe here."

"Yes, we are safe."

As we walked he seemed to ponder his own words. "We are safe on the isle," he repeated, "and yet the people of E'veria's mainland provinces suffer at the enemy's will while we stay cloistered in our libraries and laboratories." He tilted his head. "You wonder if our gifts are best contained on a little island, yes? Or if we are simply cowards, hiding behind our robes and books?"

I couldn't deny that the thought had crossed my mind.

Edru nodded and gave me a sad smile. "You would not be the first E'veri to question our traditions," he said, but then added, "nor the first Andoven."

FORTY-TWO

It was quite a distance from the Great Hall to the library. I took the time to question Edru a bit about the island and the unusual plant life I had noticed on the walk up from the boat.

"Is there a large staff to care for the grounds? They're quite beautifully kept."

"Every plant you see on the island, even those that appear as merely ornamental, are used in our healing, culinary, or textile arts," Edru said. "As with the tirandite stone, many of our plants are not known to thrive anywhere else in the world. Most of our horticulturists live on the opposite side of the island."

"Is there another castle there?"

He shook his head. "No, but there are several smaller dwellings. Manors, you might call them. There are very few man-made structures on the island. Land is a precious resource on such a small island. The buildings are made of tirandite, like the castle, but from excess stone that resulted when the interior of the castle was mined from the mountain."

So I was right on both counts, I thought, *it is a mountain and a castle!*

"We live in a relatively communal environment. There are no servants to speak of on Tirandov Isle. Each person uses his or her unique gifting to serve."

We entered a cavernous hallway; something about the space seemed familiar. "This is where we came in, isn't it?"

"Yes." With a wave of his hand, the wooden door opened. "And this is the library where the bulk of your lessons will take place."

Julien gave me a little bow. "I will remain at the door, Princess Rynnaia. Should you need anything," he paused to spear Edru with a look, "anything at all," he said and looked back at me, "do not hesitate to call for me."

"The Andoven are loyal to the King and his daughter," Edru said. "She is safe here."

"I'll call if I need you," I assured Julien, who looked none too at ease handing me into someone else's care, even though he would be mere steps away.

Edru ushered me through the door. Another slight wave of his hand and the door slid shut with a dull thud.

The room was immense. Oval in shape and at least two stories high, the walls were lined floor to ceiling with books, and a wide balcony encircled the second level. I'd thought Lord Whittier's collection was huge, but this made the library at Mirthan Hall look like a pittance in comparison.

Carved from the same opalescent stone as the castle itself, the curving bookcases put off a steady glow around the innumerable volumes they encased. The room certainly did not lack for light. Tables near every chair were graced by the glow of tirandite sculptures, and larger statues held their own positions on the floor, placed similarly to how one would arrange oil lamps.

Numerous chairs, chaises, and footstools were scattered about in an orderly yet cozy fashion. Upholstered in a deep, almost-red shade of pink, each was embroidered with the same design: a strange but somehow familiar diamond in a circle that was stitched in gold thread in such a way that it almost seemed to jump out of the fabric at me.

On this level, rolling ladders, built from an oddly beautiful greenish-white wood, were attached to a rail encircling the room. Large and sturdy with small shelves protruding from every third step, they appeared more as stair steps than the flimsy climbing devices I'd used to reach hidden places as a child.

Edru gave me a moment to explore the huge chamber. "The section you are in traces Andoven genealogies. Perhaps someday you may come back to Tirandov and study at your leisure, but due to our limited time the only genealogies in which I shall instruct you are your own." He gestured to three books on the table in front of him. "Two of these books pertain to your ancestry." He flicked his wrist and the cover of one of them opened without being touched.

"Will you teach me to do that?"

"No. Your other instructors will ascertain your abilities and decide what else you are to learn."

"Oh," I blushed. "My apologies, Honorable One."

His color matched mine as he turned and started flipping through pages of the top book, "Honorable One is a very formal address that I prefer to reserve for certain persons and occasions. You may simply call me Edru."

"I'm sorry." I sighed. "I'm so ignorant. This is all so . . ." *Overwhelming? Strange?* "What I mean to say is—"

"It is not your fault you do not know of the Andoven or our ways. Few do. Although each of E'veria's provinces offer something unique to the good of the Kingdom, only Tirandov

Isle is actively engaged in keeping its specialties within its borders."

"What do you mean?"

"Think of the people of Dwons, for example, who are known for their craftsmanship of weaponry. That specialty creates a symbiotic relationship with the Sengarra province, which is known for its excellent military training. The Sengarrans use those same gifts of strategy in trade, which creates relationships elsewhere. Sengarra's port and market cities are among the most successful in the world, and knights squired in Sengarra are given the task of defending the Kingdom."

"Two of my older brothers were squired to a knight in Sengarra."

Edru's eyebrows reached toward the already-receding hairline that aged his appearance, even though he hardly looked older than Julien's twenty-seven years. Shock painted his words when he asked, "You have . . . brothers?"

I explained my relationship to Lord Whittier's family.

"That's a relief!" He laughed and it relaxed his entire bearing. "You scared me. I thought perhaps the King and Queen had other children secreted away. Since you referred to them as your *older* brothers that would, of course, have disqualified you as the Ryn."

"But you were saying? About the provinces and what they offer the Kingdom?"

"Yes," he nodded. "As you're aware, in the province of Veetri, agriculture is self-sustaining to the province, but it is there that Storytellers are born, trained, and sent out to entertain all over the Kingdom. In Dynwatre, carpenters and shipbuilders design and build things that benefit the greater good. Mynissbyr has lumber. Nyrland grows herbs and easily preserved root crops. Stoen produces the majority of E'veria's wheat and barley crops, and their sheep and cattle feed and clothe much of the Kingdom." He took a breath. "See? Each province uses their particular areas of expertise to serve the Kingdom's needs," he said, but then frowned. "Each province, that is, except Tirandov Isle."

"But surely being an island province, and small at that, offers you some latitude," I offered.

"I suppose. But other than your knight, I cannot, in my lifetime, recall a visit to Tirandov Isle by anyone who did not have at least a little bit of Andoven blood, unless they were married to an Andoven. We have closeted ourselves away for far too long and it has been at great cost to the cause of E'veria and the cause of The First."

He cocked his head to the right. "Your Highness, when you spoke in the Great Hall you put into words what has been in the hearts of many of us for a long time. There is nothing you could have said that would have earned you more genuine loyalty than what came from your heart just then."

He smiled and my heart knew I had found at least one friend at Tirandov. But his explanation did not foster a love for his people's traditions.

But, I reminded myself, *regardless of their prejudices, they are my people, as well. They are an important part of the Kingdom of E'veria.*

"Do not despair at the traditionalists among us," he said. "You may become the catalyst to spark change even in their stolid hearts."

"I don't want to cause trouble."

Edru surprised me with a low chuckle. "I believe you were born to cause trouble, Your Highness. You are the Ryn Naia." His smile, while still subdued, was the widest one I'd seen yet.

Ryn Naia. The Reigning Lady. I grinned back at him as the words of Lady Anya's poem crossed both of our minds.

The Ryn Lady E'veria will Cobeld's curse exile.

It's more than my name. I sobered at the realization. *It's my task. My quest.*

"My tutor in Veetri was Andoven," I said, grasping on to something positive. "Don't you send out tutors and teachers? That's important."

"You are correct. Many, including your great-grandfather, are great proponents of spreading the entrusted truth throughout the Kingdom and even beyond E'veria's borders."

"My great-grandfather?"

"Yes. Lindsor oversees the Academy in Salderyn now, but in his younger days he—"

"He's . . . he's still alive?"

"Oh, indeed! We Andoven have unusually long life spans. Perhaps that is why Rynloeft has so limited our procreative abilities." He sighed.

I blinked at him. "But if this Lindsor fellow is still alive, shouldn't he be King?"

"Lindsor? King?" Edru laughed, but sobered when he noted I did not share his humor. "Lindsor is not of the Ryn line. He is the father of Meritu, your mother's father."

"Oh."

Edru closed the book he had opened and thumbed through a different one. "See here? Your mother's line." He flipped through several pages that seemed, from the few words I caught as he turned to the next name, abbreviated biographies of each person.

He started with Lindsor, whose entry took up several pages, moved to Meritu, and finally past Daithia until he reached a page that was blank, but for my name. "Since I only recently learned of your existence," he said, "and we know so little of your history, we've recorded naught about you yet. I hope to have remedied that a bit before you leave us."

"My history will be entirely insignificant," I said, "unless I find the Remedy. Perhaps we should concentrate on that which will enable me to complete my quest."

"Indeed." Edru nodded. "Dyfnel tells me you are largely unfamiliar with *The Story of The First*."

"The what?"

His eyes slid shut. He let out a long breath.

"We will speak aloud during our lessons," Edru regained his serious tone and turned back to the book, "but at times it may be difficult to verbalize questions you have. Therefore, I would ask that you refrain from blocking me from your thoughts and I will do the same. In this way we can better accomplish our task within the limited time we've been given. Shall we begin?"

He shut the book of my mother's genealogy and reopened the first book. "This volume traces the line of the Ryn."

It was a thick, interesting tome, containing not only names and dates, births, and deaths, but detailed physical and personality descriptions, as well as lists of victories, accomplishments, and defeats.

"We will concentrate on the Ryn line for now, for that is first and foremost who you are." Edru turned a few pages. "Here is your father's story, thus far."

Scanning the page as quickly as I could, I learned that King Jarryn—*my father,* I had to remind myself—was an accomplished knight in his own right before he became King. He was reported to have close bonds of friendship with his knights and a sharp sense of humor. He was intelligent and fair, but in the early years of his reign tended to act impulsively and deal with the consequences of his decisions later. However, even when he made a quick decision that seemed foolhardy at the time, he always worked diligently to amend the situation and arrive at the desired outcome.

The Andoven style of writing was about as far from a Veetrish tale as it could be. Not remotely superfluous, it neither glamorized the King's accomplishments nor glossed over his failings. Considering it was a King of whom they had written, I was more than a little surprised to see words and phrases that were not at all complimentary: descriptive phrases like "stubborn," "ill-timed excursion," and "brash." Were the Andoven so comfortable, then, insulting their King?

"Do you ever worry that something you write might offend the King?"

"No," Edru looked at me as if the question was preposterous. "We write what is true. It is what is expected of us."

I grimaced. "Remind me not to do anything really stupid, then, would you?"

Over the years King Jarryn became more cautious and methodical, though still determined in his cause. As he grew older he made wiser choices and the people's love for him grew.

Under King Jarryn's direction, a large Academy was built in Salderyn where he employed Andoven teachers to instruct his knights in the subjects of History and Truth. I paused over that.

History and Truth. Both were written as proper nouns, but weren't they one and the same? Dyfnel claimed that truth must be gleaned by one's heart, yet the King appeared to view it as something that could be taught. In recent years, the book claimed, he had widened the academic invitation to the entire Kingdom, regardless of their station.

I was touched by my father's concern for the common people. A warm rush of color moved through my mind. I closed my eyes, picturing his face as I had seen it while reading his letter.

"You have met the King?" Edru questioned, surprised.

"No," I shook my head. "While I was in Mynissbyr I read a letter he wrote and . . . I saw him. Sitting at his desk at Castle Rynwyk, I believe." A cold shiver ran down my spine. "It was a fairly ghastly experience. I was quite ill."

Edru's eyebrows rose even higher. "It's most unusual that you would be able to accomplish such a thing without proper instruction. I imagine it was rather uncomfortable." He rubbed his chin. "I am caused to wonder what additional gifts you will discover with your other instructors. You may yet surprise a few of them, as you have me." He tapped the book. "Shall we continue?"

I flipped back a few pages. "Why do all of the Ryn families have the surname E'veri? Why not use a patronymic like everyone else?"

"Not everyone else. When a woman marries, she takes her husband's name. Over the past three centuries there has been an increase in the sentiment that love unions are the most beneficial to the Kingdom of E'veria. In that, the Kingdom has taken the example of the E'veri family to heart. There are still occasions when unions are formed for political or monetary gain, but the E'veri family *always* marries for love. Without a union based on love at Castle Rynwyk, chaos would reign."

"How so?"

"Tension in a marriage not only affects the individuals, but the decisions they make. The Ryn's most trusted advisor is his or her spouse."

As he spoke, a giddy sort of joy welled up within my chest. My parents had loved each other. I wasn't sure why it mattered to me, but it did.

But had he answered my question? Did his answer explain why all the Ryns shared the E'veri surname? Or was I too thick to comprehend something as seemingly simple as my own name? My shoulders drooped as a mild despair over all that lay ahead of me while on Tirandov Isle fell upon them.

"No, Princess Rynnaia, it is I who is being thickheaded." Edru's eyes narrowed as he read my thoughts. He ran a hand through his hair and paced a few steps away and back. "And no, I did not answer your original question."

Relief sent a cooling mist through my mind.

"In the Ancient Voice, the word *veri* means *purest truth as expressed in love. Veri* is the word for an all-encompassing, sacrificial love that only ends with the end of life. Additionally, the word *E'* expresses a bond similar to the marriage covenant, but stronger and without the possibility of dissolution."

He paused and I thought on that for a moment.

"The Ryn family is given the surname of *E'veri* because they are inseparably united *with the Kingdom itself.*" Awe poured from Edru's thoughts into his voice. "Whoever marries the Ryn takes on that surname as a vow not only to the Ryn, but to the Kingdom as well."

I let out a breath, not realizing that I had been holding it while he explained. I understood, now, the significance of my surname, but this particular family tradition was an exceptional burden. Could I live up to that? Could I find a man worthy—and willing—to make that sort of commitment?

A familiar face crossed my mind.

"When a man marries a female Ryn he adds the royal surname to his patronymic and becomes King, ruling alongside the Ryn," Edru said softly. "If you were to marry the knight, his name would become Julien de Gladiel E'veri."

"I'm not—er, he hasn't—I mean, we don't—"

Had I ever blushed so swiftly? Or so deeply? I groaned. "I didn't mean for you to see that."

"My apologies." Edru cleared his throat and his own cheeks took on a pink sheen. "*E'veri* has been the official name of the royal family since the First King, Loeftryn de Rynloeft, established the house of E'veri and named his Regents and Successor. Taking the name consecrates a solemn and weighty vow. Only death can break that bond."

"And I was born already sworn to it."

"Yes." He nodded. "You were."

I stared at the teacher, seeing in his thoughts concepts that were completely foreign to my comprehension. I spoke haltingly, wondering if the words would sound as bizarre aloud as they did in my thoughts.

"So E'veria, the Kingdom itself, is united with love and . . . truth . . . as if those concepts are joined in a marriage bond?"

"Yes!" Edru's smile widened. "You've got it!"

"Well, lovely! It's so clear now."

Edru's small chuckle reminded me that he had a direct connection to my thoughts, not that the sarcastic tone of my voice had hid them well.

I wasn't sure I was going to like this arrangement.

"Understanding will come to you in time, Princess. Truth will reveal himself to you in His good timing because He *is* that love. He is *Veria*."

Now truth was a "he"? I nodded, still confused. For a moment Edru looked as if he would elaborate, but he thought better of it and turned my attention back to the book.

ℱORTY-ℱHREE

"Why, in all these years," I wondered aloud, "did the King not remarry?"

Edru had remained quiet, his thoughts subdued, while I had studied more of the E'veri family line, but when that question passed my lips his thought was like a shout.

She doesn't know!

A swirl of gray blocked further insight as he spoke aloud, "Even if he had wanted to take another wife he could not. E'verian law would not allow it."

"But," I argued, flipping back a few pages, "Queen Tifryn married Sir Lig de Reshtel, but King Lig died in battle shortly after their marriage and . . ." I paused, tracing a path down the page, "four years later she married . . . Drysdin de Willet. If the law allowed her to remarry," I flipped pages again, "just two generations before my father, surely it would have allowed him if he had wanted to."

I thought about that for a moment and looked back at the book. Trying to form a question to his last comment, I once again noted the swirl of gray that kept his thoughts hidden.

"I thought we agreed not to block each other's thoughts." I rounded on him. "Yet you evaded my question about remarriage and are now blocking me from its answer. Why?"

"I am sorry to go back on my word, Princess Rynnaia." His gaze was honest and his words rang true. "But there are some questions you will have to ask Dyfnel, because I was not aware that you did not yet know their answers."

He waved his hand and the book closed. "You have processed quite a lot of information. Enough, I think, for your first day on Tirandov Isle."

"But what about the Queen's book?"

"In time. Keeping the Remedy in mind, there are more pressing matters than history."

I could hardly argue with that.

"In the morning you are to have your first lesson with Celyse."

I glanced beyond my teacher to the curved, west-facing window. The sun was nearly set. The room was so well lit by the light-effusive statuary and furnishings that I had not even registered the passage of time

I was preoccupied while Julien escorted me to my chamber. My mind barely registered more than the next step in front of me. With so much going through my mind, I didn't even notice when we stopped in front of a door.

"Your Highness?"

When I looked up and met Julien's gaze my distraction disappeared. His left hand covered mine where it rested in the crook of his right arm and I couldn't seem to stop myself from sweeping into his mind.

Colors swirled. Deepened. Within the effusive green and burnished gold rested unfathomable depths of honor. Of nobility and . . . *something else*. Something pure and so intense that I couldn't put a name to it.

"Colors . . ." his whisper was shocked and the connection vanished. "I saw . . . colors."

I gasped. "You did?"

"It was like you'd held a sapphire to the sun and it burst into flame." He closed his eyes as if to recapture the image. "There was blue and red and orange and . . . gold. Bright. Moving like . . . flames."

"That was me." As soon as I spoke the words I knew they were true. "You saw . . . me, I think."

Julien blinked. "How?"

"I'm not sure. I think I . . . let you." I was nearly as confused as he was.

"That makes sense. I think." He shook his head. "Maybe. Or as much sense as the Andoven have ever made to me." He blinked and then smiled as he gestured to the door we'd stopped in front of. "This is your chamber."

I flicked my hand at the door. Nothing happened. Julien arched an eyebrow and I shrugged and reached for the knob. "Doesn't hurt to try."

His eyes crinkled at the corners. "No, I suppose not." He pulled a key from his pocket. "May I? I don't think we have security concerns here, but I'd like to walk through. Just to be sure."

I stood in the doorway while Julien did a thorough sweep of the room. When he finished, he gave me a bit of a sheepish smile. "While you were in your lesson, Dyfnel reminded me that your father doesn't even bring a guard along when he is here. But I've not been trained to let the Ryn enter an unfamiliar room alone."

I laughed. "I wasn't under the impression you'd been trained in regard to the Ryn at all."

"Not this particular Ryn, of course," he said. "But while we thought you were dead, your father remained the Ryn."

"Ah."

"Dyfnel said there would be fresh clothes for you in the wardrobe." His brow furrowed. "He asked me to warn you that dinner would be a rather formal affair."

"Oh," I smirked, "that must be a nice change, since the Andoven are usually so relaxed."

"Indeed," he laughed. "Is there anything else I can do for you?"

"Not that I can think of."

"My chamber is nearby. I'll be back shortly to escort you to our 'formal' dinner. Until then, Princess Rynnaia."

As I entered my chamber I had to wonder: was the formality of the meal to come for my benefit, or was it always so? And if it was for my benefit, would I even know how to respond?

Cazien had advised me to not let the Andoven intimidate me.

If only it were that easy.

FORTY-FOUR

Like every other room I'd visited in the castle, my bedchamber glowed, and the same dimensional, diamond-in-a-circle pattern I'd noticed in the library was repeated in all the fabrics in my room. The shape's internal dimension imitated the way the light of a candle or a star stretches up and out in spires when squinted at, but that wasn't what made it seem so familiar, nor did it explain why I was so drawn to it.

I turned to the wardrobe, wondering what sort of items awaited me inside. To each side of its mirrored front door, panels of inlaid wood depicted, again, the diamond-in-a-circle motif. Centered above my own reflection was yet another even more intricate copy of that shape, but the way the artist had rendered it made the design seem to jump out toward my eyes.

There was something about the design that spoke to my heart, but in a language even more complex than the Ancient Voice. It was as if this design was a key that could open a secret door, if only I could figure out a way to separate it from the wood. Lost in thought, I stared at it for a long time. And then my stomach rumbled.

Dinner. The sound reminded me. *Julien will soon come for me.*

I pulled the mirrored door toward me to find a riot of color inside. When I reached out to touch a gown fashioned in a brilliant shade of sapphire, the fabric caressed my skin like a cloud across a gentle sky. I'd never seen such rich cloth. I ran my hands along it, unable to put a name to the fiber, and pulled it out to get a better look.

A ring of elongated silver beads encircled the scooped neckline and cuff of each long sleeve. The fabric appeared heavy, but its touch was lighter than gossamer.

I laid the gown on the bed and stepped back to admire each exquisite detail. It was a gown fit for a princess. Even a queen.

I swallowed hard, closed the wardrobe door, and gazed at my reflection. Did I see a future queen looking back at me?

No. I did not.

All I saw was the red-haired version of Rose de Whittier; a simple country girl from Veetri.

The longer I gazed at my reflection, the tauter anxiety pulled my breath. I glimpsed hints of Rose, the ward of Sir Drinius, who doubted her uncle's love. And if I squinted *just so* I could even make out a bit of Rozen the Squire.

But I did not see the Ryn.

I turned away.

My bag had been brought up and unpacked for me. I found my sturdy comb in one of the vanity's drawers and I eschewed the question of my dueling identities and turned my attention to bringing order to my hair, but my hands and hair would not cooperate with each other. It seemed almost as if my hair was rejoicing at being freed from the bond of the hairpiece. It refused to bend to my desire to contain it atop my head.

Defeated, I let it hang loosely down my back but for the side pieces I secured away from my face using some silver-tipped pins I'd found alongside my comb.

I turned my head from side to side. It would have to do.

At least the pins will match the dress. I took a deep breath. *Even if the princess does not.*

When a knock sounded on the door, I jumped. But when I opened it, expecting to see Julien, I was even more surprised. "Oh!"

The Andoven woman's eyes widened at my little squeak of a gasp, but she recovered quickly. She curtsied. "Your Highness," she said. "I am Celyse."

Celyse. The name of Dyfnel's daughter. Another of my teachers.

"I thought—" I peered down the hall, confused. Where was Julien? "Am I to have a lesson?"

"No," she smiled. "I came by to bring you this." She held out a box. "It was your mother's, given to her by your father when they were wed. It belongs to you now. And," she added, "if it suits you, I will serve as your lady's maid while you are here on the isle."

"Please, come in." I took the box from her outstretched hands and motioned her into the room. I set the box on the vanity, thinking it might be better opened in private. "I thought I might wear the blue gown."

"A lovely choice."

The gown slid on to my frame and the buttons were easily secured. Celyse retrieved a pair of beautiful blue slippers from the wardrobe and I put them on. But I did not look toward the glass. For some reason, the thought of looking at myself in this dress made me quiver. I did not want visual confirmation that I looked as ridiculous as I feared.

"It would be appropriate for you to wear this, as well."

I turned toward Celyse. She held the box, now open, toward me.

Inside, a simple circlet rested on a bed of fabric very much like the gown I wore. The circlet was of the shiniest silver, formed into a vine of roses. In the front it dipped into a v-shape, which held an opalescent stone. *Tirandite*, I reminded myself. Rimmed in silver, it was cut into the diamond-in-a-circle shape and drew my eyes even more than its wardrobe counterpart. I ran my fingers over the stone and it glowed brighter at my touch.

"The Emblem of the First," Celyse said. "You are drawn to it, yes?"

"I didn't know it had a name."

Celyse removed the circlet from its case and set it on my head. She walked to the wardrobe and closed the mirrored door. "Come."

"I can't." I closed my eyes, frozen in place. I didn't want to see the contradiction I was sure would meet me in the mirror.

Celyse took my hand. I allowed her to lead me, but I couldn't bring myself to open my eyes.

"You are the Ryn. Be of good courage, child, and open your eyes."

I did not recognize the princess looking back at me. She appeared confident, strong, and regal. Nothing like I felt at the moment.

The Emblem of the First flashed orange.

"Oh!" My hand flew up at the sudden heat on my skin, but it returned to a comfortable level of warmth so quickly that I was sure I must have imagined it. "Did you see that?"

"Indeed." Celyse chuckled and met my eyes in the mirror. "Truth knows you, Ryn Naia," she said. "In time you will recognize Him, as well."

I took a step back and crossed my arms. "Are you related to Cazien de Pollis?"

"Yes, distantly." Her smile was puzzled, but curious. "Why do you ask?"

"You seem to share his talent for cryptic statements."

"Ah. Well, I claim no great fondness for pirates in general, but Cazien does amuse me. I did not mean to be cryptic. You have my apologies, Princess."

Celyse moved toward the door. "Your knight approaches. Unless there is anything else . . . ?"

I shook my head.

She nodded and moved to the door. "Then I will see you at table."

When the door closed behind Celyse I glanced again at the foreigner in the glass.

"I am Rynnaia E'veri."

The whispered words sounded weak and didn't match the conviction of my reflection. Unable to reconcile the contradiction of my appearance with my multiple identities, I moved to the door, opening it just as Julien raised his hand to knock.

He stared at me, his fist still poised in the air. He stood like that for several breaths.

"Your Highness." He finally lowered his hand and bowed. "You are . . . stunning."

"It's the dress."

"The dress is lovely." His eyes swept over me. "But it is the princess within that honors my eyes. May I escort you to the dining hall?"

Julien led me through the complex corridors as if he had lived in Tirandov Castle all his life. As we rounded the last corner I heard the clinking of crystal and silver along with soft laughter and the muted din of many quiet voices.

My stomach clenched with anxiety and my grip tightened on Julien's arm.

"You are the Ryn," Julien whispered in my ear. "Remember who you are and no one can make you feel less."

We crossed the threshold into a huge dining hall filled with circular tables. A hush moved through the room as all eyes turned to me. *Gray, gray, gray.* I recognized the act of hiding thoughts and concentrated on blocking my own from the brilliant mind readers that filled the hall.

Julien guided me to the far end of the room and the only rectangular table. Soon I was seated at its center. Julien sat on my left and Dyfnel, to my relief, was at my right and he introduced me to his wife, Argeena. Also at the table were Celyse, Edru, and, to my dismay, three quite dour old women and two men who certainly matched them in age and expression.

Directly across from me sat the most ancient person I had ever seen. I also thought him the most severe. I had not marked his face earlier in the crowd. Perhaps his age had kept him in his chambers.

The buzz of conversation returned, but the ancient Andoven did not participate. His brow only furrowed with what appeared to be centuries of concentration and worry under the thick crest of shoulder-length white hair. He seemed to find little pleasure in the occasion.

Perhaps we had that in common.

An attendant had just finished filling our goblets when the scowling Elder pushed back his chair and raised his glass.

I looked to Dyfnel for a clue.

Here we go. He spoke silently into my thoughts and rolled his eyes. I had to cover my mouth to avoid letting anyone see my amusement.

"We come together this evening," the ancient man's voice rasped like a cold, wet wind, "to honor Princess Rynnaia E'veri, Heir of E'veria, daughter of King Jarryn and Queen Daithia, Granddaughter of King Rynitel and Queen Olina, Great-granddaughter of Queen Tifryn and King Drysdin, Great-great Granddaughter of . . ."

Good fortune! I thought. *Is he going to recite my entire genealogy?*

It appeared so. I tried to turn my attention back to the speaker, but found my mind wandering. Vaguely, I wondered if even the glowing plates would keep our dinner warm through the verbosity of his toast.

Through sheer willpower I focused my mind on his words for three more generations, ending with, " . . . whose direct line can be traced back to the very Successor himself, the second King of E'veria, Stoenryn E'veri." He took a long, wheezing breath. "As Regent of Tirandov, I bid Your Highness welcome to our table and pledge to you the loyalty and resources of the Andoven, here and throughout the known world, that same which we have also pledged to your father, the King. We now lift our goblets to you, our long awaited and long *unknown* . . ." at that he speared Dyfnel with his scowl, "hope."

The Regent lifted his goblet and the rest of the room followed.

I lifted my goblet, conscious of the unnerving reminder of this afternoon. "Thank you, Honorable One," I replied and gave him a gentle smile. "It is I who am honored by your hospitality."

As the Andoven tipped their goblets to drink, I sent the Regent a personal, silent greeting. He gave a nod and a dim light entered his eyes for the first time since my arrival.

I am called Jezmyn. He offered friendship. I accepted.

Conversation flowed a bit more freely and I made a special effort to include Jezmyn, but every once in a while I caught furtive glances in my direction, and when I noticed them, swirls of gray filled my mind.

The gray swirls became thicker as the meal wore on, almost as if everyone knew something I didn't . . . or couldn't. Eventually I found it difficult to even concentrate on conversation, let alone stomach the rich food brought out, course after course. My head throbbed. With each turn of my head, my vision smeared as if I was rolling through fog with wheels attached to my feet. Somewhere along the way, the swirls of gray had taken on a murmur of their own. Weaving a low hum through every conversation, they buzzed inside my head.

"Dyfnel." When Jezmyn spoke, the conversation at our table ceased. "You are, indeed, the greatest secret keeper in this room. Not everyone is as adept at your particular gift and the princess is feeling the strain of it."

Dyfnel's eyes fell on me.

"You were charged with these secrets, Dyfnel." Jezmyn wheezed. "It will be up to you to reveal them. See to it."

"Yes, Your Grace." Dyfnel sighed, looked down at his empty plate for a long moment, and then looked my way. "If you are finished with your meal, Princess Rynnaia, I would like you to accompany me."

Without a word, I stood. I could hardly wait to escape the dining room and the suffocating deception swirling about it.

When Jezmyn caught my eyes, his were full of sympathy. "The deception you feel is not born of hostility," he explained, "but out of loyalty to a promise made to your father. If my people knew the depth of discomfort it has brought, they would rather leave the isle than continue to inflict such upon you."

That eased my mind at least a little, but still . . . whatever Dyfnel had been charged to tell me, it couldn't be good. I swallowed hard.

"Should you have need of an ear, dear one," Jezmyn added softly, "I would be happy to provide it. Regardless of the hour, my friendship is at your disposal."

"Thank you."

Julien stood. "Might I accompany you?"

"There will be a certain point where we must go on alone, Sir Julien," Dyfnel replied, "but the princess may desire the comfort of your friendship when we return. It will be good that you are near."

I was not comforted at his words, but every second the swirls of gray grew denser. Julien or no, I was leaving the dining hall. Now.

With Julien at my elbow, I followed Dyfnel out a different door and through a new system of corridors. At last we reached the top of a long stairway.

As we descended into the bowels of the castle I relaxed the guards I'd placed upon my thoughts in the dining hall. Slowly, the gray swirls faded until they were little more than background—static noise. Each level we descended seemed to lessen their throb. We turned down staircase after staircase. It seemed to go on forever, but we finally reached the bottom.

Though dimmer than the higher floors of the castle, the walls still retained enough of the natural glow of the stone to give sufficient light. We passed through a few more archways and corridors before coming to a halt in front of a door like none I had seen so far in the castle.

Whereas the other doors were carved from wood, this was stone and engraved with the—I had to stop and think of the name Celyse had given it. *Oh, yes. The Emblem of the First.* The door, of course, glowed, but the emblem shone with a glare so blue, so fierce, that my eyes ached to look at it. Dyfnel paused facing the door. His shoulders drooped.

"Dyfnel?" I placed a hand upon his shoulder and opened my mind to his thoughts.

I wasn't prepared for what I found therein. My breath caught on waves of grief. Uselessness. Failure. I dropped my hand, as if the lack of physical contact would lessen the tumult of emotion, but when it did not, I reached for the gray I was becoming more adept at finding by the hour, and blocked his thoughts. But the memory of them remained and fueled my fear.

I took a step back from the door . . . and into Julien's broad chest. "I—I can't."

"Princess Rynnaia?" Julien's voice was soft. Calm. I turned and he reached for my hands and held them to his chest.

"There is something behind that door that you need to know," he said.

"But what if it—" I didn't know how to put so many questions into words other than to ask, "What if it hurts?"

I didn't fear physical pain, but from Dyfnel's thoughts I couldn't help but fear that whatever was behind that door could break my heart.

Julien rubbed his thumb over mine. "When it touches your soul, truth is like fire," he began. "As you know, when we rest too close to the fire we quickly become uncomfortable. Too close and it even becomes painful. But that doesn't always mean we should try to elude its flames."

He lifted two fingers to his forehead. "Perhaps if you look at my thoughts, it will be more clear?"

I nodded. In low and halting words he continued to speak, but in his thoughts the layered colors of a candle's flame

separated into different layers—orange, yellow, blue, white—
and then conjoined again.

"When you experience truth it will leave its mark upon
you," he said. "Like a brand upon your soul. But even when it
is painful, it is always for your good."

"I'm scared," I whispered.

He squeezed my hands. "I know."

"Will you wait for me?"

"Always," he vowed. "With all that I am and for all of my
life." He lifted my hand to his lips.

Dyfnel shifted beside us. "Are you ready, Princess?"

I held Julien's gaze for another long moment, drawing
strength from his conviction. "No, I'm not ready," I admitted.
"But as I doubt I will ever be, lead on."

Dyfnel turned and, when he opened the door, the sweet,
warm scent of roses enveloped me.

FORTY-FIVE

The long, narrow chamber was quite warm and every bit as humid as the hothouse where Lady Whittier kept her seedlings. And like a hothouse, the space was filled with plants, mostly roses, which explained the scent, as well as many species I could not identify.

"How do you keep them alive this far removed from the sun?" I whispered, but even that seemed loud in the chamber's deathly quiet.

"The mountain from which the castle is carved receives its light from the sun and expels similar properties in the stone," he began. "We've learned to augment the stone's glow with proper soils and waters." He paused. "But we are not here to see the plants."

The far end of the room was partitioned on three sides with heavy curtains, and even though I wondered what was beyond them, I couldn't stop looking around, taking in the beauty of the roses, some as large as my head, others as tiny as a thumbnail.

"As I told you earlier, I am a physician." As my eyes roved the space, Dyfnel spoke hesitantly, quietly. "It is the most developed of my gifts and one that's been used in the service of your family for many years. I have studied the healing properties of plants, minerals, waters, and medicines for most of my life. For the past nineteen years, without success, I have tried to invent—or discover, rather—a Remedy for the Cobeld curse." He sighed. "And although I have failed miserably, my research has not been in vain. I have discovered ways to use what the earth offers in combinations that can reduce pain and often prolong the lives of the ill, the injured, and . . . the poisoned."

My eyes stopped roving the room at once, focusing on Dyfnel as I took on the full import of the words both said and unspoken.

The implication flooded my mind and dizzied me. I reached out a hand to steady myself, but my finger caught on the thorn of a rose. I gasped, but the momentary pain from the prick of the thorn cleared my head.

My breath fled to where I couldn't quite reach it. My eyes focused on the curtains, seeking a crack through which I might see what lay beyond them. No. It couldn't be. But my pulse thrummed the truth of it into the back of my skull, pounding two syllables, into my brain: *Mother.*

My mother!

"She's . . ." I paused on a hitched breath, "alive?"

"Yes." Dyfnel gestured to the far end of the room. "The medicines keeping her alive cause her to sleep for many hours each day, but she feels little pain other than the drain of constant fatigue. Her decline became a bit more pronounced recently, of course,"

"Why 'of course'?"

His eyes filled with tears, even as a weak smile forced his lips to move. "Because her blessing upon you was finally delivered. Come, child," he said. "You've both waited long enough."

Her blessing?

My head spun as I followed Dyfnel to the dark-curtained area. Gently, Dyfnel pulled back one of the curtains, allowing light to fall upon the sleeping form beyond. My stomach leapt into my throat and I regretted what little dinner I had eaten.

Even with the light so dim, I could tell the woman's hair, though faded by illness, had at one time been a brilliant and fiery hue. Her face was remarkably smooth with only a few faint, fine lines around her mouth and eyes. She was thin, and her skin was thinner, still—frailer than the delicate flower petals so prevalent throughout the room.

If I was twenty years older and dying, I thought, *I would look almost exactly like her.*

Her eyelids fluttered. Cautiously, I approached the bed. I reached for her hand and covered it with mine.

Her hand was cold, and the skin stretched thin. Fingers I imagined had once been graceful were now emaciated and bony, as if barely able to cling to the feeblest threads of life.

My free hand covered my mouth, blocking the keen that threatened to escape as I sank to my knees at her side.

"Dyfnel?" Her voice was dusky. Her eyes remained closed.

"I am here," he said, his voice thick. He placed a hand on my shoulder. "Lately she is able to experience only short bursts of wakefulness, child. Use the opportunity."

I swallowed hard. What should I say?

"Queen Daithia?" I began. "We've never met, officially, but I'm—" I broke off, took a breath. "I'm Rynnaia. Your daughter." I slid my right hand beneath her cold fingers and placed my left hand gently over her hand as if to impart some of my warmth to her. "I'm here."

The Queen's eyes fluttered open, but even as she whispered my name, her eyes closed. I despaired that she had fallen asleep again, but then she spoke. "Dyfnel? I dreamt of my daughter being carried by a bear," she whispered. "A good bear. He took her on a giant silver horse through the Great Wood."

She was quiet for a long moment, and then she whispered, "This is not a dream." She winced, as if making a great effort, and, finally, she opened her eyes. "Rynnaia, you're here." She nearly choked on a sob. "You're here!"

"Yes, M-mother."

Looking into her eyes I saw not only features of my appearance so clearly inherited from her, but love that left no room to deny who she was to me.

Mother. Although I had referred to Lady Whittier as such while traveling from Mynissbyr, I'd never had the opportunity to call anyone by that name before. I never thought I would.

"I'm here, Mother. I'm going to fulfill the prophecy. Julien will help me find the Remedy and you can return to Castle Rynwyk."

"Julien?" She blinked, fighting to keep her eyes open. "Of course. The bear." She smiled. "He would be a knight now, wouldn't he? Jarryn sent him for you."

"Yes. Julien is the best of knights." I swallowed. "He's everything a knight should be, Mother. Noble, loyal, true. I—" I broke off, feeling a blush creep around my neck and onto my cheeks. "He has become a dear friend. I am honored to have his service."

The Queen smiled and there was such beauty, such love in her face that my eyes filled with tears. With each word she spoke, she seemed to awaken a bit more. "I too once felt so moved by a knight. Of course he was also known as the *Prince* at the time."

"We mustn't stay long, Daithia," Dyfnel broke in. "I don't want our visit to tire you."

"Yes, it would be a pity for me to become tired." A note of sarcasm tinged her voice, but the cynicism did not reach her eyes. She weakly squeezed my hand. "I wish things had been different . . ."

She closed her eyes and I feared she'd fallen asleep, but they reopened. Moisture glistened on her lashes. "This is the life we have been given, Rynnaia, and we must use our gifts as well as our pain to serve a greater cause. You are here. You are alive and safe. That is what matters."

"I don't know what to do!" A sob broke through my lips. To finally meet the woman whom I'd always thought dead was life-altering, but to see her so weak and ill wrenched my heart.

I swiveled my head to look at Dyfnel. "It's my fault, isn't it?" His words finally made sense. "Her weakness."

"It's no fault of yours," Dyfnel replied as he leaned in and assisted the Queen to a sitting position. "It was a gift, given for your benefit."

"Yes, Rynnaia," Mother said. "My blessing was freely given and nothing in the world could convince me that it was a mistake." She leaned forward and embraced me with a strength that belied the frailty of her condition, enveloping me in the fathomless depth of her love. "I would give up my last breath for you."

"Please don't!"

She chuckled and rubbed a hand over my hair, much as Lady Whittier and Aunt Alaine had done when, as a young girl, I'd scraped a knee or had a fright.

"You have had truth thrust upon you, Rynnaia, rather than growing gently into its center," she said. "It is a heavy burden to carry. One I wish I could take from you." She paused to draw a shallow breath. "But I cannot. Before you leave Tirandov you will have been taught all that can be told. The rest can only be experienced and absorbed into your heart."

"The center of the flame." I recalled what I had seen in Julien's thoughts outside the door. "The white heat. The layer that causes the most irreparable damage."

"Yes." She smiled. "And the most complete healing."

I drew back and tilted my head at the contradiction.

"Rynnaia, you will find that wounds caused by the sear of that purest, white-hot truth, though they will forever leave their scar upon you, will make you stronger if you let them."

"Julien speaks of this as you do, but it all sounds like riddles to me."

"Ah, Julien." Her eyes radiated warmth. "He was a wonderful little boy. A joy to know. I am nearly as sorrowed to have missed the rest of his childhood as I am that I missed the entirety of yours."

"He speaks fondly of you, as well." I bent to kiss her cheek. "We will find the Remedy, Mother. Somehow. And when you are back at Castle Rynwyk we will bore you with every mundane detail of our lives."

Her hand shook as she reached up to cup my cheek. "I doubt that anything you could say could ever bore me." She took a labored breath. "Julien's family has searched for the Remedy for centuries, Rynnaia. But with you I believe they may finally succeed."

The Queen's smile might have been the sweetest I'd ever seen. "I have loved you all these years, even though I could not be with you. Time is short, but love is a mighty guard, dear one, and I will continue to cloak you with its power.

"Time is short," I repeated. "That's what Lady Anya told me."

"Lady Anya?" Questions filled her eyes. "But how—?"

"Not today." Dyfnel's voice was quiet, but firm.

The Queen shot him a look of defiance that almost made me laugh.

"My Queen, if you wish to spend more time with your daughter, you must keep to the schedule of your regimen."

She glared at him a moment longer, but then relaxed. "The dratted physician is correct." She acquiesced with a sigh, but there was fondness in her tone. "I must on to dreams again. But I will expect to hear that tale, Rynnaia. Soon."

"I'll be back. I promise." I arched an eyebrow at Dyfnel. "Just try and keep me away."

"I wouldn't dare."

"I love you, Rynnaia." Even the limited strength of her voice was fading. "No matter what happens, know that I have always loved you."

"I—"

I paused as a strange new warmth spilled from my heart and into my consciousness. I bit my lip. I wanted to return the words, but I knew they should not be given lightly. Could I profess to love her?

Warm, beautiful colors flowed through me, but they were not entirely mine. Subtle differences marked my mother's love—as well as her pain, desperation, and determination—as clearly as the higher, more defined set of her cheekbones and the narrower shape of her mouth and chin differentiated her face from mine. The colors were deeply honest and undeniably real and they brought fresh tears to my eyes at the trueness of their beauty.

Could I say the words aloud?

Yes, I could.

"I love you too, Mother."

Closing her eyes, the Queen smiled. "What more could I need?"

Dyfnel helped her recline on her pillows and I bent to kiss her cheek. "Sleep well, Mother. I'll see you again soon."

She was already asleep when I rose and followed Dyfnel through the curtain.

We were almost to the door when a lone thought stopped me in my tracks. "Dyfnel?"

"Yes?"

"Does the King know she lives?"

He blinked. "Of course! To keep something like this from the King would be high treason." He sighed. "You must understand, however, that King Jarryn and the Andoven at Tirandov are the only ones privy to the truth. Not even Sir Gladiel and Sir Drinius suspect that she lives. The King and Queen thought the burden of keeping you safe was enough. And she has not had need of their services here."

"He should have told me, at least!" I hissed. "She's my mother! And you!" I accused. "You could've told me before we ever reached Tirandov! You could have prepared me for this, but you didn't!" A strange taste—bitterness—touched the sides of my tongue. "Is this part of your job, then?" The words felt like poison in my mouth and my tone reflected their toxicity. "This, then, is the duty of the Andoven?"

"No, Your Highness," he said. "This is our duty in obedience to our King. This is our duty to preserve the life of the Queen."

He looked down at the floor and the fight fizzled within me.

"I led my people to believe that, if I were to find a Remedy in time, the Queen could be saved," he said softly. "That she and the King might yet produce an heir."

"None of them knew I survived? Not even Jezmyn?"

"Not even Jezmyn. As he implied, my gifting in the gray—in the keeping of secrets—is strong." His voice was quiet and filled with regret. "The knights who ferried you to safety were told the Queen had perished. And indeed," he sighed, "I thought it would be the most likely outcome of the curse she received."

He swallowed with some difficulty. The depth of his despair was carved deeply into the wrinkles surrounding his bright eyes. "Truly, it is nothing less than a miracle she has survived. But living wears on her. At times it has seemed almost cruel to go to such lengths to keep her alive when death could free her, and could yet succeed in claiming her at any moment."

At any moment. But I just found her!

"It's that bad?"

"She has fought well, child. But when you learned your name and your abilities were released, it pulled the fullness of the blessing given to you from within her. If I hadn't been here . . ." he shook his head. "I'm not sure she would have survived it."

"I thought a blessing was supposed to be a good thing!"

"Indeed. To the one who receives it." He smiled. "When you were born, she placed her hands on you and spoke using her Andoven gifts, and I can only surmise, a great deal of power granted her by The First."

"What did she say?"

"Her blessing pledged all of her own gifts and strengths and abilities to you . . . and may have imparted even more that we have yet to discover. 'I give you all that I am' is what she said." He shook his head. "It sounds simple enough, but what that could entail is anyone's guess. It could reach back generations, perhaps as far as Sir Andov himself."

"Sir Andov?"

"One of the original knights of E'veria," he explained. "The first Regent of Tirandov Isle. You'll read of him in *The Story of The First*." Dyfnel sighed. "Your mother will never regret the blessing she gave you, no matter the cost to her health. But without the Remedy?" He shrugged. "I cannot see how she will last much longer."

Grief for the years we'd lost pressed upon my soul. She had already sacrificed so much for me. "I will find the Remedy." My throat tightened. "I must."

"It is my dearest hope that you will. But you have much to learn before you're ready to take on that quest." His smile was weak as he gestured to the door. "Your knight awaits."

"I *will* be allowed to come back."

It wasn't a request, and he knew it.

The gravity of this new knowledge fell fully upon me then, strangling me, yet filling my heart with such desperate joy and fettered hope that it smothered every other emotion.

FORTY-SIX

As promised, Julien awaited us just outside the door. "All is . . . well?"

The look on his face was expectant, concerned, but with a strange flicker of hope. But my strength was too spent to address it.

"Yes," Dyfnel nodded. "All is well."

I wanted to shout, *"My mother is alive!"* but the words, even whispered, wouldn't come. It felt like a dream, and at the moment, I was too overcome to discuss what had happened beyond the bright stone door. Therefore, it was in silence we walked back through the corridors and up the long staircases. With each level we ascended a dull ache pressed more firmly against my temples, and though I felt worn, sleep was the last thing on my mind.

"Your Highness?"

Dyfnel spoke so softly that I had to step closer to hear him.

"Sometimes," he said, "when my heart is particularly heavy, I find that lying on the earth, looking up at the vastness of the night sky, allows me to feel small enough to bring things into a clearer perspective."

"Thank you," I whispered. *For taking me to my mother. For taking care of my mother. For your loyalty to the King.* I gave in to the impulse to hug him. As Dyfnel returned my embrace a wave of relief flowed through his mind.

He bid us good night, but turned back after only taking a few steps. "You may find," he said, "that neither protecting the truth nor serving it is a straightforward occupation. Do not be too quick to judge your father. He did what he thought was best with the information he had at the time."

Without waiting for a reply, which was probably a good thing considering my mixed feelings toward the King, Dyfnel turned down a hallway and walked out of sight.

I turned to Julien. "Do you feel like a walk?"

"If that is what you wish."

"It is. You'll have to find the door, though. I'm lost in this place."

"It is something of a maze," he agreed. "But I think I can find our way outside."

In no time at all Julien led me out of the castle and onto the rich-smelling lawn. For several minutes we walked in silence, following a crushed stone pathway that led down a slight hill and away from the glow of the castle.

Like a blanket that had just been brought in from the line on a sunny summer day, the ground itself seemed to give off a comfortable heat. We sat on the grass and stared out at the sea.

"There's no moon tonight."

"And not a cloud in sight, either," Julien noted.

I nodded. "All the better to see the stars." With that, I reclined on the spongy lawn to better take in the night sky.

Blue-black with pinpricks of light filtering through, there seemed no end to it, and as Dyfnel had suggested, I began to

feel small. I couldn't see Julien's face, sitting as he was, wi
me flat on my back in the grass beside him.

"What do you think a star would see, looking down at us?"
Julien didn't answer. I didn't really need him to.

"Would it even acknowledge our existence?" I continued
my wondering aloud. "Or would it be so captivated by its purpose, its obligation to pierce the night, that it wouldn't even
register something so insignificant as two breathing dots
upon Tirandov's lawn?"

Under the vast canopy of stars, my smallness came into
focus. I didn't know why the King had deceived his Kingdom
rather than just keeping us both near, guarded by his knights;
but maybe, like the stars above, there was a greater purpose
that was still beyond my comprehension.

Closing my eyes, I took a deep breath in through my nose,
and as I sent it back into the night, my anger dissolved, at
least for the moment, and the truth I had been unable to utter,
drenched as it was in layers of emotion and time, released.

"Julien?"

He angled his head back to look at me. "Yes?"

"My mother is alive."

Julien dropped his head on to his upraised knees and exhaled. After a few moments he lifted his head and gazed off
toward the sea. His breathing was shaky, each inhalation jagged, each exhalation like a stream of staccato sighs.

"I had dared to hope it," he said at last.

Leaning back on to the grass beside me, he rested his head
in his hands. "When the door opened I caught the scent of
roses. It reminded me of her, and I wondered, with all the
truths that have come to light these past weeks, if it was possible that she, too, had survived," he said. "The Queen always
smelled of roses. She put bouquets of them all over the castle.
When she died—or went away, rather," he paused and the

breath he took sounded painful, "the roses stayed in the garden." He turned his face toward me and smiled. "Except for the one she sent to Veetri, of course."

"Yes." I chuckled. "Except for that one."

We gazed at the deepness of the night, content in the quiet of our smallness. Finally, he spoke. "Is she very ill?"

"Yes." I kept my gaze to the sky, worried that to look at him would release more emotion than I was prepared to reveal. "Dyfnel has kept the poison at bay with medicines, but she is very weak. She needs the Remedy soon or she will die."

Saying the words aloud seemed to confirm them in my mind. A heavy weight settled painfully in my chest. "Nineteen years is a long time to carry poison in your body. I—" I swallowed and took a deep breath. "I don't think she can last much longer."

"The task is daunting," he whispered. "My family has searched for the Remedy for centuries without success, and unless there is some miraculous clue in those scrolls Erielle found, I'm afraid there is little hope. I'm sorry." He reached for my hand. "You have no idea how sorry I am, Rynnaia."

A fluttering surety moved across my heart as lines of Lady Anya's poetry flooded my mind.

The Ryn Lady E'veria will Cobeld's curse exile.

A tiny smile played upon my lips. "You may have sought the Remedy, Julien, but you were missing two crucial tools in your search."

Beside me, Julien turned, propping himself up on his elbow. "We've used every combination of research, force, and cunning that we could contrive. Beyond that," he shrugged, "what else is there?"

A rush of confidence gave my words a saucy edge. "Sky-jeweled eyes," I said, "and a head ablaze with fire."

$\mathcal{F}$ORTY-$\mathcal{S}$EVEN

y mother is alive!

$\mathcal{M}$ It was the first thought in my mind as I awoke, but jubilation warred with despair when the second arrived closely on its heels.

My mother is dying.

I'd dreamt of my mother all night, and if I was to fulfill my quest and save the Queen, there was no time to waste. Lady Anya charged me with finding the Remedy and exiling the Cobeld curse, so if my mother died before that happened, it was no one's fault but mine.

Fueled by a new urgency to learn all I could from the Andoven, I threw off the coverlet, picked a dress I could get into myself, and went in search of Celyse.

A young Andoven man was more than happy to give me directions and promised to advise Sir Julien as to my whereabouts.

"You are about rather early this morning, Princess." Celyse opened the door just as I was about to knock. Her faded blond hair was pulled back into a knot at the nape of her neck, but her expression was so open, so welcoming, that it didn't cause her to look severe.

"Not too early, I hope."

"No," she said with a smile. "You must be anxious to begin your lessons now that you have met the Queen."

"Yes," I nodded. "I know I don't have much time here. I would use all that I have wisely."

"Follow me."

We entered a sparsely furnished room, and with a flick of her wrist, Celyse closed the door behind us.

I will teach you that. She spoke into my thoughts. *But later. We have much to learn.*

Celyse led me to a table with two chairs. *We will not speak aloud,* Celyse began. *Rather, I will teach you to communicate more effectively in this manner. It is my charge to gauge your gifts and to see how far we can push you beyond their limits . . . or mine!* She laughed aloud at that. *Your Mother's lessons taxed me quite thoroughly when she came here the first time!*

"You taught my—"

She shook her head, reminding me to use my mind rather than my mouth.

You taught my mother?

She nodded.

My abilities will be weaker than hers, won't they?

That remains to be seen. Celyse smiled and the warmth of it colored her words. *There is much about your birth that was unique. Besides your being an E'veri Ryn, your mother's blessing was most unusual. My father believes your abilities may well surpass those of your mother. They may even surpass his own.*

I blinked. *How is that possible?*

A mystery we would all like to solve. When she laughed, the sound was audible, but it also echoed in my thoughts. *Shall we proceed with the lesson?*

I nodded.

I would like you to try and call out, using your mind, to someone within the castle. I would like you to wake them up and summon them to meet us here.

I immediately thought of Julien. Celyse's eyebrows rose.

I suggest, this first time, that you choose someone Andoven. Calling your knight might cause him undue alarm.

I hadn't thought of that. *Dyfnel?*

A very good choice, Princess.

Several long moments passed.

"I'm not doing it right."

She shook her head and put a finger to her lips. *Concentrate on his face. Close your eyes if it helps. You may say his name aloud if you wish, but it is not necessary.*

I closed my eyes and pictured the physician as I'd last seen him, wearing a dull gray robe and with his long gray beard gathered at his chest with a leather strap.

"Dyfnel." My mind visualized an unfamiliar hallway and a door. It did not open, but it didn't have to. Somehow, I gained access to the room as if the door did not exist.

I saw Argeena first, pouring tea at a table, and then Dyfnel, hunched over a book.

"He's already awake. Oh. Sorry. I didn't mean to—"

Call him.

"Dyfnel." I repeated.

Dyfnel looked up from his book. A smile parted his lips as he closed his eyes. *Yes, Princess?* He asked, opening them again and looking at me.

Celyse asks . . . that I . . . I concentrated, giving each word equal weight, *bid you to come to . . . uh . . .*

The sunrise room, Celyse supplied. *You don't have to work so hard, Princess. Let it flow, just as if he were before you.*

The vision blurred for a second. Even though I knew we were in different parts of the castle, it seemed like I *was* in the same room with Dyfnel. But Celyse was in my thoughts, too.

Dyfnel?

Good, good! Celyse silently cheered. *You got it back.*

I took a deep breath. *Dyfnel, I'm with Celyse. She asked me to bid you come to the sunrise room.*

An amused sort of affection colored the Andoven man's thoughts. *I will come in a moment, bearing your breakfast tray.*

Thank you. I opened my eyes and shifted my mind fully toward Celyse.

Well done! Is there anyone of Andoven lineage not currently at Tirandov, to whom you would like to speak?

I immediately thought of the King, but an instant later thought better of it. I wasn't nearly ready for *that* again.

Do not fear distance, Celyse explained, misinterpreting my hesitation. *Andoven communication is unfettered by the complexity of the words or the miles between those conversing. The success of your communication comes from the intensity of your desire to send the message.* She allowed me to ponder that for a moment. *It is our fear alone that makes distance daunting. Be brave, Princess Rynnaia. You have nothing to fear.*

But she was wrong. *I don't know how to be a princess!* I let out a heavy breath and dropped my head into my hands. What was the point of hiding my feelings from one who could so easily see my thoughts?

Celyse put her arm around my shoulder and guided me toward the window. *Look there.* She pointed to a fence which was covered in climbing vines. *Spring comes to Tirandov Isle earlier than it does the rest of E'veria. Those vines are already* budding. *Soon, there will be a riot of roses. All colors. It will be beautiful.*

I'm sure it will. I was less sure where she was going with this conversation.

Celyse smiled. *The oils within those roses exude an intoxicating fragrance, and contain healing properties when extracted. Their stems, however, are peppered with thorns.*

My brother Rowlen used to call me "Thorn" instead of "Rose" when I irritated him.

Celyse chuckled. *Thorns have their place. They serve to protect the flower. But they can cause quite a bit of pain to the one who handles them carelessly.*

I arched an eyebrow in her direction. *You're not really talking about flowers anymore, are you?*

She just smiled. *You must learn to understand the rose, Rynnaia, before you are able to reconcile yourself to your past. You were once called by that name, were you not?*

I nodded.

Like the roses in our gardens, that name was on loan to you for a season. A season not without its thorns.

Again, I nodded.

And yet there was beauty. There was sweetness. And love enabled you to grow bright and strong above the thorns. She smiled. *Hold those memories in your heart, Rynnaia. Learn from the thorns while you inhale the fragrance of love and sacrifice that has protected you from birth until now. Had it not been for the protection those thorny choices afforded Rose, you would not have survived to be Rynnaia.*

My eyes swung to the door. *Your father approaches.*

"Well done!"

I jumped when Celyse spoke aloud.

And again when her words were silent. *Another lesson completed! You are an apt pupil, Princess. How do you feel?*

I thought about it for a minute. *I feel . . . wide awake.* The admission surprised me. *Perhaps more awake than I've ever felt!*

Tirandov can do that to a person, she nodded knowingly. *In time you will adjust, but for now, let's use it.* She laughed and put a hand to her belly when her stomach growled. *After we break our fast, of course. You'll find your lessons increase not only your energy, but your appetite as well.*

She was right. After breakfast we worked through many skills, including how to open and shut a door without touching it, but I was not tired in the least. I was, however, glad to adjourn to the dining room for the midday meal.

Julien rose as I approached the table and, as soon as I was seated, Jezmyn spoke a blessing over the food.

He closed his eyes and tilted his face upward. He held his arms at an angle at his sides with his palms facing up and spoke in what I had come to recognize as the language of the Ancient Voice. At first I bowed my head in respect, but I couldn't remain in that position. Something drew my head up to look at his face.

The rigid formality I expected had disappeared from his countenance, replaced by a peaceful reverence that filled his foreign words with a meaning that, even though I couldn't understand it completely, revealed a lack within myself. Had I ever felt such peace as that which fairly glowed from the Regent of Tirandov?

When Jezmyn finished, Dyfnel leaned over and translated the blessing for Julien and me. "He says, 'Giver and Sustainer, you have provided for our physical needs as always. You instruct the hands of your servants in its pleasing preparation to delight our senses. May we be granted wisdom as we seek to protect truth and may we honor you within its light.'"

Julien nodded. "May it be so."

I reached for my glass. My throat felt suddenly dry and tight. In the wizened, upturned face of the Regent I had seen something I had never glimpsed in my own reflection.

All through the meal I pondered that seemingly missing piece of myself. Although the conversation at my table was lively, at the meal's conclusion I could no better recall a subject discussed than I could remember the taste of food I had unwittingly cleaned from my plate.

As we left the dining room, Julien leaned toward my ear. "Dyfnel said I could visit the Queen this afternoon."

"That's wonderful." I tried not to let him hear the tiny pang of jealousy in my voice, but I must not have accomplished my goal.

"If you would like to go with me," he offered, "or if you would rather use the time to visit her yourself . . ."

"No. You should go." I shook my head. "Of course I'd like to see her, but I have my lessons." I sighed as we approached our destination, the library. My next lesson was with Edru. "I'm sure she'll be very happy to see you. She spoke so fondly of you."

"She did?"

In his eyes I glimpsed, for just a moment, the little boy for whom the Queen held such affection. Not that I could blame her. After all, I was quite fond of the man he had become.

I smiled. "She did."

He paused at the door of the library. "Princess Rynnaia?" his voice was suddenly more formal. "Dyfnel informs me that you will be meeting with the Elder Council after dinner and that I am to accompany you. I thought perhaps afterward you might enjoy a walk in the gardens?"

"I'll look forward to it." When his eyebrows lifted I laughed. "The walk, I mean. Not the Council."

Julien smiled. "I knew what you meant."

I looked toward the door. "Do you think I should knock?" Just then the door opened.

"Princess. Sir Julien." Edru held a book out to the knight. "I found this volume in the stacks. It concerns the lineage of the knights of Fyrlean Manor. I thought if you were going to stand guard, perhaps it would help pass the time?"

"Thank you, Edru. Next time, perhaps?" Julien released my arm. "I am requested elsewhere, and since I know I leave the princess in capable hands, I have no need to stand guard."

Edru bowed his head at the compliment.

Give the Queen my love, won't you?

Julien's eyes opened in surprise as he received my thought. "I—er, yes. I will."

Edru chuckled as I followed him into the library. "I take it your lessons with Celyse were rather profitable this morning?" His cheeks took on a slight hue, which likely matched mine. "I apologize," he said quickly. "I did not mean to see, but your thoughts were . . . powerful."

His color deepened and he cleared his throat. "Few Andoven can communicate in that way with people of non-Andoven ancestry. Since we agreed to unblock our minds yesterday, I was unprepared. I'm terribly sorry for invading your privacy. Shall we begin?"

My young teacher slid a thick book to the center of the table.

"*Loeftryn de Rynloeft*," I read the title aloud. "He was the First King of E'veria, right?"

"He was The First, yes. Including the First King."

I arched an eyebrow, expecting an explanation, but none was forthcoming.

"This is his story. You may have heard it referred to as *The Story of The First*." Edru gestured for me to open the book, so I gingerly lifted the thick cover.

"It's not written in E'verian."

"It is the Ancient Voice," he replied. "Take your time, Princess."

"But—?" How was I supposed to read a book in a language I didn't know?

"You have read languages unknown before, have you not?"

The King's face swam across my vision as realization dawned. *The encoded letter.*

"Oh, no Edru." I backed away from the book. "I don't think I should—"

"You can do it. Take your time."

"No, Edru. I can't. The letter from the King was meant for me to see. Lady Anya's poem, also. But this book is ancient history!"

"Yes. And it was written specifically with you in mind." He paused. "And for others, as well. It was written for all who have a heart to know the deeper truths of this life."

An unknown fear constricted my chest. Hadn't I received truth enough?

I rubbed my hand over the page. Something about this book drew and repelled me at the same time.

Fear made me want to run screaming from the library. But I was also curious. How would the ancient First King of E'veria have known of me thousands of years ago? Was it part of the prophecy? Like Lady Anya's poetry? Why would he have recorded information for me in this book?

The memory of the incapacity I'd experienced upon reading the parchment from the King assailed my thoughts.

"I also have this gift," Edru said, "which is one of the reasons I was chosen as your tutor. It is an uncomfortable sensation at first. But it does get easier with time. But as the day always seems to pass too swiftly when we're caught up in a story, you should soon begin."

I knew his smile was meant to reassure me, but it didn't. The book was not only thick, but tall and wide as well. "I'm going to be here awhile."

"No one expects you to read it all in one day." His smile was kind. "But even once you have read it in its entirety you will not be finished, for it will call you back." He chuckled. "Truly, I often learn new things from it, and I have had it available to me for the whole of my life."

"It's a big book." I was stalling, and something quirked in Edru's eyes as if he knew it.

"If you would like, I can arrange to have a tray brought in with your dinner and you can avoid the formal gathering this evening."

A chance to avoid the formal meal? "Yes, please."

"I will take my leave of you, Princess, that you may study in quiet and privacy. Someone will alert you when the hour of your meeting with the Elder Council approaches."

"Any chance I could avoid that, as well?"

Edru smiled. He knew I was kidding. "Is there anything else I can do for you in the meantime?"

"Yes. I promised Sir Julien I would tell him if I planned to read anything . . . odd."

"I will inform him."

Edru gave me a slight bow and turned to leave. At the door, he paused. "Your fear is well-founded and wise. When words of truth are passionately recorded on paper they contain a sort of magic, transforming those who open themselves up to receive their light. You have experienced a version of this from your father's letter and also from Lady Anya's poem."

"Neither experience was entirely pleasant, Edru."

His smile acknowledged my sarcasm with compassion. "If your heart is open to it, the words within this book will alter the very marrow of you and set free all that is still bound in the dim shadows of the unknown."

"I'm not necessarily convinced that's a good thing."

"It is."

He left me then. Alone with The Book.

FORTY-EIGHT

The door whispered shut as Edru left. The book beckoned me to look at it, to discover the secrets hidden within its foreign words, but I hesitated.

I paced away from the book—away from the fear of what might happen to me if I read it. Finally, after many minutes of staring blindly out the library's one enormous window and chewing the nail of my index finger nearly to the quick, I returned to the table and opened the book to the first page.

Embral e' Veria. The first three words, written in the Ancient Voice, nearly jumped off the parchment.

"*Embral e' Veria.*" When I read them aloud, they sounded strangely familiar. Was this another Andoven gift? Or could it be that I had heard them before?

I closed my eyes and repeated the phrase. From the deeply buried place of my earliest memories, I knew I'd heard those three words before, spoken in a strong, deep voice.

My father's voice.

My eyes snapped open. The recently loosed memory of him visiting me when I was a little girl came back in a rush. He'd said the words then, I was sure of it. What did they mean?

I focused on the words, and although I was not surprised when they began to take on motion, I was surprised that I didn't feel ill.

"It's a name." I scanned down the page, finding more words, but with one commonality. "It's . . . a list of names?"

Was this another book of genealogy? I groaned. I'd had about as much of that as I could stomach the day before, but I kept reading. As I perused the list, each title lit its own brilliant color in my mind. Unlike the genealogical books, however, these were not names of a family; they were all different titles for the same person. Each hue, shade, and tint that caressed my mind gave more depth and meaning to the words. It was beautiful. I saw more of the color spectrum within those names than I ever knew existed.

The words were easy to read now. I traced the list, one title after another. *King, Sovereign, Guard, Warrior, Parent, Guide, Teacher, Master, Friend,* it said. *Creator, Giver, Sustainer, Provider, Truth, Hope,* and *Light.* Each word listed as if it was an individual entity, yet the verbiage was clear that each specific title was just one ingredient of a greater whole.

Some names on the list were more descriptors than titles: *Healer of Suffering, Merciful Warrior, Source of Light.* Other titles were put together in ways I did not understand and their duality confused me: *Violent Mercy, Living Martyr, Gentle Warrior, Humble King, Patient Fury.* The titles drew vivid pictures, combining clashing colors to paint a riotous but somehow harmonious variegation in my mind. It was terribly confusing and my mind reeled in the vibrancy of the colors.

My eyes ached. I closed them. After several deep breaths, I looked back at the first name, *Embral e' Veria.* The words shifted so I could read them: *Infinite Power contained within Unending Love.*

Another contradiction. How do you contain a power that is infinite?

The shapes shifted again as if that one phrase, *Embral e' Veria,* could be interpreted in multiple descriptions. They had almost become readable again when a knock at the door broke my concentration.

I closed my eyes for a moment, surprised to still have my balance. This reading was different than my father's letter; or maybe I was changed since coming to Tirandov. I rose to answer the door.

Julien held a tray with what I assumed was my dinner. Concern etched lines between his eyebrows. "Are you well?"

"Yes, thank you. Come in." I motioned him to take the tray to a table near the window. I didn't want to risk spilling anything on the ancient text. "I'm reading the history of Loeftryn de Rynloeft. Edru called it *The Story of The First.*"

"And indeed it is."

"You've read it? You know the Ancient Voice?"

"Yes, I've read it. But not written in the Ancient Voice." He set the tray down. "Over the years, my family has been privileged to study copies that have been translated into our modern language."

"Are these translations easy to come by?" Considering the collections of literature I had been privy to during my education, why had I never before seen a translation of this particular book?

"No. In fact, they're quite rare. But since the days of Lady Anya, it has been a high priority in my family that *The Story of The First* be studied. Ours is an uncommon tradition, unfortunately, and one few can afford." He brightened. "But there is hope that will soon change. Your father has scribes in his employ who are painstakingly copying the texts that they might be more available to the people."

"He does?"

"Yes. The Kingdom has sustained centuries of damage due to the exclusivity of the Andoven and their skewed interpretation of what it means to be Protectors of Truth. King Jarryn is devoted to the cause, but he has strong opposition."

I sighed and stirred the soup. An aromatic steam rose from the bowl, tempting me, but my mind was too full to allow my tongue to be otherwise occupied.

"This book is so complex and yet . . . so simple! All I've read so far is a long list of names, but they're all titles of the same person. It's confusing." I pressed my lips together. "And irritating. And yet . . . compelling." I pushed a breath up to my hairline. "But there is nothing for it, I guess, but to continue on and hope it starts making some sense soon."

I lifted a spoonful to my lips. It smelled good, but I couldn't define the aroma. I tasted it. *Odd.* Savory, but odd.

"It's not making you ill in any way?" Julien asked. "The reading, I mean." He gave me a lopsided grin. "Not the soup."

"No," I laughed. "Just confused. But it's kind of fascinating, even though I find myself unaccountably irritated by it."

"My translation may not be quite as thorough as what you are reading, but I would be happy to discuss it with you when we take our walk this evening." Julien paused. "If you're still of a mind to go."

"I am." I nodded. "I imagine I'll be in need of some air after meeting with the Elder Council."

"I will leave you to your dinner and studies, then," he rose. "I'll return to escort you to your chamber before the meeting."

"Thank you."

Julien paused at the door. "I'm not sure how the text is arranged in the Ancient Voice," he said, "but in my copy there is a chapter entitled 'The Emblem of The First.' It has the history and meaning of the symbol found both on my sword and throughout Tirandov. It might be a good place to start."

Of course! Julien's sword. I knew I had seen that shape somewhere! It was a bit different to see it etched in steel—and here at Tirandov it lacked the roaring bear atop it, of course. Perhaps that was why I hadn't made the connection when I had seen the same shape around the castle. Roaring bears—*and Bear-knights*, I admitted silently—could be rather distracting.

"Thank you. I'll see if I can find it."

He bowed and moved toward the door.

"Julien?"

He turned back toward me. "Yes, Princess?"

"I'll look forward to our walk later."

"As will I." His smile stole my breath and quickened my pulse.

FORTY-NINE

*N*ow that Julien had given me a suggestion for my reading, I was anxious to begin. I fixed my concentration on the text and the letters began their dance, forming words I could see ahead of me. I glanced again at the names and noted a few more that I had not noticed at first: *Truth Bearer, Truth Barer.* I paused, appreciating the differentiation of the meanings.

So he brings truth and he also illumines it from wherever it is hiding. Illumination. *Hmm.* That thought reminded me of my purpose and I flipped forward in the book.

I was a little dizzy as I scanned the pages, looking for the words that would shape themselves into the Emblem of the First. Finally, about three-quarters of the way through, I found the sought-after words, along with an intricately rendered drawing that matched the diamond-in-a-circle design.

I groaned. Had I known the emblem itself would be there I could have saved my eyes a bit and scanned for the picture. *Oh well.* I would know better next time.

I concentrated on the design, admiring the simple beauty of it, and wondered if my Andoven gift would allow some deeper meaning into my consciousness. As I looked closer at it, it almost seemed to grow on the page. The harder I concentrated on the design, the clearer and wider it became until it seemed that my vision itself must be expanding to fit its breadth.

I gasped when the emblem began to glow. I blinked, but when I opened my eyes, the glow was even brighter. I brushed my hand across the paper and felt heat. I pressed my fingertips to the page and it glowed brighter still.

"Ow!"

I ripped my hand away and looked at my first three fingers. Where I had touched them to the emblem, small blisters were already beginning to throb.

Heat from the page blew against my face. How could it be that the emblem was hot enough to burn my skin, yet it did not consume the fragile, ancient page? How was that possible?

I refrained from touching it again but I was unable to look away from the white-hot glow of parchment that did not burn.

Just as the letters had done on previous pages, the emblem began to form a new shape. It looked at first like a fist, and then a crown. Once the crown had fully formed, another figure emerged at its center.

I sat frozen in place, fascinated as the shape expanded into the form of a man, outfitted as for war. The size of the man grew, rising underneath the crown as it lowered onto his head.

White light, subtly tinged with blue, shot upward from the page as if a wind within the book itself fed its ascent. The light grew larger and larger until it became a life-sized dimension. It was so bright it hurt.

I shot to my feet, upsetting my chair as I stumbled away. Scorching rays of heat threatened to blind me. I wished to close my eyes to save them, but I couldn't. Even my eyelids were paralyzed by fear.

The light impaled my mind with the roar of a voice so loud that my bones vibrated against the sinews holding them in place.

Rynnaia E'veri!

The bright warrior spoke only to my mind, but it was like thunder—the worst kind of thunder—that rattled the very bones. But somehow I knew he spoke only to me. None in the corridors would hear him. None would come to my aid.

I was at his mercy.

Throughout my life I had been amazed by some of E'veria's most gifted Veetrish Storytellers, and even frightened by some of the images their stories had conveyed; but I'd always known they were just stories. I had *never* seen or felt anything so fearsome, so real, as this. Not even when I'd learned I had met a real Cobeld in Mynissbyr had I been filled so entirely with terror. I longed to cry out for help. To hide! But I couldn't move. What was this strange and frightful magic?

"Who are you?" I gasped, but the words let in the heat and stole every trace of moisture from my mouth. I wouldn't make that mistake again.

What are you? I raised my hands against the onslaught and shielded my head with my arms. Perhaps if he could speak into my mind, he could also hear my thoughts. *It's too bright! I can't look!*

It is not your eyes that refuse to see me, Rynnaia E'veri.

The roar became softer, almost a whisper, but with an ocean's depth and a volcano's magnitude behind it. The heat remained steady, as if its energy was focused entirely upon stealing my breath. Maybe even my life. The bright parts of me were burning away like the thinnest parchment. I had no colors of my own left to claim.

This heat consumes me! I wanted to cry, but my eyes, so dry in the heat, refused. *The light is too pure and I am dulled and . . . and gray in it!*

You have read my names, Rynnaia E'veri. Are you ready to know me?

Ready to know him? A character from . . . a book?

Who are you? I begged the answer. *What are you? I cannot even bear to look at you!*

The forceful, dry heat of the light did not lessen, but my mind was suddenly filled with other colors, beautiful colors, the full prismatic range of the titles I had read earlier. And I realized: these are *his* titles. These are *his* names.

My very skin felt like it could melt, though no perspiration formed on it. Dropping to my knees, I huddled on the floor and impotently tried to shield my head from the radiant assault.

You've read my names, Rynnaia. You have seen some of my colors. Are you ready to know me? Or will you go into battle without sword or shield?

Was I not already in a battle? It certainly seemed as if my life could be snuffed out at any moment.

I had no training as a knight. I was useless with a sword. But a shield . . . ?

Hope vied against paralyzing fear. Perhaps this Warrior King would let me live. Or at least allow me to die fighting. Keeping my eyes closed, I dropped my arms and raised my face to the onslaught.

Where do I find this . . . this shield? I stood.

Here.

The heat gentled slightly, and as I opened my eyes, the form of the warrior collapsed inward, becoming a vertical beam of light before disappearing back into the page.

The emblem glowed white, then blue and orange before it faded to resume its intricate, but one-dimensional, inked form.

Panting, I rose to my feet, righted my chair, and sat heavily on it.

Before me, the book was motionless. Dull. As ordinary as if the entire experience had been a product of my imagination. A dream.

My fingertips throbbed. I lifted my hand and examined the blisters. Bigger now, each white nub was encircled by an angry red stain.

It wasn't a dream.

My mental paralysis lifted, and with trembling hands, I turned the page.

$\mathcal{F}$ I F T Y

$\mathcal{I}$ didn't take me long to realize the warrior who had come from the book was none other than Loeftryn de Rynloeft himself, E'veria's First King. But the book depicted him in a much more human form than the one by which he'd so recently graced my presence.

I'd heard the story before, of course. I'd even seen it told in Veetri. But there was something about soaking up the words for myself that made it come more alive than even Lord Whittier's gifted hands had been able to.

The more I read, the more my fear subsided. I was drawn to the story, even to the First King himself. He seemed much friendlier as a knight than as a glowing warrior coming out of a book. But the more enthralled I became with the man and his tale, the more keenly I was aware of the separation of pages and time that kept him out of my reach.

Similar to the genealogy texts I had studied the day before, this story introduced the First King's knights one by one: *Nyr, Veetri, Mynis, Dyn, Sengar, Dwons, Stoen, Andov.* I recognized the knights from the provinces that had been named in their honor. Idly, I wondered for whom Shireya, both the mountain and the province, was named.

As I read about the First King's knights I felt especially connected to the young knight Stoen, who, though opinionated and intelligent, was easily discouraged by feelings of unworthiness. It seemed almost cruel that his insecurities had found their way into history, but I was glad, in a way, that they had. I could identify with the knight's inner turmoil.

Near the end of the chapter was the story of an epic battle and a traitor from within the First King's own ranks.

The traitor's name was Cobeld.

I shivered at the name, but continued to read. The way he was described did not paint him a goblin, as the Veetrish so often chose to; nor did he look like the wrinkled old man I'd met in the Wood! The Cobeld in this story looked nothing like my idea of a villain. In fact, I mused, if I'd cast the role of hero in this tale, I'd have been more likely to give him this knight's face rather than the regal but unremarkable visage inscribed to Loeftryn de Rynloeft.

I shook my head. I wasn't a historian or a Storyteller. Those gifts belonged to others. I was the Ryn and reading this story was my assignment. I reined my focus back in on the story.

Detailed descriptions of the grisly battle fought at the foot of Mount Shireya made my heartbeat quicken, my breath catch in my throat, and my soup threaten to reappear.

When Stoen was captured, I wept. I could feel his anguish as enemies overtook the First King on the battlefield. Even detached as I was by the boundary of the ancient pages, I cried out as Cobeld himself dealt the final blow that brought death to the First King.

It was too much. I closed my eyes for several breaths, willing the scene away. Leaning back in my chair, I rubbed my eyes, but the vision would not depart from where it had seared itself into my imagination and left its implications as questions in my mind.

The First King had been killed by the traitor Cobeld. I had seen it myself, recorded on these very pages. He was dead.

Dead.

Was it a ghost, then, that came out of this book?

A ghost who knew my *name*?

Suppressing a shiver, I returned my eyes to the story.

Only eight of the King's loyal knights remained alive at the end of the battle—the heroes for whom eight of E'veria's provinces were named. Shackled under heavy guard, the knights were forced to watch as their King's body was born away by the enemy, tossed onto a pyre, and set ablaze.

The fire burned for several days and all the while the eight faithful knights remained imprisoned in cells within Mount Shireya. Early one morning, the mountain began to tremble. So violent was the quake that I feared the knights would perish. It was so real to me, in fact, that I found myself grabbing on to the arms of the chair to keep from falling.

But the knights remained unharmed. Instead, a burst of light stilled the quake and the bars and gates of the cells shook loose and knocked the guards to the ground, rendering them unconscious.

When the knights moved past the guards and out of the mountain, they found the funeral pyre still ablaze. But the fire had a different sort of flame than when they'd last seen it. Hotter and purer, it was as if the flash of white light they'd seen inside Mount Shireya had wrapped itself around the base of the pyre. Blue and white flames wound over the pyre, a moving vortex of heat and light, until suddenly the flames parted as if ripped by a giant pair of hands, and a man walked out of it toward them, unscathed.

"Greetings, knights."

No, I thought. *It can't be. He's . . . dead.*

But if he's dead, I argued with myself, *who was just here, speaking to you, Rynnaia?*

White-hot flames leapt from his palms. He moved around the semicircle of knights, touching his fiery hands to each man's chest and speaking each man's name in turn, starting with Stoen.

"My King!" Stoen fell to his knees, but hope reigned alongside the confusion in his voice. "Are Cobeld's forces defeated? Have the people finally come to our aid?"

"Cobeld is defeated, though he will be loath to admit it." He paused, his voice a bit sadder. "The people remain as they were."

A wrenching sound tore from Stoen's throat, almost bringing one from mine. "But I watched you die on the field," he said. "I saw your body burn! How is it possible that you are here now?"

"I am The First," Loeftryn de Rynloeft replied simply. "I do not fall as men fall. True, you saw me taste a bitter sting, but I am the Highest Reigning, descended from the Reign Most High."

I blinked and the words rearranged on the page to take on their original form as written in the Ancient Voice: *Loeftryn de Rynloeft.*

Ah. So even his proper name had meaning. Loeftryn de Rynloeft. *The Highest Reigning, descended from the Reign Most High.* I blinked again and the letters rearranged so I could continue.

"I have chosen you from among your brothers-in-arms to unite my people in truth," Loeftryn de Rynloeft said. "Soon I must depart from this plane. Stoen, you are to serve as my Successor. You will be E'veria's King."

"I am not worthy of such a calling!"

"Do you love me, Stoen?"

"Yes, of course! You are not only my King, sire, but my friend, as well."

"If you love me, you will continue to be my servant as E'veria's King. You must care for my people and protect them. As King your burden will be heavy. You will be among the weariest of my servants, yet you must see that the truth is recorded, revered, and protected. You must endeavor to see that it is uplifted throughout this Kingdom and beyond. Your descendents will be charged with the same responsibility. Will you accept this challenge?"

"I will serve you, my King, in whatever position you place me. I will serve you with all that I am and for all of my life."

"May it be so." With that, Loeftryn de Rynloeft removed a crown from behind his shield and placed it on Stoen's bowed head. "I crown you Stoenryn E'veri, King of E'veria. You will be united to your people, your land, and your duty as the Servant of Truth by the power which rests within the deepest bonds of love. May you and your descendants rule justly and wisely."

When the First King granted his Successor's new name I finally recognized Stoen, *Stoenryn*, that is, as my ancestor. I felt rather dull that I hadn't made the connection before.

"Knights," Loeftryn de Rynloeft said, moving his gaze to the other men, "will you remain true to King Stoenryn and to my Kingdom?"

The seven men answered in unison, "With all that we are and for all of our lives."

Again, he reached behind his shield and brought out a gemstone the like of which I'd never seen, nor could I name. When viewed at the correct angle, the Emblem of the First glowed within each facet.

Loeftryn de Rynloeft set the stone on the ground. Removing his sword, he placed its tip at the stone's center. Grasping the hilt with both hands, he closed his eyes, lifted the sword directly upward, and then brought it down. The force of the hit sent sparks up the body of the blade. The stone shattered..

"Separate, each facet has its own beauty, as does each of your lands," he said. Moving slowly around the circle of knights, the First King gave each man the title of Regent, and into each of their hands, he placed a piece of the stone. "But unless you remain united under my emblem, you will not be whole."

The First King closed Stoenryn's fist around his piece of the stone, the very center piece that had suffered the blow of his sword. "As King you are a servant, a warrior, a leader, and a friend to your people at all times. Go in peace, Stoenryn E'veri, and lead well."

Stepping back from King Stoenryn, the First King slowly surveyed his knights. "With each stone I've imparted a gift that will make E'veria a great Kingdom. Use your gifts wisely, knights, and arise knowing that, though you may not see me, I will be with you always."

As the knights lifted their heads and took to their feet, the pure, blinding light they had witnessed earlier poured again from Mount Shireya, as if the very stone that formed the mountain was the center of a flame. When the light faded, nothing was the same.

Loeftryn de Rynloeft was gone.

Additionally, the enemy was changed. Still unconscious, Cobeld's followers were no longer the strong warriors of battle they had been. Their bodies had aged somehow—and had shrunken just as severely. Where once stood fearsome men of battle now lay straggly old men.

The Cobelds.

I closed my eyes to rest them as I digested the vivid story that explained so much about my Kingdom's history.

I inhaled deeply through my nose, and as I exhaled, I opened my eyes and cautiously ran a hand over the page I had just read. Pleasing warmth remained on the parchment, but the burning intensity I'd so recently experienced was gone.

What did it all mean?

And what about what I'd witnessed—that the First King died on the battlefield . . . but didn't stay dead? Had his voice, his form, really come out of a book and called my name?

Had that really happened?

One glance at my throbbing, blistered fingers confirmed that it had.

He said he *knew* me. He asked if I would know *him*.

I looked up from the book and toward the window. Daylight had long since fled, taking my sense of time with it. It felt like mere moments since I'd begun reading this story, and conversely, a lifetime. I shook my head to ward off my confusion, but somehow I knew images from that particular story, as well as my encounter with the Warrior King himself, would be forever burnt into my mind.

A sudden wash of green and gold forced its way to the surface of my thoughts. *Julien.*

My knight approached. I would have to ponder it all later. I had the Elder Council to deal with tonight. The rest of the story would have to wait.

ℱ I F T Y - ᎾN E

"Princess Rynnaia?"

Julien peeked in the door of the library. Even at this distance the brilliant green of his eyes shone.

"Is it time?"

When he nodded, the light caught his burnished gold hair and I had a hard time not staring. As distractions went, I couldn't ask for a more appealing one. Oh, but then he smiled.

"Are you ready?"

"Ready to go before the Andoven Elders?" I laughed, but the sound lacked a certain amount of humor. "Hardly. But I don't believe I have much of a choice."

With one last glance at the book that had burned my fingers, I stood. I needed time to change my clothes and prepare for this meeting.

Of course I had no idea what it would entail, only that my presence was requested.

Julien offered his arm. "I visited your mother today," he said as we walked.

"And how is the Queen?"

"Weak." His frown was immediate. "I stayed but a few minutes. She fell asleep."

I nodded.

"Celyse will be along shortly," he said when we reached my chamber. "Is there anything else you need?"

"No. Thank you."

I waited while Julien did a quick survey of my room. When he had assured himself it was secure, he promised to return for me in time to attend the Council of Elders and left me to prepare.

Tension coiled in my shoulders and I couldn't decide whether it was due to the expectation of walking into a hostile meeting or from the hours spent poring over the book.

But would the Elders be hostile, truly? My assumption was based on little more than the growing sense of injustice I'd felt since arriving on Tirandov Isle. *Perhaps my fears are unfounded. After all, I don't even know what the meeting is about!*

No one had confided a specific agenda for the meeting. Perhaps this was just another Andoven formality to make the royal family feel . . . well, *royal.*

Or perhaps it wasn't. Perhaps they had an agenda, a specific agenda that they hoped to accomplish with the King. Through me.

Moving to the mirror, I scowled at my reflection. Who did the Andoven expect to see at their meeting tonight? Princess Rynnaia, the clueless young girl with the strange Veetrish brogue? Or the Ryn, the flame-haired young woman prophesied to exile the Cobeld curse? Would they see me as a child in need of guidance? Or as their future Queen?

I was pierced with a longing for the days I was known as Rose de Whittier, the foster daughter of the Duke of Glenhume. Things were so much easier then. Now I couldn't even open my mouth without fearing the political ramifications of every word I spoke.

I paced away from the mirror. Speech was rather passionate and free at the duke's home in Veetri. Here among the robed quiet of Tirandov Isle's erudite residents, however, every breath was much more controlled.

I didn't feel like a princess, though I was attired as one. Nor did I fit in among the Andoven, though the gifts I'd inherited from my parents surely marked me as such. But crowns and gowns and colors flying through my thoughts hardly made up for nineteen years of ignorance. Why anyone thought me adequately prepared to attend—let alone speak to—a council of Andoven Elders was beyond me.

Andoven Elders!

I barked out a laugh. It was ridiculous to even consider it. The Andoven Elders were reputed to be wise beyond anything I had come across in my nineteen years. They'd had years to hone the gifts they had been born with, as well as the intelligence, reason, and diplomatic skills of centuries at their disposal.

If only the King were here instead of me. I dropped my head into my hands. I wished I could consult him and seek his advice before facing down the possibly hostile Elders.

My head shot up. Well? Was I part Andoven, or not?

I closed my eyes and thought of his face, as I'd seen him at his desk. "King Jarryn," I whispered.

Nothing happened.

"King Jarryn!" I said his name more forcefully. My mind traveled swiftly over sea and land to a huge castle surrounded by tall stone walls. I entered a room of the castle that held two thrones, but neither was occupied.

I put every ounce of concentration I could dredge up from my core into repeating his name again. "King Jarryn!"

Still, nothing but a view of the throne, gardens, and castle appeared. Just as quickly, it receded from view.

"Celyse." I closed my eyes. My teacher was nearly to my door.

She paused. *Yes, Princess?*

I would like to seek the King's advice before this Council, but when I call out, I cannot find him. I see only an empty throne. What does this mean?

Celyse smiled. *You are calling for the King. You do not find him because you do not address him as you should.*

What is the proper way to address the King? I thought back to Aunt Alaine's instruction in courtly etiquette. *Your Majesty?*

Her chuckle reverberated in my head. *Remember, Princess, although he is your King, he has a stronger and dearer name that is to be used by you alone.*

She was quiet for a long moment. *I am now at your door. Would you prefer I come back later?*

No. Sighing, I rose to open the door, understanding what was required of me, but not sure I was yet able to use that word.

Another time, perhaps.

Knowing my physical appearance would need to communicate nearly as much as my words, I chose my attire carefully, selecting a bronze gown with a square neckline. It set off the deeper auburn tones in my fiery hair and made me feel more mature than a lighter color might have. Celyse pulled the shimmering laces that crossed my midriff to tie in the back and I stepped back to check my reflection.

Gold threading covered the sleeves and skirt with the repeated pattern of the Emblem of the First, the diamond-in-a-circle design which now held a greater, and a little more frightening, significance for me since reading the book and burning my fingers upon it. The dress was elegant and the laces were loose enough that they didn't constrict. After pondering my hair for a moment, I decided to leave it bound up in the braids I'd worn all day, coiled about my head. Right before Julien arrived, Celyse set the silver circlet in place.

I jumped when, once again, the stone that rested on my forehead flared with heat. Someday I might get used to that. But I hadn't yet.

Julien and I didn't speak as he guided me through the corridors, but shards of a tense, silver color moved about the thoughts of nearly all those we met. This, of course, did not help my anxious mind to calm. My morning lesson with Celyse had given me the skill to see the colors of others—as well as the absence of them—without being overcome, but recognizing the stabbing silver thoughts as thinly veiled hostility, I remained wary.

We entered the Hall of Elders through a set of large double doors. The room was unlike any other I had seen at Tirandov. Covered with dark panels of wood, the glow of the tirandite walls was largely masked, but the panels were beautiful, inlaid with designs so detailed that I longed to simply stand and stare.

Some of the panel designs depicted scenes of battle. One showed a huge mountain with wood cut away to have the glowing stone beneath shine through like rays of light coming out from all sides of it. I recognized the scene as the one I had read that afternoon, just after having my fingers burned by a picture on a page.

Thinking about that experience made my fingers throb—proof again that, however fantastic, it had happened.

Julien led me to a huge chair at the head of a long table. Even as tall as I was, the chair dwarfed me. My feet didn't even touch the floor. I had the absurd compulsion to swing my legs, but stilled them before they made the motion. If the Andoven Elders wanted me to feel like a little child in their presence, they had certainly succeeded.

Even though the sun had long since set, this interior room had no real windows, no view of the outdoors. I had to wonder if the lack of windows was to keep us from noting the rising sun if the Elders tended toward long-windedness.

I was glad I had blocked my thoughts before leaving my room. Julien might not be able to read them, but anyone else in this room could.

Sharp silver threaded icy tentacles through the silence as the Andoven Elders took their seats. Directly opposite me at the far end of the table sat a woman who held an air of authority. She caught my eye several times, each time looking quickly away and toward the man on her right. Knowing the superiority of the Andoven abilities, I did not even attempt to see the thoughts of anyone in the room, concentrating instead on keeping my own hidden.

Finally, the woman stood and spoke. "My fellow Elders," she said, "it is time. Shall we call this Council to order?"

After each member gave a silent assenting nod, she turned her attention to me.

"Princess Rynnaia." Her tone made me feel like a child at my schoolwork again. "It is a rare privilege to have a Ryn at our Council." She bowed her head slightly. "Welcome. I am called Ryjitha and I currently serve as Council Chairwoman."

I gave her a slight nod.

"As the daughter of our King you are, of course, welcome to join our discussions," she said with a smile that implied she saw me as little more than a particularly adorable toddler, "though I doubt they will hold much interest for you."

Did she, now?

"On the contrary, Honorable One," I said, careful to use the formal Andoven address, but conscious of the way my lips had pressed together and my eyebrow had arched at Ryjitha's implication, "as the daughter of the King, and as a loyal citizen of E'veria, I am *exceedingly* interested in the discussions of this respected Council. I thank you for including me this night."

Ryjitha's lips formed a thin line. The man beside her, whose attention had previously been focused on the tabletop in front of him, coughed. As I met his unfamiliar gaze, I caught a sparkle of . . . humor?

I gritted my teeth. I had not intended to amuse.

Well met, Princess! His voice reached beyond the block in my thoughts, surprising me with the sparkle of pride it held.

I wondered who he was, but I was glad to have formed a unique allegiance with the stranger, even if I was a little concerned that he had so easily bypassed the gray blocks I'd constructed.

The Council worked from a prepared agenda and efficiently covered all areas of concern without the verbose overtures I had feared. Though I would never in a hundred years admit it to Ryjitha, I did, in fact, find myself quite bored with the tedious parade of agenda items. My mind wandered. Finally an item caught my interest.

"The Chair recognizes Dyfnel and wishes to hear his report concerning the lost scrolls."

Dyfnel stood. "As this Council is well aware, The Lost Scrolls of Anya have recently been recovered. I have completed the translation of the language in which they were written and have put several students to work making copies for distribution."

Well, I thought, *that was fast.*

An Elder near my end of the table cleared his throat. "Has the Remedy been identified?"

"No," Dyfnel replied, "I regret that it has not. The text concerning the Remedy is written much as Lady Anya recorded her poetry, but in a less straightforward manner." His frown relaxed almost into a smile. "It is quite an amazing piece of literature. Though written in the Ancient Voice, the translation into our modern language could have easily come from Lady Anya's well-known book of poetry. It follows similar patterns of verse and rhyme and seems almost a continuation of the story." He paused and frowned. "Although we have reasons to doubt its chronology."

"But what of the Remedy?"

"It remains unknown exactly *what* the Remedy is. However, a map of sorts is given. Jezmyn and I are piecing it together as best we can."

Ryjitha spoke again, "Is it the advice of this Council to summon the King's knights, or to send an Andoven team to claim the Remedy?"

At once, no less than thirty Elders began discussing the merits of the different plans. Voices which had started as a low hum slowly rose in anger and pitches of incredulity as the discussion continued.

As I perused the table I noticed that Jezmyn's eyes were locked with those of the elderly stranger next to Ryjitha. From the shifts in their facial expressions it appeared they were having a private discussion. Finally, Jezmyn gave a nod and stood.

As the various speakers noticed him, the sound gradually quieted until it was utterly silent at the table. Even had he not been the Regent, his bearing commanded respect.

"Honored Friends," his raspy wheeze broke the silence, "you discuss among you the merits of men and do not take into account the prophecy spoken. Even so, my gifted colleague," he gestured toward Dyfnel, "has not yet given you enough information to even consider who is to be tasked with retrieving the Remedy." Jezmyn returned to his seat.

"But this is our duty, Honored Regent!" A man midway down the table spoke. "Only the Andoven are well-acquainted enough with the entrusted truth to be able to find the Remedy."

"Indeed." Further down the table, a woman spoke. "As Protectors of the Truth, it is our duty to keep the Remedy from falling into the hands of those who cannot possibly understand the ramifications of such a substance. We cannot allow it to be squandered."

With each bigoted statement, my blood renewed its strength, pounding stronger and stronger against the blisters on my fingers.

"The King's forces are not able to interpret the Ancient Voice, let alone a code." This pronouncement came from a dry, matter-of-fact voice four seats to my left. "An important detail could be missed in the translation that would be clearer to one with greater gifts and more education."

Along with nearly everyone else, I jumped when the man sitting next to Ryjitha pounded his fists down on the table. Even as far away as I was from him, I could feel the vibration of the violent gesture as he stood.

"Greater gifts?" A dangerous glint lit the old man's eyes. "Greater gifts, indeed! All gifts fall from the same hand. And I would venture to say that the Giver does not measure the abilities He bestows upon His people by *your* prejudicially skewed standards!"

The Elder took a deep breath and his voice was only slightly softer as he continued to address the assemblage. "Friends, if you would see the fear, death, disease, and deformity the

Cobelds and their allies are causing among those you are claiming to protect the Remedy *from*, you might find compassion enough in your hearts to see these victims as children of The First, the same as you are! Instead, you lock yourselves away on this isle, unable to see that the rest of the Kingdom desperately needs hope and peace!"

Even though he appeared quite aged, his voice bespoke a passion that made my pulse thrum in my throat. But the longer he spoke, the more reddish-purple his face became. In truth, I feared a bit for his health.

"Not one person on this isle has come of age without having studied *The Story of The First*," he continued, "but generations on the mainland have had no access to it other than those tales the Storytellers deem dramatic enough to portray." His fist hit the table again. "Fulfill the reality of your purpose, my friends, not the damaging curse by which it has been profaned!"

A chaos of angry voices erupted around the table as chairs were pushed back and clusters of arguments gained momentum. I glanced down the table. Of all the Andoven, only Dyfnel, Jezmyn, and I remained seated.

Julien had moved closer toward me. His hand rested on the hilt of his sword. After a few moments he bent down and spoke into my ear. "They do not lack for conviction, Princess Rynnaia, but they do lack direction."

I nodded. "They do at that." It was clear this Council was heading nowhere good.

Closing my eyes and gathering all of my concentration, I spoke to the Elders with the force of my mind as well as the power of my voice.

"ENOUGH!"

My voice seemed to echo off every surface. The volume surprised even me.

A deafening silence fell. All eyes turned toward me at once.

"Sit down."

I refrained from adding, *"please."*

While everyone else took their seat, I stood, allowing my thoughts to open as I gazed around the room. Some refused to make eye contact with me, though others sent embarrassed words of apology that I acknowledged with a slight nod of my head.

The subtle warmth at my forehead increased. Though I wondered at the significance of the change in the stone's heat, I ignored it. A calm feeling of confidence stole through my frame. Squaring my shoulders, I addressed the Council.

"I have never been in want of books," I began, "but just this morning I was offered the opportunity to read *The Story of The First*. Never before had I been privy to a copy of this text." My chin lifted. "I am the Ryn. Yet this book, a book I've been told is essential to informing my future reign, was not available to me because it has been so very well *protected* here on this isle."

I paused for a breath. "Although I am now aware of my name, rank, and Andoven ancestry, much of who I am is grounded in my upbringing as the common ward of a Veetrish Storyteller. As such, even knowing that I am part Andoven cannot erase the offense I take from the bigoted idealism coloring the discussion of this respected Council. Indeed, as the Ryn I am distressed that the lives of intelligent and hard-working E'verians continue to be shackled by the ignorance imposed upon them by erroneous bigotry and tradition."

"Your Highness—" Ryjitha began.

"I am not finished."

Ryjitha closed her mouth and locked her eyes on the tabletop.

"Many at this honored table would deny mainlanders the chance to even *pursue* the knowledge that could quite possibly save E'veria, simply based upon the belief that others' gifts are not as seemingly profound as your own." I lifted my chin. "I cannot begin to comprehend what logic could defend such a position. As E'veria's Ryn and future Queen I am deeply disturbed that a few citizens of one of her provinces have exalted themselves so highly above the rest."

Every eye was riveted on me and not all with the warmth of friendship. When I spoke again, my voice was softer.

"There is no question that a team must be dispatched as soon as possible to retrieve the Remedy. The Queen's life depends upon it as do many others suffering the influence of the Cobeld curse. The question, however, appears to be in whose hands rests the responsibility of choosing the individuals who will go on this quest."

I paused to let the weight of my authority, as newly known as it was even to me, settle on the assembly. "This revered Council may discharge itself from the difficulty of making that decision. The traitorous acts of the Cobelds have put *all* citizens of E'veria at risk. This is not a decision to be made by scholars, though your insight is highly valued. This decision rests with the King and will be made by none other."

Confident that I had said all that needed to be said, I sat down. The heat of the stone on my forehead had increased gradually as I had spoken, though I had not made conscious note of it before taking my seat. As I moved my gaze around the table I realized that all eyes had moved from my face to a place above and behind me. Curiosity bid me to turn and see what had drawn their eyes, but I didn't allow myself to give into it until the stranger sitting next to Ryjitha spoke into my thoughts.

Look, Rynnaia, he said. *Look.*

I turned. On the panel covering the wall behind me, the wood inlay of the Emblem of the First was . . . glowing.

"Julien," I whispered, "was that . . . ?"

He leaned into my ear. "No, Princess, it was only wood before."

From the opposite end of the table, Ryjitha's voice carried a note of resignation. "We cannot deny the truth of the princess's words, for the light confirms it. The King must be contacted tonight."

She exhaled and peered at the parchment before her. "Our next item concerns the Academy at Salderyn," she said dryly, turning to the man she so recently had wished to throttle. "What update have you for us, Lindsor?"

Lindsor? My breath caught as the stranger who I now knew to be my great-grandfather rose.

FIFTY-TWO

"I bring greetings from King Jarryn," Lindsor's tone was much more reserved now, but as he raised his eyes he gave me a sly wink. "The King thanks the Andoven for the tutelage of his daughter and for your continued care of the Queen."

At that his eyes grew a bit damp and he cleared his throat. "The hour grows late, so I will be brief. The unrest and violence in E'veria continue to increase and the people are hungry for hope. The Academy at Salderyn is nearing capacity as citizens from all regions and provinces flock to the safety of the fortified city and search for answers to what plagues their land."

Compassion for the plight of the people colored both his words and thoughts. If he hadn't already won me by his passionate speech, I would have felt an immediate affection for him.

"Construction of the Academy in Luce is finally nearing completion and it will soon need to be staffed. Furthermore, the King desires to build additional academies in each of the mainland provinces and asks for Andoven volunteers to serve as teachers in Luce and elsewhere as the need arises."

"Thank you, Lindsor," Ryjitha nodded. "Council, alert our people to the King's request." She turned back to Lindsor. "Can we depend upon you to create a selection criteria for these new positions of . . . honor?"

"Of course," Lindsor nodded, and as he sat down, his gaze travelled the length of the table to where I sat. *Greetings, at last, Great-granddaughter,* he spoke to my thoughts. *You may look like your beautiful mother,* humor colored his words, *but you are very much your father's daughter. A true-born E'veri you are, child! I look forward to getting to know you.*

As I do you, sir.

The meeting adjourned shortly thereafter. Many lingered to introduce themselves to me and it was a long time before I was face-to-face with the one who truly held my interest.

"Rynnaia!" He stretched his arms and pulled me into them.

"Great-grandfather." I returned his embrace. "Two days ago I didn't even know you existed, and now you're here!"

"And I have known of you only a short time longer." Lindsor released me and looked past my shoulder. "Sir Julien!" He moved to clasp the knight's hand. "The King sends his greetings to you and thanks you for the duty you so loyally give."

"It is my honor to serve the King and his daughter thus," Julien replied.

"It is good to see you, lad." Lindsor turned his attention back to me. "Sir Julien was a pupil of mine when he was but a squire to your father. You will benefit much from his friendship in the dark days ahead of you."

His words sent a chill through my blood.

"But even darkness has its benefits, does it not?" He smiled. "A torch in the brightness of Tirandov's Great Hall would cast no shadow nor would it garner special attention. But the smallest ember uncovered in a cavern will shatter the darkness and dispel its threat. It is in darkness that light is most visible, Rynnaia. You need only open your eyes to see it."

"I confess I'm impatient to get on with it," I said with a sigh. "But I've so much to learn and so little time in which to learn it."

"You are a passionate one!" He threw his head back and laughed. "Like your mother and her father before her. Though I am proud that your father's lineage shines through to temper those tendencies." He winked. "Unlike me, you give thought to your passion before it explodes into words."

I laughed, knowing he mocked himself. "You are passionate, my gifted Great-grandfather, but I do not believe your gifts extend to diplomacy."

"No, indeed!" We visited for a while before I noticed his weariness. When Lindsor admitted exhaustion from the journey, he promised we would talk more the following day.

Just before leaving the Hall of Elders, he turned back. "Ah, the memory of this old man is not what it once was. I nearly forgot to pass on a request from the King." He shook his head. "Rynnaia, your father wishes you to speak with him as soon as your lessons have progressed sufficiently to facilitate the communication."

The failure of my earlier attempt flushed through my mind.

"Ahh . . ." He saw my thoughts. "I imagine that will be a difficult bridge to cross. Just speak from your heart, child. When the time is right, you will reach him."

With a gentle bow of his head, Lindsor exited, leaving me alone with Sir Julien.

"After all that," Julien said, "I imagine you're exhausted."

"No, actually." The admission surprised me. "I'm anything but. Are you?"

"I've done little to tire myself." The corner of his mouth lifted slightly.

I returned his smile. "I do believe I would enjoy a stroll beyond these glowing walls."

He offered his arm.

Outside the castle, the air smelled of spring, of all things green, and of the sea. We took a different path than we had the night before, one which wound around the opposite side of the castle.

From this side of the narrow isle the sea looked and sounded as a normal tide, nothing like the silent current on which our boat had come in. A sliver of the moon's reflection danced on the waves.

The soothing sound of the surf cleared away the tension of the meeting. The bright fog that kept Tirandov Isle hidden from passing ships had cleared to allow us a view of the sea's vast open waters.

"Dyfnel tells me the fog only arises when a ship draws near," Julien said as he sat beside me on a stone bench. "This isle is full of wonders, is it not?"

"Indeed."

We sat in companionable silence, appreciating the grandeur of sky and sea that made us feel so small, yet far from insignificant. A gull passed overhead and its call broke the calm, sending a shiver through me.

Julien chuckled. "The sound was rather piercing, wasn't it?" He leaned back against the bench and tilted his face toward the sky. "Shocking, almost. Like that ember in the darkness Lindsor spoke of."

I examined his profile as he gazed at the sea, loving how the breeze ruffled his hair.

"Some things are only understood with time and gentle understanding," he said. "But it's the big moments . . . a shout that breaks the silence, an ember in the dark cavern, things like that, that capture our attention."

I had to look away, lest I add "a handsome knight" to his list. I turned to watch the tide push and pull at the sand.

"I took your advice on that chapter in *The Story of The First* today," I said. "Do you think the source of that light, the light that changed the soldiers in the story into Cobelds, is the Remedy?"

"I don't believe the light is sourced from the mountain. I believe Loeftryn de Rynloeft himself was the source. The mountain was just doing his bidding."

I laughed. "A mountain is not a living thing with a will of its own. How could it *do* something for the pleasure of a man?"

"Because he wasn't a man as we understand the word. Think of his name: *Loeftryn de Rynloeft.* It means Highest Reigning descended from the Reign Most High. When you dissect the definitions of the words they can mean more than they first appear to."

"I understand that he was the First King, but *de* usually refers to a father's name. Except that the name *Rynloeft* refers to a position or a place." I wrinkled my nose. "It doesn't make sense to me! How could he be the descendant of a *place*?"

"It is a little tricky," Julien paused. "Princess, you must think about the word *descend* in its other literal meaning. To come down from."

"But that makes him seem to have no beginning. No parents, no ancestry. How can that be? Everyone has descended from someone!"

"He is The First."

I stood up and began to pace in front of the bench.

"Princess," Julien spoke after a few minutes, "look at the moon and the light it gives. Do you not wonder who hung it in the sky?"

I stopped pacing and gazed at the glowing orb. "Yes, of course I know there is a Creator." I paused, thinking back to the book. "That was one of his names, too, wasn't it?"

"Yes. And that name remains true, as does he."

"The First." I resumed my pacing. "So what you're telling me is that the one responsible for the sunrise in the morning, the blooming of flowers, the pull of the tides, even our very breath, this *Creator* is the same being as the First King?"

"He is the same."

"But he *died*. And then when they realized he wasn't dead,"—my words confused even my own ears—"he disappeared into the sky. That should have been the end, right?"

"Yes. But it wasn't. Truth is not so easily done away with. His love for us is unfathomable. Unquenchable."

"Indeed?" I turned back to face him, my hands on my hips. "Then why, if the First King cares so much about E'veria, does he keep the Remedy hidden? Why did he give the Cobelds the ability to impart death through the hairs of their beards? Why has he let my mother suffer for nineteen years? If he is such a powerful being, so powerful that he can circumvent *death*, why didn't he destroy Cobeld and his followers so we could live in peace?"

"I don't believe he gave the Cobelds their power. I think it comes from a darker source."

The shiver his words sent through me made the burns on my fingers throb. "What source would that be?"

"I don't know." Julien was quiet for a while. When he finally spoke, the change in subject surprised me. "Do you know the legend of the night sky?"

"Of course." No one could live in Veetri for as long as I had without hearing such a popular tale. Having grown up in a house with two Storytellers, I knew it by heart. "It is said that the Creator, whose garments were made of light itself, gave each day a period of darkness that his creation could have a few hours of rest and peace from the heat of the sun," I said. "But from the first night, the darkness caused so much sadness that he had pity upon his creation, tearing pieces of his cloak and throwing them into the sky."

Julien chuckled. "Were it not for the lack of Story People, I would think you one of the gifted Veetrish."

My Veetrish accent had again come to the fore while relating my abbreviated version of the famed tale.

He smiled. "Go on."

"No teasing?"

He crossed his arms. "Very well," he said with a sigh. "No teasing."

I tilted my face toward the sky and gazed at the expanse above. Just then, a shooting star passed overhead. "Did you see that?" I asked.

Julien nodded. "Beautiful."

"*A glimmer's trace for just a breath, thus ends its path of light.*" I quoted the poem from which I had, in a roundabout way, arrived at my horse's name and stopped worrying about how Veetrish I sounded. "Would you like me to finish the tale?"

"Please."

I took a breath, but kept my eyes trained celestially. "To ease the burden of darkness on his beloved people, the Creator tore his very cloak, which itself was made of light, and threw the scraps skyward. When the pieces of his cloak touched the sky," I lowered my voice to a hush, "the stars were born." I paused and spoke again in a normal volume, "From that night forth there remained within the darkness of the night sky an innumerable collection of celestial bodies giving the people hope even through their darkest times."

I stood, stepped a few paces away, and gave Julien my best attempt at a Veetrish Storyteller's showy bow.

He laughed and applauded. "A well-told tale! Do you recognize any of the First King's names in that story?"

I thought about it for a moment. "Creator, of course. That is the name with which I'm most familiar, having heard it most of my life. I've always thought of light and hope as words of description before, but I guess they're listed among his names, as well."

"Indeed." Julien's smile widened. "Even a folktale born of Veetrish imagination can contain truth at its core." He gestured to the celestial canopy above us, dotted with millions of stars. "Each star varies in size and intensity, but even the brightest are invisible in the bright light of day." He lowered his gaze to me. "It is the same for us. If we never experienced the darkness of suffering and pain, we could never grasp the depth of comfort found in the light of love."

He paused and gazed out at the sea. "We are allowed to suffer and allowed to observe the sufferings of others, which is sometimes even more difficult, so that we might better experience the meanings of our Creator's many names and discover a clearer picture of the nature of his character. And as we do, we learn to know him better."

"He asked if I was ready to know him." I sighed. "But I am not."

"He . . . asked?"

"Yes. After he burned my fingers, of course."

I showed Julien my blisters and explained my experience with the book. My next words carried a sharpened edge that was almost painful to pronounce.

"I am both ignorant and stubborn. I am Andoven, but I am unschooled in my gifts. I am the Ryn, but I have no idea how a princess is supposed to behave. And I can't even wield a sword, Julien! Yet I'm supposed to defeat the Cobelds?" I shook my head and trained my gaze on the sand. "What qualifies me to be the one entrusted with the Kingdom's hope? Surely there are many others who would be better suited to this position."

"Nay, Princess, there is only one. He chose you to be the Ryn and to take on this quest in the same manner he chose me to be born a knight of Fyrlean Manor. Because he is The First. He sees the whole and knows the parts we are each to play."

"I envy your confidence, Julien." I stared at my hands, folded in my lap. "But I cannot embrace this, or *him*, as you wish me to." I sighed. "I hope you're not too disappointed in me."

Julien reached for my hand. "This decision to accept or reject *The Story of The First* is not one to be made lightly, Rynnaia. You must give it the fullness of your consideration and not try to rush yourself."

"Yes. Don't rush. Good advice." I laughed, but the sound held less amusement than irony. "I shouldn't rush, but I must read until my eyes ache, learn to harness my Andoven gifts, and have a conversation with a stranger who happens to be my father!" The sarcasm coating my tongue increased as the list of all the things I had yet to do became more and more daunting. "Then I must figure out how to exile the Cobeld curse, and, by the way, pick up the Remedy on my way through so I can save my mother's life. No, Julien, there's no rush."

"Your burden is grave." He ran his thumb along the skin joining my index finger and thumb. "I would take it from you if I could."

"I know you would." I squeezed Julien's hand to try to take some of the sting from my words, but was forced to lift my hand to cover a yawn.

"We should go back to the castle and find our rest." He let go of my hand, stood, and offered me his arm. We retraced our steps in silence.

"You are a patient man, Julien de Gladiel," I said as we neared the glowing castle. "I doubt many other knights would serve their King as teacher to an obstinate princess."

"I'm honored you trust me with your questions," he said. "It is no burden to share my heart with you."

It is no burden to share my heart with you.

I mulled over his words as we walked. We were nearly to the castle doors when my sharp intake of breath caused him to pause mid-step and turn to face me.

"Is something amiss?"

Heat fizzled up from the core of my body and into my face. Sudden clarity dawned.

My feelings for Julien had deepened far beyond friendship to something with much more depth and tenderness.

My eyes sought the ground. Blocking my thoughts was of no use to me against this man. If he looked in my eyes I would be incapable of hiding my heart from him.

Julien's gentle hand touched my burning cheek and turned my face toward him. I kept my eyes closed, fearing what he would see in them.

"Are you in pain? Did you turn your ankle, or step on a stone?" The concern in his voice was my undoing. I saw him clearly before I even opened my eyes.

"Princess . . ."

Drenched in streams of green and gold, I was dizzied by the power his colors contained. I lost all ability to control my thoughts.

I love this man. I love him.

"Rynnaia . . ."

His hand pressed against my cheek. When I lifted my hand and placed it on top of his, a jolt of blue heat shocked me as our fingers touched.

Julien inhaled sharply. His green eyes grew even more intense as the gold in his thoughts increased. He was so beautiful I could barely stand to look at him, but I couldn't so much as blink. His head bent toward my upturned face and—

One of the castle doors scraped across its threshold. I blinked as Julien spun around, hand to his sword hilt. The colors dissolved, but I had to work to school my thoughts when I realized what that sound had interrupted.

Julien had intended to kiss me.

To kiss me!

I had no desire to share our private moment with the Andoven interloper. I sent a light gray covering to surround Julien so that his thoughts, also, would be unknown to whoever came through the door.

Julien relaxed his stance as Jezmyn crossed the threshold. Turning back to me with a look of apology, Julien whispered, "We will discuss this. Later." And he took my arm and guided me farther up the path, out of the shadow of the shrubbery.

"Hello, Jezmyn."

"Princess," the Regent wheezed. "Sir Julien." With a sweep of his hand, Jezmyn closed the door. "Dyfnel said I might find you here. Your father has been contacted, and after some discussion with the Elders, he has decided that you, Princess, are to pick two from among the Andoven to accompany his knights."

"Me?"

"You are," he said, nodding as if the King's request was the most natural thing in the world, "the Ryn." He smiled. "Your father asks only that you confer with Sir Julien before considering those choices."

"Of course." I swallowed. "I would not think of making such a decision without consulting Sir Julien." I laughed, but the sound was shallow. "I've lived quite a sheltered life. I know little of quests or the fortitude required for such adventures."

"The King would appreciate a word from you tonight."

"Tonight?" Nerves gathered in a knot at my center. "I don't know if I am able to achieve that quite yet, but I will try."

"That is all he asks." Jezmyn's smile was warm. "I am available also, should you have need of a friendly ear."

"Thank you, Jezmyn."

He nodded and continued down the path we had just come from.

Tension sizzled in the air between Julien and me as we entered the castle.

Julien cleared his throat. "Might I have a word before you retire?"

"Of course." The entryway was deserted, but still felt exposed. The library doors, however, stood open and the room was empty. "We could step into the library."

He nodded and headed in that direction. As soon as the door was closed, he spoke.

"Your Highness, I must beg your forgiveness for the liberty I nearly took earlier." His head was lowered, his eyes cast on the floor. "It was entirely improper and an ill-fitting action for a knight sworn to protect you. I'm so sorry. Forgive me, please."

He was . . . sorry?

I wanted so badly to look into his thoughts, but I couldn't form the words to seek permission and I wouldn't let myself invade his privacy without it.

I struggled to uphold the formality that he so clearly wished to maintain. "The fault is entirely mine," I said. "I should have tried harder to block my thoughts from you."

"No, the folly rests with me."

Folly?

He looked up, then, his eyes full of the regret that now colored his thoughts vividly enough that I didn't have to try to see it to know it was there.

"Princess Rynnaia, you are in the process of discovering truth and uncovering your Andoven abilities. I fear you are mistaking this humble knight for the one you truly seek to hold your heart."

"I'm . . . what?" I blinked.

Julien ran a hand through his hair. "As much as I enjoy our evening walks, Your Highness, it might be best if Dyfnel or . . . or Edru accompanied you from now on."

Understanding dawned like sunrise over the sea, sending its chilly breeze across my heart. Julien had not been drawn to *me*. He had merely been drawn into the colors I had sent out to him.

Embarrassment stained my cheeks. My ignorance of the power of my Andoven gifts had caused me to project the love I had just discovered into his thoughts. Yes, I loved him. I wouldn't even attempt to deny it. But my love was one-sided. Julien didn't love me.

An invisible fist constricted around my windpipe. *He doesn't love me.*

"My apologies, Sir Julien." I fought to keep the tenor of my voice smooth and even. "I will not let it happen again."

A hot lump of sadness threatened my ability to breathe. I swallowed and forced words through my throat. "Meet me back here after my morning lesson, if you please, and we will discuss the King's request. I will see myself to my chamber. Good night."

I didn't wait for his reply. Instead, as my vision clouded, I nearly ran toward the door. Once I had breached the hallway the tears broke through my reserve. I gathered my skirts and broke into a run. Green and gold colors swarmed after me like bees chasing a bear from their hive. I heard the sharp rap of Julien's boots crossing the library's stone floor, but their haste only urged me to increase my speed.

Please don't follow me! I thought in desperation. I heard the library door shut and the firm click as the latch caught, echoing off the stone walls. Assuming Julien's long-legged stride would soon catch up to me, I took the first staircase I found leading down and fled without looking back.

FIFTY-THREE

The late hour had the residents of Tirandov firmly ensconced in their private quarters, and I was able to
give full vent to my embarrassment without the fear of increasing it as I fled. Weeping, I ran mindlessly through corridors and down staircases without any particular destination
in my mind. I finally came to a halt a moment before I would
have crashed into the dead end in front of me.

Like the entrance to my mother's room, the Emblem of
the First was carved into stone, but I knew this was *not* the
door to the Queen's chamber. This design glowed faintly yel-
low-orange instead of blue, and an illumined carving, written
in the Ancient Voice, rested above the diamond shape.

I ran my hand over the letters. Though my hand felt no
stirring of the stone beneath it, my eyes fixed on the shapes as
they began to move and form a word I could read.

Silence.

What could this chamber be, with such a name?
Cautiously, I opened the door. The surprisingly small room
was unadorned, the few chairs and settees, unembellished.

Blank tapestries hung over most of the walls. I found the dimness soothing. It was the kind of room you could sink into and relax, a space in which you could escape from the noise of your own thoughts, as well as everyone else's, and just be still.

I was thankful the room was unoccupied, but my breathlessness, heavy-laden with tears, seemed somehow irreverent even so. I shut the door and opened my mind, but felt the presence of no other colors but my own. For the first time since coming to Tirandov, I was utterly alone. It was almost as if this room was not even a part of the castle.

I sank into a chaise and leaned into its softness, absorbing the rare and peaceful silence that hadn't touched my mind since I had learned my true name.

The chaise seemed to form to every curve of my body as if it had been waiting to embrace my wounded soul. I could not allow myself to think about Julien. *Sir* Julien, I corrected myself. He had made it clear that he felt nothing more for me than duty and friendship.

The colors of my attraction to him—nay, my love!—had collided against his reason. Not being Andoven, the oddness of it must have confused him into acting contrary to his feelings and led him to nearly kiss me.

Let it go. I urged myself. *Think of something else.*

But what?

Jezmyn wanted me to contact the King. Well, I could try that. *Again.* Celyse had said I would only reach him if I called him by the name he would expect from me.

Father.

My heart stumbled on that word. In my mind, "Father" was a term of endearment. How was I to speak such a name to a man I didn't even know? My only references to him were from other people and from the letter and from the brief childhood memory it had released.

452

It made me slightly dizzy just to think of that experience. At least I could picture his face now. Maybe if I said the word aloud it would work.

I closed my eyes. "Fa-father."

I whispered the word tentatively, trying hard to focus on the face from my memory, but other, dearer faces swept through my mind: Lord Whittier, Uncle Drinius, Lord Whittier again. Those men loved me like a daughter. And I loved them. It was easy. But it was ever so difficult to think of the King, a stranger, with that same tenderness.

"Father?" I called out, but my whisper was absorbed within the heavy, colorless tapestries draping the glowing walls.

"Father!" I gave more volume, more purpose to the word. Suddenly, I was crossing the sea. Instead of the cliffs I had seen at Port Dyn, however, I came to a sandy shore.

Where is he? I wondered, even as my mind traveled on.

As far as my mind's eye could see was sand—a sparse landscape, indeed. My mind zoomed over the terrain and it gradually became rockier, with somewhat greener hills appearing in the distance.

A massive mountain range appeared at the eastern edge of my vision, tinged pink in the sunrise, though it was well past midnight at Tirandov. *This must be a faraway land,* I thought, *to already be bathed in the rays of the sun.*

I could no longer picture the face of King Jarryn, only the word "Father" spelled out in my head. I shouted again, trying to concentrate fully on the name I was calling.

Why would the King venture so far from Castle Rynwyk during such a dangerous time?

I sped through dead brush, past vacant homes and a river whose banks were littered with the bloated bodies of dead animals and fish. I was glad to be only seeing, as I was sure the scent of death would have overpowered me.

I tore my eyes away from the sight and looked ahead to the desert where a grayish-black fortress loomed suddenly before me. Fear pricked sharply within my chest. I shouted again, but in my panic and confusion I wasn't even sure what name left my mouth.

Through the iron gates, my mind moved into the oppressive depths of the fortress itself. I passed hulking, armored guards whose faces I could not see, as well as smaller, unarmed creatures—Cobelds?—that seemed to be ordering the larger ones. I feared I would be discovered, but that fear eased when I remembered that I was not actually within the walls. Only my thoughts had entered.

With dizzying speed my mind traveled down, down, down, until I could no longer count the levels of stairs I had passed.

At once, it ended. The light was dim, but my eyes adjusted quickly.

I was in a dungeon.

Was this the King's dungeon? Or was he—I swallowed hard—a prisoner here?

Prisoners filled every cell with the heavy air of despondency. Fear was etched in each gaunt face. My chest ached for them as I looked at the bars and locks keeping them imprisoned.

Around the dull iron lock of each cell, something odd shimmered with a silvery brightness, but I could not slow my mind's journey to dwell on it.

Where could he be?

Then my mind finally stopped in front of a cell and refused to go further. It appeared I had found him.

"Hello?" *Why had the Andoven not told me that the King had been captured?* "Are you in there?"

From the darkened corner, one of the cell's inhabitants stirred. My gut clenched as a man moved toward me in the faint torchlight. In the opposite corner, another man stepped forward, and a familiar, deep voice spoke as my eyes focused better on the faces.

"What is it?"

"I thought I heard a woman's voice," the first man said. "It sounded like . . . like Rose." He shook his head. "It must have been a dream."

The man rubbed his eyes and took another step toward me. Torchlight illumined his face. My heart clenched. It wasn't the King. It was Uncle Drinius.

His eyes widened, almost as if he could see me. In his thoughts, I sensed a creeping fear for his own sanity.

"Rose?" he whispered. "Gladiel, do you see her? Can you see Rose?"

"Uncle Drinius! Sir Gladiel!" I cried, but my shock broke the connection and they faded from my view. In an instant I was back on the settee in the dim room, panting for breath with tears coursing down my cheeks.

"They're alive!" I laughed through my tears. "They're alive!"

I may not have contacted the father I had intended to reach, but I had been given a gift of hope for the uncle I had feared lost. I rose and hurried to the door, anxious to share my news with the only other person in the castle who would share the fullness of my joy: *Julien.*

I paused on the stair. In my excitement I had forgotten my reason for seeking the Silence room in the first place. Clenching my teeth, I shook my head, lifted my chin, and determined to be Her Royal Highness instead of the romantic fool I'd been before.

It took a lot longer to retrace my steps at this more reasonable pace and I got more than a little bit lost. Finally I reached a familiar hallway and found my way to Julien's door, which was just down from my own. Receiving no answer to my knock, which I thought was odd, given the hour, I sought him with my mind.

Sir Julien. With closed eyes, my mind found him. *Sir Julien!* His head popped up as I made contact with his thoughts.

He was still in the library . . . and not at all happy about it.

FIFTY-FOUR

I heard the commotion in the entry hall before I rounded the last corner. A crowd had gathered, most attired in their nightclothes. Edru stood at the library door, searching through a ring of keys.

"I apologize, Sir Julien," Edru called. "But none of these keys fit the lock. I don't know how this happened! This door has not been locked in— Well, not in my lifetime, at least."

"Nor mine," an elderly voice interjected.

"What's happened?"

A collective gasp filtered through the crowd as they all turned to look at me.

"It appears we can call off the search for the princess," the wry voice of my great-grandfather spoke from their midst.

Concern had etched even deeper lines into his wizened face. The crowd parted as he moved toward me. "Where were you, child? None of us could locate you in the castle! You've given us all quite a scare, what with your knight being imprisoned and you nowhere to be found."

"Julien's imprisoned?" I blinked. "In the library?" That seemed . . . odd. "Has he been injured?"

"He is unhurt. Are you?"

"I'm fine."

"Where were you, child?"

"I found a room whose door reads *Silence*. I needed to be alone and it suited." I didn't elaborate. "Edru," I called toward my teacher, "what happened to Sir Julien?"

"Someone has locked him in the library," Edru explained, "and we are unable to open the door."

"Who?" I asked, fearing the answer. Could an enemy have infiltrated Tirandov Castle? "Who did this?"

"That is what we are most anxious to find out."

My great-grandfather placed his hand on my shoulder and looked deeply into my eyes. "Did you lock this door, Rynnaia?"

"Of course not! I would not lock a knight in where he could not do his duty!"

But you did. I heard Julien's thought. My eyes swung toward the door. *You slammed the door behind you and I was unable to follow.*

"No, I didn't!" I shook my head. "I don't know how! I—I've not been taught how to do that!"

Lindsor's eyes sparkled and he spoke to me alone. *You must have been very angry with your knight, Great-granddaughter.*

He is not MY knight, Honorable One. And I wasn't angry . . . exactly.

Oh, is that how it is, then? The sparkle in his eyes dimmed as sympathy replaced it. He turned to the crowd. "It would seem that my great-granddaughter has uncovered another gift. If only all the Andoven were such apt pupils! As it is, however, she is the only one who will be able to unlock this door. Therefore, you may all return to your beds."

The crowd dispersed without a sound, though I knew the whispering gossip of their thoughts would likely keep them from sleep. Only Lindsor, myself, and Edru remained.

I reached for the ring of keys in Edru's hand. "Have you tried all of these?"

He nodded.

Lindsor chuckled. "You did not use a key to lock it and therefore no key will unlock it. You must use your mind." He turned to Edru. "I believe the princess and I will be able to handle it from here, young man. You may return to your rest."

Edru gave us both a small bow and left.

"To open or shut a door," Lindsor instructed, "you must respectfully accept that the object is there to do your bidding. Might I inquire as to your state of mind as you left the library earlier?"

"I was crying," I said, embarrassed. "I did not want to be seen. I wanted to be alone."

"Do you remember opening the door before you left?"

I pursed my lips as I thought back. It seemed so long ago, yet it had been less than two hours, in truth. My mouth formed an "O."

"No! It opened and I walked through it!"

"Rynnaia, the opening or shutting of a door requires little effort for an Andoven. The locking and unlocking, however, is a skill few are able to achieve. It is an ability usually inherited through families. That being said, I will tell you that my own life has been spared on several occasions by my ability to slip out of enemies' traps." He arched an eyebrow. "Unlocking them, as it were."

Julien's impatience filtered through the wooden door and into my mind.

"I don't mean to be impolite, but I need to apologize to Sir Julien. I fear he will not soon forgive me."

"I think you underestimate him, child," Lindsor replied gently. "But I can think of no reason to tarry." He quickly explained how I had locked the door in the first place, confirming that I, indeed, had been responsible for Sir Julien's imprisonment.

"The Giver has endowed all of his people with clear gifts, whether they acknowledge they come from his hand or not," Lindsor began. "To some he gave the gift of being able to till and plant the earth to bring about a bountiful harvest. To others, such as the knight inside, he gave a strong body and mind and the firm resolve it takes to defend the Kingdom. To the Andoven, he gave gifts of communication with man, beast, and matter, that we would be better able to protect the truth entrusted to our care." He sighed and I knew he was thinking of the Elder Council uproar.

"These gifts are not to be used for vanity or pride, but are to be used out of respect for the Giver. We are never to glorify the gift itself, nor the one who uses it. We are to return the honor of our gifting back to the One who gave it."

"Well," I said, "now that you've made it so clear . . ."

Lindsor smiled. "You may not yet acknowledge it, Rynnaia, but each time you use one of your gifts, you are only using it by permission of The First. Now let's attend to this door."

As he continued to describe the process I closed my eyes and concentrated on the keyhole. *Show me how you work.* My mind's eye entered the workings of the locking mechanism. I spied a piece that was able to move. *Move aside,* I requested. *Release.*

There was a clicking sound. *Open.*

"Well done, Rynnaia!" Lindsor patted me on the back. "It is good that you've learned this now. It will likely come in handy after you leave Tirandov."

As Julien's boots clicked toward us, I stared at the floor, not yet ready to meet his eyes.

"I will leave you now," Lindsor said. "I believe the two of you have much to discuss."

A moment later I was alone with Julien.

"I'm sorry," I whispered. "I didn't mean to lock you in the library and I certainly didn't mean to alarm all of Tirandov. Please forgive me."

Julien let out a deep breath, as if he had been holding it for a long time. "Of course I forgive you, Rynnaia."

I looked up. "You didn't use my title."

"Would you prefer I did?" A glimmer of undefined emotion flashed in his eyes, but I refused to look into his thoughts, though the temptation was strong. I'd never heard such vulnerability in his voice.

"No."

He smiled and a little part of me I'd never noticed before melted when the vulnerability remained.

"I fear you misunderstood the intent of my remarks earlier."

"About that." I swallowed. "I need to ask your forgiveness for what happened outside. I hope when I understand my gifts more clearly I won't—" I paused. Heat blazed into my cheeks, but I refused to be a coward with my words, even if I couldn't meet his eyes. "When my training has advanced, I will be better able to prevent my thoughts from transferring to you. Until then, please accept my apology."

He looked toward the doors. "If you're not too weary, would you consent to join me outside? Please?"

"Earlier you said we shouldn't walk together anymore."

"Earlier I was a fool and I hurt you."

"No, Julien, it was my—"

He stopped me with a shake of his head. "I have pledged my sword to you, Rynnaia, but I will draw on a greater power than its blade to protect you from . . . *me*. Shall we?"

We left the castle once again, but settled on a bench in plain view of its glow. I was silent, waiting for Julien to speak because I wasn't sure where to begin. I did not have to wait long.

"So much has changed these past weeks," he said. "My perception of the future of the Kingdom has expanded, knowing you survived, but I've also discovered things about myself I never knew. I've changed. As have you, I'm sure, in ways that I, having known you for such a small measure of your life, can't even imagine."

He chuckled then, but his eyes were toward the sea. "Less than two months ago you didn't even know your name. Now you are every inch a princess and a skilled Andoven woman, locking and unlocking doors without keys. It's amazing."

"I'm still me." I reached a hand toward the circlet of silver vines resting atop my head. "Somewhere, beneath this crown, I'm still me."

"I know." He faced me, suddenly serious. "Rynnaia, earlier in the library—"

"Please." I had apologized. Did we really need to rehash the conversation? "I don't wish to speak of it. I understand what you meant and you need not trouble yourself further. You are a knight, Sir Julien, chosen by the King to be my personal guard. I will respect your position."

"I don't think you understand as well as you think you do." His smile was gentle. "And when propriety doesn't dictate the use of my title, I do wish you would simply call me Julien."

"It seems too *p-personal*," I stuttered. "I would be more comfortable with the title, I think."

"King Jarryn never hesitates to call his knights, his *friends*, by our given names. The bonds of friendship supersede titles. Are we not still friends?"

"Of course we are." I looked down at the ground, trying to blink my tears away.

"Good. I am immeasurably glad to be your friend." He paused and took my hand. "But I am not content to be your friend."

My head swung toward his, but I quickly looked away. With his free hand he pulled my chin back toward him.

"Rynnaia, I have never felt such deep regard—" He shook his head. "No, that's not the right word. Fondness? Affection? Enchantment? Hope?" The breath that escaped him had the cadence of happiness and disbelief all rolled into one. "I feel all these for you, and more. Do you not, with all of your Andoven abilities, sense that my regard for you has increased well beyond the commonness of friendship?"

"But I mistook my own thoughts for yours. I saw—"

I paused, hoping a breath would loosen the pain tightening my throat and give me a word that wasn't as precious, nor as humiliating, as *love*. But since I couldn't deny that word was now firmly attached to my feelings for Julien, the pressure only increased. When I spoke, my words barely held the volume of a whisper. "I saw something that wasn't there. I'm sorry."

"No, Princess, you saw what was true. Look again. I'm ready for you this time." He squeezed my hand. "Please."

I closed my eyes and tried to gather my strength.

He rubbed his thumb along the back of my hand.

I opened my eyes and fell into his.

Remnants of the gray with which I had guarded his thoughts from Jezmyn still lingered. I pushed them away, but what I saw was the same as before. My feelings were on display in his mind. I squeezed my eyes shut. "I can't."

"Please, Rynnaia. Try. I need you to see the truth. I need you to see my heart."

The tenderness in his voice brought a groan of agony from my chest. He cupped my chin and tilted my face upward. A tear squeezed from my closed lashes and fell on my cheek. I reached up to wipe it away, but he beat me to it.

At his touch, colors washed over me. Blue and orange, green and gold, his colors and mine danced and twirled, never combining, but never truly separating. It was so beautiful, so real, so true.

But it couldn't be true.

"Julien, I—" I choked out a sob. "I'm sorry! I can't seem to help it. Please! It's more than I can bear!"

But he held fast to my hand. I was immersed in the exquisite dance of colors.

"Trust what you see, Rynnaia. It's real."

"But you said—"

"I was unclear." He brushed the tears from my cheeks. "You left before I could explain myself and I was quite unable to follow you."

I finally had the strength to open my eyes. "Forgive me. I didn't mean to—"

"I *have* forgiven you, Rynnaia. I could never withhold such from you. I'm not sure I could withhold anything from you."

"I've tried to keep my promise, Julien. I've tried to block your thoughts and protect your privacy. That's why I can't trust what I see now."

The realization of what I was saying and what had actually happened was slow in coming. His thoughts were not blocked from me now. I had pushed all of the grayness away. I had seen the truth. I had seen Julien. And his feelings for me.

My eyes widened. "It's true?"

"It's true." He smiled. "It's a lot to take in, isn't it?"

"Yes."

"Do you remember how Rowlen reacted to me?"

I nodded. My lip twitched upward at the memory.

"How would he respond to our spending this sort of time together, now that we've admitted our feelings for one another?"

I winced. "He would call you out. Or haul me away. Or both."

"Exactly." He chuckled, but there was something pained in his humor. "We've spent much more time alone than would be considered proper by most standards."

It was true. Between the days at Fyrlean Manor and our stay in Port Dyn, the hours we'd passed alone together were well outside the bounds of propriety. Even now, while in full view of anyone peering out of the castle, our situation might seem improper.

"But ours is not a usual situation," Julien continued, "and until this evening there was never a time that the boundaries of propriety were crossed."

And yet the heat of his hand still warmed mine as if he had no intention of letting it go.

"The truth, Rynnaia, is that I have grown to care deeply for you. And more than anything, I wish the King was here so that I might seek his approval of my suit."

I tore my gaze from our entwined hands and finally met his eyes. "You wish to court me?"

"More than even you, with all your Andoven abilities, could possibly know."

I sighed and tension escaped as if the world of winter had fallen off my shoulders and filled my heart with the promise of spring.

"But I cannot pursue that course without the King's leave," he continued, "and since we have no idea when we will see him, we are at an impasse."

A frown pulled at my brow. *Would the King give his permission?* My thoughts poured over one another with such force that I could not form them aloud.

"I don't believe I've ever seen you at a loss for words, Rynnaia." Julien's eyes sparkled. "Perhaps you wish to refuse my suit before I get the chance to speak with your father?"

Before I speak with your father. My father!

Uncle Drinius!

"Julien, I have news!" I jumped up. "While you were locked in the library I tried to contact the King, but instead I saw my uncle. Sir Drinius, that is, and Sir Gladiel!"

"My father?" He was immediately on his feet. "He's here? At Tirandov?"

I shook my head. "Sorry. No, not here." I explained my experience in the Silence room.

As I spoke, myriad emotions crossed his face. He sat down heavily, and with his elbows on his knees, rested his forehead in his hands.

I placed my hand on his arm. "At least we know they're alive. There is hope."

"Hope." He remained still for a moment before he lifted his head. "You're right, of course." He sighed. "This fortress you speak of. I know of it, though only by repute. It is a Cobeld stronghold in Dwons."

I had feared as much.

"Dwonsil warriors are cunning. I've no doubt the silver around the locks were cursed hairs from a Cobeld's beard.

466

They would know a knight would never try to escape through Cobeld-cursed bars." He paused. "The enemy must know who they are. What they mean to the King."

"Why would that matter?"

"My father and Drinius aren't only King Jarryn's personal guards, they're his closest friends. They must be trying to draw the King to Dwons."

I sat down beside him. "I'm sorry. I know if you were on the mainland you would be mounting a rescue right now."

"If I was on the mainland, Princess, how would I even know this information?" He smiled softly, but his eyes suddenly widened. "Rynnaia, do you think . . . ? No."

"No, what?"

"Would it be possible to—?" His voice was hesitant, but hopeful. "Is there any way you could send a message to my father for me?"

"Hmm." I'd gotten there once. Perhaps I could do it again. "I can try."

$\mathcal{F}$ I F T Y - $\mathcal{F}$ I V E

$\mathcal{O}$nce inside the dimness of the Silence room, I relaxed. Picking a settee large enough to comfortably share, I took Julien's hand. "I'm new to this, Julien, but I think I can do it. Celyse said the ease of my connection depends upon the strength of my desire to reach them. And I very much want to reach your father and Uncle Drinius."

He squeezed my hand.

I closed my eyes. *"Uncle Drinius."*

This time I wasn't searching in vain for someone who fit the idea of "father" to me. I was calling by name and going directly toward the exact person I wished to reach. That clarity took me over water and sand and through the difficult terrain and fortress in a flash. Before I took another breath, it was as if I stood in front of the knights' cell.

"Uncle Drinius."

"Rose?" Quickly moving into the torchlight, my uncle looked directly at me. "Is it really you?"

Quietly, now, I said. *You cannot risk being overheard.*

"How is this possible?" he whispered. "I'm not Andoven."

469

I smiled. *As it turns out, I am.*

His eyes widened. "You know."

I nodded. *I am on Tirandov Isle with Julien de Gladiel. Are you and Sir Gladiel well?*

"We've been here several months," he whispered. "In truth, we don't know why they're keeping us alive. But we believe they are plotting to use us against the King somehow." His gaze darted down the dark corridor. "You must not let him be a party to any rescue efforts, Rose. That's what they want!"

I hold no sway with the King, I said. *I'm sorry.*

"No sway?" He blinked. "No sway? Child, you're the—"

"Drinius!" Sir Gladiel barked his name as he came into the light. He turned his eyes to me. He blinked. "It can't be . . ."

He could *see* me? But I hadn't called to him!

But I had intended to.

"Rose," Drinius spoke, "you know who you are now, child. Think of E'veria's future. You must not take any risks with your safety!"

I will do what I must, Uncle Drinius, for E'veria. It will mean many risks, I'm afraid. But I will do my best to survive. At least long enough to find the Remedy.

His shoulders drooped.

You kept me safe from the Cobelds all these years for just such a time as this. Now it is my turn to put myself at risk for you and the rest of the Kingdom. I paused as a smile of pride lit his eyes. *Julien wishes that I speak to his father for him. Have hope, Uncle Drinius. And remember you have my love.*

"And you have mine," he whispered. "With all that I am and for all of my life." He motioned Sir Gladiel forward. "She's with Julien."

Sir Gladiel blinked again. He squinted. "I can't—"

I concentrated my thoughts toward Julien's father. "Sir Gladiel," I said aloud. Julien's hand squeezed mine.

"I don't know how you're doing this, Rose but, my sword!" He moved into the light. "It is good to see you!"

Julien is here with me on Tirandov Isle. He sends his love.

A possibility entered my mind. I had passed my feelings and thoughts to Julien before. Could I act as a liaison between the two men?

Without opening my eyes, I turned to face Julien and held out my other hand. He took the hint.

Keeping my concentration focused on his father, I leaned toward Julien until I could feel the heat of his breath on my face. The word, the request, came from within my heart.

Meld.

At once, his colors swirled into mine, and when a bright flash of gold touched my mind, I knew he realized my intent. Pressing my forehead to his, I released one of his hands and stretched it toward Sir Gladiel, as if I could be a bridge between father and son.

I saw nothing but colors swirling around me. I could neither hear voices nor see faces. My world shrank until it was only color: mine, Julien's, and what I assumed were Sir Gladiel's. I put all the effort of my mind and all the strength of my heart into connecting the two men, but nothing resulted but color.

Something pulled at my fingers, as if trying to disengage their grasp. I gasped and the colors disappeared, as if sucked into the vortex of my breath.

I opened my eyes and sank back into the cushions of the settee. "I'm sorry. I tried as hard as I could." I rubbed my fingers against my temples. "Maybe it isn't possible."

"You're sorry?" He looked at me with a puzzled mix of wonder. "I spoke to my father for the first time in over a year, Rynnaia! I could *see* him! It was amazing!"

"But . . ." I sat up. "I thought it didn't work! I only saw colors."

"It worked!"

Julien jumped up and pulled me to my feet. He twirled me around until I was laughing so hard I could barely breathe.

"You've given my father and Drinius hope, Rynnaia." He set me back down. "And you gave me a chance to tell my father about you."

I laughed and wrinkled my nose. "Your father was there when I was born, remember? I'm hardly news to him."

"What I meant to say," his voice was low, almost as if he was afraid someone would hear, "is that I told him how I feel about you." He reached for my hand and raised it to his lips. "Thank you."

I suddenly felt weak, but I wasn't sure if it was from the exertion of the communication or from feeling his lips touch my hand.

F I F T Y - S I X

One of the many odd gifts of Tirandov Isle was the more I learned, the more my need for sleep decreased. Celyse explained that those who lived on the island for long stretches of time eventually acclimated themselves to the energy gleaned from the glowing stone, but since my gifts were so newly revealed and I wouldn't be here for long, it was in my best interest to take advantage of it.

The short visits I had with my mother each day, however, were all the encouragement I needed to stay the course and stretch my mind. But it seemed that the more my abilities developed, the faster her health declined. This was the cost of her blessing to me.

Though my days were long, they passed in quick succession. I spent every morning with Celyse, refining my communication skills, occasionally surprising her with some of the things I had tried in the hours we were apart. Alternating my afternoons between reading the *Story of Truth* and discussing it with Edru and Lindsor, I also spent many hours with Jezmyn and Dyfnel, discussing the contents of the scrolls

Erielle had discovered. When I finally got to read them for myself, I had to agree with Dyfnel. Apart from the promise of leading to the Remedy that would save my mother's life, the poetry told an adventurous but complexly riddled story that captured the imagination.

Our journey to find the Remedy would be both physically and mentally demanding. It was to that end that I endeavored, each morning when I rose, to perform the series of controlled movements I'd learned from Julien when he'd been recovering at the Bear's Rest. And each night I paced the thick sands of Tirandov. As my endurance increased, I adjusted my routine to make it more difficult.

My mind and body became stronger every day, but as our departure from Tirandov drew near, I couldn't help but wonder: would it be enough? A growing sense of apprehension shaded every moment I studied and trained.

I dreaded seeing an end to my daily visits with the Queen. We had grown close. Well, as close as two people can become after nearly twenty years apart and when only allowed brief daily visits. But my heart had bonded to hers, and that made knowing the Remedy was her one hope of survival quite a burden to bear.

"Rynnaia."

I jumped as Lindsor's voice snapped over the stone floor of the library as I was reading a copy of the translated scrolls.

"Yes, Great-grandfather?"

"How long have you been on this isle?"

I did a rough calculation in my mind. "A little over a month, I think." He should know. He had arrived shortly after me.

"Has anything impeded the progress of your lessons with Celyse?"

"Not that I know of."

"Exactly!" His scowl nearly doubled the wrinkles on his parchment skin. "From all reports, your lessons have progressed well beyond what was expected for your first visit to the isle. If that is so," he paused to let the full shade of his disapproval sweep over me, "why, then, have you neglected to contact your father?"

I tensed. "I've been busy with my studies, Great-grandfather."

"Too busy to afford a few moments peace to the King?"

His stern tone communicated his disappointment in me as clearly as his thoughts. My eyes sought the floor. I bit my lower lip. "What if he . . . ?"

How could I put my worries into words? There were so many ways I could disappoint a King.

"Rynnaia." Lindsor stepped closer and placed a gentle hand on my shoulder. "Have you considered that the King may be as nervous about your meeting as you are? Perhaps even more so?"

The King? Nervous? No, I hadn't considered that. *But what if I'm not the princess he was hoping I would be? What if I am . . . a disappointment?*

"You are his daughter, first. Do not forget that." Lindsor moved his hand to lift my chin. His blue eyes looked deeply into mine. "You've nearly completed your first reading of the *The Story of the First*, have you not?"

I nodded.

"Have you not yet learned the power of a father's love? Your father's love will overshadow any shortcomings, real or imagined, you might have as a princess."

My fear was an irrational thing, I knew, but that didn't make it less real. I grasped at anything I could to explain my delay.

"But even the *Story* is clear that a father must be willing to sacrifice his child if duty commands it. If I fail to fulfill the prophecy, wouldn't it be easier for the King if he did not know me?"

"Let's say you do fail." The old man paced to the window and back. "Let's say the Remedy remains hidden and Daithia dies."

I sucked in a breath.

"If she dies, would you prefer that you had never met the Queen?"

"Of course not! She's my mother and—oh."

No argument Lindsor could present would be more damning than my own words. With a sigh, I closed the book. "If you will excuse me, Great-grandfather." I stood. "The time has come for me to speak to the King."

Approval shimmered in his eyes. "May I walk with you?"

"I would welcome your company."

We took our time making our way through the castle to the Silence room. I knew that I could be anywhere when I sought the King, but the quiet peace and dim glow of that particular room seemed to impart a special sort of solace that I hoped would ease the tension of our meeting. When we reached the door, Lindsor put both hands on my shoulders and looked in my eyes.

"Your heart is expanding along with your mind and your abilities, child. Although truth is sometimes unnerving to confront, always at its core is *Embral e' Veria*. The Limitless Power governed by Unerring Love."

"*Embral e' Veria*," I repeated. "That's the first name listed in *The Story of The First*."

"Indeed."

Lindsor had recited the definition a bit differently than I remembered reading it, but his words held an element of wisdom that could not be argued.

"Each bit of truth you have partaken has set free a part of you that you were unable to reach into before. You have accepted *The Story of the First* in your mind. You believe its history. But there is more. Much more."

"I doubt my brain can hold much more."

"Some things," he smiled, "can only be understood when you come to the end of yourself."

His words did not exactly contain the encouragement I had hoped to receive in his company.

"So what you're telling me," I couldn't keep the irony from staining my words, "is that I will remain confused until I die?"

"It's not as bad as that, child." He chuckled. "Although I must admit there is something to that statement! None of us will have a complete understanding until we have no more distractions." He smiled down at me. "But that day is, I hope, a very long time away for you." His expression turned serious again. "What I'm referring to now, however, is what comes when you discover that all of your abilities and gifts, all of the strength of your character, and all of the help you have been given from the hands of others, are simply not enough; and that you must surrender all that you are in hope of a help greater than what you can accomplish with your own strength."

"In other words," I said, crossing my arms, "in order to understand truth I must become clueless, helpless, and alone." I arched an eyebrow. "Why, Great-grandfather, you make it sound so appealing. I can hardly wait."

He chuckled, but his eyes grew moist. "Neither can I, child. Neither can I."

A sudden lump came to my throat, bringing with it a certain measure of longing—an acute awareness of that empty inner place I had ignored since the evening I'd recited the tale of the night sky for Julien.

Lindsor gave me a gentle, lingering embrace. "Your father loves you, Rynnaia. But that, also, you will have to learn for yourself." He pressed a kiss to the top of my head, turned, and walked back the way we had come.

The Silence room was just as I'd left it. Settling into my favorite chaise, I pictured the face of the King as I remembered it from reading his letter at the Bear's Rest. I was just about to call out to him when I paused.

Would this be a convenient hour? He was, after all, the King. Presumably, he would be quite busy, with the war and whatnot. Maybe I shouldn't...

"You promised Lindsor," I reminded myself.

I took a shaky breath. "Father."

As if Salderyn was simply a step away, I was immediately there. But, as I feared, it wasn't a good time. He was not alone.

Surrounded by men who bore the telltale knight's beard, he stood at a table that was covered with scrolls—maps, from the look of them.

Rynnaia. Without looking up, his rich voice spoke to my mind. *Please wait.*

Of course, Father.

At that, he did look up. A smile of pleasure lit his face as he began to roll up the map closest to him.

"You're dismissed," he said to the knights. "We'll continue this later."

The knights filed out of the room and the King moved to a chair.

He closed his eyes just long enough to say my name, "Rynnaia." And then he looked straight into my eyes. *I confess*

I feared you'd never seek me out. Are you terribly angry for all of the deception?

This was not at all how I expected our first conversation to begin.

So *that* was what Lindsor had meant. The King thought I was avoiding him because I was angry.

Not now. I was. Before. I bit my lip. *For most of my life, if you want to know the truth.*

I do. He nodded. *And I'm sorry, so very sorry it had to be this way.*

I know. And suddenly, I *did* know. Finally speaking to him—seeing the sorrow in his heart—made it easy for me to forgive him.

I'm sorry it took me so long to contact you. I was unsure of myself. I'm sorry if I caused you pain. There was a pause in which neither of us seemed to know how to continue.

Thank you for sending Julien for me. I filled the awkward moment with something familiar and true. *He has become . . .* I reached for the smallest strand of gray and hoped he didn't notice . . . *a dear friend.*

I am glad to hear it. My fear evaporated as the colors of his love wrapped around me, bright and deep and true.

At once fiercely protective and wondrously tender, the colors reminded me of the overwhelming emotions that had incapacitated me the night I read his parchment at the Bear's Rest. Tears formed at the edges of my eyes.

You surprised me that morning, Rynnaia. He saw the memory I had recalled. *I had not expected to hear from you so soon.*

You were hiding something from me, weren't you? I searched, but caught none of the swirls of gray, black, and gold that had caused me such discomfort that day. *My mother.* I realized.

Yes. I was afraid the knowledge would put you in further danger. I'm sorry. I didn't want you to know until you reached Tirandov. He paused. *I understand you and your mother are growing quite close?*

You speak with her?

Indeed. Grief clouded his answer. *Not as often these days, I'm afraid. And more briefly, it seems, each time.*

It was the same for me, though in person. *I'm sorry.*

We have no regrets.

And yet it was the blessing given to me that continued to drain her health.

You seem to have found a solid place within your great-grandfather's heart, as well. Lindsor tells me you have quite a gift for . . . what did he call it? He chuckled. *Oh yes. "Forceful diplomacy," I believe, is how he termed it.*

I laughed out loud and he smiled at the sound. *Not every Andoven counts among the friends of your heir. But they accept me, nonetheless.*

The King sighed. *I've had much the same response these many years. But they are loyal, even when they disagree with the position of the crown. You will not find an enemy among the Andoven,* he gave me a wry smile, *but your patience may be tested by their stubborn hold on traditional bigotries.*

I grinned, finally feeling a connection to the stranger I called "Father." *I think you and I have much in common, Father. I look forward to meeting you soon.*

A look passed over his face that I could not gauge and he did not speak for a moment. When he did, I was surprised at the turn of the topic.

Have you chosen the two Andoven you wish to join my knights in retrieving the Remedy?

Yes. Dyfnel has agreed to accompany us. His familiarity with the scrolls will be invaluable and, should anyone need a physician, his knowledge will be appreciated. I also would like to take my teacher, Edru. He is just a young scribe, but I believe he has the heart of a knight. If we survive, he will be able to record our quest from firsthand experience and I believe he will serve our cause well.

My father's brow creased. *You will not be going to retrieve the Remedy, Rynnaia. My knights will escort the two Andoven and you will take your place at Castle Rynwyk.*

So, Dyfnel had not yet shared the contents of the scrolls with the King. I sighed. *Lady Anya's prophecy was just the beginning. The scrolls confirm that I must go.*

No! A fierce, violent stubbornness radiated out from him. *You will not.*

I took a deep breath. Something about his stubborn refusal wrapped itself around my heart, pulling it tightly and giving me the strength to defy the King.

I wish it could be another way, Father, believe me. When you read the scrolls you will understand. I related to him my experience at Fyrlean Manor with Lady Anya's poetry. *I am the Ryn Naia spoken of in the prophecy. Even without the message from Anya, even without confirmation from the scrolls Erielle found in the Great Wood, my physical appearance and royal birth would confirm the path I must take. I cannot relinquish my duty to E'veria any more than you can ask me to as our King.*

The King was silent. A wealth of emotion played across his face as he fought to deny my claim.

Gladiel and your mother have tried to convince me of this—to ready me for your necessary entrance into danger—for years. I had hoped they were wrong. I should have known better. Your mother is rarely wrong. His smile was grieved. *I've taken the liberty of picking a few valiant knights. I would rather send you with an army, but stealth will be a major factor in the success of your travel through Shireya. The knights I've chosen are among my best. They await you at Holiday Palace. As do I.*

He was in Port Dyn? I would see the King . . . my father . . . in person! Pleasure lit up my thoughts. *I will not keep you waiting long.*

His smile warmed at my response. *My knights have finally been told of you and of your mother's survival and they are anxious to meet their Ryn.*

All our talk of the quest and knights brought something to mind that I'd been tossing around in my head but had yet to put into words. I paused to gather my courage. *There is another person, one not of Andoven lineage, who I think would be an asset to the team.*

You are the Ryn, he said, as if my title gave an extra measure of credibility to my request. Perhaps it did. Even with the King. *Who did you have in mind?*

I took a breath. *Is Erielle de Gladiel still at Holiday Palace?*

Erielle? The King blinked. Clearly that was not a name he expected, but I rushed ahead, not wanting to give him the time to deny my request.

I know she's young, Father, but she's as skilled and as brave as any knight. As a descendent of Lady Anya, she is better acquainted with the prophecy than anyone I know. Even though she wasn't able to translate the scrolls, she is the one who found them, Father. And—

Finally, I did pause, for what I had to say next was based not on fact, but on something much less defined. *I can't explain why, but I have the strange feeling Erielle will play a part, an essential part somehow, during our quest.*

The King's lips pressed together. He didn't look angry, but neither did he look pleased. *What has Julien to say about this?*

I hadn't exactly mentioned it to him yet. My silence said as much.

I've already secured Gerrias de Gladiel for the team and Julien, of course, will lead the quest. He shook his head. *To ask Lady Gladiel to send all three of her children into harm's way while her husband remains missing seems cruel, don't you think?*

I hadn't thought of that. I scowled, trawling my mind for a solution that would allow Erielle to help us seek the Remedy. *Would Gerrias be overly disappointed if he were to remain in Port Dyn?*

The King sat up straighter. *You would have me send a young girl in place of one of my best knights?* His gaze pierced mine. *I don't question Erielle's bravery, and Gladiel saw to it that she knows her way around a sword, but she is not a knight.*

I lifted my chin. *Perhaps she should be.*

When the King crossed his arms I felt like a little girl, arguing to stay up past her bedtime.

Why are you so intent on having the lass with you?

I pondered my conviction a moment. His argument was entirely valid while mine was vague. I couldn't explain why I felt so certain that Erielle should be included, but I couldn't escape the urgency that it just felt . . . *right.*

Much of the text in the scrolls has been written in riddles that we may only be able to solve when we come upon their answers. Men and women don't always look at things in the same way. Erielle has a keen mind in addition to her ready sword. Beyond that, there are certain, more, um, delicate reasons. My words were colored by the same pink tinge as my cheeks. *Reasons that would make another woman a welcome addition to our company.*

The King furrowed his brow. *Surely, Rynnaia, there is an Andoven woman, someone older and wiser, who would better serve in that capacity than Gladiel's daughter!* Loyalty and concern for his missing knight added to his resolve. *Erielle should go home to Mynissbyr.*

I determined to convince him. *The Andoven are not encouraged to face hardship or danger, as you well know. I can think of many who would gladly join me, but none better equipped than Lady Anya's own.*

A fresh wave of assurance calmed me, though I couldn't fathom whence it came. *I can't explain how I know, Father, but I am confident, absolutely confident, Erielle should come. I cannot promise she or Gerrias or even Julien will be kept safe for their mother, but I do have news of Sir Gladiel that might bring Lady Gladiel a glimpse of hope.* I relayed the information to him of the captured knights.

His look was grave. *I have recently received intelligence that you confirm. Be assured every effort will be made to bring them safely back home.*

They believe they are being used as a trap to bait you toward Dwons, I cautioned.

The Cobelds have chosen Drinius and Gladiel because of their relationship to me, not knowing one with an even dearer claim to my heart exists. He smiled. *I will not leave while my daughter is on such a dangerous road. Rest assured that every effort will be made to rescue the knights, Rynnaia. But I will not abandon you to seek them myself.*

And about Erielle?

He took a deep breath. *I will not stand in the way of your choice if you are sure. Erielle may go.* He shook his head and when he spoke into my thoughts again his tone was dry. *I've no doubt she will embrace the opportunity.*

Indeed. I laughed, wishing I could be there when he delivered the news. *Thank you, Father.*

He did not look convinced at the wisdom of my request and I could tell he would lose sleep over it.

When should I expect my princess to arrive?

Two days, Father. My time on Tirandov Isle had passed swiftly, yet the atmosphere was so serene that the rest of the world sometimes felt like a vague memory. *Dyfnel has already secured our passage.*

Aboard Meredith, *I hope?*

Yes.

Very good. Until then, Rynnaia, rest in my love and be of good courage in the truth.

I will try, Father. Thank you.

My stomach growled as the connection was broken, reminding me it was time I left the Silence room to dress for dinner.

$\mathscr{F}$ I F T Y - $\mathscr{S}$ E V E N

$\mathscr{I}$ sought solitude that evening. Or at least as much solitude as a princess can expect to find. Julien followed at a short distance as I walked the paths outside the castle. I made my way to the northern beach and continued past the longboat in which we had arrived until I came to a lower place on the beach where the castle was no longer visible. I sat down and removed my shoes, curling my toes in and out in the sand, longing to find the peace eluding me.

I lifted a sparkling handful of sand and let it run through my fingers, glad for the warmth it retained even in the coolness of the night air. As it glittered through my grasp, it awakened the need that, no matter how I'd ignored it, had stubbornly clung to that empty space inside me.

My heart was gripped by a sudden desire to be in the water. It pulled me like the tide, whispering that a swim could wash away all the tension, all the uncertainty in my heart, that the vastness of the sea could swallow my fear and replace it with the confidence I lacked.

I stood and started toward the edge. *Come, Rynnaia!* It seemed to call to me, drawing me near. *Come for a swim.*

But for the obvious lack of trees, the strange stillness of the current made the bay resemble more of a secluded woodland pool than a gateway to the open sea. The warmth of the water surprised me, but I reminded myself we were in the southern sea and that the warmth of tirandite stone would surely permeate the surrounding waters.

Exuding peace and tranquility, the bay invited me to wholly enjoy what it offered, tugging at the inner part of me that longed for comfort. The need to be fully immersed within its warmth would not be denied. I lifted the hem of my skirt and stepped deeper.

"Princess, stop." Julien's boots sloshed in the water as he moved to my side. "I don't know what creatures reside in these waters."

On this side of the isle the otherworldly stillness of the sea felt not of tide, but of time and knowledge. Somehow even the uncanny calm of the isle's entry point held an awareness of what danger its magical current would soon deliver me to. Using my Andoven gifts, I trawled the water but, although I was aware of a great mystery and a deep, urgent longing, I sensed nothing that would do me harm.

"Fear not, Julien. There is naught but comfort here tonight."

"And you know this . . . how?"

"I'm Andoven."

His only response was to deepen his scowl at the water.

"I would like to go for a swim." I knew propriety would not allow him to stay. "Would you allow me to dismiss you?"

"I will not leave you alone, Rynnaia. I'm sworn to protect you."

I sighed, knowing what he said was true, but unable to assuage my desire to be held in the water's embrace.

"Perhaps I might swim with Her Highness?" Celyse's voice cut through the darkness. "I saw the princess from my window and deduced her intent. You may wait just over that rise for us, Sir Julien. Be assured we will call for you if we have need of your services."

Julien was not pleased with the arrangement, but was unable to find a good reason to deny me.

I put my hand on his arm. "Please don't worry."

"I cannot promise *that*," he said with a little smile and a nod toward Celyse. "I will be near." Grudgingly, he went back to the path and over the small rise of the dunes.

"I brought an extra robe for after your swim," Celyse said. "It would be difficult to put your gown back on when you are wet. Shall I help you out of your gown?"

"Thank you." I nodded, taking a few steps back onto the dry sand.

Soon I was divested of my outer garments. Wearing only my shift, but feeling unashamed with only Celyse as witness, I began moving again toward the water.

Celyse was similarly attired, having removed her robe also. "I will stay a safe distance away, Princess Rynnaia. Your first time in the Bay of Tirandov should be private."

I waded into the stillness. The surface of my skin was rough and dry from the many hours spent within the pages of books and the saltwater stung my hands. But the sting quickly faded, caressed away by the water's silkiness.

The water had an entirely different feel than that of the Veetrish ponds where I'd learned to swim. It was almost as if it seeped through my skin and into an undefined region of my soul, and I had to question my definition of water when compared to the liquid consolation in Tirandov's bay.

When the depth reached my shoulders, I laid back in the water and floated under the sea of stars. The darkness of the moonless sky invaded every corner of my vision. I emptied my thoughts and simply enjoyed the comfort, knowing from someplace within the deep recesses of my mind that in these brief moments I might experience a sort of peace that might not be mine again for a long time.

I shuddered at the thought, and from the corner of my eye, saw a shimmer that lit the water.

I gasped and quickly found my feet.

Glimmering, miniscule lights surrounded me, thicker and brighter the closer they came to my skin. All around me the water sparkled, as if tiny slivers of stars had fallen into the sea.

"You have awakened the enikkas, Your Highness." Celyse chuckled. "Do not be alarmed. They are gentle creatures, made for beauty and of light. They are drawn to you for your pleasure at their company."

I brushed my arm through the water. A trail of light followed it. The feeling of peace that had taken hold didn't leave me, but it was enhanced by a new emotion. Beyond mere happiness, I was overcome with breathless wonder that such creatures existed. And awed that I'd been allowed to experience their beauty.

As I made a slow turn in the water, my self-made current illuminated with multi-colored sparklers. A surprising sound flowed from my mouth. It was not the laugh of one who had been entertained, but an expression of joy that came from the depths of my spirit, as if my soul did not have the ability to contain such wonder within and had been forced to crack open and allow pieces to escape.

At my laugh, the water glowed even brighter, as if millions of the creatures had been awakened by the sound. I cupped a handful of water and brought it close to my face to see them better.

The tiny bodies of the enikkas were barely tangible, but luminously visible in their incandescence. Greens, pinks, blues, and golds glittered just beneath the water's surface. It was light and beauty and utterly fascinating.

"Do they always come like this when you swim here?"

"They come quite often, Princess." Celyse's expression mirrored the wonder of mine. "Although I must admit I've not seen so many at once for a very long time. It appears as though the enikkas have been waiting for you to seek them."

"Celyse, I—"

As suddenly as my laughter had come, tears sprang to my eyes and began joining the salty water around me. Overcome as I was by the beauty and comfort of this water and its creatures, I was unable to speak, so I sent her my thoughts instead.

I want to share this with Julien. I want him to know of this before we leave Tirandov.

"Neither he nor the King would approve, Princess Rynnaia." Her voice did not hold censure, but was filled with understanding. "Might you suggest he come to swim on his own later? For propriety's sake?"

Will they stay? Will they wait for him? The water is lovely on its own, but the enikkas are enchanting. So comforting.

"I believe they might," she nodded. "But bear in mind that, although they came to you, Princess, they would not have come without being called."

My mind filled with questions, but the glow around me was so wonderful that I was still unsure of my voice.

How could I have called them? I did not even know such wondrous creatures existed!

The glow increased for a moment, as if the enikkas themselves were warmed by my praise.

"They are not creatures who speak or reason like men, but they are an extension of the Light by which all things came to be. They come and go at His bidding, providing the comfort of their beauty to those whom He desires to receive it."

They were sent? This sweet water, these beautiful creatures, this supreme comfort was meant specifically for me? My hand fluttered to my lips. I was overcome by this manifest display of affection and care.

This moment was a gift. A gift from The First. A gift of *Embral e' Veria.*

The first name recorded in *The Story of The First* danced through my heart. None other would have been capable of endowing such an all-consuming comfort. Only the one I had been studying could be capable of such Gentle Power and Mighty Love.

The colors of his names caressed my mind with unbearable tenderness. I gasped as a legion of enikkas surrounded me. Their brilliance was enhanced again by their increasing numbers. They flooded my thoughts with their own unique form of communication.

Their touch was subtle. As the glittering enikkas brushed against my skin I felt a slight increase of warmth at the precise point of their connection, though none was bigger than an eyelash on its own. Their light swirled as my eyes filled with the wonder of understanding that such a moment of beauty had been created for my personal experience.

For me.

White lightning flashed through my mind, melding the truth I had read about into my discussions with Julien and the Andoven teachers. In that brilliant flare of enlightenment the eyes of my heart were torn open.

My hands flew to my chest, seared by the heat of my discovery. Scraps of history and information that I'd been frustrated at trying to connect on my own were, at once, inseparably fused together within my heart. The reality of *The Story of The First*, and its implications to my own existence, was finally illuminated.

Above the water, from the sky, and from underneath my feet I felt a rumbling—a fearful, joyous sound. I turned, but Celyse had her back to me as she moved toward the shore, oblivious to the sonorous vibrations.

Rynnaia. The Voice spoke for my ears alone. I closed my eyes and lifted my face to the new, warm breeze that gently stirred the water.

Thank you, my heart breathed to the Fearsome, Gentle, Conquering Voice. *Thank you.*

I am Loeftryn de Rynloeft. I am the Highest Reigning descended from the Reign Most High. I am the Pure Light of Truth and the Mercy that Consumes. I am Embral e' Veria. I am the Power of Love in its Purest Form. I am The First. And I am holding your past, present and future.

Comfort swelled and filled me.

I knew you, Rynnaia E'veri, before you were conceived and you are known by me still. You are here by my appointment and none other. Are you ready, now, to know me?

Was I ready to know *him*?

In the library he had shocked me with the forceful heat of his presence, but having gained my attention, he now romanced me with beauty and the gentle warmth of comfort in order to win my heart. Was I ready to know him?

A sob broke through my chest. I had never felt so exposed nor so naked with joy and awe and fear.

I'm ready.

Are you certain?

The overflow of my heart sang out through the words of my thoughts. *With all that I am and for all of my life, I am yours!* My throat filled with emotion. *I am yours, Embral e' Veria. I am yours!*

The blazing pain of love, pure love, constricted my chest, and then loosed itself within me like an explosion of stars across the sky.

You are mine.

As the words entered my consciousness, the pressure lifted from my body. My sense of awe remained, but my fear was replaced by an unnamable peace.

At the urging of the enikkas I allowed myself to be pulled under the water. Their brightness wrapped around me like a fluid blanket of light. As the water closed over my head, healing restoration seeped through my mind and body.

All doubt and confusion were washed away by the water's warm illumination. Suspended beneath the surface of the sea, I was completely new. As if the core of my identity had been lying dormant, it had now awakened after a lifetime of sleep.

Be of good courage, Rynnaia E'veri, the Voice of The First caressed my very soul, *for I will be with you. Always.*

The rumble ceased.

I rose from beneath the water, thousands of glittering enikkas dripping from my hair, my shift, and my skin. As they trickled back into the sea I whispered my thanks for their part in the beauty that had brought clarity to my heart by way of my eyes.

Wrapped in her robe, Celyse sat on the sand, waiting for me. "You have been changed," she smiled.

"Irrevocably so." I nodded, doing a final sweep of my hand through the glittering creatures. "Please stay," I entreated. "Dear enikkas, I wish for my friend to see you."

Their glow decreased for a fraction of a moment, and I had the odd sensation that they had bowed to me and granted my request. "Thank you, sweet creatures, for the service you have rendered me this night. I hope I may someday serve you as you have so wonderfully served me."

Another moment of a lessened glow, but they remained. I dipped my head, blew them a kiss, and waded back to the shore.

Celyse held a robe, but my spirit was so alight within me I wouldn't have needed its warmth, but for propriety's sake. I fastened the sash around my waist as she gathered my discarded gown.

"Julien!" I called in the direction he had gone. I couldn't wait to share what had just transpired in the water . . . and in my heart.

He was at my side but a moment or two later. His voice was breathless as he rubbed his thumb across my cheek. "You've been crying." His gaze narrowed on the illumined bay behind me. Concern lined his brow. "Rynnaia, have you been harmed?"

"Beyond anything in my experience." Although joy stretched my cheeks, my eyes welled up again. "My very soul has been torn and mended this night."

"You look . . . you look as if . . ." he trailed off, but hope shone in his eyes.

"I am *his*, Julien. I am his."

Julien's expression turned into nothing less than pure satisfaction. Before I could recover from the jolt his smile sent through me, he pulled me into a fierce embrace.

His heart beat an intense rhythm against my cheek. I sighed from the sheer pleasure of the moment and tipped my chin to look at his face.

"What is that in the water? I've never seen such a sight!"

I turned to face the sea, but Julien didn't let go of me. Instead, he simply adjusted his arms. "They're called enik-kas," I said.

He rested his chin on the top of my head. "They're beautiful. I've heard of them, but I never imagined . . ."

"They were sent by The First," I said, but I was sure he already knew that. "Julien, you should swim."

"I should escort you back to the castle."

"Celyse will see me back to the castle. Allow yourself this joy, Julien. You will not regret it."

Releasing me from our comfortable embrace, he stepped back. "I believe I will take you up on that offer, Princess."

"I will leave you to it, then."

A warm bath awaited me in my chamber, but I didn't linger in it. For the first time since coming to Tirandov Isle, I felt sleepy.

As I settled into bed, I let my gaze rest on the design of the Emblem of The First woven into the canopy above me. In my imagination, it took on an enikka-like glow, and I smiled as the good-night kiss of unquenchable love settled peacefully upon my soul.

I drifted to sleep feeling better equipped for my quest than I had thought possible and slept in bliss, floating through dreams of glowing water and a tender Voice that lovingly spoke my name.

FIFTY-EIGHT

*F*illed with joy from the fresh memory of my time with the enikkas, I had to share the fullness of my heart with my mother. As I approached the door with the bright blue glowing Emblem of the First, however, I was keenly aware that her very survival depended on the success of my coming journey.

I will be with you, the tender Voice echoed through my heart, imparting a new strength and peace that allowed me to face her, even knowing this time together could be our last.

The curtains on her bed were drawn back and she sat up, alert. She had been waiting for me. "You have been changed."

I sat in the chair across from her. "I'm sorry it took me so long."

"Only the skies bring us light on a schedule, Rynnaia," she said with a smile. "Illumination would not have come to you before you were ready to receive it."

Her eyes shone with unshed tears. When she reached for my hand, however, her skin felt thinner than it had before. A cold, prickling dread dusted over my shoulders. Her condition was worsening.

"I'm sorry." The words spilled out before I could censure them.

"You need not apologize, my dear. You needed time and rest after such a momentous event."

While I was sorry I didn't come last night, that wasn't what I was apologizing for. But I didn't correct her. I was sorry—no, *sorrowed*—that the blessing she'd given me, while strengthening my own abilities, was draining the very essence of her life a little bit more each day. I turned my head and blinked my tears away.

"You're here now. And I want to hear all about it."

"I can hardly find the words," I said. "But . . . the enikkas!" A fresh burst of wonder pressed a laugh up from my heart. "To realize what it means *to be known* by love itself—er, himself," I laughed again. Somehow I had lost the ability to finish a sentence.

Her laugh was like music. It defied the Cobeld curse that normally gave tremble to her voice. She squeezed my hand. "Rynnaia, you may not understand this yet, but your trust in that complete love is a much stronger protection than any secret we could devise to keep you safe. It is a shield that can parry the thrust of many a deadly weapon."

I nodded, remembering that just such a defense had been offered to me when the glowing form of Loeftryn de Rynloeft had seared my eyes and burned my fingers.

"*Embral e' Veria.*" She took a breath and closed her eyes. "Your father has always been partial to the foremost name in *The Story of The First.*"

I nodded. "It says it all." I paused. "But without rendering any of the other names insignificant."

"Indeed. Limitless power, bathed in a sweet covering of unfailing love," she said with a serene smile. "It's a beautiful name. A true name. Let it be your guide as you forge into the unknown."

The picture her words painted gave new depth to my understanding of that name, having been bathed in that love, literally, the night before.

"Let yourself melt into that strength, Rynnaia," she said. "Trusting in *Embral e' Veria,* and in the constancy of the provision of The First, will not remove the danger from your path, but it will make it more easily borne."

I nodded. The scrolls promised danger, but The First promised a shield.

"When you are in doubt, or when fear itself seems as if it will overpower you, concentrate on the many titles of the First King that you have studied these past weeks. You will be reassured by them."

When my mother lifted her smile toward the ceiling and whispered the name again, somehow I knew that she was no longer speaking to me, but, rather, on my behalf.

"Gentle Warrior, My Keeper and Friend," her tone, as well as the names she chose by which to address The First spoke of reverence, comfort, and trust. "Keep my child within your arms and see her safely through what is to come. You are our Hope and our Light. Help us to depend upon you alone while we await your provision."

Her shoulders trembled as she took a breath and my own caught in my throat.

"May it be so," I said.

She squeezed my hand and opened her eyes. "May it be so, indeed."

"I will do everything within my power to succeed, Mother."

"And when your power is expended?"

"Then I will call to The First, whose power is . . ." I thought to the list of names and smiled when my mind landed on one entirely appropriate to her question, "inexhaustible."

She leaned back into her pillows. Death stalked her every breath, but the colors of her love swept over me with a blinding force that took all other thoughts from my mind. When they faded, I knew our time together had come to an end.

I leaned in and kissed her forehead.

"Dream sweetly, now," I whispered the phrase Lady Whittier said over me when I was a child, "and wake with joy." My last words were transported more by color than by sound, "I love you, Mother."

"My Rynnaia. I love you so very much," she whispered as sleep claimed her.

Quietly, I left her chamber, seeking the privacy of the Silence room instead. There, without anyone able to witness my thoughts or my tears, I wept.

FIFTY-NINE

My belongings were packed and sent ahead—in an unmanned boat!—to the ship awaiting us beyond the fog. Mindful that later that day I would arrive in a busy port city that did not yet know the Ryn lived, I dressed in the same simple gray traveling dress in which I'd arrived and coiled my hair in a simple style that could be easily hidden beneath the hood of my cloak.

"Even in these clothes, you look different than when you came." Celyse held my cloak and I slipped my arms into it.

I nodded. "I am the Ryn."

She beamed. "That you are. Are you ready to go?"

I took a breath. "Not quite. Why don't you go on." I wanted a few moments alone. "I'll be right along."

With a small bow of her head, Celyse exited.

I stepped in front of the wardrobe's mirror.

Flanked on each side by the inlaid Emblem of the First, my reflection was, at last, accurate to my own eyes. My cheeks were flushed with confidence and my eyes shone with knowledge that went far beyond the comprehension of my mind and into the utter depths of my heart. I stood with my back straight, unashamed of my height or the flame-colored hair I had inherited from the Queen. Even the simplicity of my dress and cloak could not hide my identity now. And the absence of a crown did nothing to disguise the surety written across my face.

I am Princess Rynnaia E'veri. I am the Ryn.

I reached above the mirror and ran my hand over the Emblem of the First, remembering the heat that had blistered my fingers within the pages of *The Story of the First*. The wood was cool to my touch, but my heart was warm with the memory of the tender patience with which *Embral e' Veria*, The First, had revealed himself to me.

You are mine, he had said. I could no longer deny him. And I had no desire to.

"I am yours," I whispered.

I took one last look around the room in which I'd spent most of the last month, and then I swept out the door, through the corridors, and into the entry hall. I was surprised to find it deserted after the flurry of activity that had gone on earlier. Where was everyone?

I closed my eyes and followed the colors of the Andoven to the front lawn of the castle. With a wave of my hand, an ability that I rarely gave a second thought to now, I opened the tall, arched door and stepped across its threshold only to gasp at the sight before me.

On the lawn in front of Tirandov Castle were all of the Andoven and their families. Hundreds upon hundreds of them. They covered every inch of grass, gravel, and sand from the bottom of the castle steps nearly to the shore.

"Well . . . hello," I said.

"Tura hathami Ryn Naia!"

Long live the Reigning Lady. I didn't even have to think about the translation anymore. My mind was attuned to the Ancient Voice as naturally now as if it were commonly spoken.

The lone voice was followed by hundreds of echoes and not a few exclamations of, "May it be so!"

My great-grandfather stepped forward. "The Andoven have provided gifts to speed your journey and contribute to its success."

Ryjitha laid a pack at my feet. "The light of Tirandov, Princess. May these tirandite-tipped torches light the dark places you must go."

My throat tightened with gratitude as other Andoven stepped forward and presented me with gifts.

"*The Story of The First,* translated into the modern voice," said an older scribe.

A vial was pressed into my palm. "Sand from the shore where the enikkas visited you."

Finally, Celyse stepped forward, her eyes bright with unshed tears. She held up a necklace. The silver-edged pendant was made of the glowing stone of Tirandov, carved into the Emblem of the First. I examined it more closely. At its center, a long-stemmed rose, its thorns still intact, was etched in relief.

"Your mother commissioned this design, not only to remind you of your own history, but to help you remember how the past has shaped you in order to face the future. Wear it as a token of your mother's great love for you and of the power you now have access to through The First."

She moved behind me to fasten the chain around my neck. Like the stone in my silver circlet, when the pendant's gentle heat touched upon my skin, it flared to a warmer, brighter glow before settling back down.

I was moved by the gifts and by the hearts of the people before me. "Thank you so much," I said. "For the services you have done for me and for E'veria, I am forever grateful."

My traveling companions gathered the gifts as the crowd parted. Julien, Dyfnel, Edru, and I walked down the pathway and stepped into the longboat. As soon as we were all on board and settled, the water pulled at the boat without the need for casting off.

I turned in my seat and waved at the Andoven until the bright, pinkish fog enveloped us and I could no longer see the people or the Isle of Tirandov.

Beyond the fog, the Seahorse ship *Meredith*—and Cazien, of course—awaited us. When we docked I would finally meet my father the King, and soon after begin my quest to fulfill a prophecy spoken hundreds of years before I took my first breath.

"Dyfnel!" A thought startled me from my musings. "You do have the scrolls, don't you?"

Sitting at the head of the boat, the Andoven man turned, patting the pouch slung across his body. "Yes," he said with a wink. "I have the scrolls. And translations of the scrolls. And copies of the translations of the scrolls."

"I have copies as well, Your Highness," Edru added.

"Oh." I blushed. "That's . . . good. We're going to need those."

"And it's about time, I say!" Julien laughed, but his eyes turned suddenly serious as he reached for my hand and gave it a gentle squeeze. "Are you ready, Rynnaia?"

"Yes, I believe I am." I breathed deeply of the warm southern sea air. "With all that I am and for all of my life, whatever may come of it, I am ready."

About the Author

Serena Chase contributes book reviews, author interviews, and features for *USA Today*'s Happy Ever After blog as well as for *Edgy Inspirational Romance*. A life-long lover of fairytales who admits to being mildly obsessed with pirates, Serena lives in Iowa with her husband, two daughters, and a white Goldendoodle named Albus. *The Ryn* is her first novel.

ACKNOWLEDGEMENTS

$\mathcal{M}$any thanks are necessary to those who have helped me carve this road to publication, but I'll start with my husband, Dave, who wears "the knight's beard" with pride, and whose graceful provision and encouragement made it possible. My True Love, I'm sure that over the past nineteen years of marriage (especially the seven spent refining this book!) you've had moments in which you've thought, "Whoever wrote this episode should die!" (Yep. *Galaxy Quest* reference.)Thanks for supporting me in chasing after my dreams, for watching the show, and for keeping me sane (or at least as close to it as possible) through it all.

To my beautiful girls, Delaney & Ellerie: thank you for listening to me talk about imaginary people for years on end, for being excited when all of this finally started coming together, and for being the brightest, loveliest stars in my universe. I love you.

A special sort of thanks goes to those brave few who, years ago, read the exhausting and poorly crafted first draft of this novel: Connie Hutchcroft, Delaney Van Ness, Donna Perdelwitz, Manon Bushman, Jessica Hellberg, author Nicole Johnson (really embarrassed about that one. Believe me: it's better now!) and author/adventurer Michael Tison. Thank you. And to my brother Tod, whose engineering expertise made Ayden's plumbing actually work, my thanks.

To Heather Perdelwitz: from the first draft of the first chapter until now, you have read countless versions of this story, talked me down from ledges, and witnessed my various neuroses concerning character, plot, setting, sentence structure, etc... and you are still my friend. Thanks are not enough, which is why your name is included in the dedication.

To my Strive Wednesday Small Group: Ali, Allison, Jordyn, Kara, Marissa, Morrgan, Alex, Sam, & Corliss, and to the MHS Color Guard girls: I love you guys and pray this story speaks a fresh sort of beauty into your already-beautiful hearts.

This book would not be in your hands, nor would its path to your heart be as clear, without the help of the editors and coaches who found the holes in the story and held my hand while I filled them. My heartfelt gratitude goes to Sandra Byrd (http://www.sandrabyrd.com) who has been not only an editor and coach on this project and others, but also my mentor, encourager, and friend. Thank you, Sandra. Also, editor Jenny Quinlan of Historical Editorial http://historicaleditorial.blogspot.com : your eye for clarity and story added a grace to this book that I could not have achieved on my own. You are a valuable asset to have on my team! Thank you so much! And to author Tamara Leigh: thanks for that extra bit of spit and polish. It really helped to bring the shine. I am honored.

To Joy Tamsin David who invited me into her adventure at Edgy Inspirational Romance www.edgyinspirationalromance.com : Joy, you have played such a big role in my career and you appreciate my sarcasm as only a true friend could. Thanks! And to Joyce Lamb, curator of USA Today's Happy

Ever After blog: thanks for building a tall platform and then offering a hand to help me climb up it. You rock.

To the book blogging community who embraced me when I first joined Joy at Edgy Inspirational Romance and who are now helping to bring my stories to the world, I am so grateful. *wipes eyes* Extra tight hugs go out to Rel, Christy, Amber, and Juju.

For my beautiful book cover I must thank the team that made it happen:

For the character images, my deep thanks to photographer Lincoln Noah Baxter and model Megan Wilson. Also: Donna Perdelwitz (for making Rose/Rynnaia's lovely blue cloak) and photo session helpers: Sue Wilson, Delaney, Ellerie, & Dave —& Jerry Woods, who happened to be there and knew how to turn on the lights.

For photo editing, scenery images, and design: a huge hug, some chocolate, and a ginormous thank you goes to graphic designer Jodie Gerling of JG Designs, who combined Lincoln's photos with her ability to translate the crazy in my head, and was willing to Skype for 4-hour-long tweaking sessions to produce a book cover that rocks my world. GO TEAM SEAHORSE!

To my Mom & Dad who kept that pink book of Grimm Fairytales within easy reach and didn't scoff (well, not too much) when I climbed into the old wardrobe, time and again, with the hope that I might find a lamp post: thanks for your love, your patience... and for setting the stage on which I fell in love with fairytales.

And finally, Dear Reader, I thank you for taking the time to read this novel. I pray your heart would glimpse, find, and hold on to the love that woos you even now.

I would love to hear from you! Please drop by my Facebook page http://www.facebook.com/serena.chase.author , say hello on Twitter @Serena_Chase, or visit my website www.serenachase.com to find out what is coming next in the Eyes of E'veria series! You can also find me on Pinterest where I have a boards specifically dedicated to the Eyes of E'veria series.

All My Best,
Serena

Continue Rynnaia's adventure in
Eyes of E'veria, book 2: THE REMEDY
The Remedy is available NOW for e-readers
& coming soon to paperback

& begin a new fairy tale adventure (with pirates!) in
EYES OF E'VERIA, BOOK 3
Coming Summer 2014

www.serenachase.com

Made in the USA
Middletown, DE
28 May 2020